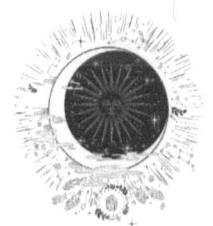

Under

the

Bronze Moon

Richard J. O'Brien

Red Grit
Books

Book Design by the author

Cover Design by the author

Red Grit Books

Second Edition: August 2021

First Edition of this book originally published by Sinister Grin Press, Copyright © 2018

The Red Grit Books name and logo are trademarks of Red Grit Books.

The publisher is not responsible for websites (or their content) that are not owned by the publisher.

ISBN: 978-1-7377027-6-4 (paperback)

Acknowledgements

A special thanks goes out to Alana who returned The Godfather's favor, the reference librarians at the Haverford Township Free Library who gave me access to their special collections room and left me there to travel back in time, and my father-in-law Phil who, at a moment's notice, supplied historical information regarding early twentieth century trains and trolleys (including a copy of Stein's Philadelphia Trolley Guide from 1915). Several history books on The Great War were consulted in shaping parts of this novel. If there are any historical inaccuracies, the fault lies with me and not those historians like John Keegan and others. As always, I offer a heartfelt thanks to my wife Jessica who, incidentally, unearthed an effigy of Lot's wife in our home a few years ago, proving, yet again, that stories can be inspired by the most unlikely of circumstances.

Dedication

In Memory of Philip G. Craig

The pages are still blank, but there is a miraculous feeling of the words being there, written in invisible ink and clamoring to become visible.

~Vladimir Nabokov

Part One:

Standing in Two Worlds

Chapter One: The Great Rumor— Pittsfield MA, 2012

Toward the end of his life the reclusive writer R.J. Hyatt had only one trusted friend. Her name was May Weldon. It had been speculated in many literary circles that Ms. Weldon, Hyatt's only surviving confidant, was in possession of an unpublished manuscript penned by Hyatt and completed just before his death. Such haphazard theorizing, however, never resulted in hard evidence. Armchair speculation failed to uncover any physical evidence of Hyatt's unpublished second novel, but still, it was no secret that May Weldon was the sole executor of Hyatt's literary estate, and that she was very protective of her deceased friend. In the decades following the writer's death, several attempts had been made to convince Ms. Weldon of surrendering the fabled manuscript; however, those efforts, despite large sums of money offered to her, proved unsuccessful. May Weldon always categorically denied the existence of any such manuscript.

Richard J. O'Brien

In the spring of 1998, the question was put to Ms. Weldon in an interview published in The Atlantic. *"There is no second novel,"* she had responded to the question. *"I do wish people would just accept that. It's been thirty-two years since Robert passed from this world. If he left a book behind I think I would have cracked by now. Next question."*

Harold Miller, professed bibliophile and professor of Modern Literature at The University of Massachusetts—Amherst, was the last of a dying breed. Slight, tall, and gray-haired, Miller had been a terminable wallflower at public gatherings ever since he was a young boy, but he led a secret life. Since he had gained his tenure at UMass-Amherst, he spent his free time, at the behest of his publisher Rhineholt, hunting down unpublished manuscripts from deceased writers and bringing them into the public spotlight. To his credit, Miller, in the twenty years since he first began moonlighting as a member of the publisher's clandestine services, had unearthed a dozen novels and short stories. Rhineholt was venturing into new territory, buying up manuscripts, printing them, and selling them as 'undiscovered writings' from American writers who had met their Maker long before their popularity waned. Miller's secret calling was a delicate process. Rarely were the executors of a late writer's literary estate ready to hand over unpublished and, often immature, works rendered when the author was yet-to-be-discovered and his style unpolished, at least not without sufficient recompense. Rhineholt ultimately paid those estates well enough, but Miller himself never made quite enough money to sustain himself.

In 1995, Harold Miller published *Memory and Dust: A Life of R.J. Hyatt.* The work took him nearly a decade to write, and his research in earnest began in 1987. In 1990, he was granted several interviews with May Weldon. His wife had already died, and Miller, not knowing what else to do with himself, immersed himself in his work. His daughter Elinor was already a graduate student. When the Hyatt biography was released it was the first in-depth look at the reclusive fabulist. The

2

biography won Miller modest accolades and it had been the only full-length biography about R.J. Hyatt until 2010 when Wade M. Kincaid published his Hyatt biography. Most reviewers remarked, correctly, that Mr. Kincaid's book seemed derivative of Miller's work, offering nothing new. Miller's work continued to sell at a steady trickle, as biographies do, but within the past year sales had come to a near halt.

It was a cold spring morning in Pittsfield, the kind that made New England unique in winter's ability to wear out its welcome when Miller received a phone call from his editor. The original editor of the Hyatt biography had retired the previous year, moving to Spain where it was rumored she divided her time between writing a novel and bedding young Spanish women half her age. Miller's new editor, Schuyler Heddings, was an aggressive, sharp-witted thirty-eight-year-old native Tennessean and Vanderbilt graduate. Heddings came from an old family who once rubbed elbows with the likes of Robert Penn Warren and James Agee. He was filled with a raw vitality that men like Miller barely remembered in their old age yet were deeply envious of whenever they found themselves in its presence. He was among the new breed of editors, a businessman first, a predatory hit man who calculated dollars and cents as easily as he turned near-perfect manuscripts into flawless ones.

"How are you getting on, Dr. Miller?" Heddings asked.

"Fine," Miller told him.

"I was thinking about your Hyatt biography," he said. "It's been on my mind a lot."

"Oh?"

"I'm not going to sweeten it up, professor," said Heddings. "Numbers are down. Fewer dollars in sales inches a book closer to going out of print."

"When?"

"Oh, we're not there yet," he said. "I am thinking we need an updated, expanded version."

"R.J. Hyatt died before you were born, Schuyler," Miller reminded him. "There's not much to update. Unless he's come back from the dead then I suppose there could be. Have you heard anything?"

"Very funny, Dr. Miller," he replied. "Look, we all know how great this biography was. Hell, it made this publishing house a shit ton of manure if you don't mind my saying so. And you're right. R.J. Hyatt hasn't come back from the dead. But you know who may soon be booking passage to the other side?"

"Me?"

"Good lord, professor," he said. "Hell, no. I was reading an alumni newsletter from Bryn Mawr College just last night. It appears that the esteemed May Weldon is in poor health."

Miller felt an uneasy ache in the pit of his stomach.

"I am not sure how much more she could tell me," he told Heddings.

"Maybe May Weldon has been pulling the wool over everyone's eyes," the editor said. "Maybe she'll have a change of heart on account of her pending sit-down with her Maker. And maybe I can talk to accounting. Maybe we can offer her something."

"Schuyler, you know the history of this as well as I do," said Miller. "I hope you're not suggesting she's hoarding anything?"

"Anything? No," he said. "But a big old stack of papers with prose and page numbers and chapter headings? I don't see why—"

"You can't be serious."

"She donated a handful of letters to the Smithsonian just last year," said Heddings. "Maybe she's holding on to something else."

"I've seen the letters at the Smithsonian," Miller reminded him. "Five letters to his editor at Allen and Unwin don't necessarily make the case for an unpublished novel penned by R.J. Hyatt."

"It could be that she is sitting on something big," he said. "Maybe she is, maybe she isn't. But we won't know until you go down there and talk to her yourself. Hell, she may be in a generous mood. She may hand over—"

"Schuyler, this is madness. There is no evidence to suggest that R.J. Hyatt wrote another novel."

"Stranger things have happened," Heddings said. "You remember Claude McKay? A grad student found McKay's novel this year. Do you want that to be your legacy? Undone by someone like that?"

Miller had always prided himself on being a humble man. He was considered by and large to be an expert on all things concerning R.J. Hyatt. In class and at symposiums across the U.S. and in Europe, for nearly four decades, he defended his stance concerning the quantity of Hyatt's work. What infuriated Miller was that his editor would align himself with those who believed that a little old lady in Haverford Township, Pennsylvania kept a second novel manuscript from the world, a literary treasure chest of gold, a previously unknown novel penned by the enigmatic R.J. Hyatt, an author who turned his back on the publishing world and chose a life of seclusion. Miller had met such ill-informed optimists at every turn: in his classroom, at seminars, even once during an odd stroll in New York City. No matter where he went someone would inevitably pose the question that he loathed most: Do you think R.J. Hyatt ever wrote another novel? They came out of the woodwork, crackpots convinced through some delusional divination that a second novel existed, though nothing had ever been found to suggest such a manuscript existed beyond the fragile realm of speculation. They came at him through every channel—phone calls, letters, emails—and all of them with nothing more to support their distorted claims than their own fanciful, albeit misguided, wishful thinking. They pinned their hopes on this belief, a belief that perhaps they hoped would serve as deliverance from their sordid, fractured lives. The greatest rumor among Hyatt fans of this sort maintained that an elderly woman, once the writer's lover when they were young, honored a dying man's wish by stonewalling anyone who came searching. The unhinged collective reality some shared about Hyatt's lost work was not one that interested Miller. For his editor to insinuate that this myth was somehow based in reality was what troubled him. The last time Miller had interviewed May Weldon was when men like Schuyler Heddings were barely teenagers. He knew the truth. He had peered into the eyes of a woman who once lived under the same roof as Hyatt. None of the writings left behind by Hyatt after his death, mostly letters and a few essays, hinted even remotely that he had been at work on anything else except poems toward the end of his life. Miller knew because he had scoured them all. Then the day came when he had met May Weldon, and he knew in his heart that there wasn't a second unpublished novel. The heartache still visible in May Weldon's eyes, long years after Hyatt had passed away, was proof enough.

"Look," Heddings said, at last. "How would you feel about bringing May Weldon in on this one last time?"

"In what capacity?" Miller asked.

"She could write a new introduction to your biography."

"What compensation would you offer?"

"The standard, of course. Unless—"

"May Weldon conjures Hyatt's secret second novel from thin air," said Miller. "Story at eleven."

"Come on, Harry," his editor said. "There's no need to be like that."

"Who's to say she's even capable?"

"May Weldon went to Bryn Mawr College," Heddings said. "Granted, you know that already. I'm sure she can still write a brief essay about her dearest friend."

"I meant," Miller said, "because of her health."

"What's wrong with May Weldon?"

"You said she was in poor health."

"I did," his editor said. "Old people get that way, Harry. It's called entropy. Things fall apart. Just reach out to her."

"No one just reaches out to the executor of R.J. Hyatt's literary estate, Schuyler."

"You did it before," he said. "No lawyers, no fuss. Remember? It will be like a reunion."

"I don't know," Miller said. "When I began writing the biography it was different back then, a different time, and things were—"

"You slept with her?"

"I beg your pardon?"

"Never mind," Heddings said. "The biography needs new life, old friend. The accounting goons are making cuts everywhere. I can't keep the wolves at bay forever. And I'd sure as hell hate to think that your life's work will go out of print."

"There are alternatives."

"Really? Enlighten me."

"I could take my book to a university press," Miller said. "That's one alternative."

"And charge people fifty-two dollars a copy in this economy, Harry?" he asked. "Oh, I don't think so. Let me know how it works out."

Miller spoke next but the line went dead. He didn't bother calling Schuyler Heddings back. Instead, he thought about the last time he'd been to Philadelphia. It had been too long, and now there was the Constitution Center which he'd always wanted to see. He thought it might be nice to spend a long weekend in Philadelphia, and then drive to Delaware County where he would call on the one woman in the world who would just as soon see Miller drop dead than show up on her front porch.

Chapter Two: The Land Of Dust And Honey—The Hollow Hill Gate

Runyon Barth, dogged and raw, hungry and fever-stricken, wandered in those early days like a ghost over the landscape. His mind was rattled, and his ears played tricks on him. He heard distant cannons where there were none, and artillery shells exploded overhead in silence. He remembered little of the battle; even now, only momentary glimpses of the dead who lay scattered and broken, once among the living, now gone, reduced to butcher scraps. Burnt flesh and scorched bone littered the trench where he lay. His gas mask tightly fitted to his face so when the rain came, it rendered him nearly blind as the mask's dusty lenses became dotted with raindrops. Barth wiped them with his hands, but his actions made things worse. It was late in the afternoon when the artillery shelling stopped. He lay in the trench with only the dead to keep him company. Soon, the Germans would make their final advance. Barth waited. The minutes passed. And still they did not come. He waited for someone to blow the whistle; one of the officers who rendered the all-clear once the lowest-ranking soldier had removed his gas mask and took a deep breath. But there were no whistles. In that blurred world Barth was the last man standing. If the Germans came now it meant one of three possible scenarios: he could play dead until one of the German soldiers stuck him with a bayonet over and over until he died, he could shoot and hope their return fire would kill him instantly, or he could remain alive and be taken prisoner. The last was not an option. Barth had seen firsthand how the German infantry treated prisoners of war. Sometimes the bodies that had been left behind were intact; other times they were barely recognizable. As he laid there in the trench, he witnessed the coming of night. And still the final German attack did not materialize. In the dark, he took off his gas mask. The air he breathed was damp. It carried the smell of gunpowder and burnt flesh. The rain continued its relentless assault for hours, and when it stopped, Barth climbed a damaged ladder to the rampart wall above the trench. A fog approached, its dewy gray shade growing thicker until it blotted out the mile-wide pockmarked pasture that served as the no man's land between Barth's infantry unit and the Germans, the boundary between the dead and the victors.

The first order of business that evening was to traverse the trenches and search for survivors. What struck Barth as he moved among the dead was not the bloodied, singed, blistered, and rank bodies of his brothers-in-arms; what got inside him, what made him feel weak and less than human, was the silence, the utter absence of voices. He moved from one dead soldier to the next, recognizing those faces that still kept their shape. Faces like one that belonged to Kyle Leucht, a private who had come from Minnesota, whose face was frozen in a mask of agony when the shrapnel shredded his chest and stomach to bloody ribbons, chewing away skin, bone, and organs until only a chipped and scorched spine remained. Then there was Barth's company commander Captain Henry Reed, of the Boston Reeds, a Princeton graduate who loathed Germans almost as much as he did the Yale football team. And there were others, so many others; body after body, most missing their faces, but he could not bring himself to get too close. The front-line trench where he stood was connected to others via narrow communication trenches. The support trench had been reduced to a hasty graveyard made from sandbags, earth, twisted corrugated metal, and splintered wood. The company headquarters dugout had been turned into a crater—here a boot stuck out, there a helmeted head detached from its body.

Darkness slowed Barth's movement. He climbed out of the support trench and low-crawled beneath reams of barbed wire. On his belly he made his way across two hundred yards of bombed out earth until he reached the reserve trench. The last of the dead awaited him. Broken teeth glistened inside bloodied mouths. The burned and mangled bodies of men Barth once knew resembled a surreal acrobatic of corpses pressed into the earth, frozen in mid-performance as if turning cartwheels in anticipation of a glorious victory that never came, replaced instead by the concussive certainty of German artillery rounds.

He wanted nothing more than to lie down, to sleep for a million days, and to wake up only after the pasture had rejuvenated itself; to remember in the years to come the flowers in that field, flowers tended by angels who would offer him sweet water to make him well, to forget the memories of war, but he knew his lot was to remain in Hell among the dead.

Barth thought that the artillery barrage had rendered him deaf. He had not been able to hear the rain when it fell late that afternoon. There was no place within the trenches for him, as every empty space belonged now to the dead. So, he dug a space for himself into the communication trench that ran perpendicular between the reserve and the officers' trenches. No sooner did he cast aside his shovel than he heard an owl's hoot. The noise startled him. When the owl hooted a second time he knew that the sound had come from somewhere within the forest that bordered the pasture. If he closed his eyes and listened, the hoot might take Barth back to Ardmore, back to Smith's Powder Mill where he walked at night as a boy (against his mother's wishes) during autumn nights, hoping to glimpse the one the townspeople called Gathis, as he pondered what myth remnants the original Welsh settlers loosed upon the eastern Pennsylvania landscape when they first arrived; and later, as a teen, within those same woods, always one step ahead of Smith's ancient dogs that roamed the property after dark, when he discovered the soft, pliant flesh of Brigit Mahoney, a local girl four years older than Barth, whose voluminous red hair contrasted greatly with her pale breasts and wide hips, as she stood naked one night beneath a harvest moon. People in town considered Brigit queer, demented, a woman given over to carnality before God. Barth encountered the strange and beautiful woman three times in the woods near the creek. The first time she ran away when she realized that she was not alone. Upon his second glimpse of her, Brigit stayed put, taunting the young Barth with questions until Gathis's silhouette emerged from behind a giant, oak tree. The third time Brigit and Barth were alone. The third time was different. Barth had gone into the woods caught between childhood and adulthood; in the woods he had known Brigit, and in the woods he had become a man. When the owl hooted again, Barth opened his eyes. The spell was broken. Ardmore was gone now; likewise, the woods around Smith's Powder Mill and the lush curves of Brigit Mahoney.

From somewhere else out in the fog came a new sound, distant yet menacing all the same: the voices of German soldiers. Barth heard no more than six of those voices. If they belonged to a patrol, he needed to hide. The cutaway he had dug was not large enough to conceal him and the idea of crawling back into one of the main trenches among the rain-soaked corpses repulsed him. If he played dead, he might live. It was a slim hope, one that he did not want to chance in case the German patrol wanted to wet their bayonets that night. Barth imagined taking one or two of them by surprise, but the remaining patrol members would surely kill him. The conversation in the fog drew near. The six soldiers were close enough now that Barth heard them fix bayonets on their rifles. The German patrol would spend hours in the trenches, stabbing the dead to ensure they remained that way. Then they would sweep through once more, robbing the fallen of whatever they deemed valuable.

Barth lit out of the reserve trench and ran away from the patrol, away from the dead, and headed toward the owl that continued its lonesome lament. A few hundred yards to the west lay the tree line that marked the edge of the forest. Barth couldn't see it through the fog, but he knew in which direction to travel. The woods would provide better cover if the forest wasn't teeming with another German contingent already. Still, a likely death that may lie ahead was a better chance than the certain end behind him. He had not traveled far into the pasture when a rifle shot rang out.

"Halt!" one of the soldiers cried.

Barth kept going. The German patrol opened fire. With the night and the fog on his side, Barth hit the ground. The Germans quit shooting. Barth stood up and sprinted the remaining distance toward the woods. His only weapons were a pistol and a bayonet.

Once Barth entered the forest he removed the bayonet from its sheath in his boot. He chose a wide tree to hide behind that offered a fog-enshrouded view of the opening through which he had entered the woods. The first German appeared like a shadow, drifting slowly into the forest. Barth kept the blade of his bayonet concealed under his arm for fear of the steel gleaming in the dark. The German soldier stepped right past him. Barth slipped one hand over the German's mouth and, with his other hand, buried the blade into the base of the soldier's skull. Gently, he lowered the dead man to the ground. A minute passed before a voice could be heard.

"Heinrich?"

A branch snapped somewhere. Barth heard the remaining five men conversing as they weighed their options. He watched as two more Germans entered the woods. The other three remained at the pasture's edge.

Barth planted his bayonet in the ground and took out his Enfield revolver. As the two soldiers drew near he saw that they were mere boys, no more than sixteen years old, dressed in uniforms a size too big. One of them opened his mouth to say something. Barth shot both boys in their faces.

"Franz?" another voice called out. It sounded older. "Thomas?"

"Yah," Barth snapped.

The remaining three stepped right next to a tree where Barth stood waiting for them. Barth shot the closest one in the head and fired two more shots, hitting the remaining two in their stomachs. That left him with one bullet. He cast two of the survivors' rifles out of reach. Next, Barth picked up the rifle belonging to the German he had just shot in the head. He stepped over the closest one and fired a round into his face, killing him. The third German twisted in agony as he crawled on his side toward the pasture. Barth tossed the Gewehr 88 aside. He pulled his bayonet out of the ground, advanced on the wounded German, and kicked him over onto his back. The soldier wiggled on his back, gripping the wound in his stomach. Barth kneeled on the man's arms.

"Nein," the surviving patrol member whispered. Blood bubbled in his mouth. "Nein...Bitte...Mein Gott—"

Barth took a deep breath as he touched the man's chest with his bayonet, leaned forward, pressing all his weight behind the bayonet, and stabbed him through the heart. The German's mouth opened as he coughed blood; wide-eyed, his body offered a final death spasm. Barth withdrew his bayonet from the dead man's chest. He rolled off the dead German and lay on the forest floor. The few treetops he could see appeared like dark ghosts through the fog. He lay there for a minute or more, listening. None had come to follow the patrol. Barth got to his feet, feeling for the first time that night the fatigue of war, and began to walk.

Chapter Three: A Man Of Two Worlds—Ardmore PA, 1909

On most days, the townspeople saw him at dawn and again at dusk. Rain or shine, he showed himself, never before dark and never after the sun peeked past the eastern horizon. The old German immigrants and their families had a name for him; the Irish did too, but none dared share those names with him face to face. He was a tall man, broad-shouldered and thin at the waist, regal to some, quite barbaric to others. He never walked on a sidewalk, choosing instead to walk the road as if he and the newly paved streets were somehow connected on some metaphysical plane, aspects of one another permeating any number of realities in a single moment. No one knew if he had a wife. In time, people came to know him as Yates, or, when not in his presence, the Centurion. At night, mothers told their daughters of the dangers they might find when walking alone with boys along those roads that led down to Cobbs Creek. *Stay away from the creek after dark,* the mothers said. *Stay away or he will come. And no boy, no matter how strong, will be able to save you.* Young and old men alike gave him a wide berth. None challenged him when he walked the streets of Ardmore, for they envied what they sensed in this stranger: a man with his feet in two worlds, impervious to pain, and blessed with gifts spoken of only in the darkest of places devoid of hope as if he embodied the very soul of ancient men long gone like those of Sparta or the warring Visigoths. In secret, children believed he was God's keeper of balance, an antithesis to the better angels whose names graced the pages of the good book. He never wore a hat; his hair and beard colored salt and pepper were a tangled, long mess. Yates walked with a staff—a beautifully carved five-foot length of mahogany-stained dark wood and etched with a language long forgotten in the world. In truth, only children ever got close enough to view the many etchings carved into the staff. The writings on the stick were not culled from a dialect spoken when the continents were still conjoined; the language was old Welsh, not spells as many were led to believe, but one long love poem to a girl Yates had known in his youth who vanished before he sailed for the new world.

In the new country, around Ardmore and Haverford, the Centurion kept to himself. The people suspected that he squatted in an old tenement house near the old wool mill, but no one knew for sure. Yates preferred walking the woods near Cobbs Creek at night, especially when the moon was new, and the woodlands cast into pitch. Among the people were those who spoke secretly about him, telling tales on long nights of doorways in the woods that led to dimensions swayed not by God's good grace but by His utter absence, places that even the Devil refused to tread. It was believed by many that the Centurion retreated to these realms from time to time to nourish his incalculable strength and his arcane knowledge of things long dead, of magic whose incantations were penned by fallen angels who passed through the world on their way to Hell.

There was only one who knew Yates beyond the town myths and gossip, twin currents that ran faster than the creek's rapid waters. Her name was Abigail Sweeney. She lived with her mother in the old widow's tenement house near the gunpowder mill. Patrick Sweeney, Abigail's father, had died when his daughter was six-years-old.

The death of Patrick Sweeney began in earnest when the mill owner, Jeremiah Addison, had offered to pay Sweeney half a week's wages to paint the upper half of the press house chimney stack. It was a spring day much like any other in the

Delaware Valley, and a hint of humidity heralded the coming summer heat. Sweeney had spent the morning that day drinking just enough whiskey to settle his nerves. His fear of heights was something he would not let interfere with making some extra income. Money was money, after all, and Sweeney had known people who did worse for it. Scaffolding had been erected around the lower half of the megalithic chimney the previous week. When Sweeney found out that three other mill employees had also been chosen to paint the top half of the chimney, he went directly to Addison.

"I can do this work myself," he told him.

"All the same, Sweeney," the owner said. "Each man will do his part."

Sweeney had calculated that he could make a little more than two weeks salary if he had been permitted to do the work alone. Addison saw it differently, understanding that the division of labor would not hinder production in the mill.

Outside the mill, located one hundred yards from the powder magazine, stood the press house. It was a squat structure, save for its colossal chimney, constructed from wood and stone, and devoid of nails or any other metal for safety's sake. In recent years, Addison received pressure from the local authorities to paint the chimney in tri-colors, the top being red, on account of an increase in short-range flights made by aircraft aficionados as well as the Navy out of Philadelphia. A crew of men, hired by Addison from the American Bridge Company, had suspended rope seats from the top of the chimney. Sweeney dreaded the idea of dangling on a wood seat attached to ropes so far off the ground. Addison assured Sweeney and the others that these were the very same seats the American Bridge Company used during the construction of the Flatiron Building in New York City. That may have been fine and well for Addison, Sweeney thought. But two things bothered him. He'd never seen the Flatiron Building, and he would have preferred a ladder atop the scaffolding that had been erected half-way up the chimney's circumference. Addison forbade any use of ladders. He swore to Sweeney and the others that the rope seats were safe. Addison's foreman, Leo McMahon, was of another and perhaps more informed opinion.

"I hope you have your affairs in order," McMahon said to Sweeney. "Hanging by a thread one hundred feet above ground. That's no place to be. If the good Lord wanted you dangling like a giant spider, He would have given you six legs. But the job's got to be done. Now, don't be acting the maggot when you get up there. You're likely to fall and meet your end."

Sweeney considered McMahon a jackass of the highest order. Still, McMahon was Jeremiah Addison's foreman; as such, he possessed the uncanny ability to see danger where others remained blind to it. In the gunpowder business, even Sweeney knew that was an admirable quality. Still, Sweeney, who considered himself a realist of the highest order, would not be dismayed by McMahon's superstitious banter.

With the foreman's words still ringing in his ears, Sweeney climbed atop the scaffolding. He was the first one there that morning. The harness seats hung where the American Bridge workers had left them.

Ten minutes later, McMahon showed up. He climbed up the scaffolding with the other men. There was no mistaking McMahon's purpose. He was there simply to make sure that the work got started properly and on time.

The morning was cool. Sweeney was the first one to ascend to the chimney top. The harness seat wasn't bad, but it still made him nervous. A paint can was affixed to the rope and better than half the paint splashed out as he used his wide brush to paint an area only a few feet square. There were guide ropes that were supposed to be used to pull one's self either left or right. Sweeney got the hang of it just as his paint can emptied. He lowered himself to the scaffolding for a reload. One of the other men, Ciardi was his name, refused to go back up. Sweeney was hoisted up high once more, fresh paint and brush at his disposal. By noon the temperature had risen. Sweeney sweated out the whiskey he had consumed early that morning.

By the time the lunch whistle blew he wasn't hungry, but he was ready for more whiskey.

For Sweeney it felt natural to be back on the ground. When the lunch break was over, he stalled for as long as he could before he was secured back into his harness seat. The painting that day was an effort of Sisyphean proportions. Sweeney and the two others continued to sling paint, and no matter how much they put down the chimney appeared as old and weather-stained as ever, as if the stone drank in the wet paint.

Somewhere after three o'clock that afternoon Sweeney had lost count of how many times he'd been lowered to the scaffolding, given another fresh can of paint, and hoisted once more, high over the town of Ardmore. Storm clouds gathered to the west and a strong wind kicked up. Lightning streaked the sky. Sweeney looked down. McMahon was far below, a sunburned ant on the ground screaming his head off about something while he flailed his arms as if caught in the throes of a seizure. The other men on the chimney were lowered first. Sweeney didn't know what to do, so he slung paint as fast as he could until he felt the ropes move. Lightning struck the top of the chimney. Sweeney was already out of his harness seat and scurrying down the scaffolding along with the other men when lightning struck a second time. All of them, including Sweeney, were blown off the scaffolding, falling more than thirty feet to the ground; all of them were miraculously uninjured save for one. Sweeney hit his head against a large rock. The blow fractured his neck and crushed the back of his skull.

The unfortunate act of nature that caused Sweeney's death weighed heavily on Jeremiah Addison. Before nightfall he had arranged for Mary and her daughter to move into the widow's tenement building. The structure offered ten one-bedroom apartments, two bathrooms that were shared by the tenants on both floors, and a common kitchen where a cook prepared lunch and dinner five days out of the week. Addison had his foreman McMahon take the mill's Lippard Stewart E-Express truck and see to the Sweeney widow's move from town onto the mill grounds.

When Mary Sweeney and her daughter Abigail were fetched from their rented house, McMahon explained that there had been an accident. He informed Mary in private that her husband had expired. In hindsight, he wished he had used a better word instead of equating Sweeney and his life to that of a jar of milk or strawberry preserves.

What Mary, Abigail, and McMahon had not anticipated was the body of Patrick Sweeney being left on the ground through a horrendous thunderstorm while the millworkers sought shelter far away from the powder magazine and the press house until the lightning storm passed. As a show of further disrespect for the dead, McMahon himself had run over poor Patrick Sweeney's body upon returning to the mill with the widow and the dead man's daughter. The truck got stuck in the mud, and a gang of millworkers had to carry a distraught Mrs. Sweeney and her grieving daughter Abigail to higher ground. Flush with embarrassment and convinced he was destined for Hell for his actions, McMahon was left to scrounge up help to push the truck out of the mud. After several attempts, it became apparent to all that the truck would remain stuck unless something was put under the rear tires for traction. The problem that presented itself was that Sweeney's body was beneath the rear tires, pressed eight inches below the muddy surface of the mill yard. McMahon conferred with Jeremiah Addison. The two men came up with a plan.

It happened that Mary Sweeney and her daughter Abigail watched from afar as Addison and McMahon placed timber in the mud in front of and behind the rear tires as the rain continued to pour down. The impromptu engineering feat did the trick. The truck was freed from the muddy pit. In the process, the rotating tires on the rear axle had splintered the timber. At least that's what McMahon thought when he heard the cracking sound coming from underneath the rear of the truck. The cracking sound came from the late Patrick Sweeney

19

as the femur bones in his legs and his spine snapped in several places from the truck's weight. The timber did in fact splinter. Sharp slivers of wood had pierced the skin of Sweeney's muddied, dead body. By the time Addison, McMahon, and a few other men pulled Patrick Sweeney's mangled and bloodied body out of the deep mud, the widow Sweeney, watching the fiasco along with her daughter from the porch of the widow's tenement building, had already fainted. Unaware that her mother had collapsed, young Abigail leaned over the porch railing and vomited.

Two years after Patrick Sweeney was laid to rest (a closed casket, of course), a nine-year-old Abigail went missing. Until that day she had played the role of servant to her mother after school. Mary Sweeney had resigned herself to spending her time in the bedroom, propped up by pillows as she stared at a dirty window that looked out over the woods behind the widows' tenement house. Her daughter conveyed meals from the house kitchen to her, but as the months progressed following Sweeney's death, mother and daughter barely communicated. It was as if Mary Sweeney had lost the will to speak. It happened one morning that Abigail walked out of the widows' tenement house just after sunrise. By lunchtime that day Mary Sweeney's screams could be heard as she cried out for her meal.

McMahon pooled together a dozen men from the mill to search the surrounding woods. He paid special attention himself to those areas others may have overlooked like the new Beechwood Bridge, built in 1907, that connected Beechwood Road with Karakung Drive. McMahon and the volunteers worked in expanding circles, crisscrossing each other's paths. Jeremiah Addison called in the police chief who had a few squad members bring dogs out to the mill site. The search lasted all day. McMahon and the mill workers were unsuccessful in locating the girl; the same went for the bloodhounds that the police department used. The dogs followed Abigail's scent down to the creek. After that the trail went cold. The water was clear. From the bank everyone involved in the search had a clear view of the creek's bottom. As the day wore on, many began to suspect that Abigail had been abducted. Murmurs of justice floated in whispers—a justice that did not necessarily involve the police or the courts.

"The widow cannot know," Addison told McMahon. Nightfall was fast approaching, and the men were exhausted. "Gather lanterns, as many as you can find. Tell the men I will pay them to stay late and continue to search."

McMahon believed that Abigail had drowned. He told Addison as much that evening.

"Where?" the mill owner asked.

"If she found her way to Naylors Run she could be underground," said McMahon. "I should take some men down that way. It's only a few miles away. Even a little girl could have covered that ground if she moved all day."

A fog settled on the mill grounds, having creeped up from the creek that formed the western border of Haverford Township. McMahon doubted that lanterns would be of any use if the fog continued to grow thicker. Still, he did what he was told. He enlisted the help of a half-dozen men to get the lanterns lit and ready to go.

"McMahon!" Addison called out.

The foreman turned to look. Out of the foggy gloom of eventide, near the mill wheel, two figures materialized. A child and a giant strode toward the place where Addison stood.

In the years that followed the dam break in 1918, McMahon would always remember the first time he saw the savage they called Yates, the wanderer of the woods, the one some of the Irish around Ardmore believed was the esteemed guest of an Elfin court. A guardian sent from beyond on the day Abigail had gone missing and the man tasked with finding the missing young girl and returning to the living world the sole link that Mary Sweeney still had.

Upon laying eyes on Yates, the men around McMahon whispered in the dark about the stranger working the most

21

heinous sins against Abigail. Some of them wanted to rouse the Haverford police into action, while others spoke of a more expedient method that caused a dull pain in McMahon's lower abdomen when he heard the word 'castration.'

"We should get a doctor to examine the girl," said Ciardi. "If he's abused her—"

"Never mind the doctor," cried Osborne, another mill worker. "We should make it a police matter. It's kidnapping, pure and true."

"Let's rush him," Ransom suggested as he stood behind other men. "I don't care how big he is. He can't take all of us."

All eyes turned to Ransom now. He retreated, realizing the others would make him approach the big man first.

"Why isn't he trying to run?" another man inquired.

"Look at him," Ciardi said. "*Il mostro*. If we let the monster go, he will come back for her."

In the end, as the millworkers who had searched all day for the missing girl now took up position around Abigail and Yates, it was McMahon who called upon cooler heads to prevail. Before Yates could wander off into the mist once more, the mill physician examined Abigail. The doctor declared the young girl physically well and mentally intact. Yates was permitted to leave on his own accord.

"It's better it turned out this way," Addison told his foreman later that night.

The men had all gone home to their families. Young Abigail was returned to her mother who by now was able to scarcely grasp the events that had transpired that day.

"How so, boss?" McMahon asked.

"You know as well as I do the thoughts that plague a man's heart," Addison replied. "Those men wanted blood tonight the moment they laid eyes on Yates."

"I wonder who he is."

"He's no ghost, that's for sure."

"If he was, he'd be the first good wraith I'd ever seen," said McMahon. "He must have kept her hidden between the worlds for a spell today."

"Your problem is you're too superstitious, Leo," Addison told him. "Yates is just a vagrant who still possesses a shred of decency."

McMahon pursed his lips, as if some final word tasted sour in his mouth. He scanned the woods, a few fawns bounded past, followed by their mother. Then, with his lips still pursed, he whistled an old reel he remembered from his childhood. One glance from Addison told him that the boss was in no mood for music. So, McMahon quit whistling. He sat there quietly now, thinking about the big man as he listened to the mill wheel creak as it spun ever so slowly in the dark.

Chapter Four: A Keystone Of Dark Blue—Haverford Township PA, 2012

On spring nights, when the air was still warm after sunset, the sky turned dark cobalt as the first stars made their presence known, and the voices of teenagers wandering to and from the Skatetorium reached further once the wind had stopped. Families within their homes along Chelten Road went about the business of clearing their dinner tables and readying small children for bed. Traffic along Darby Road returned to normal after the rush hour that had prolonged itself each passing year. It was during this hour when May Weldon left the confines of her home and ventured into her backyard, a cup of licorice-flavored tea in her frail slender hands, and a book tucked under one arm. May placed her tea and her book on a cast-iron-framed glass-top table and sat in a cushioned wood chair beneath a tall oak that faced away from her back porch. She practiced this nightly ritual in those warmer months, during which she would read a book until the last vestiges of daylight prevented her from seeing the words on the page.

Long ago, decades past now on a night similar to this one, a young May Weldon entered the backyard from the sidewalk, coming home from an errand, and saw a light beneath her back porch. Back then, lattice work had covered the perimeter of the porch between the deck and the ground. That night a portion of the lattice had been removed. It was a night that proved to May something she had maintained in her heart for a long time: of all the emotions she had experienced in a lifetime, it was love that she remained powerless against. Love was a wave that stretched far and wide, washing over her, a feeling so pure yet difficult to endure. It was a fond memory once, seeing that light beneath the porch; but, as the years passed, it became more intolerable; for that memory called to mind the press of her beloved's body against hers, the beloved who had left the world long ago, the beloved from whose absence she had never recovered, knowing that the years would be long and difficult before she saw him again as she had remembered him. And while other women she knew had married, raised children who in turn gave them grandchildren—in other words, women who had lived, loved, and died, May rebuffed other men. She learned to be content with her arrangement; for in her heart she carried the secret knowledge that her love affair, while separated by distance and decades, was far from over. There were many days ahead before the reunion May cherished above all else, and above all else there were plans to be made; plans that caused her to feel a sense of déjà vu, to feel as if she had already traveled down a road strange and new. And for this, she preferred not to see the back porch while she sat in her yard. Some memories, she knew, tended to snag time, to slow down life's gradual and linear march. The light's absence did not always mean darkness. There were things far worse than that, things that wore the heart thin. Determined as she was in those final days, it was much easier to avoid the one reminder that caused her so much anguish.

The book she chose that evening was *Wuthering Heights*. She opened the book to the third chapter. There was something about the coarse landscape, the biting wind that Emily Bronte wrote about that set her mind at ease. In another book she loved, she knew a place where the wind did not blow so cold, where the sky remained her favorite shade of blue, that dark cobalt she had loved for so long, and where a magnificent tree bloomed on an otherwise empty expanse, a canvas that

God had abandoned long ago to create something crueler and more akin to his Likeness.

Inside her home the kitchen phone rang. May paused her reading when she heard the back door open.

"Miss Weldon?" her nurse, Virginia Noonan, called out. "There's a man on the phone."

Virginia was a late addition to the household. The young nurse visited once a week to administer May's chemo treatment. On days when the pain proved too much to bear, May wondered which malady would do her in first: the nurse who had invaded her sanctuary or the cancer.

May did not dislike Virginia, but the nurse was too curious about things beyond the scope of her duties. The first time Virginia had visited May's home there was an air of superiority about her. The confidence she exuded, culled from her youth, and her knowledge of medicines meant not to cure but perhaps prolong her charge's suffering, was easy enough to deal with. It was Virginia's inquisitive nature that upset May most. The first time Virginia stepped foot into the basement she was instantly drawn to the root cellar door. May dismissed her nurse's questions, stating that no one used the root cellar, that it was a whim of her father's, having built it during the Second World War. It had come about when May's father was assisted by their tenant one autumn. Every day after school May came home to find Hyatt hard at work, hauling buckets of dirt into the backyard. Her father and Hyatt used wood joists to construct a stone arch that would support the existing foundation. May's mother worried that the house might collapse. Even when the stone arch had been completed and crowned with a keystone of dark blue stone Hyatt had brought home from Europe, Mrs. Weldon remained skeptical. She knew nothing of the stone arch's strength, and she refused to go into the basement until the heavy oak door was hung. After the job was done, when May was still a young girl, she began to hear Hyatt moving around their home at night. She knew he went to the basement, but she never dared to follow him.

"So, you have no idea what's in there?" Virginia had asked.

"I thought you were going to do a load of laundry?" May pressed her.

"I was," she replied. "I am. Aren't you curious?"

"The key to the padlock was lost long ago," she told her. "My father was an odd man. He used to keep potatoes stored there. After the war, the key was lost. And I have no interest in damaging the lock."

May didn't like lying, even to strangers, but she had no intentions of entertaining Virginia's constant line of inquiry.

That was weeks ago. Since that day May forbade Virginia to do any laundry. That night when she visited, before May went out to read her book in the yard, Virginia commenced her campaign once more. May was grateful for the phone call that served to deflect her inquisitive nature. A nurse, she reasoned, should never be so easily distracted.

"There isn't much light left," May told her. "Let me be."

"He says it's important," Virginia insisted.

"Tell him I'm washing my hair."

"Do you want me to take a number?"

"If you wish," said May.

She went back to her reading. A minute later, the back door opened again.

"Miss Weldon?" Virginia called out.

May rose from her seat and turned to face Virginia as she stood on the porch.

"What is it now?" she asked.

"The man is very persistent," she said.

"Aren't they all?"

Virginia stood there. Her posture told May that dealing with phone calls was beyond the scope of her duties as a home healthcare provider. Again with the attitude, May thought. Her cancer may have advanced, but she had not lost her faculties. She had a good mind to give Virginia a kick in the ass. Sadly, the meds she had been administered as of late had sapped her strength.

"He's a telemarketer," said May. "Just hang up. Honestly, Virginia. If you can't perform that simple favor, then I'll come do it myself."

"Miss Weldon," Virginia said, "he's not trying to sell anything."

May started her way across the yard toward the porch. The light had already changed and it was too dark to read.

"Next time," she told the nurse, "don't answer my telephone."

"I think he said his name is Hyatt," Virginia stepped aside as her charge climbed the steps.

May stopped.

"That's not funny," she said.

"I'm not trying to be funny, Miss Weldon," her nurse announced.

In the kitchen the receiver lay on the countertop. May picked it up.

"Who is this, please?" she asked.

When the caller identified himself, she pleaded for a moment, then May cupped her hand over the mouthpiece.

"Virginia," she said, "you better go."

"You can call me Ginny," she told her.

"Ginny sounds like a waitress name, dear," May replied. "It's a name hardly fitting your profession."

"Are you sure?"

"Or perhaps a hooker's name," she answered, "but I see no call to be rude."

"I mean do you want me to go?" Virginia already had her bag slung over her shoulder as she stood by the back door.

"Yes," said May. "This may take awhile."

"Do you want to lock the door behind me?"

"My dear Virginia," her patient said, "I've lived here my whole life. I never locked my doors and I'll be damned if I'm going to start now. Good night."

May waited until she heard the back door close. She sat down at her kitchen table, twirling the telephone cord around her index finger.

"And to what do I owe this distinct pleasure?" she asked the caller.

"I apologize for the hour," Harold Miller told her.

"If you felt that strongly then you would have waited until tomorrow."

Overhead, from the second floor, a soft footfall sounded the way it always did as night approached.

"I would like to talk to you," said Miller.

"Aren't you? I mean, right now? Talking to me?"

"My publisher was wondering if you would be amenable to possibly—"

"Good-bye, Dr. Miller," said May.

She stood up slowly and held the receiver away from her ear. Miller was still talking when she hung up on him.

Chapter Five: Slade The Errant Knight—Ardmore PA, 1915

It was the second Sunday in May when Robert Jonas Hyatt first met Megan Sullivan. He was a robust fourteen-year-old high school freshman and she a divine creature of well-proportioned cheek bones and dirty-brown, curly locks who stood near the mill wheel, one arm across her chest as she stood staring at the creek. Her pale linen dress caught the setting sun's rays just so, allowing Robert to study the shape of the lithe girl. At fourteen years old, he already knew that the widow Sweeney's daughter Abigail did not wear undergarments beneath her homemade dresses. This knowledge came second-hand from some boys at school who said that Abigail Sweeney would lift her skirt for a nickel and allow the coin-bearer a glimpse of her copper-colored pubic hair. Abigail was sixteen-years-old, two years older than Robert, and already well on her way to developing a reputation that small-town girls would just as soon avoid. With Megan Sullivan, however, it was different. She was a mystery to Robert. Just watching her, he knew that such a girl would be incapable of entertaining such a notion, much less carrying out such an act for money. Presently, as he watched Megan slip her right foot out of her shoe and toe the cold creek water, Robert had to look away.

When he was a little boy Robert had learned from his father Theodore to look people straight in the eye. Still, Robert could not bring himself to lock eyes with Megan Sullivan, even though his father had told him that it was important to make eye contact when first meeting someone. Theodore, in a rare rational state of mind, also informed his son that a gentleman never extended his hand first to shake a woman's hand when making her acquaintance.

"It's untowardly," Theodore had told his son. "And in such a simple gesture much can be read and none of it good."

"Why is that, papa?" young Robert asked that day.

"It's not civil," his father replied. "And that type of forwardness may cause you to run afoul of a woman's husband."

"What happens if she's not married?"

Robert's mother, busy clearing plates from the dining room table that night, shook her head and laughed.

"He's got you now," she said.

"If the lady is not married and you try to shake her hand first," his father replied, ignoring, for the time being, his wife's comment, "then you will find trouble with her father. When you're older, I will explain it all to you."

"You would do well to listen to your father," said Helena Hyatt. "I might have married a king if it were not for your father's staid customs."

"And my charm," Theodore added.

Helena grunted. A faraway look fell over her that night, one that Hyatt would not soon forget. It was an expression his mother often wore whenever his father talked about himself too much. A look that made young Robert uncomfortable. She carried a small stack of plates to the swinging door that led out of the dining room, paused, and went into the kitchen.

Robert's eyes remained fixed on the swinging door that night. He thought about his father, how for as long as he could remember he had felt sorry for him.

Theodore was a tanner by trade, but the trade had not been kind to him. When Robert was ten-years-old his father took a job as a trolley operator on the Ardmore/Llanerch Line #16. There was a fair amount of favors being done for people related to public transportation workers. Theodore made it in by the skin of his teeth when two other candidates, cousins of the hiring manager, suddenly died: one in a barroom brawl in Philadelphia and the other by heart attack. The wages were barely enough to support his family. Theodore's wife Helena taught high school English at the new Oakmont School on Eagle in Haverford Township, but the family needed more; so, Robert's father also worked late afternoons at Addison's Gun Powder Mill along Cobbs Creek, a job his wife would have preferred him not to take. Theodore's wife suffered nightmares from time to time of the mill's powder magazine blowing up. In each dream, Helena saw her husband enter the powder magazine, a windowless wood shed of some size, just before it exploded. During those early days of Theodore's new employment, his wife would awaken from the dreams of exploding powder magazines. As time went on, however, Helena learned to sleep through the most horrid versions of that dream. She never shared the workings of that dream with her husband, and she felt guilty some mornings when she woke up refreshed and happy despite losing her spouse in a dreamtime blast.

Helena did not make much money teaching high school English, but, despite the low pay, she prided herself on her students. In those days, nearly half of all students never finished the eighth grade. Those who went on to high school knew the value of a good education. It was this sentiment that drove Helena to teach her own children to read at an early age. Both Matilda and Robert learned to read before they were old enough to attend school. It moved Helena that both children had discovered the magic and the power of words so early in life just as she had done, and she marveled at how her children devoured books the way her gluttonous husband wolfed down food at the dinner table. When there were no books to be had, Matilda and Robert made up their own stories when they were little, creating elaborate tales such as The Goblin King, The Witch of Windsor, and Slade the Errant Knight, in which they both acted out parts. For Helena, teaching meant more than she could put into words; her children's natural love of stories, however, eclipsed her fondness for teaching.

Robert abandoned his impromptu acting career at the age of twelve. His focus shifted to recording those tales onto paper, with Matilda's help.

Presently, as he watched Megan Sullivan, Robert remembered a tale about the knight Galahad who was wounded and bleeding. What such a seasoned vassal might make of the vision before him troubled Robert, but he didn't have time to ponder such a thing for long. His sister Matilda took hold of his hand and gave his arm a tug.

"Mother says you must eat," Matilda said. "And I won't eat unless you do."

"You go," he said. "I'll be along shortly. Tell mother I am not hungry."

"But I am hungry now," his sister said.

Matilda stared at her brother with her large hazel eyes. Her blond hair had been cut short just a few weeks before that Sunday. At eight-years-old, her eyes already revealed the old soul her young body carried with such care.

"Stop that," he said.

"What am I doing?" Matilda asked. Then, "Who is that girl?"

"You see her too?"

"She's pretty," his sister announced. "Are you going to marry her?"

"I don't even know her name," said Robert.

"Wait here."

Matilda let go of her brother's hand. She walked down to the creek where she joined Megan at the water's edge. The two spoke in hushed tones. Then Megan leaned forward and whispered into Matilda's ear.

So, it happened that the first time Robert saw Megan he stood transfixed, unable to move, and relied upon his young sister to make initial contact.

"What were you two whispering about?" Robert asked after his sister returned to his side.

"I told her the truth," said Matilda. "You are a shy invalid whose mental defect makes you a social pariah. In many respects you are much worse off than Yates the Centurion, I told her. Do you know she's never seen Yates? I find that hard to—"

"Matilda, what did she whisper to you?"

"A secret."

"What kind?"

"Don't be a dolt," Matilda said. "There's only one kind of secret, Robert. Besides, you won't talk to her so what's the point?"

Robert took a step forward, intent on finally talking to the girl by the mill wheel. When he did, a voice called out from behind him.

"Megan Ann Sullivan!" the woman cried. "I thought the fairies took you!"

"There are no fairies in America, ma," the girl replied.

"She's Irish," Matilda told her brother. "From County Cork. That's in Ireland. In case you wanted to know."

"I know where—" Robert began.

"Just the same," Megan's mother said now. "Come and eat. Mr. Addison was kind enough to have this picnic for his workers."

"I'll be there shortly," the girl replied.

"If you don't move now," Mrs. Sullivan informed her daughter, "I will box your ears and embarrass you right here in front of your friends. Now, let's go."

Megan walked straight toward Matilda and Robert. When she reached them, she stopped and caressed Matilda's cheek.

"Your sister says you're a mute," Megan said to Robert now. "I guess that explains why you didn't come over to the water and talk to me."

"I'm not mute," Robert informed her as he took hold of his sister by the scruff of her neck.

"Megan Ann," her mother shouted. "Now!"

"The old girl gets easily excited," Megan said, nodding at her mother. She winked at Robert, and added, "Come and find me later, if you like."

Chapter Six: The Land Of Dust And Honey—The Hollow Hill Gate

In the foggy dark, the woodland proved more treacherous than Barth had anticipated. Trees were snapped in two everywhere. Branches formed jagged obstacles—some on the forest floor, others hanging by a sliver of damp bark. The German artillery bombardment had begun there. Barth remembered standing on a ladder in the forward trench, binoculars in hand as he spotted the rounds exploding at treetop level within the forest. It didn't take long for the German unit to adjust their artillery fire, walking the shells from the woodland out onto the pasture until those artillery rounds rained down over the trenches where Barth's unit desperately awaited reinforcements. A company-sized element of British infantry had been scheduled to relieve Barth's group in the trenches and link-up with the remaining British battalion in the pasture a quarter-mile south. Making his way slowly through the forest, it didn't take long to discover what had become of the British. Visibility was still poor, affording him a glimpse of only ten or twenty yards in every direction. A foul scent affixed itself to his uniform—the rank odor of the dead.

The ancient maples and oaks that made up that part of the forest had stood for at least two hundred years. Most of them had been reduced to stunted, splintered trunks. The British dead lay scattered amidst shredded branches and fallen trees. Of the many bodies he stumbled upon none were left intact; here, a torso missing its head and arms; there, legs and lower bodies in a tangled and singed heap. The ground beneath his boots was moist with blood. Barth moved slowly through the kill zone, inspecting torn backpacks and bloodied cargo belts for food, water, and ammunition. He had only been at it for a few minutes when he heard the voices of German soldiers and the metallic clatter of their gear as they marched through the forest.

Barth estimated that he saw a company-size element, judging by the faint shadows, moving in a line not thirty yards away from him. He hunkered down next to the corpse of a British sergeant whose lower body had been shredded to ribbons. The Brit's face, frozen in the moment of time when he bled out, appeared horribly contorted, as if glimpsing the afterlife caused more fear than the artillery shells that had exploded all around him. Keeping an eye on the column of German soldiers, Barth was lulled into a stupor as he listened to the cowbell clang of metal on metal as their mess kits rattled against ammunition magazines. He considered the fallen Brit beside him lucky, as he did those who lay dead in the trenches. For them, the war had ended abruptly; for him, it meant another day of madness. Death was like a jackal cackling in the dark. It taunted him, wanting him yet refusing to leap, in league with that devil charged with making men beg for death.

A hole was torn in the hypnotic metallic clamor when an artillery shell exploded. Barth's body went rigid. Cries of terror and confusion filled the woodland. One among the German unit had stumbled upon unexploded ordnance. Barth counted a dozen men crying out in the dark. He heard the officers barking orders as the wounded were dragged deeper into the forest.

He had no way of knowing how much time had passed when he could no longer hear the German soldiers. Barth sat up slowly, listening for the slightest movement. Before long, the report of small arms fire could be heard. The shots, nearly muted by the fog, rang out from a good distance away. The Germans dealt with their severely wounded differently from everyone else in the war. It was less a form of barbarism as it was one of expediency. The injured made healthy soldiers vulnerable, and soldiers were no more than a commodity to be traded and bartered with among the invisible powers at play—

lethargic, apathetic demons and angels whose respective purposes as they trolled this earthly realm were staving off death for those who would trade their souls or facilitating a man's end so that others may live. It was a ridiculous game because Death never harbored any interest in playing by the rules.

When Barth moved again he headed north, away from the British dead whose body parts littered the forest floor like so many autumn leaves, away from the unexploded ordinance that waited in the dark. Soon, he walked among trees untouched by German artillery. It did little to clear his mind, to assuage the fear of inevitability—that his efforts would not permit him to stay concealed for long. The forest grew older the further north he moved. He paused at various intervals to listen. In the dark there were more than owls and other nocturnal creatures making sounds, for in the wide and deep expanse of night came a new noise, the succinct bone-wrenching silence that marked the absence of war, a stillness on all sides, a space devoid of the great folly. In that static hum of sad silence, and in that steady murmur of nothingness, another fear took hold. Out of nowhere, from deep within the dampening, deafening fog, the war would return to him. And when it did he would seek not the valiant escape a soldier often does when faced with enemy forces that outnumber him, embracing a firefight like an old friend; no, the sanctity of survival would move him to hide once more like a scavenger, waiting for the war to pass him by the way it had done earlier that day.

Surveying his present position, Barth spotted a giant oak tree, the top half of its massive root system exposed atop a low rise. He did not know how far he had wandered to escape the enemy. Stopping was dangerous, but Barth was exhausted. Slowly he approached the rise, pausing to pick up a long stick. He squatted in front of the exposed root system and jabbed the stick several times into the dark cavity beneath the tree. When he was satisfied that there were no errant bears driven mad by the artillery bombardments, or ravenous wolves whose food supply had fled the area in protest against the war, hiding there, he gathered broken branches and stacked them haphazardly against the exposed root system, leaving a small opening through which he could crawl in and out.

It wasn't long before Barth discovered that the hollow hill beneath the great oak was much more spacious than he had first anticipated. The ground was damp. The roots over his head and to his left and right gave off a faint phosphorescent glow, turning the convex roof and walls into a starry sky. His body heated the hiding place. He stretched out on the ground and his eyelids became heavy. Sleep fell over him.

A hole opened in his mind. He often dreamed in this fashion, for as long as he could remember, with the opening starting no larger than a fist, but then growing in size, a gradual blossoming that offered Barth glimpses of worlds where color was more vibrant, the air crisper. The longer the hole in his mind stayed open, the more vibrant the colors appeared. A gateway into a new world appeared to him, no matter how ephemeral. At present, with the war going on all around him, with the landscape stripped bare of colorful vegetation, and with the sky once filled with abundant stars now turned opaque with smoke, Barth's dreams were different. When he could sleep he dreamed of the faces of the dead, some with their chests and stomachs reduced to empty cavities stuffed with kindling and set ablaze by unseen hands to stave off the cold that only the dead knew.

He woke up with tears in his eyes, shocked by the realization that he too may already be dead. Perhaps his penance for killing was to serve on a battlefield for eternity. In war, each suffered his own hell, dwelling in that place, ignorant of the moment the body gave up the ghost to go on existing in an afterlife that replicated the worst moments of a man's life in continuous loops until space and time, light and darkness, good and evil, matter and spirit all rushed toward the singularity which was God's breath: an inhalation drawn in one cosmic moment of disbelief, followed by the divine gasp when He realized that Creation had missed its mark, instead that men created in His image had resorted to war; they had given themselves over to shadows aping angels, proving that all was lost.

Barth wiped his eyes. The glowing roots were still visible. From somewhere deep in the darkest recesses of the hollow hill came a ringing sound that sounded like Sanctus bells at mass. He sat up, inhaling the aroma of the wet earth, and listened as the chiming continued unabated. Called by the bells, Barth crawled on his hands and knees toward the sound's source.

The further he moved down the gradual slope the drier the ground became. After crawling on his hands and knees for twenty yards he was able to stand up and walk. For a short distance, the root system overhead remained within reach. Then it gave way to more cavernous surroundings and even the soft earth beneath his feet was slowly replaced by loose rocks. His pace slowed as a result of the rocks, but it gave him time to take in his new environment. Several times he stopped, listened for the bells, and heard the ringing increase, leading him deeper into the hill until he reached a stream.

He knelt at the water's edge, washing his hands, his face, and his neck, and then he cupped the cold water into his hands and drank. With each handful he felt renewed. All the while the bells continued to call to him. He stood up and moved once more, wading through the knee-deep stream. On the other side of the water, a gradual incline led him through sparse trees until the land crested. At the top of the next low rise, he came to a rocky outcrop where a heavy and ancient wood door stood. The door was framed in an arch hewn from dark stone riddled with veins of white and gray; the keystone over the arch, pale blue in color, glowed with its own inner moonlight. Barth pressed his ear to the door. The bells he had followed were ringing on the other side now, and they still beckoned him. He leaned his shoulder against the door, gave it a slight shove, and opened it.

A warm gust met him from the other side. Tall trees stretched high toward strange constellations. Turning back, Barth glimpsed the outline of a root cellar built into the side of a hill from which he had emerged. He attempted to push the ancient door shut, resting his hands on its surface until his fingers pressed through the rotted and brittle wood. The door collapsed into pieces. The dark stone arch caved in next, and the keystone came to rest atop the heap as it continued to emit its strange silver-blue light. The doorway that had led him into that land was gone now, and before him, only the hollow hill. Behind him, towering trees loomed laced with countless vines, their massive trunks ringed by brushwood and bushes. A primitive forest awaited him, as ancient as the stones that lay at his feet, a paradise unscathed by the war.

Chapter Seven: The Fool's Daughter—Pittsfield MA, 2012

Harold Miller sat in his study. It was nearly nine o'clock at night. He stared at the phone on his desk, contemplating the call he had just made to May Weldon. Her abruptness did not surprise him, nor did it offend him. He had always felt they shared an intrinsic connection, since he first met her all those years ago, when his academic career was still on the rise, and he a widower for one year. Miller's wife Ann had died in an auto wreck on the Massachusetts Turnpike. He had been in Amsterdam, attending a symposium on fantasy literature. It was his daughter Elinor who had delivered the bad news when she called him in his hotel room. The connection was not good. His daughter, of all people, had to inform him that his wife of twenty-five years was dead. At the time, Elinor had not been much older than Miller had been when he had married Ann. Despite her adulthood, Elinor lacked maturity. She blamed him for his wife's untimely death, as if it might have been averted if Miller had not gone to Amsterdam.

The funeral was a modest one, Presbyterian, and attended by family that consisted of Ann's two older brothers, and Ann's younger sister by five years. Ann's siblings had been aloof throughout their marriage so the cold reception he received from them at the funeral came as no surprise. Along with Ann's siblings there were a smattering of cousins, some close and some distant, and friends who had remained in Ann's life since her days at Emerson College. A solemn luncheon at

Miller's home in Pittsfield followed the burial. Elinor stood dutifully by her father's side until the last guest left the house late that afternoon. Then she left him alone in his study. It was there that Miller broke down and sobbed for hours. He regretted not being close to Elinor.

At times, before and after Ann's death, he found himself envious of friends who had large families. To Miller, having more than one child meant a chance to become a better father to each successive one. He considered himself a failure in that respect; for him, fatherhood had remained a mystery. With each passing year, Miller felt as if he was missing some important part of that equation; somehow an essential part of the formula had eluded him. By the time Elinor turned thirteen, the divide between them was already so wide that Miller had given up any serious attempts at crossing it; instead, he began to reconcile himself to that rift, recognizing his own role in its creation. Miller's relationship with his daughter was strained enough while Ann was alive, but with his wife's passing, the divide deepened. In the days since his wife's death, Miller often resented how he had immersed himself in his work and pretended that he could have done things differently. He knew beneath the pretense, though, that if he had not spent long nights and weekends pouring over the passages of R.J. Hyatt's great novel, his relationship with Elinor would have remained the same. No amount of father-daughter time would have averted the unequivocal dis-ease they shared, that theirs had always been, and would undoubtedly remain, a strained and distant relationship. The fissure stretched back for as long as either one could remember, and forward into the foreseeable future; too wide a gap, it seemed, for Elinor or her father to take that first step.

The winter after his wife died, Miller had made up his mind to write a biography about R.J. Hyatt. For all his intensive studies of *The Land of Dust and Honey*, for all the explications he had written about Hyatt's poems, for all the long hours Miller had spent mapping out the cadence of

Hyatt's prose, a feeling remained that he could not shake: the further he delved into the written works of R.J. Hyatt, the more distant R.J. Hyatt the man became. The task itself, telling the story of a life far removed from his own, appeared daunting, but Miller knew of no other biography about Hyatt in existence. No matter the odds, no matter the obstacles he might face, he knew the undertaking would be worth the effort.

Miller pitched the idea to his academic publisher, but upon considering the subject matter, it was decided that his needs would be best served by a mainstream publisher. Hyatt's only novel was immensely popular, and fans of the writer's work would delight in a well-researched biography. Miller knew nothing of selling a proposal to the likes of big publishing houses. He also understood that most academic publishers were not interested in works of general readership. Biographies about writers who lived on the fringe, writers who shut out the world, writers who rarely maintained relationships with anyone they did not create on the page, were less about biographical information and more about further solidifying a writer's ephemeral existence. The biggest obstacle Miller faced was not finding a publisher (he ended up submitting his proposal to Rhineholt, the same publisher who published a new edition of Hyatt's novel every few years), but the overall lack of living people who had known Hyatt during his lifetime.

"What do you think?" Miller had asked his daughter one day when she was home for the Christmas holiday.

"About what?" she asked.

"Me writing Hyatt's biography."

"Oh, that's cool," she said. Then added, "I guess."

Elinor had just entered her first year of graduate anthropology studies at Harvard—her area of study: archaeology. Her PhD thesis would be on Bronze Age settlements. The only reason she had come home to Pittsfield at all was not out of some sense of familial duty. No, Elinor wanted her father to know that she intended to spend another summer abroad. Half of Elinor's gift from her father when she completed her undergraduate studies at Columbia University had been to cover her travelling expenses for a summer in Europe.

"Not Europe again," Miller said.

"No, dad," said Elinor. "Papua New Guinea."

"Big contribution to the Bronze Age from Papua New Guinea?"

"You're such an ass," was Elinor's reply. "You're still sore about the whole Europe thing?"

Along with paying his daughter's way to tour Europe for six weeks after she graduated Columbia, Miller also presented Elinor with a used and battered copy of *The Land of Dust and Honey*. When his daughter had returned from her trip in early August, Miller asked her about the book.

"It was ok," she had told him.

"That's it?" he asked.

"Dad," Elinor said, "I don't have to like everything you do. Even if it is a book that you spent a lifetime studying. It doesn't mean I love you any less."

Miller was shocked. The admission that his favorite book in the world meant little or nothing to his daughter overshadowed Elinor's admission of love. He experienced a bitter taste in his mouth, unsure of which may have impacted him more—her genuine sense of love or her lack of admiration for her father's life's work. Miller, as much as he would never admit it to his own daughter, was still grieving his wife's death. He maintained a rigid exterior—a gift he had inherited from his New England born and bred father.

"Well," he said at last, hugging his daughter close, "I love you even if you hate Hyatt's book."

Elinor cried. She did a good amount of that in the weeks and months following her mother's death. Later, she would remember the moment between her and her father as an awkward and uncomfortable union between ghosts composed of oppositely charged particles. Elinor missed her mother, and her father was no substitute. This feeling she would never admit to her father. She knew that her father's make-up was different than hers, that she was more like her mother than she cared to admit, and that her father never cared for bandying about the word 'love' the way other people used it. For Elinor, it was one thing to lessen the meaning of a word by constantly using it, and it was something else entirely when her father refused to say the word.

For Miller it was a tipping point, a deciding moment in which he chose to move forward with the Hyatt biography. He would dedicate the work to his daughter, and through the light he would shed on Hyatt's stark, reclusive life, Elinor would, as she matured, come to realize the value of *The Land of Dust and Honey*, and its impact. The work would be a welcome relief for Miller. For Elinor, it meant little. It proved nothing except that her father had not grieved the way most men do when they lose a wife. Instead, he carried on as a widower as he had once done in marriage, putting behind him flesh and blood relations while setting his sights on a man long dead who spoke to Miller from some realm removed from the living world.

After Ann's death, the house had changed. There was something in the permanent absence of another that could never be undone. Miller was grateful when his biography research took him away from Pittsfield, but eventually he had to return. When he sat down to work in his study it was enough to keep his head down and pour over his notes and other research materials. Now and then, late at night, especially as summer turned to autumn, the old house settled on its foundation—a belabored giant made from concrete, wood, brick, and glass hunkered down for a long winter's hibernation—and the creak of floorboards took on a familiar cadence, not unlike the soft pad of his late wife's footfall. Ann had gone through life treading lightly wherever she went, even when they lived in their tiny, two-bedroom apartment in Providence, as Miller completed his dissertation at Brown, fearful that any sound she made might distract her husband. Now that the house was empty save for him, every noise caused

Miller to stop. It began in earnest right after her passing. Ann's absence made the house hollow, taking on a cavernous quality that amplified every sound, from a pen dropping on Miller's desk to the hourly chime of the grandfather clock in the living room. For this reason, and to Elinor's detriment, Miller donated the clock to an auction house. When Elinor was a young girl she had been fascinated by the clock, and though she rarely visited him after her mother had passed, Miller felt certain on those few occasions that she noticed and disapproved of its absence. His wife had been a different story. Ann had tolerated the clock but saw no reason to keep such an antiquated timepiece. She complained some nights that time would not allow her to sleep. After Ann's death, Miller still felt her presence in the house, as if her spirit had somehow eluded passing on to some paradise beyond the pale, and instead of rejoining whatever source the spirit came from, she instead fused herself with the very essence of the house. Miller did not admit to himself that he'd hoped removing the clock would encourage her spirit to depart, to move on to the place where the dead dwelled, and, in doing so, let him study and write uninterrupted. Alone, Miller viewed the hollow house as more and more intolerable. If he had been a superstitious man, he might have considered that Ann was somehow trying to tell him to move on, to sell the house and start anew, but his intellect did not allow for misgivings about an afterlife; the body, charged with energy, was born, lived and died; in Miller's clouded recollection of a physics class or two, the energy released upon death could not be destroyed so it became something else the way the body in decomposition did. He was a stoic man, a stubborn man whose resolve forced him to push on and refuse to give in to the ghost that sought to separate him from his work.

Presently, Miller rocked forward and back as he rubbed his eyes. His desk phone rang. He lunged for it.

"Thank you for reconsidering," he said when he answered.

"Reconsidering what?" Elinor asked.

"El?"

"Hi, dad," she said. "How are you?"

"I'm well, thanks," he said. "How is the world treating you?"

"You know how it is," his daughter answered. Then, "So, I am free this weekend. I thought I might drive up for a visit."

Miller said nothing. A noise escaped from low in his throat.

"What is it, dad?" Elinor inquired. "Were you expecting someone else on the phone?"

"Work," he said.

"The university?" she asked. "Or the other thing?"

Whenever Elinor spoke of her father's extracurricular interest, convincing a writer's estate to part with unpublished works of the deceased, she made it sound illicit.

"My publisher wants me to update the biography," he told her.

It had been years since Miller referred to R.J. Hyatt by name to his daughter. He understood that she preferred it that way. It was one of those things, another mystery meant to elude a daughter's father, that proved how little he knew about his only child.

"That's good news," Elinor said.

"I am in a bind," he said.

"How so?"

"If I don't come up with a new introduction or something heretofore unknown about Hyatt," he said, "the biography will go out of print."

Try writing about someone else, Elinor wanted to tell him.

Instead, she said, "Well, if I can be of any help let me know."

"Elinor, I was thinking about driving down to Philadelphia," he said. "Perhaps comb through the archives at—"

"Some other weekend perhaps?"

"Sure."

"Call me when you get to Philadelphia."

"Good night, Elinor," he said, writing the word *Philadelphia* on a Post-it note.

Miller hung up. He sat still, listening to the old house settle. During moments like this, he often called out Ann's name, imploring her to bring something to drink. Then he would feel foolish remembering that she had been dead for years. And after that, a certain melancholy would take hold. He imagined Ann, in those moments, as a ghost on the ground floor, shaking her head in quiet disbelief, wondering when her husband had become such an old fool.

Chapter Eight: A Severe Distrust Of The Irish—Ardmore Pa, And Elsewhere, 1915

The monthly Sunday picnics began shortly after Abigail Sweeney had been returned safely to the powder mill by the one they called Yates. Jeremiah Addison, a devout Presbyterian—in a community burgeoning with Irish, Italian, and German Catholics—believed that his task was to do good for others, especially the disadvantaged. And in emulating his Savior, Addison had often been accused of being a Communist.

No sooner did he set his man Leo McMahon to task, imploring his foreman to see to the details, Addison caught wind of the men working for him murmuring amongst themselves that if the big boss had enough money to throw lavish banquets, then surely, he had enough money to see that every man in his employ could get at least a penny more an hour.

Opinion changed after the first picnic. The powder mill workers soon realized that all Addison wanted was to develop a sense of community and offer thanks for a job well-done. Among the workers were a few who kept spreading rumors that Addison was a Communist, that his efforts to feed workers and their families one Sunday out of the month were nothing more than a ruse to recruit others into the Party. Those men shied away from the picnic at first, amidst rumors of Pinkerton detectives and other more nefarious types descending upon powder mill grounds with ill-intent in mind. As the months passed, nothing of the sort happened. And each of the workers in turn, at first so vehemently convinced of Addison's affiliation with communists, eventually came around and attended the Sunday picnics along with their families.

The company picnic turned out to be nothing like the lavish banquet some had suspected. Barbeque chicken and roasted pig made up the main course. Workers and their families were encouraged, but not required, to bring inexpensive homemade side dishes. Desserts were supplied by Addison's wife Loretta and the members of the Ardmore Ladies Auxiliary Club. Volunteers were called upon to clear the mill grounds by day's end; otherwise, the task was left until Monday morning. Leo McMahon was also charged with keeping a tally of those workers who skipped out early before a clean-up detail could be mustered. By the time the third monthly picnic was drawing to its end things began to shape up, each man doing his part. By the following spring, the picnic operation ran like a well-oiled machine.

When they joined their parents at the picnic table, Matilda and Robert both wished they had stayed down by the mill wheel. Theodore Hyatt, quite drunk and red-faced, held court with several families as he wove the intricate, and by no means truthful tale, of his family's ancestry.

"You see, after the Norman Invasion, things became dicey for my kin," Theodore said.

"He hasn't gotten to Robert the Bruce yet, has he?" Robert asked his mother.

"Hush," said Helena.

"It is true that we Hyatts were instrumental," Theodore shouted over the din of the picnic-goers, "in a great many pivotal epochs in English history—"

"Did your people steal Erin land from my ancestors?" a man spoke up, his brogue thick and threatening.

Laughter erupted. Robert took hold of Matilda's hand. His intention was to back away from the scene and rescue his sister from any further embarrassment, but their escape attempt was thwarted by Helena.

"Don't go," she said. "We are going to eat if your father can ever get to the part where the Hyatts sailed for the colonies."

"And it wasn't Robert the Bruce," Matilda corrected her brother. Then, to the crowd, "It was William Wallace himself who felled the first Hyatt."

"My daughter knows her history," Theodore announced. "Poor Henry Hyatt was trampled underfoot by Wallace's horse just scant hours before the great Scotsman was defeated at Falkirk."

Robert saw the fifth of whiskey in his father's back pocket. Mr. Addison forbade liquor on the premises, but he was willing to turn a blind eye unless men took to fighting.

"Hyatt!" Leo McMahon shouted.

"Yes, Mr. McMahon?" Theodore shouted back.

"Give those tales of cunning and deceit a rest. Feed your family, boy-o," the foreman told him, "before you starve to death what's left of your proud lineage!"

As the crowd erupted in laughter once more, Theodore turned to his wife as he reached for the fifth of whiskey in his pocket.

"You heard the foreman," he said. "Take the children and I'll be there directly."

That night it was already dark when Robert walked his mother and his sister home. His father, having had too much to drink, decided a nap was in order so he wandered off into the woods near the mill. Robert insisted on going after him, but his mother had other plans.

"Leave him," said Helena. "Maybe the wolves will have a go at him."

"Mother," said Matilda, "there are no wolves in Pennsylvania."

"An unfortunate thing."

"What?"

"Never mind," her mother said. "Time to go home. You and Robert have school tomorrow."

Helena was a stickler for school. She had been to college, graduating Bryn Mawr at nearly the top of her class. Afterward, she taught English at the Llanerch School in Haverford Township on Darby Road. She married Theodore soon after that. When the new high school opened on Eagle Road in 1912 she accepted a position there.

The summer before she met Theodore, Helena took a train to Chicago to hear a lecture given by the great educator himself John Dewey. She sat on the edge of her seat, listening to Dewey extol the virtues of education and lay out a plan for the future of American intellect. Helena respected learned men, the great philosophers of her time. Like so many philosophers, Theodore possessed a gift for words. It was the thing that had attracted her to him from the beginning. As the years passed, however, things changed. Helena encouraged her husband to write, but Theodore considered a life of letters as one better suited for women and dandies.

"What about Jack London?" Helena asked. "He's no dandy."

"Labor union pimp," Theodore said. "Getting rich off the common man. I will not have you speak of Socialists in my house."

Ultimately, like so many intelligent men plagued by their own thoughts, Theodore drank more and more, and at times accused his wife of the most heinous betrayals. That Helena was beautiful no one ever disputed; her charm, however, was what drew men—ordinarily intimidated by such beauty—near to her like moths to lamplight. For Theodore, it became a source of pain; for Helena, a burden to bear over the years as she resigned herself to the fact that in her neck of Delaware County there were no men on a par with the likes of John Dewey or Jack London, least of all, her husband.

When Helena Barker was nineteen-years-old, two things happened that changed her life forever.

The first had to do with her grandfather Heinrich's farm in the Lancaster region. Her father's father, an immigrant from Germany, had been in a long-term dispute over the proposed boundary of his property. His neighbor, a man from County Cork, Ireland named McNally, owned the farm adjacent to the elder Barker's land.

It was rumored that McNally had in his possession a survey drawing dating back to 1805 in which his property extended fifty yards into the Barker farm for the length of ten acres. It was by all accounts a profitable track of land that the Barkers had worked ever since Helena's father was an infant. Before McNally, the farm was owned by an Amish family who had sold it to the Irishman and moved to Ohio. Within a week of settling into the new homestead, McNally plowed under a considerable stretch of corn that the elder Barker had planted.

The feud went on for a decade or more until the Lancaster County Sheriff, a Swede by the name of Jorgen, convinced both men to settle the matter at court. McNally brought his old survey drawing and his deed. Heinrich Barker brought with him the bill of sale for his property along with his copy of the county survey drawing. After careful review of the documents, and further consideration of a bill of sale dated 1809, in which the previous owners of McNally's and Barker's farms, one Elijah Chupp and one Mordecai Yoder, respectively, had entered an agreement. Elijah Chupp, the father of the former owner of McNally's farm, had sold a portion of his land to Mordecai Yoder, a strip of land that measured half an acre by ten acres, and the court ruled in Barker's favor. The matter was settled, or so Barker thought.

That night as Heinrich Barker lay sleeping next to his wife Joan someone broke into their farmhouse. Helena was just twelve-years-old at the time, living on a farm in Springfield, PA along with her father Jonah and her uncle, Jonah's twin brother Herbert. The intruders bound the sleeping couple to their bed, doused them with lantern oil, and set them on fire. The farmhouse burned to the ground, as well as the barn which housed a few horses, some cows, and several chickens.

No one, not even Jorgen the sheriff, could prove that McNally and his sons, Constance and Francis, as half-witted and full of hate as any thugs that ever walked God's good earth, were complicit in the Barkers' deaths. Helena's grandparents were buried; that is to say, two empty pine boxes were placed into the ground since their bodies had been consumed, flesh and bone together, in the inferno.

The destructive power of fire had not seen its last days in Lancaster County. Seven years to the day that the Barker farmhouse and barn burned to the ground, another fire consumed the house of McNally. Unlike Barker and his wife Joan, McNally and his sons managed to escape the blaze. Eileen McNally never made it out of the house. Out of the darkness three rifle shots rang out in succession: one each felling McNally, Constance and Francis in that order. Only Francis survived his gunshot wound, though it severed his spine. Choking on the smoke that billowed across the front yard, Francis shielded his eyes from the blaze that burned the farmhouse. He saw a slender figure in a long black dress approach. The shooter raised her rifle as she advanced out of the darkness. On her face, a look of anger emerged as she stood over him. Francis opened his mouth to curse the young, beautiful, dark-haired angel of death in her funereal dress, but before he could mutter the 'f' in 'fuck you,' she shot him in the face.

Afterward, Helena developed a severe distrust of the Irish. For a few weeks she dreamt of Francis McNally laying in the grass, his lower body paralyzed, as he hissed like a snake. Each time the dream ended with Helena raising her hunting rifle and shooting the Irishman in the face. It was around this time that her otherwise ardent interest in quail and pheasant hunting had lapsed. Until she shot Francis McNally, Helena had looked forward to her excursions into the field with her father and her uncle Herbert. After killing the murderous Irishman, hunting no longer mattered.

Not long after the execution of the McNally men, Lancaster County Sheriff Jorgen visited the Barkers farm in Springfield accompanied by the Springfield Police and the sheriff of Delaware County. Jorgen was convinced that the Barker brothers and one other assailant were responsible for the deaths of McNally and his sons. However, upon thoroughly searching the house and the small barn where the Barker brothers raised chickens, the Lancaster County sheriff could find no rifles, much less those that may have been used in the execution of the McNally men.

The second thing that happened to Helena Barker was this: upon returning from Lancaster County one afternoon, along with her father and her Uncle Herbert, she saw a young man walking along West Chester Pike as she rode a trolley from 69th Street. The train ride from Lancaster to Philadelphia lasted nearly five hours, and then Helena, her father, and her uncle took the Philadelphia West Chester Trolley out of the city. The previous day, Helena's father and her uncle had just sold the farm where her grandparents had been killed seven years earlier, in fact, the McNally farmhouse nearby lay in smoldering ruins. Having leased the land to an Amish family for a time, Helena's father and her uncle were relieved that, as dreadful as it was to sell the land for cash, they could begin to put the past behind them now that the old farm belonged to someone else.

In Upper Darby, just a mile or two before their stop in Haverford Township, Helena spotted a young man. He was tall and lanky. In those days Theodore Hyatt wore a green bowler hat that, when Helena would later tell the story, looked better fitted for a performing monkey or a dancing elephant. Suddenly, Helena was possessed with the idea that she had to find out more about the man in the green hat. To her father's chagrin, she stood up when the double-block trolley pulled to a stop at the next block. Helena was already on the sidewalk when her father joined her. Uncle Herbert, having fallen fast asleep, remained on the No. 34 trolley.

"What's this all about?" her father asked.

"You there," Helena called out to Theodore, ignoring her father for the moment.

Theodore pointed at himself. Helena had gained considerable confidence in her first year at Bryn Mawr. Her parents worried that their daughter might absorb too much independence and bravery, and never find a man to marry. When Theodore stood before Helena and her father, his hat looked even more ridiculous than it had when she first viewed it from the trolley. Helena was about to dismiss the man, claiming she had confused him with another, when she looked into his eyes for the first time. Until that moment she had been prepared to write him off as another Haverford dandy. But something happened that afternoon that caused young Helena to reconsider.

"Good afternoon, sir," the young man said. "Theodore Hyatt. Pleased to make your acquaintance."

Theodore and Helena's father shook hands.

Helena felt lightheaded staring into Theodore's eyes that were colored blue like the sky on a cloudless day. At Bryn Mawr, she had learned that independent women did not swoon, that free-thinking women were not taken with 'the vapors.' Silently, she admonished herself for having such thoughts.

Helena's father had more than one worry, the least of which was whether his daughter would ever be married. Johan Barker believed that his daughter's education might lead her toward a ruinous path or, worse, lead to her alignment with the Women's Suffrage movement that was gathering steam. Johan also worried that the events of seven years ago had affected his daughter in ways that were now only starting to show. That his daughter had been accepted into Bryn Mawr was cause for celebration, but he still feared that the road to righteousness was besotted on both sides by ruination. If Helena continued to bask in free ideas and critical thinking, Johan wondered if his only child would end up with an unwanted child. Perhaps a life far away from that outcome, but equally distressing, was this: living a life devoid of men and secretly falling in love with women in some city like New York or even Paris where Johan had it on good authority that men were free to love men and women encouraged to share intimate and sensual encounters with other women.

"Do we know one another?" Theodore posed the question to Helena.

He removed his dark green bowler hat and looked warily up and down West Chester Pike.

"Are the police after you, Mr. Hyatt?" Helena asked.

"No, no," he looked nervously at Barker as he spoke. "Nothing of the sort, I can assure you."

"That look suits you," she told him.

Having judged that Theodore was not a lecher, Barker stepped to the curb for the moment to seek another trolley. There were none in sight.

"Which one?" Theodore asked.

"That one," Helena said. "Without that ridiculous hat."

"But a man should not be without one," Theodore countered. "Do you agree?"

Helena spotted her uncle Herbert walking toward her and her father. When he joined the group, introductions were made, handshakes were exchanged, and the Barker men quietly excused themselves to step into a tap room for a draft.

"Where do you go to school?" Helena asked.

"I don't," Theodore replied. "I work. And you?"

"I shall return to Bryn Mawr this fall," she told him. "I am studying English literature."

"My ancestors are from England," he said.

Something in his voice made her laugh.

"What's so funny?" he asked.

"Nothing," she said.

"I will take a trolley to see you at Bryn Mawr College," he said, at last. "And if there are no trolleys, I will walk."

"I don't think you will be allowed on campus."

"Then I'll stand across the street until you notice me."

"Please don't wear that hat."

Theodore tossed the hat into the street. A beer vendor in a horse-drawn carriage pulled to a stop at the curb. Helena and Theodore watched as the horse shook its head and shit on the dark green bowler hat.

"Well, then," said Theodore. "That takes care of that."

"I need one more favor," she said.

"Anything."

"Please go retrieve my father and my uncle from that barroom," Helena instructed him. "It is hot, and we have miles to go before we are home."

"Where do you live?"

"Springfield," she answered. "Now please, go and get my father."

In the years that followed, Theodore would do what he was told. Jonah Barker thought it was an admirable quality. Helena entertained vague ideas about weakness. After the children came along, and Helena's father had passed away, Theodore stopped doing what he was told.

That night, walking home from the Addison Powder Mill picnic, Helena was less concerned about her husband's obstinacy and public display of drunkenness, as what alarmed her was her son's fascination with the Irish siren she had caught him talking to at the creek earlier that day. And to compound matters Helena understood that the Sullivan family had come from County Cork like the McNally clan once did. She knew that no good would come of Robert's association with the Irish girl. What was more upsetting, as she considered her blood, and Theodore's blood running through Robert's veins, was that she would be powerless to stop her son from falling in love.

Part Two:
Outside the Boundaries

Chapter Nine: The Door Ajar— Haverford Township PA, 2012

After R.J. Hyatt passed into the next world, May slept in her living room on the ground floor of her home. She could not bear to sleep in her room on the second floor, with such close proximity to the third-floor apartment that Hyatt had once occupied as it weighed on her like a great stone.

In those early days she tried to carry on as well as she could. For nearly two decades she had slept in her living room every night. Her waking hours had become consumed with meetings in Philadelphia with Hyatt's attorneys. At night, however, it was another story. Her old house on Chelten Road took on a life of its own, emitting noises the way old houses did. Ever since the writer had taken up residence on the third floor when May was a young girl there were noises in the night—some familiar, others inexplicable. If her parents had been aware of Hyatt's penchant for pacing through his apartment at all hours they never said a word, not even when Hyatt took to leaving the third-floor apartment and wandering through the house in the dark. Some nights he went down to the basement. May knew better than to follow him. By 1950, when May was a young woman, she had become accustomed to the strange nightly journeys of R.J. Hyatt. Often May heard conversations being conducted in the third-floor apartment. The first time she heard a female voice May didn't talk to Hyatt for a week, as such was the only way she knew to cure her wounded heart. In time, those voices existed as if on the edge of a dream.

After the writer passed over, May did the sensible thing. Haunted by those dream-like voices, she retreated to her living room at the front of the house and avoided the second floor. The living room became her sanctuary. From that room she had no view of the kitchen either. That meant that whatever passed through her house at night was welcome to come and go as long as she was not disturbed. In time she discovered the truth concerning the voices, the late-night footsteps.

It took her decades to make her peace with those elements that shared her house, and shortly after her sixtieth birthday May resumed sleeping in her bedroom on the second floor. The strange comfort in her situation was a secret one. Though she lived in her house alone, considered by her community to be *that old spinster* on Chelten Road, May never lacked for company. R.J. Hyatt left her when she was just thirty years old. By the time she was forty years old she had come to accept the residual energy he had left in his wake. In truth, she knew that he would never leave her behind. He loved her too much for that. And while he had to leave the world, Hyatt had made sure that certain arrangements were in place. He had chosen May as his sole heir; his estate, by the time he moved on, had amassed considerable wealth, as each year his novel became more popular, and each year the money grew at an exponential rate. She remained grateful and humbled by his generosity.

Once Hyatt was gone she traveled—Europe, South America, Africa, and Asia—but each year, after spending many months abroad, she returned home. Europe was especially difficult for her. In France she had felt as if she was following the path Hyatt had once walked, only the trail had grown cold ever since the First World War. She remained the dutiful benefactor of the man who had turned his back on the world, a man who chose to create another world of his liking. At home, May learned that her world was much more interesting beneath the surface; indeed, it was more infinite, and over the years, through her travels, she had developed a sense that the world she thought she knew had grown much smaller. For May it was a welcomed inversion. Hyatt had initiated her, and more than all the money he had left behind, May cherished the notion that her present world was mere prelude.

That notion began taking root when May was still mostly a child, shortly after Hyatt had slid a copy of Ovid's *Metamorphoses* across a library table. One day when she was eleven years old May decided to call upon Hyatt in his apartment. She wanted to see the great writer at work, to glimpse the process of genius at play. That day Hyatt turned her away, but May Weldon's infatuation caused her to remain undeterred.

The following week, on Friday, May ascended to the second floor, determined. The door leading to Hyatt's third-floor apartment was ajar. She seized the opportunity. As she climbed the narrow stairs that led to the writer's flat, she heard him reciting poetry. His voice filled the room; an invisible barrier of sound that prevented the girl from reaching her destination.

"Mr. Hyatt?" she called out.

Despite her curiosity, May understood little about how her parents' tenant worked; much less, at her age, about how a writer created something from nothing. All she did know was that the man who rented the third-floor rooms wasn't like anyone else she had met. She was determined to find out more, no matter the cost.

"What is it?" Hyatt asked.

"Nothing," May stood at the top of the stairs.

She retreated after that. A hollow feeling filled her that afternoon.

Several weeks later May returned home after school. Her mother cornered her in the kitchen. There were freshly baked muffins on every surface. The table, chairs, and window sills were filled with pans bearing blueberry, cranberry, pumpkin spice, and banana nut muffins as they cooled. Alice Weldon stood with her fists pressed against her hips like a general surveying the recently conquered ingredients of her labor, a ringmaster of her own culinary circus.

May reached for a pumpkin spice muffin. Her nimble fingers felt the heat, her mouth watered as she called up taste from memory. The anticipation of this rare delicacy was too much, since her mother rarely baked, but when she did, it was as if she had conjured delicious cakes, muffins, and cookies from the ether.

"Don't you dare," Alice said.

"Just one?" May asked.

"These muffins are for the Ladies Auxiliary Auction," she said. "I am to make six baskets. The money we raise will be used to send writing supplies to our boys overseas."

May knew little about the Ladies Auxiliary except that a good number of the members wore too much make-up and perfume. She found it unnerving that beneath the talcum and the perfume on the older ones she could still detect something rotten, as if those old women were dying slowly from the inside out. Thinking about it made May sick. She never wanted to grow old. She never wanted to carry the scent of decay the way those ladies did.

Her mother raised an eyebrow, a warning shot. May lowered her hand.

"All of them?" she asked.

"Yes," her mother said. "All of them. Besides, your father will be home soon. We will eat dinner at six. Now go wash up. You can help transport the baskets to church."

"Mother, I have homework."

"The homework can wait," said Alice. "The Ladies Auxiliary cannot. Now, go."

"Where is Mr. Hyatt?"

"And that is another matter," she said. "You must not disturb Mr. Hyatt the way you do. You are always meddling where you shouldn't be. Mr. Hyatt is a writer, my dear. An artist. He's not like us. His kind doesn't do well with children underfoot."

That afternoon Alice Weldon drew a line, but her tenacious daughter had already crossed it. During the first weeks of Mr. Hyatt's residence on the third floor, Alice would interrupt the final few busy moments of her cooking and table-setting, climb the stairs, and call Mr. Hyatt to dinner. As time went on, though, she realized that Hyatt was a quiet man of dignity and respect, possessed of old-fashioned charm. Alice saw that he was no threat to her child, so she delegated the chore to her daughter. Elated by this new responsibility, May had accepted the task with glee. For she had refused to accept that Hyatt disliked her; moreover, she knew something about the writer her mother did not. The previous week May had traversed the narrow stairs leading up to Hyatt's rooms. The door leading to the third floor was ajar. A thrill coursed through her. All afternoon she heard the tenant pacing back and forth, and now, like an invitation, the door was open.

That day, when her mother instructed her to call Mr. Hyatt to dinner, May did not hesitate when she found the door ajar. She walked up the narrow stairs and peered into the writer's sacred space. Hyatt sat at his desk, poised over a thick ledger journal, fountain pen in hand, staring into the empty space between the desk and the wall. May was already in the room, padding across the floor, when she saw the ledger journal was open and the pages blank.

"Mr. Hyatt?" May said.

He turned to face her. In his left hand the pen hovered only an inch from the blank page.

May took a step closer. The fountain pen Hyatt used to compose his work was old, the kind which her father kept at his office in Philadelphia and was an instrument that the skillful could use to draw ink from a jar, and in less capable hands often resulted in the inept dousing their clothes with ink.

"My mother said that dinner is ready," said May. "She said come downstairs before the food gets cold."

May moved closer to the desk. Suddenly, she wished she had brushed her hair. She blushed as she kept her hands clasped behind her back, aware of her bare knees and the skirt she wore that made her thighs itch.

"Were you writing a poem?" she asked.

"Yes," he replied. His voice sounded distant. Then, "I mean no."

"Do you always begin in the middle of a ledger?" she asked. "Or are there other pages finished?"

"There are some," Hyatt said.

"May I see them?"

Hyatt emptied his fountain pen into a black jar. He placed the pen and the jar into a desk drawer. Next, he blotted the pages with a separate sheet of paper and carefully closed the ledger journal.

"Come, Miss Weldon," he said as he rose from his seat. "We mustn't keep your parents waiting."

May led the way down to the second floor. In the hallway she sensed that Hyatt had stopped. When she turned to look at him, he leaned against a closet door.

"What's wrong?" she asked.

"Do you go into your basement often?" he asked.

"Oh no," she said. "Once I saw a spider. And another time, when I was six, the lock got stuck on the door in the kitchen. A light bulb went out and I was stuck in the dark."

"Not a good thing," Hyatt straightened up now, "to be left alone in the dark."

What May wanted more than anything was to throw that conversation in her mother's face, to prove to her that she was not meddlesome, that she stood on level ground with their odd tenant, and that, despite the years between them, she and Hyatt shared something in common—a mutual respect for darkness and vivid imaginations. Instead, May kept it to herself. On some level she knew that Hyatt's questioning her about the basement had been a test, an initiation that marked her passing through some boundary that was part of many that made up the tenant's world. More than anything, May wished that she was older, possessed of a woman's body and a mature intellect. She wanted to spend more time with Hyatt, but she didn't want to be just some bothersome little girl. The following day, Hyatt and her father began work on the root cellar in the basement.

Presently, May lay down on her sofa, spread out a sheet over her body, and remembered those decades past when the two men removed earth from the ground night after night. Her mother protested the excavation at first; she was fearful that the house might collapse. But then Hyatt used the dirt removed from the basement to build her a small, terraced garden in the yard. It took Hyatt and her father less than three months to build the root cellar. The entrance in the basement was marked by an arched doorway capped with an odd keystone. It was Hyatt himself who hung the heavy, oak door. He had allowed May to see the door when he had finished. May was disappointed. She had wanted to see what was inside the root cellar, convinced that Hyatt was hiding treasures he had brought home from the First World War. In time, she found out that something far greater than any war loot lay behind the oak door.

The pain in her body pulled her ever so slightly toward a different world now. Lying there on her sofa, as she drifted in and out of sleep, May remembered that day in the second-floor hallway once more. Hyatt had been right. To be left alone in the dark was never a good thing.

Chapter Ten: The Land Of Dust And Honey—The Eldritch Bells

A small fire burned in the hearth as daylight relinquished its grip over the valley. Tilly Smith sat by the fire, mending the hem of her dress. She appeared to be no more than ten years old, though time and circumstance had made her age beyond those meager years. She lived in a cottage beside Lake Vanassara, drinking a cup of cold, clean lake water every day at dawn, as the nymphs had instructed her when she had first arrived. Back then she found the cottage in a state of disrepair, uninhabitable almost between the thick dust that covered every surface and the various insects who squatted there. In those days, many decades ago, Tilly was near death, malnourished, dehydrated from being lost in the forest, driven nearly to madness by strange dreams that she inhaled; dreams that were songs in the dense fog that flooded the forest late at night; until one morning she saw through the trees a shimmering in the distance, a shimmering like a million pocket-sized mirrors laid out side-by-side, reflecting the sun's rays at once. Branches whipped her face, her neck, her arms, and vines snagged at her shoes, slowing her down, as she ran through the forest toward the water. When she reached the lake shore she collapsed at the water's edge, dunking her face beneath the water and drinking down her fill. Beneath the water the nymphs saw her face and swam up to meet her, embracing the lost child and pushing her toward the air again, fearing, they did, that Tilly might drown.

Presently, seated by the fire, Tilly remembered how kind the nymphs were, kind enough to warn her that she should never travel to the lake's west side after dark, for that was the time of song, and the songs the nymphs sang every evening manifested themselves as a mist over the lake, blowing westward through the forest until the mist was breathed in by creatures large and small, creatures who knew the grace of such songs, creatures whose magnificent dreams afforded them a glimpse of eternal harmony, a glimpse the human mind clouded with its own fears and prejudice. A blessing of song turned into something vile and threatening. Spirits of the earth and air shared a secret knowledge with all living things, the nymphs had told her, but man had long ago turned a deaf ear to that knowledge. The young remained in tune with the spirit knowledge for a time; if she wished to remain a child then she could drink from the lake once a day, they told her, and never again venture into the western forest at night. Tilly did as she was told.

In those first weeks, when the days were still warm, Tilly did what she could to clean-up the cottage and make it livable. She explored the forest on the eastern side of the lake every day, taking full advantage of daylight to search for her brother Cecil. She and her younger brother had become separated during a summer storm. Cecil was only six years old. And when evening came, once the sun set behind the woodland to the west, she kept a watchful eye on the far shore of the lake; though she waited year after year for him, she never once glimpsed his small form emerging from the forest.

On the afternoon she and Cecil had become separated they were playing near the caves within woods that bordered her family's farm. Tilly's parents had forbidden the children to go near the caves, believing in local superstitions about fauns, green men, and all manner of fairyfolk who dwelled in and around the caves. The elder members of the local village told of gateways between the worlds. Tilly was apt to listen to her parents. As for Cecil, he had been inquisitive and rebellious from the time he could walk. The tales the old people told were too tempting for a boy like him. He stole away to the woods whenever he could, hoping to glimpse an elf, a goblin, a brownie, or any other Fae said to inhabit what the elders called the place between places.

What started as a game of hide-and-seek soon turned into Tilly's worst nightmare. Unable to find her brother, she feared that he had fallen deep into one of the caves. Her frantic search was hindered by strong, rain-laden gusts that muted her voice each time she called out Cecil's name. Even the caves, always anxious on clear days to render an echo for the children's benefit whenever they shouted into the dark recesses, remained mute in the wake of the intensifying storm. Lightning struck a tree nearby. Tilly retreated into one of the caves for cover. Had Cecil done the same? There she would wait for the storm to pass, knowing that it would take more than thunder and lightning to scare her brother. Tilly reminded herself, as she stood in the mouth of a large cave, that her brother knew his way home, that in some respects he was better versed in the woods than she; still, it would be impossible to return home without her brother, for without Cecil she would have to admit to her parents that she and her brother were playing by the caves, and when she did, presenting her case alone, she would wish for a quick death rather than face her parents' anger.

Lightning flashed. A face appeared in the woods, nearly concealed by drooping vines and low-hanging branches. It was a face that resembled a faun's, old and grizzled with twisted dead branches for horns and dark hollow eyes, the way they were depicted in storybooks. Another lightning flash revealed that the face wasn't a face at all, but simply a knot in a tree trunk. Tilly was ready to call out Cecil's name once more but stopped. A sound came from somewhere behind her, originating deep within the cave. Tiny cymbals jingled, like a tambourine, and Tilly thought that maybe the storm was playing tricks on her. She covered her ears for a moment, but when she removed her hands the jingling continued.

The tone she heard put her mind at ease; the notes varied, but there was no particular melody to the noise. The clinking called to mind her most prized gift, which was one that was given to her shortly after her grandmother Ester had died—a wind-up box that chimed a slow song as a porcelain ballerina pirouetted on top.

The tinkling in her ears drove her deeper into the cave. For the moment, she forgot about Cecil and followed the chiming bells. The cave floor sloped downward. Tilly traversed the gradual decline with ease, scampering at the very end like a crab on her hands and feet, careful not to soil her dress, until she reached level flooring. The slightest light, a blue hue like the lightning outside, graced the wide space.

Old timber lay strewn about near the walls of the cave, along with shattered earthen jars. Tilly's father had told her that men once mined for precious stones in the caves, long before the turn of the century. Not locals, he had informed her, but men from as far away as Holland, France, Germany, and even America. In those days, Tilly's father explained, Britain was sore over having lost the colonies, and so the British Empire had one more go at the new country, setting fire to the nation's capital before the tide of war turned. The last of the miners to leave the caves in centuries past were the Americans.

Tilly's father Abraham attributed it all to greed. Abraham told his daughter that greed was a horrible thing, going all the way back to the war of the angels; half the story of the war in Heaven having never been told. The church, according to Abraham, never mentioned what became of the conspirators who supported Lucifer's charge on Heaven's ramparts and even the Bible was vague on accounting for those angels who fell from grace by proxy. Some, like Lucifer, took up their fiery weapons against God, thus sealing their fate, and were cast into Hell; others, also stripped of God's grace and cast out, those malevolent angels who, for reasons known only to them and their Creator, supported Lucifer's offensive, but never took up arms and joined in combat, were not cast so far as their warring brothers. For God in His infinite wisdom was a just god and mercy dictated that punishment for their crimes, while severe, may not be the same for all. No, Tilly's father had claimed, these cowardly and malicious angels fell away from divine grace, far enough to no longer bathe in the Lord's richness, yet close to remember that no matter the penance they served they would never be allowed to return, so these disgraced angels became the fairyfolk. Over time, Abraham told his daughter, these angels fallen to Earth endured their own evolution, living outside the boundaries of that great and abundant garden called Eden. And since that fateful day when their golden wings of brilliant light were torn from their backs by the hand of the All-

mighty, they suffered a collective amnesia, a condition so severe that it caused them to forget their former heavenly home. At the same time these fairyfolk were permitted to see in man the divine spark, the soul that God had created in His image, it was a constant reminder to the fallen angels on earth that another had taken their place in the light of God's grace. Jealous with rage and plagued with envy, the fairyfolk tormented mankind through the ages, operating, as they often did, outside the boundaries of good and evil, their tireless effort to lead man toward a different ruination than the one Lucifer sought to unleash, and it would have worked, Abraham said, had it not been for the age of iron that gave man the necessary weapons to combat them. But not just swords and pikes but other instruments such as rods and bars and other wards like the common horseshoe, which the fairyfolk avoided at all costs.

This then was the lesson Tilly's father had taught her, that greed had driven angels toward war and treason, and that man, while having nearly vanquished the fairyfolk on Earth, was susceptible to greed that begat other sins, that the energy of man's sin sustained the fairyfolk, allowing their remaining numbers to thrive in hidden places untouched by humankind; or abandoned places such as the caves where men in another century toiled for wealth that brought them no closer to Heaven. Abraham had estimated that madness, despair, greed, and treachery dwelled within the confines of those caves, and if strong men made hard by working underground were driven toward such predilections, then what chance did children have lurking about in places taken over by the fairyfolk? Tilly understood that her family farm struck a sense of balance between Heaven and Earth the way all things did that offered equilibrium; rather than taking and not giving back, farmers like her father understood how balance worked—a lesson, her father had told her, that many angels never learned.

Another two hundred yards into the underground chamber Tilly discovered three passageways. In each the eldritch bells jingled, but the sound was louder in the tunnel to her left; so, she set off into that tunnel, no longer able to hear the storm as it continued its relentless assault against the forest. Halfway into the left tunnel she discovered large holes cut away in the walls. The jingling of tiny cymbals continued, drawing her along the tunnel she had chosen and suffused with the same pale blue light in the cathedral-sized chamber she had just left, the tunnel led another three hundred yards to a dead-end. Embedded in the wall, a wood door framed in an arch fashioned from smooth polished stone that was capped by a keystone emitting a magnificent blue light that beckoned the lonely and tired girl. Tilly pressed her ear to the door. From the other side came the unremitting jingle of cymbals, enticing her to open the door and journey to the other side.

Chapter Eleven: The Ill-Advised Dream—Ardmore PA, 1915

Every day after school, Robert Jonas Hyatt stood in front of Whitaker's Stationery Store on Haverford Road. Minutes slipped past, having no effect on his inertia as he stood there enchanted by what he saw. In the store window were numerous fountain pens, each placed meticulously in their display. Robert remained transfixed every time he stopped in front of the stationery store, no matter if the display window looked the same each day. A rushing noise filled his ears, drowning out the daily bustle along Haverford Road, as he pondered what magic those pens on display might yield in a capable writer's hands.

Now and then, as Robert stared at the pens, one of his mother's friends would pass by and stare at him as she did. He remained oblivious to them; likewise, he never acknowledged John Whitaker, owner and operator of Ardmore's finest and, by Robert's estimation, only stationery store.

The first time Robert had set foot in Whitaker's store was when he was five years old. Helena had taken him one crisp November day to purchase Christmas cards. Robert remembered the store as long and cavernous, glass countertops to his left and to his right that were ripe for young hands to press against and leave their indelible mark. Looking back now, he remembered that this had been his first impulse, the laying of his hands on glass and, when he thought no one was looking, pressing his little nose against the thick panes to view fountain pens, mechanical pencils, stationery, rubber stamps, cardstock, and more. Ever watchful, clairvoyant almost, in the way mothers can be when their backs are turned on their children yet still aware of their every move, Helena admonished her five-year-old. But more than the memory of being scolded, Robert recalled staring at fountain pens in one glass case, as if the instruments had called to him, but at such a tender age he could not comprehend the latent magic of ink and paper.

"Hello, Mrs. Hyatt," Robert heard a man's voice from behind the counter. "How nice to see you again."

"Hello, Mr. Whitaker," Helena replied. "I am here for my Christmas cards."

"Of course," the voice replied. "They came in late yesterday afternoon."

Young Robert could not see Mr. Whitaker. As his mother completed her transaction with the store proprietor, he wondered if Whitaker, with his disembodied voice, was a ghost. For a child to believe in such things was expected, and a wraith who provided the same services to the community as he did when he was alive was not beyond the scope of his tender and impressionable imagination. No sooner did his mother place her change into her purse than Robert heard five loud footsteps.

Mr. Whitaker traversed the steps that led up to a platform behind his glass counter. He appeared behind Helena, a man in miniature compared to the likes of Robert's father.

"This is your son?" Whitaker asked.

"Yes," answered Helena. "And despite my protestations, the devil continues to rub his hands over your glass showcases. I must apologize."

"Oh, that's no trouble," he stood in front of five-year-old Robert now. "How much of an impression can a little hand make?"

Whitaker held up his hand to show Robert.

The boy, ordinarily shy around strangers, studied the little man's hand and the rest of him from head to toe.

Whitaker's hair, curly and long, was white like his thick moustache. His ears were large, too large for the little man's head, and from inside them grew tufts of wiry gray hair. He stood nearly five feet tall, barely a head over young Robert, and he wore a vest that he was unable to button because of his rotund midsection.

Presently, as the teenaged Robert stared at the window display, John Whitaker appeared at the shop entrance. When Robert made to leave, the presence of the little old man shaking him out of his quiet reverie, Whitaker took hold of his arm.

"I've been meaning to have a word with you," the store owner said.

"You did?" Robert asked. "I mean you have?"

"Yes," Whitaker said.

He guided Robert into the store and closed the door.

"Every day," the old man began, "you hang around outside my shop. It's bad for business."

"Listen, Mr. Whitaker," Robert said. "I don't want any trouble."

"It's too late for that, young squire," he told him. "Are you casing my joint? Planning to rob me?"

"What? No—"

"Welsh?"

"I beg your pardon?"

"You are Welsh?"

"On my dad's side."

"Your mother? Mrs. Hyatt?"

"German and Greek."

Whitaker reeled backward a moment, as if his little feet could no longer maintain his ample weight.

"I wasn't expecting that," he said. "But, if that is the case, then your mother is half-good in my book."

"And what book would that be, Mr. Whitaker?" Robert asked.

75

"Young man," he said, "Let me offer you some free advice—"

"My father says there's always a price for advice."

"Your father is also Welsh," said Whitaker. "In my learned and astute opinion, that makes him not much better than being Irish. Both races are steeped in drinking, superstition, and stealing. Though, I admit, not necessarily in that order. And these traits are compounded by the Greek blood of your mother's that runs through your veins."

"With all due respect, Mr. Whitaker," said Robert. "You were going to offer me advice?"

"Advice? What? No," the old man said. "What I propose to offer you is a job."

"I have never interviewed for a job," he said. "How did I do?"

"Not so fast. Tell me, which pen in the window do you like best and why?"

"It's black with an inlaid pearl band around the cap base," Robert told him. "It looks like the best fountain pen in the store. Otherwise, why place such an item in your window?"

"Why are you so interested in pens?"

Robert blushed. "It's foolish," he said.

"Come on," Whitaker said. "Out with it."

"I want to write books," the teen confessed.

"Wouldn't you be better served working in a library or perhaps a bookshop?"

"I imagine that either place must be hell on earth for an unpublished writer."

Whitaker lowered his head. His shoulders shook as he stroked his moustache, attempting to stifle a laugh.

"So," he looked at the boy now, "it's a life of letters for you? Perhaps you'll be the next Jack London? Perhaps America's answer to Kipling?"

"Why, yes!"

"Misery, disappointment, starvation," Whitaker informed him. "And nothing of the ensuing madness that you will surely endure. Do your parents know about this ill-advised dream?"

"My mother teaches at the new high school in Haverford Township. She—"

"And your father?"

"He works at Addison's Powder Mill," Robert said. "And afternoons for P&W Railway."

"A trolley operator?"

"Ticketmaster," he said. "At the Ardmore Station."

"A teacher and a ticketmaster," Whitaker announced. "Agony and bliss. So, what do you say?"

"I don't even know what the job is."

"A few hours after school each day," the little man said. "And Saturdays, of course. I need help with stock and sales. Once you learn the paper, I will teach you about pens."

"I'll have to ask my folks," Robert said. "And my mother will want to speak with you."

"Tell her to come in tomorrow or the next day," he told him. "If you want the job, show up Monday after school."

Robert extended his right hand, the way his father had taught him. Whitaker gave it a good hard shake.

"A writer?" the little man said. "You should study law. At least you won't go hungry."

"My mother wants me to follow in her footsteps," Robert said. "Go to college and all that. But my father thinks all the colleges are filled with anarchists and socialists."

"But your mother went to college."

"At Bryn Mawr."

Whitaker yawned. "Anyway," he said, "come back Monday. The pay won't be great, but you can at least buy some girl dinner and take her to a play in town."

"Thank you, Mr. Whitaker."

"Poetry or prose?"

"I beg your pardon?"

"Which will you write?" he asked. "Poetry, novels, stories?"

"I suppose all three."

"For poetry, Shelley, Keats, and Whitman," said Whitaker. "As for prose, you need to remember only two names. Balzac and Dostoevsky. Read those two and you will never go wrong."

"I'll remember that."

"Balzac wrote one hundred novels in his lifetime," he said. "One hundred!"

Whitaker was still praising Honoré de Balzac as Robert left the store.

That afternoon he rushed home, remembering not to run. Helena had told Robert that a gentleman should never run in public. When his mother arrived home shortly after he did, Robert told her the news. Helena did not say no. That was a good sign.

Chapter Twelve: The World Takes—Philadelphia-Bound, 2012

The train ride from Springfield to Philadelphia gave Harold Miller plenty of time to think. For as long as he could remember, he detested trains. His father used to make him ride the regional rails in Chicago where he grew up, starting when Miller was just seven years old, to remind his son that better men than them had already built a nation through diligence and grit. If Miller had to ride a train at all, he insisted on a seat that faced the same direction the train was headed; riding backward always made him ill.

It was on a warm morning in May that Miller sat in a forward coach car on an Amtrak train headed south. Early that morning he packed a suitcase and a couple of suits in a garment bag. It had been his intention to drive to Philadelphia but driving meant that he could ultimately do only one thing; namely, agonize over how he had blurred the lines between professional research and personal intimacy. He opted for the train instead knowing that he could at least read and go over some notes he had made concerning updates for the Hyatt biography. For Miller, riding the train meant a different sort of agony, remembering his father and how he looked down upon Miller's continuing education. Even so, at least a review of his notes would prevent him from thinking too much about his past with May Weldon.

When Miller was growing up in Chicago, his father worked as a brakeman for the Illinois Railroad. Their relationship was strained for as long as Miller could remember. Miller had wanted to believe that his father wanted him to do better than him in life, the way successive generations always gained a little more. It was the American dream, but not for John Miller. He was a working man, a union man who harbored discontent toward 'the suits'—a conglomerate of businessmen, civic leaders, university professors, and any other man who never got his hands dirty doing what John Miller considered an honest day's work.

"They're all communists!" John Miller had told his son when Harold was in high school, referring to college professors. "And you want to be one of them?"

John Miller saw his son graduate with a master's degree in American Literature from the University of Chicago. Then, six days later, he suffered a massive stroke in a railroad yard. Harold was just twenty-four years old when he lost his father. He carried with him a sense of guilt over his father's passing. The pension John Miller left behind was a modest one, and it afforded Miller's mother Eileen a simple life. As the only child, Miller felt obligated to send home whatever money he could to his mother. It was only fair, but his mother refused it, often returning envelopes unopened when he began his PhD dissertation at Brown University.

Miller's daughter was only three years old when her grandmother died. Elinor didn't remember his mother, and for that Miller had been sorry. His mother had only met Elinor once when she was just a year old. Eileen Miller did not approve of apartment living. It was, in her estimation, no way to raise a child. After Elinor had been born Miller promised himself that his relationship with his daughter would in no way resemble the one he had with his parents.

Where John Miller saw books and writing as propaganda, a way the communists manipulated the young impressionable students who populated universities and colleges all over the country, Eileen maintained that for the oppressed there was no greater escape than through literature. Miller spent quiet moments in his life wondering how two decidedly different people could come together, marry, and have a child like him. His relationship with his mother started and ended with books; otherwise, she exercised as much might as his father in raising him. And where his father considered the working man possessed of a redemptive soul, the only one worthy enough to gain God's good favor, his mother, despite a strict Catholic upbringing, had become a pre-determinist. Everyone, according to Eileen, had a path and a destination laid out for them at birth, and it was the Bible that revealed the map.

Eileen cursed her son for questioning the existence of God when it was fashionable to do so during Miller's undergraduate days, and she made no secret of her dislike for her son's wife from the moment they had met since Eileen was convinced that Ann was an atheist. Miller's mother worried herself to the brink of physical illness that her son was going to raise her granddaughter in a godless world. Still, regardless of how he felt about his parents, he wished that his daughter had gotten to know his mother. A girl, he reasoned, should know her respective grandmothers.

As the years went by, Miller knew that his relationship with Elinor was even more strained than the one he had with his father—if such a thing could be at all possible—because he carried a resentment akin to his father's. John Miller always wanted a son who would become a carbon copy of him. Likewise, Miller also wanted a son. After his daughter had been born, he resigned himself to making the best of it. As time passed, however, he began to see that she would never be interested in the things that he was, she would never want to know everything he knew. Elinor was for him what he had been to his father: someone incapable of emulating him, for better or worse, someone who would grow up to believe that a father was little more than a curiously weak creature who compromised his way through life more often than he stood on principle. As the years passed, and Miller became consumed by his academic work, he saw clearly that he had become like his father, forced to raise a child who would remain alien and strange to him.

As the train continued its journey from Hartford to Penn Station later that morning the gentle rocking lulled Miller into a stupor. In the seat beside him lay a file folder crammed with handwritten notes, some as old as Elinor, and bound shut with two thick rubber bands. The bulk of the notes Miller had already used when he wrote R.J. Hyatt's biography. There were, however, a few sheets in the folder that contained questions Miller never got around to asking May Weldon. He had every intention, but the timing was ruined many years ago. A series of unfortunate events cast Miller out of May's life. There was no way to return in time and capture the initial dynamic. So, he went with what he had. It was enough for the biography, but the unanswered questions were not academic in nature; an inquiry that bordered on fringe science, speculation and rumors that had never been substantiated.

In those days after Ann had died Miller never gave other women more than a precursory glance. He was as much a man as the next, aware of the opposite sex and on some level desiring of a woman's touch; even so, he could never bring himself to act on impulse and pursue a woman for the sake of sheer intimacy. The moment he met May Weldon that changed.

Miller saw in her eyes a sadness similar to that which coursed through him. It went beyond losing a loved one; a sadness more pronounced than that. Beyond the experience of loss there was another realm, the realm of absence, the place one journeyed inwardly, taking a profound and stark comfort in the secret knowledge that absence was not love lost, but something greater. It was a short-lived comfort, however, for in absence the grieving convinced themselves that love was never found, but a cruel trick of the universe that brought two people together only to leave one alone in the world when the other one ceased to exist. Long ago, Miller resigned himself to his inability to become a conduit of the burning love, the animal passion, that a man experienced in his youth, for even in youth he knew that he and Ann never harbored such ardor. What drew them together was not passion but reason, a rationale concerning love that was guided not by their hearts but by their minds. Their union was a practical one, a pooling of intellect, money (mostly hers), and material resources, even their lovemaking from the very beginning became a regimen, both of them knowing that there were physical desires to be satisfied, an Eros of efficiency geared not toward some mystical union between two souls but a mutual physical relief. Later, as the years went on, their intimacy became obligatory but once Elinor had come into the world, the sex life that had already slowed became a star that shined less and less each night until it had extinguished itself.

Miller was fifty years old when he first met May Weldon. Prior to that initial meeting, he had done his research on her. In an old alumni newsletter published in 1961 by Bryn Mawr College, there was a photograph of May delivering a lecture on Ovid. Her sleek body in profile, dressed in black, struck an imposing figure. Her hair, a torrent of curly dark locks, contrasted with her pristine, porcelain face. Miller had learned that May's thesis at Bryn Mawr had been on Ovid and his use of shadow in *The Metamorphoses*. What struck him most about the photograph, and what galvanized his longing for her, was how at ease she appeared, as if she remained unaware of the photographer's presence.

When the day came for Miller to finally meet May he traveled by car to Haverford Township, PA. As he traversed familiar roads that Ann and he had once traveled, he feared that the loneliness he experienced since Ann's passing might somehow hinder his goal. He was about to interview the only known living friend of R.J. Hyatt. In the passenger seat beside him lay a gift. Before leaving Amherst, he had stopped at a rare book shop, remembering May Weldon's passion for Ovid, and he had purchased a volume he hoped she would like. The book cost more than he had intended to spend, but the price was nothing compared to the wealth of information she would share with him about R.J. Hyatt.

Miller arrived at May Weldon's home late in the afternoon. It was an early spring day, the kind that offered a false sense of summer's approach with unseasonably warm temperatures. He had checked into a hotel beforehand on City Line Avenue located in Lower Merion Township. Along Darby Road, the town looked quiet, quaint in a way that many older American towns that bordered cities did with their mix of red brick row homes and old colonial-style houses. At Brookline Boulevard, just blocks from May's home, Miller stopped at a traffic light and watched as people waved to one another on the street. Half-way down the block, a young man spoke to someone on a payphone outside a firehouse. Witnessing these events, each one of no great consequence, lulled him into a stupor that left him unprepared for the maelstrom that was May Weldon when she opened her front door.

She had a pretty face, pale skin with high cheekbones, a slender nose, and lime-colored eyes. Thin, tall, long-legged with a short torso, she appeared much younger than her sixty years. In that instant Miller envisioned May Weldon as she may have looked back in the 1950s. Wearing a light-colored summer dress, she looked completely at home, a highball in one hand and a Viceroy cigarette in the other. She stood in high heels at a backyard barbeque, not feeling the slightest bit overdressed for the occasion, while she fended off the rehearsed and flawed flirtatious advances of young men, men she knew from the neighborhood only marginally, and contemplated the one man who remained an enigma to her. In Miller's daydream, May Weldon was a study in quiet confidence. Despite being surrounded by curious suitors, her eyes belied her desire to be elsewhere.

"Hello, Ms. Weldon," he said. "I'm Harold Miller."

Her hair was still long and curly, the way it had been in the photograph taken at Bryn Mawr, but now several strands of gray showed, which was a contrast May Weldon displayed proudly, making no attempt to conceal it.

"Miss Weldon, my dear," she replied. "Ms. Weldon implies that you take me for some militant feminist, Dr. Miller. And I will assure you that I am no such thing, much to the chagrin of my Bryn Mawr alumnae."

"This is for you," he presented her with the gift.

The gift-wrapped book was a rare hardback edition of Ovid's work translated in the 19th century by Gustav Schmidt.

"Thank you," she said, taking the book from him. "It's so rare I have a gentleman caller."

May removed the wrapping paper from the book. She considered the weight of the tome in her hands.

"It's nothing," Miller shifted his weight from one foot to the other.

"Rarer still," she went on, "a gentleman caller who presents me with a shit translation of a literary work I cherish above all others."

"Schmidt was admired in his day."

"He was a conservative, Mr. Miller," said May. "His uptight view of the world marred his translation. Why don't you come inside, and I will show you what I mean."

That afternoon Miller spent an hour listening to May as she read from Ovid in Latin, translating various lines into English as she did. Afterward, they shared a bottle of Riesling and talked about R.J. Hyatt. It was already dark when the second bottle was opened. Miller became morose after that. Tears formed in his eyes when May asked him about his late wife. She held him close, wiping the tears away. When he leaned in to kiss her, May held him back with a steady hand.

"Dr. Miller," she said, "not like this."

Later that night, still drunk, he drove back to the hotel.

The next morning he woke up late, feeling as if someone had set fire to the inside of his skull. He called May Weldon from his room.

"I feel like I should apologize," he said.

"Not at all," she replied. "Come for lunch and we will get through the interview."

The next day Miller arrived empty-handed at May's house shortly after 1:00 p.m., though he had briefly considered bringing her flowers. Instead, he carried a sense of guilt over misinterpreting his host's kindness. Lunch consisted of cold-cut sandwiches and May's sincerest apologies. They talked about R.J. Hyatt over several cups of coffee. Miller remembered that time to record the conversation.

The information he wanted could not be gathered in one sitting. He had pages of questions he wanted to ask. After an hour of listening to May speak extemporaneously about Hyatt, Miller changed tactics. He inquired if it would be permissible to tour the third-floor rooms where Hyatt lived until the end of his life.

"I will answer you any question you ask, Harold," she told him. "But I cannot allow you to see the apartment. You see, Harold, there are sacred places in the world where not everyone can set foot."

A deep sense of defeat filled Miller. He lowered his head as if he had just been scolded. When he had committed himself to writing R.J. Hyatt's biography it had been his original intention to hire a professional photographer who would take photographs of the space where Hyatt had composed his later poems. No one, to his knowledge, had ever taken a picture of the writer at work. A photograph of the room where Hyatt once worked would have been the next best thing.

"May," his eyes met hers now. "If you won't allow me access I can respect that. Perhaps you yourself have a picture of your friend at his desk. I could have a copy—"

"Oh, you're good," she said. Then, "come with me."

She led Miller out of the kitchen where they had eaten lunch, through the dining room and into a short hallway that led to the front door. The hallway walls were adorned with numerous framed photographs that Miller did not have a chance to view when he had first arrived the previous evening.

And that afternoon May had made sure she whisked her visitor through the hallway with much the same speed as when she had shown him out after his failed attempt to kiss her. Now, however, May was quick to point out a few black and white framed prints of parents, a somber couple in their old age who appeared to be vexed by some heavy burden. None of the photographs, Miller noted, were taken indoors. The faces of her parents, in all the photographs he glimpsed, looked as melancholic as the shadows were long behind them. In another photograph, taken perhaps in the late 1930s or early 1940s, May's father stood poised with a shovel as he stood in front of a large mound of dirt.

"Is this your yard?" Miller asked.

"Yes," May replied.

There was only one picture of R.J. Hyatt, also taken outdoors on the Weldon's back porch. He wore a long coat and a cigarette dangled from his mouth.

"Did you take this?" he asked.

It was one of two known photographs of R.J. Hyatt in existence. The other one had been the portrait used on the dust jacket back for his novel *The Land of Dust and Honey*. As for the photograph on the wall, Miller had first surveyed a print of it at Haverford College where May had donated Hyatt's papers, letters, and other effects after he was gone.

"I did," May said, at last. "I was a young girl. Robert had just come back from one of his many trips to the market. He enjoyed that. Shopping for groceries, I mean. Cameras were another matter. He could do without them. He was always shy that way."

Many photographs in the hallway were of May at various ages in her youth. Two photographs showed May as a young girl of no more than five years old standing beside a dark-haired girl whose face in each picture was hidden by shadows cast by tree leaves overhead.

"Who is that?" Miller asked.

"Her name was Tessie," said May. "A cousin, I was told. I don't remember her. She stayed here only briefly."

The rest of the photographs chronicled May's life from her tenth birthday into her teens, and then into adulthood.

Two other photographs, one black and white and the other in color, drew Miller's attention more than any of the others. In the black and white, a teenaged May Weldon was caught laughing and turning from the camera's lens as she held up a cautionary hand. The color photograph portrayed May in her mid-thirties as she stood in a dry stream bed where exposed roots as thick as redwood trees stretched out behind her. A haze of ochre clouded the air, nearly obscuring May's face.

"This is incredible," said Miller as he pointed to the framed color photograph. "Is this the General Sherman tree?"

"No," she said, flatly. "It is not."

"So where was it taken?" he pressed her now. "Africa? India?"

"Further," came her reply. "If you like, Harold, you may use the photograph of Robert in his long coat for your book. I don't know how it all works. But perhaps you can work it out with your publisher. This one is the original. It is a better quality than the one at Haverford College."

"That would be great," he said.

"And now I must ask you to leave," May said. "Come by the same time tomorrow."

Miller returned to May's home for four more days after that. The interviews went well. It seemed each day that the reclusive writer's confidant was more eager to share her knowledge of Hyatt's life. On the last day, with the memory of his drunken fumbling for affection far behind him, Miller offered to take May to dinner. To his surprise, she accepted.

After dinner, May insisted on seeing Miller's accommodations. He was staying at the Hilton Hotel on City Avenue in Philadelphia. They had a few drinks before and after dinner. Miller felt as if a door had opened, a light had graced his otherwise dismal life of letters, the weight of being a widower had been lifted, and when May kissed him in the elevator he knew that there was no sin in accepting affection from this new and curious woman.

The next morning Miller rolled over in his hotel bed, the musk odor of sex still fresh on the sheets. May was gone. After he climbed out of bed, Miller checked his research materials. The notes, the cassette tapes, and the questionnaire he wrote months beforehand, they were all there. What caused his fear that May had absconded with his materials he could not say. She had given him no indication that she had second thoughts about the information she had provided. He felt foolish. Worse, as he thought about his late wife, he became racked with guilt.

It was 7:00 a.m. Miller considered telephoning May, but he knew it was too early. For all he knew she could have slipped out of the room only minutes before he woke. So, he showered, dressed, packed his bags and went down to the lobby restaurant for breakfast.

When he finished eating, he checked out of his room at the front desk. There was a lobby house phone. Local calls within the area code were free. Miller stood there, staring at the phone on its narrow desk, and he wondered if there was a point to calling.

The previous evening no words had been exchanged during their lovemaking. In bed, the decade in age that separated them meant little. He wanted to hear her voice. He wanted May Weldon to whisper a carnal incantation in his ear as she hovered over him. He wanted her to cry out like a witch at her Sabbath, but she barely made a sound. Ann had been the same way. Lovemaking between Miller and his wife lacked spontaneity, and it lacked the torrid secret language of passion. With May it had been different. With May there had been a recklessness which made up for the lack of verbal banter. Her abandon induced a hypnotic effect on Miller. More than once, in the dimly lit hotel room, he thought her face took on several different identities. At one point, as May straddled him while he lay on the floor, Miller saw the face of his late wife looming over him. Later, he would chalk it up to grief and alcohol, but, during the moment, deep within he felt that this woman above him was every woman and none. It was akin to a spiritual ecstasy to make love to the woman who had shared a life with a man he had devoted a lifetime to studying, the only woman that had shared a sensual relationship with R.J. Hyatt. There was never any evidence in the letters and papers the writer left behind that alluded to or otherwise proved a physical relationship had occurred between May and the writer, but Miller convinced himself of their sexual liaisons, imagining himself as Hyatt when he closed his eyes and felt May engulf him. She had cast a spell that night, an enchantment that evaporated the moment she departed. Later, his sleep was filled with fitful dreams.

The lobby phone remained in its cradle. Miller got into his car and lost himself in the morning rush hour traffic. It wasn't until he was an hour outside of Philadelphia, heading north on the New Jersey Turnpike, that he realized the only regret he carried from the previous evening was not that it had to end, but his remorse was that he had grown old enough to forget that only in the dark could such magic between two strangers be so strong and strange.

After his initial visit to May Weldon's home, it had taken him several weeks to finally telephone her. He wanted to update her on the progress of the biography. When May answered her phone, she sounded annoyed and expressed how she thought it would be better if he didn't call her again.

That was the last time he had spoken to her before calling again only a few days ago. As the train rolled toward Philadelphia now, Miller glimpsed his reflection in the window. In their time apart they had both grown older; in their time apart all the magic in the world had gone away. The price for Miller was one of sullen existence marked by increasing bouts of forgetfulness. And for May it meant cancer. It was Miller's hope on the train that day that the years had passed slowly enough to put behind them whatever wasn't said the night they had slept together.

For him, there was only one true solace in life. He reached into his satchel and took out a tattered trade paperback copy of *The Land of Dust and Honey*, the one he had used in class that was littered with his own notes and marginalia. As Trenton shrunk away behind the train into a memory of concrete, steel, and despair, Miller opened the book, turning to a section he coveted most, and began to read.

Chapter Thirteen: The Land Of Dust And Honey—Beneath The Hollow Hill

Barth wandered in the dark forest for hours. Before he set out, he had combed the rock formation where the door was before it had crumbled into dust. What he had mistaken for a root cellar turned out to be a rocky outcrop covered in wet moss and laced with thick vines that grew from an otherwise low hill topped with twisted and ancient maple trees. What bothered him was not the vanishing doorway, but the keystone atop the arch that bordered it; the inner light that glowed from within the wedge-shaped stone, calling to mind moon rays, and an otherworldly luminescence that made him feel ill at ease. He knew his ancestors had come from South Wales to settle in Pennsylvania. And he was no stranger to the wild myths his ancestry invoked. Worse, he considered that perhaps he had never survived the German artillery barrage, that it was not his physical self wandering lost now; instead, his soul clinging to what was familiar: his uniform, the grit beneath his fingernails, the sour taste in his mouth that had been there even on the troop ship before he set foot on European soil. The war and the memory of war, death and the memory of death, anger in the faces of the French who seethed with fear and hatred not just for the Germans, but for the Canadian forces and other units who had come to liberate them. There was fuming over the presumptuous nature both sides exuded in their quest to further enhance war's machination, as all of this was the reality he had known. And here he was now, far from the war yet still somehow in it (or at least he assumed it to be so), chasing ringing bells through a hollow hill and stepping through magical doorways that vanished and turned to stone. The forest he traversed, the rocky outcrop in the dark, and the old magic he had experienced (if not hallucinated) made more sense to him than the war ever did.

That night he moved north, in the opposite direction from where he remembered the German army had entrenched themselves. Several miles to the west of his original position, where fallen members of 4th Canadian Division lay dead in their trenches, including many Americans who had traveled north over the border to join Canadian forces when the war began, the 3rd Canadian Division also suffered heavy casualties. The original plan, as his superiors had spelled it out, was for his battalion to overrun the Germans so that the Canadian unit in the rear could advance and relieve his unit. The German artillery bombardment, a storm of rounds that rained down for hours, prevented his battalion from achieving its objective. The last he had heard was that the 24th British Division was to the north. He followed the moss that covered the trees on one side and hoped that he could reach the British unit before the Germans got to him.

By now Barth was familiar with the story of the poor officer who had been crucified by the Germans in 1915. He had heard this story not long after the original incident from a soldier who had just transferred to his unit from the Dublin Fusiliers. The crucifixion was bad enough, but the more time he spent on the Western Front, the more he understood how man's essential nature led toward barbarism, and that all acts of humility and kindness were in fact foreign to modern man. His only hope that night was that a German outfit had not somehow managed to wedge themselves between him and the British.

The forest terrain slowed his movement. Vines and underbrush interfered with each step, causing him to take more than an hour to cover one mile of the woodland. The forest floor inclined as he continued north. Judging the landscape, Barth guessed that he was still near Vimy Ridge, but it was hard to tell for sure. With the rising incline of the land, his travel was made more treacherous.

Barth found himself climbing over fallen trees or slithering beneath them. This last form of movement, low-crawling on his stomach, provided him with an added bonus, because for his troubles he came face-to-face with a large rabbit. Before the creature had a chance to scamper into the brush, Barth caught it by its hind legs. He crawled out from beneath the fallen tree, swung the rabbit in a wide arc over his head, and smashed the rabbit's skull on a rock. Next, he fashioned a sack from his coat, stuffed the dead rabbit into it, and slung the carry-all over his shoulder.

After making his way another two hundred yards up the incline, expecting at any moment to encounter either Allies dug into defensive positions for the night or Germans on the move, Barth discovered a level clearing surrounded by a ring of tall, oak trees. He gathered kindling and built a fire, caring little if anyone smelled the smoke or saw the flames. There was something about the clearing where he stood now, something that told him he was the only one there. Fatigue had pushed him beyond the point of worry; there were, in his estimation, worse things to suffer than being caught by the Germans. With a fire burning, he set about skinning the rabbit with his bayonet. He carved off strips of meat after that and cooked it over the fire. The spit he fashioned from sticks worked well. When at last he ate the meat, it tasted gamey and raw. Hunger had beat out waiting for the rabbit to be properly cooked.

Later, after he fed more branches to the fire, he lay back and stared at the shadows that shook between the large oaks. Barth removed his canteen from his web belt. The canteen was nearly empty, and the water tasted metallic. Tomorrow would be another day. Tomorrow he would continue on, keeping his eyes open for any water source. If he had an extra shirt, or even an extra set of socks, Barth could have pulled wet moss from the trees and extracted water; though such measures were good in theory during basic training and again when he reached England before being shipped over to France, they hardly adapted well to combat conditions. Water was everywhere, water could be found, water itself was easier to come by than the means to extract it. He would need water by tomorrow, and he would find it tomorrow. The fire was good. It cast its primal light in the dark; flames danced, calling out of the ether shades and shadows, luring them into the present. A casting call for performers, magic men, shamans, witches, and others who answer the call through time, yet remain on the boundary that exists between the fire's light and the otherworld, which is the eternal plateau that divides the physical world in its forest aspect and the dark canyon of chaos, where the souls of the prehistoric dwell, forever hunting wooly mammoths in the dark, lugging torches through caves to paint their exploits, to commune with their cosmology, at one with the earth, the stars, the infinite, believing they yet live though their bodies have returned to dust. Shades and shadows blended together that night beyond the perimeter of fire's light, beyond history; a secret pageant for Barth to witness, the perfect marriage of gnosis and myth. All of this to show the soldier that he was no longer part of the war, that he was no longer part of the world.

Longer after midnight the fire burned low. Sleep came in fits and starts. A mist marched through the forest and the shades of dead Paleolithic children amassed in the cold dark, all of them searching for the eternal mother. A mist low and thick that moved over the land until it found the sleeping soldier. On its back the mist carried secret songs that the living inhaled in their sleep. Barth breathed in the singing mist as he lingered between the world and somewhere else, an ideal, a mirage of muted aspects, his mind crowded now with the voices of archaic archetypes, Akashic angels who chose true freedom before war broke out in Heaven against a zealot and his oppressor. Mist, the water Barth longed for even now as he lay on the ground exhausted, unconscious, vaporous and pure, and laden with the song of sylphs who first pushed the fish onto dry land. It became one with Barth. And then the dreams began.

Chapter Fourteen: The Well At The World's End—Ardmore PA, 1915

In the days between the job offer from Mr. Whitaker and when Robert started working, he grew increasingly excited about the prospect of earning his own money, no matter how small the amount. Not to have it to spend, but to contribute to the household. Robert knew that many of his classmates did the same thing; some even went so far as to quit school so they could work full-time. He knew Helena would never allow for that. In their home, education was cherished above all else. His father often spoke of how, when he was a boy, he became a man before his time, quitting school to go to work and paying board at his parents' house until he could afford a place of his own. Despite Theodore's proselytizing about the responsibilities of manhood, Robert had it on good authority from his Uncle Myles, Theodore's older brother, that the burden of contribution fell on his shoulders and not his father's as the boy was first led to believe.

"Your father lived high on the hog on my buck," Uncle Myles had told Robert. The conversation had occurred just six months earlier during one of those rare visits Myles made to Delaware County. "Your grandfather would never think to bother the prodigal son about wages. No, sir. Not the dreamer. My younger brother lived like a prince."

"I went to work at twelve years old," Theodore argued. "All that mining has turned your brain into goulash."

Under The Bronze Moon

"Be that as it may," Myles made a great show of rolling his eyes as he spoke now, "yours, young Robert, is a different lot. You are like me. The oldest must make do. That much is true, but remember to dream, young man. And dream well."

"Since when did you become such a poet?"

"Never mind that, Teddy. Just see to it that the boy does not work his fingers to the bone."

Robert never liked when Uncle Myles went away. His uncle had always been a source of excitement and mystery and the infrequent visits and sudden departures often left Robert with the vague fear that he may never see Uncle Myles again. He knew of no other man who sailed the high seas in search of adventure. The tales of foreign lands that Myles told were elaborate ones peppered with characters that young Robert thought could only exist in story books: great diamond mines in Africa where the Dutch fortified their investments better than most countries could their borders, gold mining in California; surviving the sinking of a frigate bound for Antarctica. Myles wove tales that kept Robert and his sister riveted for what seemed countless hours before Helena ultimately broke up the session and sent the children off to bed.

Robert's excitement about the job offer made sleep difficult. His thoughts kept returning to Uncle Myles. He listened from his bed hoping to hear his parents come to what was, in Robert's mind, the right decision, and give their approval for him to begin work on Monday. From when Robert was first old enough to lie awake at night, he would often listen to his father and mother through the thin walls of the second floor, eavesdropping as they conversed in the kitchen. Most of the talk between his parents through the years was forgettable, centered around Matilda, Robert, money, and the rumors of a planned neighborhood just south of Ardmore adjacent to Haverford Township, but one night, when he was twelve years old, Robert heard his parents talking in hushed tones about Myles and the years he had been missing and presumed dead. There was talk of a telegram, a South American prison where

Myles, in Helena's words now, was undoubtedly languishing in his own filth and praying to the god he had turned his back on years beforehand for a quick death that would end his suffering. Theodore told his wife, "I don't know about all that. What is God's business is not mine." On and on it went for what seemed to young Robert like hours until his father mentioned the name of names, the one who struck fear into the hearts of all men in and around Haverford Township and Ardmore. At that hour, with a new moon amplifying the darkness in Robert's room, the invocation caused Theodore's son to curl up in his bed. The mere utterance of such a name in darkness could only mean conjuring the elusive shade who haunted the woods around Cobbs Creek—the name of Yates, the Centurion hauled into the Ardmore Police Station that very night under the suspicion of murder, the killing of another ghost, though one Robert knew to be of flesh and blood, his Uncle Myles Hexton Hyatt, the eldest of three brothers who spent most of his adult life abroad on some adventure or another. He never stopped long enough to start a family—though it was rumored that Myles had indeed fathered children on all seven continents. And now, according to the conversation the twelve-year-old Robert was listening to, Myles was not languishing in some God-forsaken cell in South America, but had met his grisly end at the hands of the very man rumored to walk between the world of the living and the dead. The rumor that evening was that Myles had indeed returned to Ardmore and had run afoul of Yates. Helena, dismissing the charge as mere hearsay, raved about the poor use of resources on the part of the Ardmore Police as they searched for a body. "Yates didn't do this," she told her husband. Theodore wasn't so sure. He reasoned that if there was a man who could snuff the life out of his brother it was Yates. Robert's parents went back and forth that night, trading theories that concerned why Yates would kill a man he didn't know and why Myles did not call on Theodore when he arrived in town the way he always did when he returned home. Maybe Robert had the story all wrong.

Straining to listen to the muffled voices, he convinced himself that he had missed some important part of the tale; perhaps, he reasoned, lying there curled up beneath a thin bed sheet, it was Yates himself who had been dispatched by his Uncle Myles, and that the legend of Delaware County had finally met his match, but if this were true then who was being held in the Ardmore jail? Would Robert's father allow Myles to stay behind bars? Or maybe the original tale had been true? A body had not been produced because the Centurion knew the way to the other side and now all Yates needed to do was bide his time until the police gave up their search.

Myles's story did not begin with his run-in with the shade they called Yates. This young Robert found out from his mother the next day. He knew from a very young age that not many men were worthy of his mother's praise; fewer still were those from the Hyatt clan.

"If you were to look up the word 'scoundrel' in the dictionary," Helena had told the boy that morning, "then you would see your Uncle Myles's likeness included there."

"Why do you hate him so much?" he asked.

"I don't hate him," his mother replied. "I despise his ways."

"Is there a difference?"

"Let me tell you something about your Uncle Myles," Helena began. "But you must promise never to tell your sister any of this. A lady should not be subjected to such tales of skullduggery and sinister schemes, even if it has to do with her own family."

"I promise," said Robert.

"Fair enough," she said. "Uncle Myles is...was... one of those men who—"

"Is he dead?"

"Whatever gave you that idea?"

"I heard you and father talking last night," her son told her. "Did Yates murder him?"

"Murder?" Helena pressed the palm of her left hand to her bosom. "Yates? Heavens, no. The man who lives in the woods

99

near Cobbs Creek? Never! I don't think that Yates is capable of such an act."

"Mother, do you know Yates?"

"I know of him."

"What is he doing in the Ardmore jail if he didn't kill Uncle Myles?"

"You have a vivid imagination," his mother said. "Now, shall I continue this tale?"

"So, Yates is not in jail?"

"Your Uncle Myles," said Helena, ignoring her son's inquiry, "is the kind of man who possesses a curious mind. Coupled with what my mother often called itchy feet, a need to travel, and often. It is the kind of thing that leads a man toward ruin. In your uncle's case trouble has always been the wind in his degenerate sail.

"Before the turn of the century, Myles Hexton Hyatt did find a number of adventures. He prospected for gold in California and narrowly escaped being hung at the gallows when the men he worked with died in an explosion. There were those who believed Myles tossed a stick of dynamite into a cave. But the official ruling by a judge magistrate was that one of the miners had struck a hidden reserve of gas underground. All but Myles died. So, you can imagine why some men would point a finger at him.

"You would expect that Myles would have struck it rich after that," Helena went on, "since there were no partners left in his prospecting company. Sadly, the opposite was true. He came back east penniless, more broke than the day he left.

"Some months later, after borrowing money from your father, Myles went to New York City to find work. It was there he found himself in the company of some cutthroat Latvians who claimed to know the location of an ancient treasure buried somewhere in Mongolia—"

"Was there a treasure?" Robert asked. At mention of the treasure his interest in his mother's musings became renewed. "Did he find it?"

"If there was," she said, "Myles never spoke of it. Your father received telegrams and postcards from time to time over the years, but then it all stopped. Do you remember the gift Uncle Myles sent you?"

"Of course," he said. "*The Well at the World's End* by William Morris. It is one of my favorite books, mother."

"Indeed," said Helena. "You always went in for those tales of the fantastic. Even as a little boy you wanted me to read from Lewis Carroll and that dreadful book by MacDonald—"

"*The Princess and the Goblin*," Robert cried. "And now it's Matilda's favorite!"

"Young girls have no business reading such tales," his mother said. "But you and Matilda both are dreamers. What I would give if you would embrace realism as you get older."

"You mean all those bleak tales by Dickens and such? The world is bad enough, mother. Why would I read about such things?"

Helena stifled a laugh. "There are no hidden kingdoms, Robert," she said. "There are no fairy treasures, no magic wells, and no borderland realms waiting to be discovered. Your Uncle Myles thought otherwise and look what happened to him. I would save you the agony of that lesson before it consumes you."

Robert remembered the conversation with his mother as if it had happened just that morning. Though his uncle had come and gone a few times since Robert was that twelve-year-old boy who had feared that Myles was dead, he still dreamed of faraway lands, fairy treasures, and hidden realms.

In the few days since Whitaker had first offered him the job much had happened in the Hyatt household. His mother remained adamant that her son did not succumb to the enchantment of working part-time, for she believed that as much as employment would build good work ethics for a teenager, it was more important to focus on schoolwork.

"You should go to college," Helena had told him that evening after dinner.

"I can do both," Robert countered. "I can go to college and work at Whitaker's Stationery Store."

"I meant *go away* to school," his mother said. "Besides, we don't know anything about Whitaker."

"You buy your Christmas cards there every year, mother."

"Business is one thing," she informed him. "Knowing a man's quirks, his habits, his secrets, that's quite another."

On Thursday night the matter was settled, but not by Helena; nor did Robert exercise any proxy vote or other sleight-of-hand trick. It was Theodore who came home from the train depot with terrible news.

"What do you mean you lost your job?" Helena asked.

"It's no secret," Theodore began, "that Reilly and I don't get along—"

"Reilly and I," Matilda corrected her father.

"Do you see?" he asked, gesturing at his daughter. "Do you see what you are creating here?"

"I fail to see how a young girl correcting her father's English is a mark against her," said Helena. "Now, please. Continue."

"Of course you don't," he said. "You're a teacher."

The Hyatt family sat at their dinner table. Matilda and Robert toyed with their mashed potatoes. The roast beef continued to cool on their plates.

"What will you do now?" Robert asked.

"Your father will go back to Mr. Reilly," his mother said, "and apologize for whatever offense he caused."

"How is it that this is my fault?" Theodore demanded to know. "Why do you always assume the worst from me?"

"History, perhaps."

Matilda giggled. Robert kicked her under the table. His sister stopped laughing.

"Very funny," Theodore said. "I prefer not to discuss this any further in front of the children."

"Children? Mr. Whitaker has employed our son," Helena said. "Robert has a job after school. I think he should hear it."

"Matilda and I can sit in the living room if you prefer," Robert said as he stood up.

"Sit down," his father snapped. "You're not going anywhere."

Helena sat back in her chair. She folded her arms across her chest and stared at her husband.

"Tell me what happened," she said.

"Reilly is a blowhard and a stuffed shirt," said Theodore. "He thinks he's high and mighty like God on his heavenly throne. But I see right through him. All the boys at the station do."

"And did they lose their jobs too?"

"No," he answered. "I don't know what this country is coming to if a man can no longer speak his mind."

It was decided that night, by all parties present, that Robert would accept Whitaker's offer, provided that the new job did not interfere with his studies. Helena made her husband swear in front of the children that he would find another part-time job soon. Theodore appeased his wife, telling her what she wanted to hear. Once he had said his piece, however, Theodore left the table without a word and put on his coat and hat.

"Where do you think you are going?" Helena asked.

"I guess you didn't hear the news at school today," said Theodore.

"What news?"

"Yates is getting sprung tonight from the Ardmore jail."

"And how does this involve you?"

"It was Myles who paid the big man's bail."

Helena clutched her chest. "You mean," she said, "Myles is here?"

"No," her husband told her. "He wired the money through Western Union. Doesn't that beat all? Old Yates getting his bail paid by his alleged victim?"

Theodore left the house through the back door. Helena sat slack jawed, unable to speak.

Robert winked at his sister. He considered her lucky. Matilda who toyed with her food and never got into trouble for doing so, Matilda who traipsed through life like the innocent Fae creatures who populated the fantasies that both she and Robert liked to read, who had never seen Yates from more than a great distance, and who did not fully understand what had been discussed in those moments before Theodore left the house. For Matilda was too young to remember Uncle Myles, though she had sat as a younger girl listening to his wild tales of travel and adventure, transfixed as easily as her older brother had been. In the place of a fixed face, the way Robert remembered it, Matilda had little more than a phantom's presence to go by whenever talk of Myles Hexton Hyatt came up. And here, this very night, the news that Uncle Myles had paid the Centurion's bail proved that a deeper bond than Robert knew existed between those two mysterious men.

By Sunday afternoon the fog of the Yates affair, as it came to be known, had lifted. Rumor had it that the solitary man returned to his favorite haunt—the woods near the powder mill where, the more superstitious residents of Ardmore believed, existed a threshold to some borderland only Yates knew. Life in Ardmore returned to normal.

It was that Monday afternoon following Yates being let out of jail that Robert reported to Whitaker's Stationery store for his first day of work. Upon entering the establishment, he smelled lemons. Robert walked up to Mr. Whitaker who was hunched over a ledger with a fountain pen in his hand.

"Mr. Whitaker?"

The little man looked up. He slammed the ledger shut, but not before Robert realized that the page was blank.

"Master Hyatt," said Whitaker. "Are you ready to begin?"

Chapter Fifteen: An Empty House
They Build—Boston, MA—2012

Elinor held her breath when her father answered her call. She had spent the better part of the day attempting to track him down, and now that she had him on the phone, she wasn't quite sure what to say.

"Dad?"

"Ellie?"

"Where are you?"

"Down in Philadelphia," Miller said. "Is everything all right?"

"I was going to ask the same of you," Elinor told him. "What are you doing there?"

"I didn't tell you?"

"Tell me what?"

"I am updating Hyatt's biography," he said. "Further research."

"In Philadelphia?"

"Haverford Township," he replied. "I am paying a visit to May Weldon—"

"Dad," Elinor cut him off, "did you see Dr. Moran?"

There was a long pause. Elinor wasn't sure if the call had dropped.

"Should I know this Dr. Moran?" Miller asked.

Six weeks beforehand, Elinor had scheduled an appointment for her father with a neurologist. Dr. Moran came highly qualified, his specialty being the early detection of

Alzheimer's disease and its subsequent treatment. It took some delicate negotiations on Elinor's part to get the appointment at such short notice.

"Dad, the appointment was today," she said. "Do you know how hard it was to—"

"Ellie, I am not senile," her father told her. "If that's what you think."

"Dad, over the past year you have exhibited many of the early signs of Alzheimer's," Elinor blurted out. Until that moment, she and her father had never openly discussed the term. Now, it was out there. "I am worried," she concluded. "That's all."

"Ellie," he said, "I'm fine. You are just like your mother. You worry too much."

"And what happens if..."

"If what?" Miller's voice came like a spear now. "I have another episode? For Christ's sake, Ellie. People get lost sometimes when they drive. It doesn't mean they have dementia."

"Dad, it was the same route you've taken for years," she countered. "And it has happened more than once. Don't you remember that time you called me? The last time it happened? You were frantic."

The phone call was still fresh in her mind. Her father had called from a gas station. It was raining, an autumn rain that made the Berkshires look frayed and dull. If she hadn't known better, she would have dismissed the call. But her father was crying, distraught over having lost his way home.

After she was able to calm her father down, Elinor offered to leave her campus and drive out to get him. Miller refused, arguing that it was nearly a two-hour drive from Boston to Amherst. He opted, instead, to dig out the GPS system Elinor had bought him for Christmas two years prior and let the navigation tool do the work that day. It meant Elinor had to remain on the phone and talk him through how to set up the GPS device; only, it became complicated once her father ran out of quarters. It worried her that her father could not remember how to drive home from the UMass-Amherst campus where he had worked for nearly thirty years. And he had called from a pay phone. That meant her father had either lost his cell phone, or he could not remember where it was. Elinor refused to believe that he had become so far gone that he forgot he owned a cell phone. Whatever was happening to her father, Elinor had reasoned, she was sure that the knots that kept the fabric of her father's life together were slowly coming undone.

"Ellie," Miller was saying, "I was upset about your mother. Sometimes it's hard. It still is. But now it is different. I have learned to cope. Yes, I have learned to do that. But Alzheimer's disease? I don't think so."

"So, get checked out anyway," she said. "If it turns out to be nothing then I will leave you alone about it."

"I have to go, Ellie."

"Dad, wait."

"What now?"

"Are you really updating the Hyatt biography?"

"No, I got on a train and ended up in Philadelphia," said Miller. "I have no recollection of how I got to the train in Springfield—"

"That's not funny."

"To me, it is."

"How long will you be down there?"

"A couple of nights, I guess," he said. "I will call you when I get home."

"Call me tonight," Elinor said.

"I love you, Ellie," her father told her. "But sometimes you can be intolerable."

She pictured the night she had received the call from her father. A cold and rainy evening, the kind of late fall weather that puts people into a permanent state of depression. Her father had been crying, though he denied it later; but, listening to his voice that night, she had known. His tone had been the same as it was on the day her mother was buried.

Miller's dilemma that night had not been brought on by a mistake. McCleary's, the gas station where he had called her from a pay phone, had been a landmark on South Street for decades, marking the half-way point between the turnpike exit and the Miller home. She had even told him to turn around and look at the sign, but he had been in such a state.

"No," he said, sniffling. "You don't understand. It's all different now."

"Dad, you are not lost," she assured him.

"Maybe your mother will come get me," were his next words after a stretch of considerable silence.

In the days following the incident Elinor wondered if her father had suffered a break with reality. It was only later, as he continued to show other signs, that she changed her mind. She read up on the subject of Alzheimer's disease, at times lying awake at night until nearly dawn. Then the thought seized her that perhaps at that very moment her father may be out traipsing through the wooded dark of the Berkshires. Elinor struck from her mind any further thought concerning her father being in physical danger. What she could not suppress was the science of heredity, the impact her father's condition might have on her one day. Will I end up like him? Like her father, Elinor pursued knowledge and had become a professor, in part, to share what she had learned, and to engage students in debate, even if opinions were unpopular. The thought of a disease wiping clean the knowledge she had accumulated frightened her more than the prospect of cancer. Of course, if there was a silver lining in all this, it was knowing that when the disease struck in full most people maintained little or no knowledge at all of their former selves; in such a condition, she reasoned, there was little room for mourning the loss of memories gained over a lifetime.

"And Schuyler is being completely unreasonable, of course," Miller was saying now. "How many biographies do you know about R.J. Hyatt?"

"What?" Elinor snapped to. "Dad, what are you talking about?"

"Schuyler Heddings," he said. "Are you even listening to me?"

"Heddings is still your editor?" his daughter asked. "You would think he would have died from some venereal disease by now."

"Oh, Ellie," Miller scowled. "You never talked like that when your mother was alive."

"And you never went off without telling anyone—"

"At least your mother understood what I was doing," he told her. "There were conferences, visiting lectures, and trips to Europe. Your mother—"

"Is dead, Dad."

"Ellie, don't be crass."

Now it was Miller's turn to consider what came next. He wanted to assure his daughter that there was nothing to worry about, that he indeed missed his wife, that, yes, there were times when he became absentminded, confused; but, considering recent events, any such admission would cause his daughter further anguish.

Life had not always been this way. There had been a time in Miller's life when things were simple. There were adjunct jobs, and there was love. Then, like so many others in his field, he began publishing in journals. It was Ann who had encouraged him to rework his doctoral thesis on R.J. Hyatt's *The Land of Dust and Honey*; his wife who had always wanted him to follow his passion, to make leaps, to take chances, and through it all, Ann harbored enough reason and intellect to steer Miller away from any luckless pretense of writing fiction.

"It's never the same," Ann had once said, and Miller had never forgotten her words. "Sure, some academics try their hand at the novel as a form. But it's no more than an empty house they build. No, the novel is better left in the hands of those beyond university walls."

Lovely Ann, saint of reason, who always knew what to say at just the right time. It was she alone who had inquired as to why no one had ever published a biography on R.J. Hyatt. For three nights following that conversation, Miller could not sleep. Instead of fretting over sleeplessness, he used the time to pour over his old notes, scouring his original doctoral thesis, a dozen essays he had published about Hyatt's lone novel. Only a few months would pass from that night until the first time he met May Weldon.

"Dad," Elinor was saying, "I am going to reschedule your appointment next week."

"Ellie, please," Miller stood his ground. He turned to face May's house. "Allow me to make that decision. I will be home in a few days."

When Elinor heard her father disconnect, she gritted her teeth and hissed. At her desk, she stared at the wall. At that moment, she wanted to scream. Then a knock at her office door kept her from doing so.

Chapter Sixteen: A Blessing And A Curse—Ardmore PA, 1915

The end began in earnest that summer. It would take two more years before the root took hold and the bitter seed flourished. Matilda, graced by long rays of afternoon sunlight, was unaware of what awaited her. She wove her way through various groups of mill men and their families, searching for the one true person she wanted her brother to meet.

For Matilda, it was as if an evil witch had put a hex on her brother. In the course of a few short weeks, it seemed that Robert had forgotten his love for Megan Sullivan. All her brother talked about now was his confounded job. Who wanted to hear about that musty old shop and that despicable little man? What thrill could exist for anyone surrounded by all that blank paper and writing instruments? If work made a person forget about their hearts, Matilda reasoned, then she didn't want anything to do with a job when she was older. Not now, not ever. The way people toiled these days was not the way that God had intended it. In the time that her father had worked at the mill and the train station, he appeared to have grown old faster than he should have. It was true that Matilda worried about her father, but for different reasons. And now that he worked only one job there was more tension at home because her father wanted to go out to the tavern at night, and her mother, who held the strings to the nearly empty family purse, refused to let him do so.

That Sunday was the first time since her father had told Old Man Reilly from the train station what time it was that she and her family attended the powder mill picnic. Summer was drawing to a close, and Matilda wanted to work every last drop of satisfaction out of these Halcyon days. She knew it wouldn't be long before she too might have to go to work after school or on the weekends. Her friend Susan Constancia was one year older than Matilda and Susan had already had one job tutoring the Ryder boys, but that didn't last long since Susan got with child. Susan was barely old enough for high school, and about to become a mother, Helena had said one day when she thought no one was listening. But Matilda had heard her mother. No one in town said it, at least not in Matilda's presence, but it was suspected by her mother and other women that it was Mr. Ryder who had caused Susan Constancia her current dilemma. Such was the sin that weak men committed, she had heard her father tell her mother one night, when his wife refused him conjugal relations. Matilda did not know about conjugal relations. She suspected that it was a way—perhaps some magic existing between husband and wife—that kept young adolescent girls from becoming pregnant. Whatever the case, Matilda missed her friend ever since Susan was sent off to live with her faraway relatives in Chicago.

Meanwhile, Robert was busy with his own thoughts, teen troubles of a male variety. And while he adored his sister, he found himself having less time to entertain her hypothetical questions about Susan Constancia, the Ryder family, and the fate of the girl now that she had gone off to live with relatives in Chicago.

On the road to the mill that day walked several families besides the Hyatts: among them, Megan Sullivan and her parents. No sooner did Matilda spot the lithe, pretty Irish girl, she tugged on her brother's right arm.

"Yonder walks your love," Matilda told him.

"Don't be a nitwit," Robert shook off her grip.

"Robert," Helena cried. "Please don't address your sister that way."

"Is it possible," Theodore proposed, "to walk to the picnic without carrying on like a bunch of savages?"

"You're one to talk once you start drinking," his wife said. "And you better lay off the whiskey today, Teddy. Remember the last incident?"

Theodore did not, but his son did.

The Whiskey Incident, as Helena referred to it, began one night three weeks prior to the picnic. It was after ten o'clock in the evening when a knock sounded at the door. Helena instructed Robert to answer the door.

On the stoop stood Mickey McMaster, a spry plug of a man dressed in a suit that looked two sizes too big. McMaster busied himself by smoothing down the sparse hairs atop his pale, sweaty head with one hand while he held his hat tightly in the other. Initially, Robert thought McMaster was a vagabond looking for a handout. That's when the short man offered a sly buck toothed grin.

"Hello, boy," said McMaster. "Is your mother at home?"

"Where else would my mother be at this hour?" asked Robert, still unsure of the sight before him.

"Point taken," he replied. "I mean no disrespect."

There was a stain on McMaster's shirt. At first, Robert thought it was mustard.

"What can I do for you?" Robert asked.

"For me? I am afraid my salvation is beyond your meager means, boy" he said. "I come bringing news of your father. Don't worry. He's not dead."

"What's this all about then?"

"Your father has taken ill at O'Malley's Pub," McMaster revealed. "He will need assistance getting home."

"Who is at the door, Robert?" Helena called out from the kitchen doorway.

"It's Mickey McMaster," her son replied.

"Who?" his mother strode through the dining room and into the living room.

"Michael McMaster, ma'am," the short man pushed his way past Robert and entered the living room. "I sincerely apologize. I was just telling the boy—"

"Robert," Helena said. "That's his name."

"Yes, indeed," said McMaster. "As I was just telling you boy here—"

"Robert."

"No," he said, stifling a belch. "My name is Michael. But I get that all the time. Please, call me Mickey."

"Mr. McMaster," said Helena, pinching her nose with two fingers to ward off the little man's stench, "state your business."

"Ah, yes," McMaster stood on his toes for a moment, and nearly fell over. He steadied himself by taking hold of Robert's shoulder. "To business then, yes. Right you are. It appears that Ted will need some help getting home. You see, Mrs. Hyatt, a few of the boys from the mill, including me and Ted, stopped by O'Malley's Pub after the whistle blew this afternoon. You understand how we men are?"

"No," Helena crossed her arms over her chest now. She arched her left eyebrow, and added, "I am afraid I do not."

"It appears that time, that unconscionable whore, if you'll pardon my Gaelic, well, she was got away from us and—"

"Is my husband drunk?" she asked. "Again?"

"Oh," McMaster crushed the brim of his hat in his hands. "Indeed, he is. And then some, I'm afraid."

He reached into his coat and pulled out a fifth of Royal Kentucky Bourbon Whiskey, unscrewed the cap, and wiped his mouth with his hat.

"Mr. McMaster," said Helena. "You would do well to put that bottle away if you are interested in keeping your head attached to your neck."

"As you wish," he said.

"Robert?"

"Yes, mother?" her son asked.

114

"You will accompany Mr. McMaster to O'Malley's Pub and assist your father."

"But I have—" Robert started to say.

"Now," she told him.

"Yes, mother."

Outside the house, the mystery of McMaster's shirt stain was solved. Robert stepped out of the way just in time when the little fat man vomited on the sidewalk.

"Jesus and the Holy Ghost," McMaster exclaimed. "Ready for round two, I suppose."

Robert and the drunk made it half-way down the block when McMaster stopped, patted his coat pockets, and then snapped his pudgy fingers.

"Come along, Mr. McMaster," Robert said. "Let's go get my father."

"Do you have a wagon?" McMaster asked. "Or a wheelbarrow?"

"No. Why?"

"It's your father," he replied. "He's not exactly what a doctor would call ambulatory."

Robert led the drunk back to his house. His father kept a wheelbarrow in the shed. Robert made McMaster wait on the sidewalk, which was no easy task, given that the drunkard wanted to see the backyard, and retrieved the wheelbarrow. As he made his way back down the narrow path between his house and the Warzniecks' next door, he stopped. Mickey McMaster had climbed atop some trash cans on the side of the Warznieck residence.

"What do you think you're doing?" Robert hissed.

McMaster craned his neck to look at the boy. As he did, he lost his footing and fell to the ground. When he did, the trash cans tipped and crashed into one another, and the ensuing metallic clang reverberated between the houses.

A porch light on the side of the Warznieck home went on. McMaster stumbled away toward the street before Lech

Warznieck exited the house; his gargantuan form blocked out the porch light as he stood on the edge of the steps.

Robert stood still, gripping the wheelbarrow handles, scared to the point of paralysis.

"Is that you, Robert?" Warznieck asked.

"Yes sir," he replied.

Mr. Warznieck was a big Pole, barrel-chested, broad-shouldered, and armed that evening with a length of two-by-four lumber. The Warzniecks were new to the neighborhood. All Robert knew about them was that they had two little girls, twins whose names Robert could never remember. Warznieck's wife Rosalyn spoke no English. All the boys in the neighborhood loved Mrs. Warznieck. She was young, voluptuous, and prone to hang her laundry out in the backyard wearing a sheer housecoat that accentuated her attributes when the sunlight stretched across their yard in the morning hours. Like most of the teenage boys in his neighborhood, Robert was not immune to the charm of Rosalyn's physical endowments. At night, he often lay in his room masturbating as he considered the symmetry of her heavy breasts, how they would feel in his hands. The only thing that kept Robert from pissing in his pants that night, as Lech Warznieck's stood there hefting his two-by-four club, was the burgeoning erection he experienced the moment Rosalyn, dressed in a white nightgown, no longer than a shirt, of some sheer material through which Robert could see her large areolas, appeared in the doorway behind her husband.

"What are you doing?" Warznieck asked.

"Me?" Robert replied. "I'm bringing this wheelbarrow to Mr. Davis down the street. My dad said to bring it to him."

Rosalyn said something in Polish that brought a smile to Warznieck's face.

"Just a raccoon," the big man said to his wife. "Go inside."

Rosalyn offered a wave to Robert and went back into the house.

"Well," said Robert, "I have school tomorrow and—"

"Raccoons always knock over my garbage pail," Warznieck announced. "Always the same pail. Always trashcan right beneath my bathroom window. Always when wife is bathing."

"That's strange," he said. His palms sweated; his erection took on new vigor at the mere mention of Rosalyn Warznieck in her bath. "Maybe you should move your trash cans."

"Robert," his neighbor said. "You see raccoon tonight, you tell raccoon that if I catch him I crush his whiskey-soaked, fat skull."

"Yes," he looked at the two-by-four. "I certainly will."

Seconds later, Robert found Mickey McMaster fast asleep beneath an azalea bush in the Warzniecks' front yard. He gave the Irishman a swift kick in the side.

"Apologies, constable," McMaster sat up and wiped the sleep from his eyes. "I lost my house keys beneath this shrub and...oh, it's you. Did you get your father yet?"

"Lech says he will kill you if he catches you stealing peeks at his wife again," said Robert.

"Who the hell is Lech?"

"Mr. Warznieck. The bricklayer? Hauls hundreds of pounds of bricks all day long? Comes home to a pretty wife—"

"Rosalyn!" McMaster exclaimed.

"Be quiet."

"Rosalyn," the little man whispered, and pressed a dirty index finger to his lips.

He stood close to Robert now; his breath rancid, an equal mix of whiskey, vomit, and rotting teeth.

"Can we go now?" Robert asked.

McMaster staggered backward, pointing at the wheelbarrow.

"What is that?" he asked.

"The wheelbarrow you asked for," the boy said. "Remember?"

"Say, why don't you haul me back to O'Malley's," said McMaster, "so I can save my strength for last call?"

Robert pushed the wheelbarrow past the fat little Irishman. O'Malley's was three blocks away. Some nights, Robert watched from the living room window as men walked down the street, their destination the pub, and wondered what the attraction was about standing in a saloon all night drinking whiskey and beer. His father had told him once that a trough made of stainless steel had been installed in the floor along the length of the bar. There were spigots that could be kicked, spraying water like a water fountain when the stench of piss became overwhelming. Robert's first taste of alcohol came when he was fifteen years old. Old Granddad Whiskey. His friend Winston Rydell had stolen it from his father and brought it to Darby Creek where boys met at night in the woods to drink and talk about women. Robert was sick the next day and swore never to touch whiskey again. There were many boys in the neighborhood that, when they got older, would follow in their fathers' footsteps. They also frequented the pub. Robert did not want to be like them. He didn't like O'Malley, the saloon owner, and he wished that his father would give up drinking. Every time his father got drunk his mother delivered a stern warning concerning the inherent evil spawned by imbibing in spirits. Men turned to alcohol, Helena often preached, because they had weak moral fiber. Robert, at sixteen years old, knew it was something more deep-seated than that; only, at his age, he could not articulate the emptiness that dwelled within men like his father, men who drank too much, trying to fill that void, and wasted away from the inside out.

Presently, two men Robert did not know exited O'Malley's and staggered up the street toward him. One of the men tipped his hat at McMaster and kept going. The other one stopped in front of a Chinese laundry shop and relieved himself against the window.

"Bring the wheelbarrow inside," McMaster instructed the boy as they approached the entrance.

Inside, a dozen or more men stood drinking at the bar. The smoke inside the saloon stung Robert's eyes. Ruddy-faced

Tommy O'Malley stood behind the bar pouring a draft. He stared at Robert a moment, a smirk slowly forming on his face as he studied the wheelbarrow, then nodded to his right.

Against the wall across the room, Theodore Hyatt sat propped in a chair. His head hung low, his chin resting against his chest, and his long legs were stretched out in front of him. His left foot was missing its shoe.

"Mr. O'Malley," said McMaster.

The bartender reached down and produced Theodore's shoe. He threw it at McMaster who ducked. The shoe bounced off the wall and came to rest at Robert's feet.

"A man should never walk home to his wife with one shoe," McMaster said as he picked up the shoe. He set about placing it back on Theodore's foot. "This way I figured your father would stay put under the watchful eye of Tommy O'Malley. Do you know Mr. O'Malley?"

Robert did not, but he knew Sean O'Malley, the bar owner's son. They had both played baseball one summer after the eighth grade. Sean was shy, fearful of the world; his left eye was a lazy eye, peering off in a different direction. Robert's mother said that people with a lazy eye had a gift. Helena had told her son that Sean had the gift of being able to see into the spirit world; to glimpse the mistakes his ancestors made and avoid them if possible. Robert was of an age where he began to doubt his mother's esoteric musings. He didn't believe that Sean O'Malley could see beyond the present world. All he knew was that Sean's lazy eye made him different from the other boys, an outcast, and that made Robert feel sorry for him.

"We should do this soon, I suspect," McMaster was saying now. "I'm sure Mr. O'Malley wants to close up the bar so he can go home and give the wife—"

"Watch it, McMaster," O'Malley's face reddened as he lifted a cudgel into view. "I won't lose sleep tonight if I spill that dog shit you call brains all over the barroom floor."

Several men laughed. O'Malley started out from behind the bar, but one of the patrons stopped him.

119

"Let it go, Tommy boy," the man told him. "He's just having a bit of fun, that's all."

"Take your father and go, boy," O'Malley said to Robert. "And when he comes to tell your old man I'm cutting him off. He's bad for business."

"When I come to," Theodore said, his eyes still closed. "I'm going to kick your Protestant ass up and down Ardmore Avenue."

"You want to threaten me in my own place?" the bar owner asked. He pointed his cudgel at Robert. "Out, now! Before I smash your heads."

McMaster helped Robert lift Theodore and place him in the wheelbarrow. Robert folded his father's arms across his chest. When he turned the wheelbarrow around toward the door, he stared at O'Malley. The bartender lowered his cudgel, then lowered his eyes.

Outside the bar, McMaster fretted with his hat. He drew a deep breath, and exhaled. The smell coming out of his mouth was nearly enough to make Robert faint.

"You'll be alright," said McMaster as he walked back into the bar. "Hey, barkeep. How about a nightcap?"

"Get the fuck out of my bar, you half-English piece of shit," O'Malley shouted, "before I jam this here baton up your ass and turn you into a poofter."

McMaster backed out of the entrance. As he stood on the sidewalk now, he looked at Robert.

"Oh dear," the little man said. "O'Malley's being most inhospitable."

McMaster commandeered the wheelbarrow and pushed Theodore up the street to his house. Robert held his father's legs up the whole way, attempting to balance the dead weight. It was no easy feat, but the two of them managed without any mishap.

By the time they pushed Theodore into the backyard, their passenger was awake. It took several tries to get Robert's father out of the wheelbarrow and onto his feet. Each time Theodore refused to stand up.

"Take a step back," McMaster said to Robert. "Give the old boy some room."

Robert did as he was told. McMaster tipped the wheelbarrow. Theodore rolled out onto the grass.

"A good night now to you both," the little man tipped his hat. "Give my regards to Mrs. Hyatt."

He disappeared into the darkness around the corner of the house.

"Come on, Dad," Robert took his father by the arm. "On your feet."

"I'm not your father, kid," Theodore mumbled as he struggled to get onto his hands and knees.

A loud metallic crash sounded between the houses. A light on Warznieck's side porch went on.

"You're talking nonsense," said Robert to his father. He gave his father's arm a tug. "It's late."

"I don't need your help," said Theodore, shaking free from Robert's grip. "This is all that bastard's fault—"

"Theodore!" Helena's silhouette appeared at the back door now. There was no telling how long she had stood there in shadow watching them. "Get inside the house and stop making a spectacle of yourself."

And so ended the Whiskey Incident. It had happened three weeks prior to the mill picnic. Robert was plagued by both embarrassment and questions. He wanted to believe that his father had spouted drunken nonsense, that somewhere in the wanton excess of whiskey his father meant to teach him a lesson about the perils of excessive drinking, a lesson that showed Robert how a man should not act, but his father's words that night cut deep. Robert walked around in a daze following the incident. He was not sure what to make of the emptiness that welled within him now. He felt like the wounded fisher king from the Arthurian legends his mother had loved so much; a keeper of some secret injury that was unable to heal.

Nearing the powder mill grounds now, carrying that hollowness within, Robert did his best to forget the whiskey troubles. He watched as Megan Sullivan stood by as her father spoke to two millworkers. Megan turned and looked back at Robert, her chin resting on her right shoulder. If Robert had seen the look she gave him it was lost, for another distracted him as she walked quietly just ten yards away, a wraith within the tree line.

Abigail Sweeney wore a summer smock that barely covered her calves. When she saw Robert she left the trees and walked toward him. He guessed that she wore no undergarments; her full, heavy breasts swung freely beneath her dress. The other thing that enticed Robert at that moment was that Abigail walked barefoot. His eyes followed her as she turned and made her way along a path that led to the widows' tenement. He glanced back at Megan Sullivan who stood facing him now. Megan folded her arms across her chest and, the moment Robert looked at her again, turned away.

"Someone's in it now," Matilda said.

Before Robert could respond, Helena took hold of her daughter's right arm.

"A lady does not speculate about such things, Matilda," her mother said.

"Yes, mother," her daughter replied.

"And as for you," Helena's stare bore down on Robert, "it is not polite to stare at a woman, even if she is just an illiterate Irish lass."

"She's right," Theodore spoke up. "Your mother does not allow me to stare at her, and I married her."

"Isn't it time for you to join the other men," Helena told her husband, "so you can drink beer and tell coarse jokes?"

"Hot damn!" her husband exclaimed.

"Brute."

"And I love you," he replied.

"Such as it is," Helena mumbled. "Run along, Teddy. I want to speak to the children."

"Yes, ma'am."

Theodore performed a little jig and set out to join a gaggle of men who stood in a circle around a roasting pig, each with a beer in hand.

"And Teddy!" Helena called out.

"I know," he shouted. "No whiskey!"

Theodore bowed before he turned his back on his family and joined the other men.

Later that afternoon, Robert walked near the creek by the mill wheel. Matilda accompanied him, feigning a clinginess that some siblings do, but acting under the auspices of her mother's contempt for her son's wandering eyes. She was given strict orders to make sure she interfered with any attempt her brother might make to have contact with 'that Irish girl.'

"Which Irish girl, mother?" Matilda had asked.

"How many are there, child?" Helena inquired.

"Well," she said, "there's Megan Sullivan. She goes to Robert's school."

"Oh yes," her mother said. "I met her mother. Mrs. Sullivan had the audacity to ask me why I do not teach more Irish literature in my—"

"I like Yeats."

"Please, Matilda," said Helena. "Do not interrupt me." Then, "Wait. What other Irish girl?"

"The Sweeney girl," her daughter responded.

Matilda fell into a stupor, recalling the conversation she had had with her mother. Robert studied her for a moment, the way she stared at the rolling clear creek water. To his right, he saw Abigail Sweeney a few yards away. She was seated on a rock, the only ray of afternoon sunlight coming through the treetop canopy graced her pale form, turning her long, red hair golden bronze. One bare leg dangled from the side of the rock; her left foot immersed in the creek.

Matilda snapped to, ready for action. Her mother had been clear about interrupting her brother. *In my absence,* her mother's voice echoed in her head, *you must ensure that Robert does not become beguiled and corrupted by those ignorant girls.* Matilda was ready to do what was necessary. Seeing Abigail Sweeney stretched out on the sunlit rock, a shameless siren calling her brother toward ruin, made the girl's skin crawl. Lascivious was a word that Matilda had read in a novel not long ago. She could not recall the author's name, but she knew what the word meant.

In that moment, a blessing and a curse fell upon brother and sister. Three girls from Matilda's school descended upon the creek bank. Robert did not know their names. All he knew was that his blood turned cold every time he heard the three of them cackle like Macbeth's Weird Sisters. The girls swooped down on Matilda and whisked her away in a cacophony of high-pitched squeals and whispered ruinous secrets. Alone now, he approached Abigail on her rock.

"Enjoying the picnic?" he asked. Idiot, he thought.

Abigail turned to look at him. She smiled. He blushed. She withdrew her left foot from the water and drew it up on the rock. Her skirt slid down, revealing the underside of her pale thighs and the fleshy folds of her sex between her legs.

"I don't care much for company," she said.

"I am sorry," he said. "I should not have disturbed you."

"I hear you work at Whitaker's Stationery Store," said Abigail. She sat up, crossed her legs, and smoothed out her skirt. "You got any money?"

"No," Robert told her.

"That's okay," she said. "I want to show you something."

Abigail climbed down from the rock. Her bare feet sunk into the mud, but she paid her predicament no mind. Taking hold of Robert's hand, she led him behind rocks piled high behind the mill.

The noise of the picnic faded. Robert's heart raced.

Abigail leaned back against the rocks. She toyed with the shoulder straps of her smock.

"Make sure no one is coming," she told him.

Robert did as he was instructed. He peeked around the corner of the mill. His sister and the other girls were huddled together some distance away. He did not see Megan Sullivan either; her absence weighed unexpectedly on him as he returned to the place where Abigail waited for him.

The widow's daughter pulled down the straps on her smock, allowing them to slip from her shoulders. She reached into her top and pulled out her right breast and then her left. Robert nearly jumped when she took his hands in hers.

"Touch them," she whispered.

Robert obliged her. Abigail's breasts were soft, heavy; each one too large for his hand. He took a step closer, but the widow's daughter stopped him. She stuffed her pale breasts back into her top and pulled her straps onto her shoulders.

"Meet me here at midnight," Abigail said. "Bring me some money. I'll let you see more than my tits."

After that, she marched past him and vanished around the corner of the mill.

Robert waited a minute before he emerged from the hiding place. His hands felt warm. He closed his eyes, remembering how her nipples had hardened at his touch, the way pale blue veins spider-webbed their way out from Abigail's pink areolas. It was still summer. Robert was sixteen years old. As he made his way back to the picnic, he plotted how he would take his pay from his dresser drawer and bring the money to Abigail. He longed to see her naked in the moonlight, to rut like animals in the woods by the shadow of the mill.

Midnight was hours away; an eternity for him. Robert remembered his mother telling him that the widow Sweeney was in a bad way. His father had warned him about whores who did it for money. The conversation had made him uncomfortable. These thoughts and more spun around in his mind, causing him to feel dizzy by the time he reached the picnic table where some boys he knew from school were seated. Robert listened to the boys talk about news they had heard on the radio, but he could not concentrate on what they were saying, as his thoughts kept going back to Abigail and her bare breasts. More than anything he wanted to tell the boys at the table what had happened, but some part of him knew that if he had, it would no longer be a secret, and without being a secret, the moment's magic would be lost forever. The banter at the table continued; the words spoken there sounded foreign to Robert. The prospect of midnight seemed incalculable; a point in time far removed like some aspect of myth.

Robert soon spotted Megan Sullivan, but she would not look at him. And further away, on the other side of the creek, a large silhouette, backlit by the late afternoon sun, moved between the trees. There was no mistaking the wild mane atop the silhouette's head. Robert kept his eyes trained on the man as Yates turned away from the creek and lumbered deeper into the woods until he blended with the shadows and vanished.

Part Three:
A Patchwork of Flesh and Stitches

Chapter Seventeen: The Angel Of Light—Haverford Township PA, 2012

The house at the corner of Darby and Chelten Roads looked more robust now than it did the first time Harold Miller had called upon May Weldon. The gray stone façade was accentuated by tall maples that spotted one edge of the yard while old cedar trees out front bore strong, untrimmed, low-hanging limbs that gave Miller the impression they were meant to dissuade unwelcome visitors.

No sooner had Miller placed one foot on the front step, ready to ascend and ring the doorbell, his cell phone rang. The call was from his daughter Elinor. He ignored the call and placed the phone back into his coat pocket.

"Annoying, is it not?" a familiar voice called out from behind him.

Miller spotted a wraith at the corner of the house. His jaw tensed as he took in the sight of her. Gone were the curly locks May once wore, replaced now by a silk kerchief the color of emeralds. Her skin had lost its vibrant, pale tone; but, he noted as she slowly approached him, her eyes had lost none of their luster.

"Is this a bad time?" Miller asked.

"If memory serves me," said May, "with you it's always a bad time."

"I could come back later," he offered.

"Or go away for good," she countered. "Would you honor the dying wish of the keeper of secrets?"

"I am sorry," Miller told her. "Perhaps when you are..."

"Feeling better?" asked May. She laughed. "I have cancer, Dr. Miller. I will not be feeling better any time soon."

"I did not know."

"Well, it's not like I go around telling people over the telephone that I am soon bound for another world," she said. "And don't be sorry. You have nothing to be sorry about."

"I tried calling again," he said.

May took her time climbing the front steps. She removed a key from her sweater pocket and unlocked the front door.

"No, you did not," she informed him. "Why would anything change?"

Miller remembered the night they had slept together, nearly fifteen years ago, before his book had begun to take shape. It seemed like another lifetime now. Over the years, he had come to accept that May was like no other woman he had ever known; even his wife Ann, he knew, paled in comparison, and he felt ill whenever he acknowledged the fact. Still, he wondered if her illness, her treatment, and her medication had somehow blurred her memories of that time. No woman, especially one as learned and ferocious as May Weldon, held a grudge for that long.

"I feel like I owe you an apology," said Miller. "Better late than never, I suppose."

"Do they have a pill for that now?" she asked. "In academia?"

"A pill for what?"

"Pomposity," said May. She opened the front door, indicating they should go inside. "Do you want some tea?"

"I don't want to impose," he began.

"Listen to me, Dr. Miller," she said. "No one drives six hours without feeling they are owed something."

"I took the train."

"Well, I guess your carbon footprint doesn't stink," she replied. "Lucky for you, I had advanced notice."

"Oh?"

"Young Schuyler Heddings was kind enough to phone," May told him. "I did not realize he was a Vanderbilt man."

"You were impressed?"

"On the contrary," she said. "He's a twit of the highest order, but he has manners."

Miller followed May into her home. The foyer was how he remembered it, festooned with photographs of a life; among the framed pictures the one that had haunted Miller for decades, the one in which a laughing May Weldon, much younger, radiant, stood at the base of an enormous tree. So much was familiar about the foyer, even the slightest hint of mold, masked now by the stronger musk of pine oil on the hardwood floor. Among the photographs, however, there were two new additions since Miller last visited. One picture, in black and white, depicted May Weldon in a black cocktail dress, her regal white locks as full as ever, holding a wine glass as she stood in her backyard. Other people populated the background, moving about in blurred motion behind her. The other photograph, in color, showed a paler, gaunt May, her white curls gone, her bald head visible, as she stood in front of the colossal tree trunk, her demeanor much more somber than the one taken years before in front of the same tree.

"These are new," Miller almost tapped each framed photograph on the wall and thought better of it.

"A going away party last summer," said May.

"When you went back to this place?"

Miller nodded at the newer picture of May in front of the gargantuan tree trunk.

"No, Dr. Miller," she said, "nothing like that."

"I would love to know where this tree is," he went on.

"Not as far away as you think." The twinkle in May's eye made Miller feel uneasy. "Are you hungry?"

"Some tea would be nice," he replied.

"Come," she led him into the dining room. "We will sit in the kitchen, if you don't mind."

"Not at all."

"Years ago," said Miller, "you had a photograph with a cousin—"

"Tessie," she cut him off. "The photo was damaged. I had to get rid of it. Now, come along."

Miller followed her into the kitchen. He sat at the table near a window as May prepared a pot of Earl Grey.

"My nurse thinks it's morbid," she said.

"What is?"

"My having had a going away party."

"People do...what they must, I suppose."

"You were going to say strange things."

"No," said Miller. "I would not."

"It doesn't matter," said May. "You get to a certain age, and you realize just how much you don't know."

"No denying that."

"What is it you are after?"

"Heddings didn't give you any indication?" Miller asked. "That's so typical of him."

"I meant in life."

"Oh, happiness," he told her. "Comfortability when it comes time to retire. My daughter thinks..."

"What was that?"

"Nothing," said Miller. "My daughter worries too much."

"We should be with the ones we love," May said. "If I have learned anything, it is that."

"I agree," he said.

"Now," she said as she placed two saucers and cups with steaming hot tea on the table, "what is it that you want from me? Mind you, I don't have much time."

"I wanted to visit R.J. Hyatt's home one last time," Miller said. "And I was hoping you may be amenable to writing an introduction to the next edition of his biography."

"You mean your biography, Dr. Miller."

"Well, I—"

"Let's not mince words," said May. "Biographers may write about the lives of others, but their work is as much about themselves as it is their subject."

"That may be true," he said. "I guess there's enough of me in my work."

"Young Heddings is not your ally," she announced. "He wouldn't know a good book if it fell on his head."

"He is a different breed," he conceded. "But I suppose you have to be a shark in today's publishing world."

May sat down at the table. She poured milk from a small pitcher into her cup and stirred it.

"It's not easy," she said.

"What do you mean?" Miller asked.

"Being at the end of your stay here in this world," she answered.

A woman appeared at the back door, causing May to start. Miller nearly dumped tea all over himself.

"That prowler would be my new nurse," May whispered as the woman let herself in with a key.

The nurse's name was Beverly Scott. She was a redheaded pixie who stood just shy of five feet tall.

"Am I early?" said Beverly as she closed the back door behind her. "Oh," she looked at Miller, "I am so sorry. I did not know you had company."

"This is Dr. Miller," May told her.

"Is everything all right?"

"An English professor," she clarified.

Beverly relaxed and heaved her bag onto the kitchen table.

"Dr. Miller," she said. "I'll be administering some medicine to Miss Weldon. If you don't mind, perhaps you can wait in the living room—"

"No need," May announced. Then, to Miller, she said, "It doesn't help, you know."

"If you want privacy," Miller took up his tea cup and saucer in hand.

"Don't be ludicrous," she told him. "It's a simple injection. Too bad you were not here last week for the bloodletting."

"Miss Weldon," said Beverly, "please. You make me sound like I am from the Dark Ages."

"If I had one of the humors," she said, "I'd be fit as a fiddle by now."

The nurse ignored her last remark. She set up the drip beside the kitchen table.

"Honestly," May said, "I don't know why I bother. It won't cure me. It only prolongs the pain, but at least I know I am alive. Isn't that right, Dr. Miller?"

"I suppose," he said, and sat back down.

"The best part is," she went on, "in the next place I will not need medicine."

"Dr. Miller," Beverly said. "What do you teach?"

"American literature," Miller told her. "Post-1930, mostly."

"Beverly, dear," said May, "tell the professor about your favorite book."

"The Land of Dust and Honey," she said. "It was such an honor to find out that Miss Weldon was *the* May Weldon. The first time I read R.J. Hyatt's book I was just fourteen years old. It changed my life."

"How so?" Miller asked.

"It made me aware of hidden things," said the nurse. "I've read that book a dozen times now. Each time it's a different experience. How about you, Dr. Miller? Do you believe in hidden things?"

"I'm more of a realist, I am afraid," he replied. "For me, Hyatt's novel was an allegory for—"

"Now, don't you go scaring off the help with your academic doublespeak, Dr. Miller," May said. "No offense, Beverly."

"None taken, Miss Weldon," the nurse said. To Miller, "Isn't she adorable?"

"Indeed," he replied.

"It's a pity that R.J. Hyatt didn't write another book," said Beverly. "I do wish he had done so."

As Beverly and Miller entered into a dialogue about Hyatt's novel, May closed her eyes. The task of being the keeper of secrets, of hiding the wondrous in plain sight, was a difficult one. More than once in her life she had been nearly overcome by the natural desire to share what she knew. Over time she so desperately wanted to relieve herself of the burden, as if divulging the secrets she hid from the world would somehow alleviate the discomfort of the alien growth within her. There were times when May almost failed to keep her promise. Now, she simply prayed that her aging, ailing body would hold out just long enough to see a promise fulfilled.

When she opened her eyes again, May was not aware of how much time had passed. There were echoes of the conversation between Beverly and Miller about Robert Jonas Hyatt's book, as well as the adoration Beverly expressed for Miller's biography. In all of her years, in all of her reading, May never experienced anything that came close to the life she had known with Hyatt, brief though it had been. She carried little tolerance for men like Miller who relied on textual analysis to get to know the man. In the end, words were never enough to paint a realistic portrait of the writer. For while words and sentences may have helped reconstruct the body of a man, his soul was forever hidden from view.

"Dr. Miller," May said.

"Yes?"

133

"I am quite tired now," she told him. She watched Beverly intently as the nurse packed up the tools of her trade. "I wonder if you would be kind enough to come back tomorrow when I am feeling better."

"I will stay with you until you lie down," Beverly announced. "Do you want something for the nausea?"

"No, dear," said May. "No more drugs. Thank you."

"I am sorry, May," said Miller. "You should rest. I will be at the Hilton on City Avenue."

"If it's not too much trouble," May said to him. "Perhaps you can join me for lunch tomorrow."

"Call me in the morning," he said. "I can show myself out."

In the foyer, moments later, Miller stopped to take in the photographs that hung on the wall. He became transfixed once more by the picture of May standing at the base of the giant tree, studying every rut in the thick bark, the way pollen had frozen in mid-air all around May, and in that instant, he thought he should know the tree, that it, like so many aspects of R.J. Hyatt's novel, were not only universal but timeless, themes that dated all the way back to prehistory in a sense that it was knowledge men had known, and through the various ages of subsequent recorded history, had forgotten. When May and her nurse passed him in the foyer he was barely aware of them.

"You're still here?" May asked, her voice laden with sleep. "Of course, the tree. And the fount. We cannot forget the fount."

"It's the medicine," Beverly explained to Miller as she ushered May up the stairs.

"Of course," he said. "Feel better, May. I will talk to you tomorrow."

May waved her left hand, nearly slapping Beverly in the face when she did. The two women turned the landing and disappeared.

Under The Bronze Moon

Miller let himself out through the front door, thinking about the photograph, the deep crevices in the tree trunk, the pollen suspended all around the beatific and beautiful May Weldon, and how it came to be that after all these years, try as he did, he was unable to recall the thought that had entered his mind when he glimpsed the photograph on his way out. It was as if someone had placed a blank slide in his head in the place of the one that contained the memory he sought. The feeling made him uneasy. As he stood on the porch, it took him another minute to remember where he had parked his rental car.

Chapter Eighteen: The Land Of Dust And Honey—Beneath The Hollow Hill

He was a boy again, walking with his father to Smith's Powder Mill where on Sundays the mill owner hosted a picnic throughout the spring. Barth saw a dark aura around his father's head, a cloudy nimbus that blocked out the sun. In the shadow of his ailing father the dreaming Barth saw flowers wither on their stems; robins, cardinals, blue jays—dropped from their perches and lay dead on the ground. Twice, Barth's father stopped. The first time he pointed to a man standing in the woods. From where Barth stood it was difficult to see the man, but in the dream he knew it was his grandfather, his father's father who had died before Barth was born.

"I should go to him," Barth's father announced.

"No, papa," the boy pleaded. "You can meet him later."

"But he's here now."

"Don't," Barth took his father's hand.

Father and son continued down the path that led to the mill. When Barth looked at the woods again he saw his grandfather was pacing them. The boy studied the ground where the grass met the tree line. The dreamer understood that a boundary existed there, a line between the here and now, between the living world and the next one. He held his father's hand tightly, tugging him toward the path's center for fear that his father may be led astray.

Barth saw that they weren't far from the sawhorse tables where the workers would sit with their families, enjoying the meal the mill owner provided. And later, when the men stood around drinking beer as the sun set behind the woods, the children would run off to play. Barth's favorite spot was at the creek where a millwheel kept time with the world, spinning ever so slowly while the world itself spun on its axis hurdling along its elliptical path around the sun. The previous weekend his quiet reverie was interrupted by Catherine Mulroney, a redheaded thirteen-year-old girl whose father had been injured when his right hand got crushed in a grinder. The mill owner did not pay Catherine's father while he was out of work, but he allowed Mulroney's family to attend the Sunday picnics that spring. It was the mill owner's intention to hire back Mulroney once his hand healed. Yet, everyone knew that Mulroney was not going to be able to perform the same duties he did prior to the accident. Barth liked Catherine because of her blue eyes and her long, curly hair, and because she was built robustly like her mother, but what he loved most about her was that she liked to dip her pale feet into the creek. But in his dream, he saw no sign of the Mulroneys. The mill grounds were empty despite a huge picnic spread atop the sawhorse tables.

After a time, Barth's father stopped. He clutched his chest. Barth came to his father's aid as the elder Barth sat on a bench. The air around them was still. Young Barth heard the mill wheel creak as it continued its endless spin.

"Go on," his father said. "I'll be fine."

"I want to stay with you, papa," the boy told him.

"You stay here," he said. "I have to go into the woods now."

Barth's grandfather waited beneath a tree. He waved to his grandson. Suddenly, a rush of voices overwhelmed Barth. Men stood in a circle looking down at the ground. Children his age stood motionless; toddlers cowered behind their mothers' skirts. Behind him, the turning mill wheel stopped. The voices around him faded. On the ground lay a dead person; the face was all too familiar.

He awoke with a start. The night sky had given over to a dark blue shade. It was time to move on. Barth gathered himself and set out through the woods once more—to the east the land sloped downward. The lower ground would provide water.

Richard J. O'Brien

As he moved through the dark wood, aware that there existed a certain muted quality to the air, he considered how a soldier needed the sounds of war to function, that without the war he had no purpose in being a soldier, and the absence of exploding artillery and mortar rounds, the deficit of small arms fire, nearly drove him mad. If his purpose was not to be a soldier, then he did not belong there. What drove him to that brink was treading the razor edge of silence and knowing that because the war had appeared to leave him alone it meant only that the quiet dark wood might acquiesce at any moment to the war's brutal influence. From nowhere might come the machine gun fire that might end his life or the mortar round whose shrapnel would tear through his flesh, severing his spinal cord, like that kid from Montreal, no more than seventeen years old—his legs missing, his lower torso sliced into ribbons only to become a patchwork of flesh and stitches meant to hold his intestines in place. The Montreal kid Barth had seen in a Paris hospital last year, the kid who banged the back of his head against the wall where his wheelchair had been positioned, the kid who repeated his mantra "I can't walk, I can't make love" over and over again. From that moment on the choice had been clear for Barth. He would rather die than return to the States a cripple. His desire had nothing to do with any notion of heroism or dignity. The first artillery bombardment he had ever endured had caused him to shit his pants. He was not alone. It was the kind of thing he wished the Canadian Corps had put on their recruiting posters rather than the now absurd renderings that showed valiant men without a trace of fear. Barth believed, right or wrong, that part of being a soldier meant choosing your own way to go out. In subsequent battles leading up to Vimy Ridge, he had witnessed men leave the confines of a trench and walk into a hailstorm of German bullets; weary-eyed, shell-shocked men who had lives once upon a time in whatever towns they had come from, lives that were reduced to fragmented dream sequences. Men who chose to throw themselves at the mercy of their German aggressors in order to achieve a final peace of mind, for in life there were few pains a man could endure like the ones inflicted in wartime.

138

These thoughts weighed so heavily on Barth that morning that he was not aware, at first, of the shadows moving between the trees all around him; mere mirages that dissipated as the first rays of light stretched from the east past the trees along the forest floor. By the time Barth saw the shadows he understood that the silent forms lurking about were not the enemy, nor were they anything of the world he knew. Some primal part of his mind understood fully what his consciousness could not, that he was witnessing the joining of two worlds, the familiar and the other one, the one that his grandmother had told him of in tales from the old country about the fairyfolk, those veterans of the first war ever fought, long before man was pulled from the clay, fallen angels who were pushed out by sunlight every morning from the dark confines of their hiding places in this world, retreating to the unseen place until night returned.

The mist evaporated as the sun rose higher that morning. It turned out to be a clear day. A dry wind blew the treetops, causing them to sway back and forth, giant hands scratching the belly of the blue sky. Birds darted back and forth between tree limbs, taking turns to descend to the forest floor where they poked their beaks into the ground before they took flight again. Barth spotted a few deer. A lone fox lumbered along until he smelled the traveler and scampered off into a dense thicket. For the first time since entering the forest Barth felt relieved. The forest did not appear in daylight to be the fantastical, dark landscape he had witnessed the previous evening. For that, Barth was grateful.

Alone for too long a man must take care not to become a prisoner of his own mind or a slave to the musings carried on in those solitary and desperate hours. Barth's father had given him this advice prior to Barth's departure for Canada. Now, barely two years had passed since he left North America, holed up in the bowels of a troop ship that pitched and rocked night and day against the Atlantic's relentless currents, and while his father had done his best to prepare him for manhood, Barth was only just beginning to understand that in war there was little time to contemplate simple and eternal things. In war, he learned that even in death there was no guarantee of everlasting life, no certainty that the soul carried on after mustard gas singed the lungs or shrapnel and bullets tore through human flesh. Everything that Barth had seen in the war thus far led him to believe that there were places from which God had hidden His dark and infinite wisdom; the battlefield and the trenches were places where neither angel nor devil held sway. It was this absence that forced some men to dream of home, to believe that they might transport themselves from battle if only they concentrated hard enough. What they did not understand, what Barth was only just starting to figure out himself, was that any essence of home died when a man put on his uniform, that God altered the place man called home so that it would never be the same if he was lucky enough to return. What he wanted, what Barth needed, was not a way home but to discover a new and neutral place, a place untouched by the hands of God and men. Some new plane infused with the alien residue of some other creator who pulled up stakes before the world, the sun, and the stars were born.

He kept walking, hoping to find that place; instead, he encountered only fatigue and hunger as the day waned. It struck him hardest when he reached the top of a rise. His throat had become a cylinder lined with sandpaper, his stomach an empty knot. That was when he saw shards of shimmering light. It was a lake that stretched as far and as wide as Barth's weary eyes could see.

Chapter Nineteen: The Darby Rail Boys—Ardmore PA, 1915

Long walks that brisk autumn did little to calm the unrest that took root in Robert's heart. In his head, a fire roared, a hollow burning bright that had blinded him to all thoughts except one. Ever since the summer's last picnic at the powder mill, his focus shifted from the past to some possible future with Megan Sullivan. The days that led up to the start of the school year were excruciatingly long—minutes ticked by like hours and the hours seemed abysmal. For Robert, there was no end to the torment that plagued him, a crucible secret, multilayered, and true.

These were the long dog days of summer. At night, the situation worsened. Robert lay awake, feeling conflicted over his midnight meeting with Abigail Sweeney. He told no one about what had happened, as to do so would mean bringing shame upon his family. What stoked his carnal longing had been Abigail's pale breasts and what led to his near-ruination was her cunning and deceit.

It happened like this. After the picnic, Robert returned home with his family. The sun had already set, and his father, to everyone's surprise, remained relatively sober; that is to say, Theodore was able to walk home without stumbling or needing aid from his children to steady him. Matilda insisted that Robert play cards with her. She had recently learned the intricacies of gin rummy from her friend Isabella Rosanetti, an Italian girl the same age as Matilda who was already changing into a woman with fuller hips. Robert knew Isabella well, but he shunned her for fear of falling into a hypnotic trance. The girl's eyes were dark and mysterious and, though it shamed Robert to think of her in such a way, filled with forbidden knowledge. That night, after the picnic, his father had gone straight to bed. Matilda kept after him about the card game. Her brother gave in, playing a few hands until Helena intervened.

"Time for bed," Helena announced.

Matilda put up a fight. It was a fruitless attempt, and she continued to argue with her mother as Helena escorted her daughter up the stairs.

So as not to raise suspicion, Robert obliged his mother without incident. He kissed Helena good night and went up to his room. There he lay, anticipating his pending midnight encounter. At eleven-thirty, he climbed out of bed, still dressed, took six silver half-dollars he kept hidden in a sock beneath his bed, and placed the coins in his pocket.

Sneaking out of his parents' house was nothing new. One bedroom window overlooked the back porch roof. The window was already open. The problem Robert faced was that his parents' bedroom window also faced the backyard. Robert did not remember hearing his mother go off to bed. It was no secret in his family that his mother often stayed awake throughout the night, pacing the darkened first floor as a way to exorcise whatever demons tormented her.

Many a morning he descended the stairs to find his mother curled up on the couch, in cooler months with a quilted cover cast over her body, and in warmer seasons lying on the sofa in nothing more than her nightshirt. When Robert was seven years old, he woke up to the sound of his father snoring so loudly that he could hear him through the wall. But that night there was another sound as well. It came from downstairs, his mother's muffled cries. He left his bedroom, padded down the hall until he reached the stairs that always creaked whenever someone traversed them. He found his mother alone in the living room and heard the back door close. Before he could ask any questions, his mother marched him back up to bed. He never spoke of the incident, but it remained with him always.

For several minutes, Robert sat at the end of his bed. He listened for movement within the house. All was still. At last, satisfied that no one would hear him, he climbed through the open window. The air outside was cooler, but humid as it had been when the sun was up. He crouched low on the back-porch roof, listening. It took him less than ten seconds to scamper to the roof's edge and shimmy down a wrought iron post. After that he leapt into the yard, landing softly as he crouched down a second time.

In that late hour, it took only a fraction of the time it normally did to walk to the powder mill. His mind vacillated between the beautiful Megan Sullivan, how he yearned to see her when the school year began, and the temptress Abigail Sweeney who, in Robert's secret musings, had become less of a young woman and more of an elemental aspect of the creek and the woods that surrounded the powder mill, an embodiment of all that was good and true, carnal and palatable. Unfettered, the widow's daughter was, by the mores that people within his community so desperately clung to with the hope of some salvation after they were dead; for him, she was the very dream of desire, the word of Aphrodite made flesh.

There were two ways onto the powder mills grounds. One was the road, but Robert knew that Addison employed a former Pinkerton detective by the name of Stevens who patrolled the grounds from sundown to sunrise and who kept a watchful eye over the main powder room. For in 1915, many cities had their fair share of anarchists who wanted nothing more than to steal enough black powder from mills like Addison's to wreak havoc against the establishment. Philadelphia, the mill owner was unabashedly vocal about this point, harbored such miscreants as did any other major American city. Addison let it be known publicly at the family picnics that any ne'er-do-well whose intent was to steal gunpowder from the mill would not be subjected to the federal judicial process.

"Such trouble-makers," Addison had announced one afternoon before everyone was allowed to eat, "would ruin my business. And I for one would rather them go down with a bellyful of lead than make off with my gunpowder."

Little did Addison know that his biggest threat was not from the faceless anarchists he so feared, but from Mother Nature herself who would, in a few years' time, weaken a dam further up Cobbs Creek, and obliterate Addison's Mill. When the waters would recede, there would be not a trace of the old mill left except for the toppled bricks of the press house chimney.

Still, for those aligned to propagate evil in the name of freedom from tyranny, the anarchist criminals Addison so detested would meet their end not in a courtroom but when they came face to face with old Stevens and his Colt .45 pistol.

"And the same goes for any sympathizers of the Troubles in Ireland," Addison had gone on to say. "Stealing my gunpowder to ship to the Emerald Isle to further the cause will get you dead. Now, let us give thanks to the Lord for this bountiful picnic."

It had been rumored that, as a young man, Stevens had cut his teeth out west with the Pinkerton Agency in the 1880s. Robert's father had told him once that Stevens breathed with a wheeze after getting knifed at a strike rally in Arizona.

"Said he shot the man who stabbed him right where they stood, Stevens did," his father told him. "A cold-blooded killer if ever there was one."

Robert wasn't sure if he believed the story about Stevens. What he understood, however, was that his parents likened such antics, sneaking out at night and raising hell the way some boys did, to a station beneath the one to which they hoped their son aspired. *Miscreants,* his mother had called a group of boys who were apprehended after midnight for vandalizing the Haverford Friends Meeting House on Brick Lane. Helena had read the story in The Philadelphia Bulletin. In no uncertain terms she declared that her son should not harbor such frivolous and ruinous notions of sneaking out of the house after dark. Some boys Robert knew like Sean O'Malley who, despite his lazy left eye, snuck out of his house at night more often than anyone else, and had turned the art into a science of sorts, learning to elude his father who came home late six nights a week after closing the pub. It helped that Mr. O'Malley was a bigger drunk than Mickey McMaster and Robert's father combined. It was Sean who told Robert that Stevens, the former Pinkerton detective, slept in a chair propped against the door to the powder room, no matter the weather, and snored with the fury of Cerberus himself. Others, like Jack Stubbs, a boy a year older than Robert, claimed to have been chased off the powder mill grounds by Stevens who fired his pistol blindly into the dark. Whatever the truth, Robert knew that he could not access the mill via the main road. So, he chose an alternate path through the woods, hugging the creek until he reached the place where the creek's width ran narrow enough to cross by leaping across three stones. He was about to cut into the woods when a familiar voice came from behind him.

"Myles?" a rather drunk Mickey McMaster called out.

Robert turned to see the little Irishman following him. McMaster kept his distance, a dog loyal to his abusive owner.

"Go home, Mr. McMaster," the boy told him. "I am not Myles."

"Are you his ghost? God bless your weary soul—"

"It's me, Robert. Teddy Hyatt's boy."

"Let me buy you a drink?"

"No, thank you."

"Then how about you buy me a nightcap?" asked McMaster. "I seem to have siphoned off the last of this elixir."

Robert stood an arm's length from the drunk. McMaster busied himself by sticking his tiny pink tongue into the neck of an empty fifth of Old Grand-Dad. In the quiet night, the slurping sound the little man made was the only sound in the street.

"Here," Robert handed him a silver half-dollar. "Now, go on your way."

McMaster accepted the boy's charity. He regarded the empty bottle a moment, took a long sniff of it, and tossed it over his shoulder.

"The saints be with ye," he said as the bottle shattered on the street.

Robert did not wait to see if anyone had heard the breaking glass. He turned his back on McMaster and bolted for the tree line. As he entered the woods, he heard McMaster singing:

"God save Ireland, said the heroes
God save Ireland, said they all
Whether on the scaffold high
Or the battlefield we die..."

In the woods that night everything became amplified. Shadows appeared darker; tree limbs, still during the day unless moved by the wind, appeared to reach out to one another over his head; the old stones removed from the mill grounds years ago, and dumped into Cobbs Creek emitted an eldritch glow. In those first moments that Robert had entered the woods he paused to listen. The rushing creek waters sounded like breakers at the beach in Cape May where his parents had taken him once when he was eight years old and Matilda was still a toddler. His eyes darted left and right, hoping to glimpse a deer or perhaps a stag or, better yet, the reclusive Yates whose giant form haunted the woods along Cobbs Creek. It was not meant to be. Robert was alone in the woods that night, fingering the coins in his pocket before he took them out and palmed them for fear of making too much noise.

Before long, Robert made it to the mill grounds. A dirt road at the north end of the grounds led into the woods. He knew it wasn't used for anything except for when Addison had several stones removed from near the powder room, for fear of

146

some metal tool scraping against them and sending off sparks, and had the stones dumped into the creek. Where the road that led out of the woods met the grounds proper there was a wood gate, reminiscent of a ranch gate. Robert found it odd that there was no fence on either side of it.

Away from the powder room, down by the mill and far from Stevens' alleged post, the standing stones where Robert had first glimpsed Abigail's breasts stood like ancient sentries, guardians of some invisible path that led to the underworld. Approaching the standing stones now, he remained wary of the old Pinkerton detective who, in a drunken stupor, might mistake him for some anarchist out to steal gunpowder. Robert did not know much about guns, but he understood that a stray bullet meant as a warning shot could ricochet off the standing stones and do him serious harm, if not kill him.

Lost in myriad thoughts of how Stevens might shoot him in the back, Robert started when he realized that Abigail Sweeney stood waiting for him between two standing stones, as if she had just stepped out of the hidden realm that he so desperately wanted to be real; a sacred space, concealed from the uninitiated, that he was sure existed side by side with the world he knew. Transfixed by the vision that waited for him, he stared at the gauzy white smock Abigail wore.

"Did you bring the money?" she asked.

"I did," he said. "Five silver half-dollars."

"Is that all you think I'm worth?"

"That's all I have," said Robert.

Abigail placed her hands on her ample hips. Her fingers worked the hem of her smock up past her knees, past her thick thighs, until Robert could see the tuft of red hair between her legs.

"If you're nice to me," she said, "I'll let you kiss it. And if you're good, I might return the favor. Do you like that deal?"

"Yes," he answered.

Abigail turned her back to him, keeping her smock above her waist. She allowed Robert a good look at her buttocks before she darted to her right and disappeared behind one of the stones.

Robert followed her, stepping between the tall, standing rocks. Abigail waited for him; her breasts already bare as she leaned back against a smaller stone.

As he took a step forward, a blow to the back of his head dropped Robert to his knees. Someone kicked him hard in the back. He went sprawling face-first into a bed of dead leaves. Turning, he saw his assailants—four older boys dressed in overalls, cotton engineer hats, and heavy hobnailed boots—all four, Robert knew by the way they were dressed, were members of an Irish immigrant gang who called themselves the Darby Rail Boys. Their exploits, ordinarily confined to West Philadelphia and Upper Darby, were notorious among citizens who lived in the surrounding communities. The Darby Rail Boys' preferred method of dispatching someone from the earthly realm was stomping on a person until his back was broken or his brains spilled out of his crushed skull. Sometimes, when the mood suited them, they did both.

"Hold him down," one of the Rail Boys said, the one carrying the two-by-four.

"Check his pockets," Abigail said. "He has money."

The other three held him down, one on each leg as the third kneeled on Robert's arms and punched him in the face three times.

"Take his shoes," the leader said. "And his pants."

One of the Rail Boys dug his hands deep into Robert's pockets and gave his balls a hard squeeze for good measure.

"I said take his pants," the leader said.

"I've got a good mind to put my pecker in his mouth," said the one kneeling on his arms.

Robert clenched his mouth shut.

The two holding his legs removed Robert's shoes. Then they pulled off his pants, leaving him bare from the waist down.

"Put him on the rock over there," the leader instructed the others.

The other three beat Robert into submission and dragged him to the rock where Abigail stood. She stepped out of the way. Another blow to Robert's head brought him close to unconsciousness.

Two of the Rail Boys held his arms stretched out over the rock. The one with the two by four hit him across the small of the back. The searing pain brought Robert back to the present. He struggled to free himself, but his efforts remained fruitless.

The leader's face brushed against Robert's neck from behind now. Robert smelled whiskey on the older boy's breath. The odor of spirits did little to mask the smell of tooth decay as he spoke.

"I am going to stick my cock up your shithole," the Rail Boy leader whispered.

Robert heard a hollow thump as he clenched his buttocks together. The two boys holding his arms let go. Robert looked up to see each boy get hit in the face with a rock. Abigail remained fixed where she stood, unable to comprehend what was happening. The fourth boy came hurtling through the air, his arms flailing before his head crashed into one of the standing stones. Robert saw him twitch once before the boy lay still. Out of the darkness came Robert's shoes and pants. He didn't bother to put them on, choosing, instead, to run back the way he had come. He stopped when he was nearly twenty yards away from the scene and looked back. The giant Yates lifted Abigail by the neck with one hand. Abigail kicked wildly, but Yates shook her like a doll until her life left her. After that, Yates tossed the dead girl aside. Robert fought back nausea, cupping his mouth with his free hand. He did not stay to see what happened next. Instead, he ran deeper into the woods, stepping through the shallow, cool, creek water until he reached the other side.

In the weeks that followed, three things happened, or rather, didn't happen. No one found the bodies of the Darby Rail Boys. No one ever saw Yates again. It was believed by the more superstitious residents of the community that the wild man had stepped out of the world, passing from the earthly realm into another hidden from view. And news came from the mill that Abigail had vanished. The rumor was that she ran off with Shane McGowan, one of the Darby Rail Boys. People in town spoke of seeing her in the young man's company quite often that summer. As each week passed, rumor solidified into truth; for this, Robert was grateful. He would carry the burden of that gruesome experience at the standing stones throughout his days until the day he too would leave this world.

Chapter Twenty: The Shamans Of Old—Boston Ma, 2012

"Come in," she said.

"Elinor?" the voice belonged to Reginald Davies.

Christ, she thought. Not now.

The door opened. Elinor pretended to be interested in a stack of student papers she had yet to grade.

"Oh, splendid," said Davies. "You are here."

"Uh, yeah," she rolled her eyes. "I think the giveaway was my saying 'come in,' but I could be wrong."

Reginald Davies stood nearly six and a half feet tall, and he was as thin as a reed.

"I am busy, Dr. Davies," she said. "What can I do for you?"

As soon as she posed the question, she regretted it. When Davies wasn't busy teaching graduate astrophysics, he made the circuit around campus, a sullen satellite searching for a sun to call his own. Twice divorced, once a widower, the lanky Brit with thinning long gray hair, mutton chops, and tufts of matching hair growing out of his large ears, Davies had long ago introduced himself as 'Dutch' when he offered himself to Elinor at a faculty cocktail party. As Davies stood blocking the doorway to her office, Elinor contemplated the window behind her as a means of escape. She hated the air of superiority about Davies, the way he treated all non-Brits as provincial and narrow-minded, but even more she loathed the way he sucked his sizeable teeth.

"There is a delightful Ethiopian eatery that just opened," Davies informed her.

Elinor arched an eyebrow. The gangly scientist offered a lascivious grin and, predictably, sucked his teeth.

"I am sorry, Reggie—"

"Please," he said. "Call me Dutch."

"Dr. Davies," Elinor began. "You are a highly educated man. A man of science, a man of reason. So, don't take it the wrong way when I decline."

"Well?"

"Well what?"

"Are you going to decline?"

"Yes," she told him, curtly.

"How about Kruncher's Deli? Plenty of witnesses in broad daylight," he countered, and sucked his teeth once more.

Davies was to female professors what a tsunami was to islanders; most days, the waters appeared calm, but there was always the chance of an earthquake that might trigger a butterfly effect, in this case, the catalyst for the disastrous visit being Davies himself exiting the Science Building and stoking his own confidence (though Elinor refused to speculate just how he achieved such a thing), the way a killer wave did over a great distance. Sooner or later, Elinor would have to seek safety at higher ground.

"Honestly," she stood up, stuffing student papers into her satchel, "I forgot. I have a doctor's appointment."

"My apologies," said Davies. He made no move to vacate the doorway. "Please, do not let me keep you."

"If you would excuse me," said Elinor.

Davies stepped out into the hallway.

"Oh, dear," he said. "I almost forgot to tell you. I started reading that splendid biography your father wrote. Yes, yes, I know. I am only a decade late. Back in the seventies, at King's College, before I came stateside to do my doctoral work, there were two camps in my dormitories. The Tolkienites who believed in all things Middle Earth, and the Hyattians who continually searched for a gate into the Land of Dust and Honey."

"Fascinating," she said. "But I have to go now."

"We never found it."

Elinor clutched her satchel to her chest. "Found what?" she asked.

"A way in," he replied. "You see, R.J. Hyatt wrote about trans-dimensional travel as if he had experienced it firsthand. Oh, I know. It sounds ludicrous, of course. But as a novelist he seemed to know..."

"What, Reggie? Know what?"

"There are hypotheses concerning parallel worlds," said Davies. "Way back when Hyatt's novel was published, no one with a reputable standing in the science community would have ever entertained such notions. Now, it's commonplace. And there exists now the mathematics and formulae to back it up."

"But you're an astrophysicist," Elinor said. "And *The Land of Dust and Honey* is just a novel, a fantasy. Nothing more."

"That is probably true," he told her. "But back then we wanted to believe. What intrigued us about Hyatt's novel was that it was all so matter-of-fact. Exquisitely written, yes. Did it smack of magic realism before magic realism came into vogue vis-a-vis the Latin American writers like Garcia Marquez and his ilk? Without question. Hyatt's genius, and this is just my humble opinion of course, was that he was master of not so much making his reader pine for what did not exist, but of forcing his reader to recall that which may have existed at some point in human history—namely, the ability to travel body and soul, as it were, to some other dimension. One might say just as the shamans of old were said to be capable of. Yes, quite right. You see..."

Davies was still talking when Elinor reached the exit. She thought he said something about a world tree, but then she was out of the building. The heavy steel door banged shut behind her.

Chapter Twenty-One: A Tapestry Of Falsehoods—Ardmore PA, 1916

That winter, once Whitaker's regular customers had picked up their Christmas cards and gifts, business at the stationery store slowed down as the holiday approached. The new year rang in with new hope: Robert no longer feared any repercussions from the night when Abigail had set him up to be mugged and worse. Theodore had told his family that the Ardmore Police had conducted a thorough investigation of Abigail Sweeney's disappearance.

"Within a week they were crawling all over the mill grounds," Theodore had said at dinner one night. "They turned over every stone...well, not literally. I don't think even Yates could do that."

"Dilettantes," his mother said. "The police in this town couldn't find a dead body if they tripped over it."

"There was a dead body?" Matilda spoke up now.

"No one died," Robert told her.

"It doesn't surprise me," Helena said. "Not at all."

"What's that, dear?" asked Theodore.

"It's what becomes of a woman who parades around without undergarments," his wife said. "Good riddance, I say. And I hear that her mother was not aware she was gone."

"The widow Sweeney has been in a bad way for quite some time," Theodore said.

The subject changed after that to a retelling of Patrick Sweeney's untimely demise.

"And to think they drove that truck right over his dead body," Theodore said, and added, "twice."

"That's enough," Helena announced.

That was the last time the Hyatt family spoke of Abigail's disappearance; although, when the school year began, Robert's friends were still speculating about it. As the weeks passed from the long, warm days of September into Thanksgiving, the story took on a life of its own. Some said that Abigail Sweeney had tired of caring for her mother who had slipped so far into the chasm of despair there was no hope for her return and others maintained that Abigail, having grown weary of caring for her mother, perhaps glimpsing into a desolate future in which she would do so until her mother passed from the world, chose to light out in the middle of the night once she had stowed enough money away to do so. Perhaps, as many believed her money was earned through illicit means, she booked passage back to Ireland where she might live as the prodigal daughter returned. From there the story took on mythic and, to Robert's ears, absurd proportions when people on the street, among them his father's mill coworkers, spoke in hushed tones not meant for children's ears of some otherworldly abomination absconding with the wanton Irish siren to parts unknown. A favorite among the superstitious Welshmen employed at Addison's Mill being the tale of the Leeds Devil himself who, having not found a suitable wife in the New Jersey Pine Barrens, took flight one night, crossed the Delaware River, and, from high in his position near the stars, became enamored with Abigail's pale form traipsing near Cobbs Creek one moonless night.

"They say his kingdom is invisible to the uninitiated," Theodore had told his son a week before Halloween. "They say the Leeds Devil was here before the Delaware River formed."

Helena tapped her fork against her plate.

"Teddy," she said. "Don't tell tales at the dinner table."

"I am just repeating the news," he told her. "Do you know Maxwell Blackbarrow? From Addison's Mill? He saw the Leeds Devil one night—"

"Honestly, Teddy—"

"No," he slammed his palm on the table. "I'm trying to make a point here."

"Don't be angry, father," said Matilda.

"I am not angry," he said. "I am trying to prove something to your mother."

"There's no such thing as the Leeds Devil," Robert spoke up now.

Theodore faced his son, red-faced. "There is an entire secret history of the world," he said. "It's a tangible thing, right under our noses. And yet, despite our best efforts, it remains elusive. So, we settle for the lies told to us. And why? Perhaps because it is much easier to digest those fabrications rather than remain hungry for the truth."

"I will not have any of that Rosicrucian gibberish at my dinner table," Helena pointed her fork at her husband. "It's those Welshmen who pollute your mind with such nonsense."

"Rosicrucian gibberish," Theodore said and made a face at Matilda. "Have you ever heard of such a thing?"

Matilda blushed as she kicked her feet beneath the table. She had no idea about the Rosicrucians, or what they stood for, but the way her father said it made them sound funny.

"I detest all of that pagan talk," Helena went on. "If you want to be a party to it among the millworkers that's one thing. But do not bring that poison to my table. And I better not find any of their ridiculous pamphlets in this house. If I do, so help me God, there will be Hell to pay."

"Pagan, she says," said Theodore. "Well, the Rosy Cross aside, the point I was trying to make is that Max Blackbarrow has it on good authority from a vicar in Bala Cynwyd no less that the Leeds Devil from New Jersey is alive and well."

"Teddy—"

"And just a month ago," he slapped his hand down on the table once more, "the Philadelphia Bulletin printed an article detailing yet another sighting. This one in Philadelphia. A dog was killed. Old Blackbarrow was scared shitless—"

"Teddy!" Helena cried. "Such language. Children, cover your ears."

After that night there was no more talk of the mysterious devil born in the New Jersey Pine Barrens, nor was Theodore permitted to speak the name of Maxwell Blackbarrow or otherwise invoke the Rosy Cross in any of its permutations. Robert knew that his mother was an educated woman, a woman of reason who had no time for secret societies or the hocus-pocus musings of his father. Away from his family he encouraged others to weave tall tales of Abigail's disappearance, at times lending some false truth to the event so that it became murkier and more complex. Robert's father was just one stitch of innuendo among many who added to the broad tapestry of falsehoods—a stitch of speculation here, there a patch of hearsay. Before long, to Robert's relief, the blanket of rumor that had settled over Ardmore became so thick he was certain the light of truth would never shine through it.

Amidst these rumors there was other talk at school among boys Robert's age, stories that had nothing to do with Abigail Sweeney and her disappearance. The news in those days from Europe was filled with political intrigue, abuse of power, and rumors of war. Teenage boys boasted of wanting to go to fight. At night their mothers wept in the dark over the prospect of their sons being killed on foreign soil. It seemed that a new shadow was fast approaching, and it was one that made the business of Abigail Sweeney's demise appear inconsequential. Robert did not know what to make of the stories he had read in the newspapers. And his father's brand of fanaticism did little to assuage his fear of America and other countries being drawn into battle on terrain indifferent to the lives lost there.

At home, a battle endured between his parents. Their constant bickering did little to calm the fire that raged in his heart, a fire that clouded his head with a pale, thick smoke that made even the simplest decisions an arduous task; for, despite the eminent threat of world war, despite Helena's antagonistic views on the Irish race, and with Abigail Sweeney no longer in the world as a force to be reckoned with, Robert had fallen in love with Megan Sullivan, and she with him. Thus consumed, he existed in a constant state of tension, a state which did not subside with an act as simple as looking upon the one he loved. He needed more. While other boys speculated what it might mean to join the cause, he wanted more than anything else for the love he and Megan shared to move from the platonic to the physical. At night, he experienced fitful dreams in which he chased Megan through the woods that bordered Cobbs Creek. Some nights, he could not catch her. Other nights the dream rewarded him with visions of catching Megan, of her offering herself to him, of them consummating their love like animals with only the trees and the stars as their witnesses.

As it was, this love between a boy and a girl offered more hardship than anything else. Helena's rants against the Irish had increased in intensity since Abigail Sweeney had vanished; often as not, Robert's mother took to the repulsive habit of spitting on the floor at the mere mention of the Irish race. By now, Robert had heard the tale of Helena's grandparents' death in the farmhouse fire that an Irish neighbor had set, an Irishman whom, Helena proclaimed, the Devil himself had concocted a new punishment for in Hell. Of course, Helena would never disclose that it was indeed she who had perpetrated retribution against the Irish farmer; such a confession would mean that she was as cold-blooded a killer as McNally and his sons had been. And to compound matters more, Megan had told Robert that her parents refused to allow her to see the son of a *gypsy woman*. Robert knew that this hateful sentiment was not held by Megan, but he understood at some level that his mother's poisonous tongue had come back to sting her children. Megan rather liked Helena, believing that she was a modern woman, the very definition of independence, but the disdain that Helena carried in her heart, compounded with Megan's parents' *gypsy* decree, caused Robert's heart to become heavy. His head fueled with such rage, he found it difficult to remain at home for long for fear of going mad.

Chapter Twenty-Two: When One's Moon Wanes—Philadelphia PA, 2012

Pale, homogenous light from the hallway crept beneath the hotel room door, illuminating a six-inch stretch of well-worn carpet. Miller lay on his bed dressed, careful not to upset the housekeeper's hard work. He turned onto his back, ignoring that pitiful band of light, and stared at the ceiling, thinking about the original charm he had known years beforehand when he stayed at the hotel; now that allure was gone. Intermittent flashes played out before him: May Weldon in varying stages of undress and his dead wife Ann. Throughout the years he had carried a sense of guilt over having gone to bed with May, even though his wife had been dead for years when that night came, as if he had not only betrayed his deceased wife, but in a strange way May as well. He felt as if he remained incapable of ever loving anyone the way he had loved Ann. May had never given him that inclination all those years ago. He knew that she never wanted him that way. What happened between them was the fulfillment of a physical longing—no more, no less. Their need was a simple one, and the hunger for flesh upon flesh turned out to be as fleeting as the years were long.

In the near dark of his room Miller contemplated his one night with May. In many respects, because that night had been perfect, his guilt was compounded by how he could not recall ever wanting Ann the way he had wanted May. In the time following Ann's death, there had been other women, of course. Helga Stoltz, a German scholar Miller had met at a symposium in Amsterdam, was a robust, fair-skinned woman who taught modern European literature in Berlin. Helga's body, as Miller remembered it, had been pliant and fleshy, as if at any moment she might consume him. Two years after Helga, there had been another. Her name was Kamiko. She taught American literature at Spokane University. She was fifteen years younger than Miller, and, despite his preconceived notions about Asian women, anything but demure. Kamiko's tastes ran toward the extreme. Miller considered himself as liberal as the next aging academic, but he could not bring himself to urinate on Kamiko in the shower, no matter how much she had insisted. When he refused, the evening turned sour.

Upon returning east from Seattle where he had been invited to conduct a presentation on Hyatt's novel, Miller did his best to forget his encounter with Kamiko. Back in the Berkshires, with the memory of the sterile lighting in the hotel bathroom on an oddly warm winter evening in Seattle behind him, Miller committed to writing four new essays about R.J. Hyatt's sole collection of poetry and swore off bedding any more women remotely related to academic studies.

Now, lying atop a bed in a hotel on City Avenue in Philadelphia, he remembered Kamiko once more; how she had been built like a gymnast, how she wore glasses and no make-up, nor perfume (nor deodorant Miller had soon discovered), and how her hair had been cut in a close-crop no-mess style. That night, back in Seattle, Kamiko had worn a simple black dress beneath which she wore no underwear. Over drinks in the hotel bar, he had learned two things about the professor who had been born in Okinawa: Kamiko had written a novel that she was too afraid to show anyone, and, as an undergraduate, had sought treatment for compulsive sexual practices.

"Nymphomania," Kamiko had told him as if she had been diagnosed and treated for bronchitis.

"Interesting," was all Miller could think to say.

"Oh, I have it quite under control now," she said. "My therapist told me it stemmed from—"

"Did you enjoy—"

"God, no!" came her reply. "I don't think I had my first orgasm until I was thirty-five years old. And that was with a woman."

"I meant the lecture," said Miller.

"Quite honestly," she confessed, "I know next to nothing about R.J. Hyatt. But your presentation on shadow and spirit impressed me."

"That's very kind of you to say."

"Strangers," she went on.

"I beg your pardon?"

"They were all strangers," Kamiko announced. "I lost my virginity to a boy at summer camp when I was fifteen. It was consensual, not that you were going to ask."

"I wasn't—"

"He wanted me to fellate him," she said. "But, as a teenager, I thought that blowjobs were gross. Plus, in case you didn't notice, I have a small mouth."

"Well, you are very petite," Miller felt uncomfortable. He never liked when strangers were compelled to share their darkest secrets with him. "Tell me, will you be at Harding's lecture tomorrow? I think he's a brilliant deconstructionist."

"Truck stops," she said, and laughed.

"Excuse me?"

"I was just thinking about my junior year in college," said Kamiko. "I was driving back from visiting my aunt in San Francisco. My parents had moved to Orange County when I was three. Anyway, I stopped for gas. That's where I devoted much of my free time after that first encounter."

"I am not sure—"

"At rest areas, truck stops, I didn't care," she said. "Sometimes, they wanted to give me money. But I never took it. I wasn't a prostitute."

"I think I am going to need a stiffer drink," Miller told her. By now, he was sweating.

"Do you like Scotch?"

"Single malt?"

"Of course," she replied. "I have some in my room."

Kamiko's room turned out to be a suite. There she and Miller toasted the success of the symposium. Afterward, when he complained of a headache, Kamiko massaged his neck. They kissed. Kamiko got up and turned the lights down. Minutes later, they were naked in bed.

Presently, as Miller tried to think of something else besides Kamiko, a plan of action for dinner, questions he wanted to ask May upon his next visit, anything as he stared at the popcorn ceiling, the room phone rang and startled him.

"Ellie," he answered. "Please leave me alone."

"Damn," Schuyler Heddings said on the line, "whoever she is, she must have done a number on you."

"Sorry," Miller said. "I thought you were my daughter."

"Right, listen," he said. "How did it go? Is the old lady dead yet?"

"She speaks highly of you."

"When you got it," Heddings said, "you got it. Even the old broads can sense it. I don't know why, but they do. I always wanted to—"

"Schuyler, is there—"

"—do that," he went on. "Just go out and pick up some sixty-year-old woman. Maybe when I am done with her she can't walk straight for a week."

"I am very tired, Schuyler."

"Exactly."

"No," Miller said. "I meant me."

"It's four in the afternoon," he said. "Anyway, I am just checking in to see how things are going."

"Miss Weldon is very ill," he told him.

"No one's contesting that fact," Heddings said. "Will she write the introduction like we discussed? Before...you know."

"She has agreed, yes."

"That's fantastic," he shouted. "So, level with me. Did you bang her?"

"Schuyler, the woman is terminally ill," Miller rubbed his forehead with one hand. "Do you have any idea of how incredibly insensitive you are?"

"No, not really," the editor replied. "Should I?"

"Good-bye, Schuyler."

"Don't hang up," he pleaded. "Try to get to talk about her relationship with Hyatt."

"Have you read the biography?"

"Sure, sure," he said. "Truth be told, only eggheads, and I mean no offense, and old virgins want to read about some old broad looking back to when she was ten years old and getting all wet over some famous writer. We need more. You know? For the expanded edition."

"We?"

"Don't get all semantical on me," Heddings told him. "I am just saying you might sell more copies if the old broad opens up a bit, no pun intended."

"You are intolerable." Miller wondered where the disconnect was with Heddings. Had New York made him that jaded? "And I mean that in the sincerest way."

"Look," he said, "what I meant was the time may be right for May to lay all of her cards on the table. She's dying, right? So, what does she care if people know that Hyatt fucked her?"

Miller sighed. "I will see what I can do," he said. "But I will not make any promises."

"When do you see her again?"

"Tomorrow."

"Perfect," said Heddings. "I sent an in-house photographer down to get some shots of the house. Inside and out. See to it that she lets him in. I need to see what the third-floor apartment looks like these days. Those photographs in the current edition were taken when I was still growing hair on my balls."

"Anything else?"

"Try to be persuasive."

"It's a delicate game," Miller informed him.

"Anyway, the photographer's name is Cardin," he said. "Like the fashion designer. He will meet you tomorrow in the lobby. You can't miss him. He's—"

Miller hung up the phone. After that he dialed the do-not-disturb code, got off the bed, and readied himself for dinner.

Ten minutes later, having ridden the elevator down to the lobby, curious about the most recent occupant of the elevator who had apparently dropped the joint he or she had been smoking, Miller sat in an armchair outside the hotel restaurant. The hostess had told him the wait would not be long. Miller had traveled enough to know that she meant the opposite. He drummed his fingers against the annotated copy of *The Land of Dust and Honey* that lay in his lap. At his feet, a briefcase, a soft leather number colored black, from the local Staples store in Pittsfield, sat on the floor. The briefcase was crammed with old notes, transcriptions from his original interview with May Weldon, and a small digital recorder, one that Miller admittedly did not know how to use very well and, having come to grips with the inevitability of his old age, he understood that, sooner or later, the younger generation would force him out of academia. The push, once upon a time, had been publish or perish, but now, with the exponential growth of new technology, the key to longevity in his line of work had transformed into a new norm: adapt or perish. A conspiracy of hipsters who worshipped the contraptions of the elder information technology gods, those silica tycoons who had birthed a world that offered stores of information at the speed of light, and, in doing so, stripped away the need for old-fashioned research. In the time it used to take him to walk across a campus, enter a library, and retrieve hard copy materials needed to construct a formidable essay, this younger generation, to his chagrin, could cull the same information online and, in turn, pump out a similar work by the time a member of the old guard like him thanked a reference librarian for their assistance and exited the building. What was it that Ann had told him one night? Back when they shared a one-bedroom apartment in Providence, as he slaved over his doctoral thesis? He was convinced that he had already lost a good portion of his sanity, peeled away like layers of garlic skin. *If a famous chef in a five-star restaurant cooked as slow as you write*, Ann once told him, *the well-to-do customers would soon resort to cannibalism.* No, despite his late wife's enthusiastic euphemism, Miller understood fully now that his moon was waning; whatever dignity he had left he would save, and, in doing so, he would avoid the wrath of the soulless like Schuyler Heddings. Once the updated biography was completed, the proofs were corrected, and the advance copies sent out for review, for better or worse, he would retire. As of late, he conjured grand visions of moving out of the country, perhaps finding a little cottage in Ireland, or a small house in a warmer climate; but, more than anything, he longed to see the place where May Weldon had her photograph taken in front of the giant tree whose trunk appeared like a small mountain behind her. He would give Schuyler Heddings new material, licentious or otherwise, but not before he pressed May about the photograph on her wall.

Peering across the lobby now, Miller caught the hostess's attention. The young woman offered a meek smile and shrugged. While he still had her attention, he made a show of looking at his watch before opening Hyatt's novel. The chair upon which he sat had been designed, like all hotel furniture, with only one true purpose in mind: to get its occupant up and moving again. As he read, the rhythm of the prose rendered a hypnotic effect on him, causing his eyelids to grow heavy. Miller drifted into a light sleep, aware of the lobby sounds that surrounded him, the clink of china and silverware from inside the restaurant, the errant conversation at the front desk, muffled beyond comprehension by distance. He traipsed on the border of consciousness and sleep, comfortable along that mysterious line of demarcation, a sensation that allowed him a brief, lucid dream.

There was a white sofa upon which he sat and walls of dark wood, polished to a high sheen. Before him, in the place of windows or a wall, a room-sized opening led to a large, screened porch and beyond the porch, pine trees in full bloom, dense and dark needles masking the depth of the woodland. In the place of grass, moist, vibrant green moss grew, stretching far and wide beneath wild bushes, tall pines, and an ancient weave of vines. Over the pines, patches of sapphire sky became visible, giving over to shades of purple and black; a lone star shone in the eventide, suspended over the tallest pine, radiant against the darkening sky.

When they came out of the dark they appeared as mirages at first, shimmering anthropomorphic shapes that basked in the woodland's phthalo green. Slowly, as they reached the opening between the tree line and the house, the two figures revealed themselves. They were dressed in loose-fitting smocks and pants colored fallow and raw umber. The two men were pale-complected—one old, the other young, no more than a teen by the look of him. Both with hair long and white that was tied off in errant braids.

Driven by this curious sight, as if called forward by them, Miller left the sofa where he sat and went out onto the porch. As they drew closer, he saw the old man carrying a bundle under his arm wrapped in a coarse, brown cloth. The young one kept his right arm across his chest, his wrist tucked beneath his left arm, obscuring any view of his right hand. When the two men reached the steps, Miller opened the screen door. The young man stumbled forward, falling through the opening, and sprawled face-first onto the floor. The young man's right hand was missing.

"Help me," the old man said as he stepped onto the porch. He placed the bundle on the floor beside the young man. "Turn him over onto his back."

Miller knelt. The young man offered no resistance when the old man and Miller gently rolled him over. On the young man's right arm, there was a scar where the wrist had once been. Miller was careful not to touch it.

The old man unfolded the bundle that lay on the floor, revealing the young man's right hand. He picked it up, held the young man's right arm in place, and pushed the severed hand against the nub that had been the young man's wrist.

Miller remained on his knees, staring into the face of the young man whose gray eyes, devoid of pupils, never left his.

The old man began chanting. The young man closed his eyes and followed suit, offering the opposite tone for every note the old man muttered. Within seconds, both men had joined in a syncopated song; both produced reed-like sounds along with low, guttural chants, recalling, for Miller, an Inuit throat singer he had heard perform during a visit to Washington State. As the men sang, a pale light appeared, seeping through the old man's fingers as he held the young man's right arm and severed hand in place. The song intensified; the light grew brighter. Several more seconds passed, then both men abruptly quit singing. The young man wiggled his fingers on his right hand. The old one let go. Miller shimmied backward on his knees when the young man sat up and regarded his newly reattached right hand, twisting it this way and that, flexing his fingers wide and closing them into a fist a few times. Afterward, with Miller's help, the young man got to his feet.

"Someday," said the old man, reading Miller's thoughts, "your people will develop their full potential. When all possibilities are realized, magic and miracles will not be mysteries, but medicine."

"How did he lose his hand?" Miller asked.

"You must leave this place," the young one told him. "Here you are alone and vulnerable. Here, they are many and strong."

The two men exited the porch, descended the steps, and paused for a moment, listening to the absence of sound in the darkening wood. And then they were off, vanishing between the pine trees in much the same fashion by which they had first revealed themselves.

Miller looked down. The cloth the old man had used to conceal the severed hand lay on the floor. He bent down to pick it up, seeing a word embroidered in the coarse cloth. He strained his eyes to get a closer look but stopped when someone tapped him on the shoulder.

"Dr. Miller," a gentle voice called out.

He opened his eyes, startled for a moment before he regained his composure. The sights and sounds of the hotel lobby rushed back to him.

"Did I scare you?" the restaurant hostess asked. "I am sorry if I did."

"That's quite all right," he told her.

"Good," she said, and smiled. "Your table is ready."

Chapter Twenty-Three: So Vague A Notion As Liberty—Ardmore PA,1916

The only place Robert found any solace from the torment of his life was at Whitaker's Stationery Store. He did not much like waiting on customers, but he discovered a new world in the stock room amidst the surplus supply of pens, ink, paper, and card stock. When Mr. Whitaker manned the sales counter, Robert was tasked with processing new freight that was delivered via the mail. Paper and card stock arrived from places like Chicago, Pittsburgh, and other cities, while fountain pens came from other countries like Switzerland, France, and England. Often, the packages containing paper were damaged, but at times, Robert was able to salvage the contents. When he did, Whitaker would give him a ream of damaged paper, not torn but smudged or wrinkled to the point where they had no resale value.

"You can pen your first novel on it," Whitaker told Robert whenever he handed over the damaged paper. "Sooner or later, though, you will need a typewriter."

The young clerk was grateful, and while he could see the words that he wanted to write in his mind, when he faced the paper alone, he felt stymied, unable to put down those tales he dreamed. Random lines of narrative and dialogue haunted him. At night, lying in his bed, drifting along the narrow pass between consciousness and the chasm of sleep, there were voices that sounded real enough though they belonged to no one the would-be author knew in his waking life; voices that belonged to people with faces, faces as distinct and imperfect as his and his family's. Before long, he developed an affinity for these spectral emanations that came to him in dreams; so much so, he envisioned them down to the smallest flawed detail; yet, try as he did, when he sat down at the small desk in his bedroom, having first finished whatever homework his teachers had assigned him (his mother, ever the educator, insisted that his lessons always be the priority) he remained paralyzed by an entrenched fear that, despite his best efforts, he could not yet write so eloquently as to do any of his characters the justice they deserved. The tedium gnawed at him. Compounded with his tenuous relationship with Megan Sullivan, his quandary now doubly disastrous, Robert needed help.

"When we close shop," said Whitaker one evening, "there's something we need to discuss."

The hour that passed between the time the little man made the announcement and the moment Robert lowered the blinds on the store entrance seemed one long excruciating eternity. Once the merchandise was removed from the windows that faced the street, Whitaker asked Robert to accompany him to the stock room.

The young clerk feared that Mr. Whitaker was going to tell him that his services were no longer needed, that he was going to lose his job over some detail he overlooked in the receiving ledger. Whitaker cherished his ledger and treated it with careful hands the way a priest might The Holy Bible. Robert found it difficult to breathe. His heart raced.

"Mr. Whitaker," Robert began, "if there is some way that you can give me another chance—"

"Relax, Robert," the little man told him. "I am not about to sever ties with you, if that's what you think."

Robert slumped into a chair beside the stockroom desk where Whitaker sat. He discovered that it was still difficult to breathe, and he feared he might pass out or, worse, suffer a seizure.

"Thank you," he managed with some difficulty.

"No," said Whitaker, "what I want to talk to you about is not work-related."

"Oh?"

"Truth be told," the store owner went on, "for weeks you have wandered around like that bastard from the Old Testament with the sword over his head."

"Damocles? I don't think he was in the Bible."

"That's not the point," he said. "I can tell by the forlorn look on your face these past weeks that something is gnawing at you. Are you writing anything?"

"No," Robert stared at his shoes.

"Then it has to do with love," Whitaker surmised. "Am I correct?"

Robert fidgeted in his chair. "There's a girl at my school," he confided. "She's Irish. My mother does not approve of her."

He went on to tell Whitaker about how his parents, mostly his mother, did not much care for Megan Sullivan. In turn, he explained, Megan's parents had forbidden her to see Robert socially because his mother was half-Greek.

"Do you love this girl?" Whitaker asked.

"I find it difficult to think straight," said Robert. "I am unable to sleep at night. My head feels like there are a thousand winds all blowing at once inside. My heart has swelled to the point where I cannot eat. Is that love?"

"Close enough, my boy," he replied. "Do you talk to this young lass?"

"Sometimes at school," he told him. "Last week she got into trouble because she tried to slip me a note in the schoolyard. A teacher saw her and intercepted it."

"Did her parents find out?"

"She won't say."

"Her parents know. If she's not telling you, then they found out."

Whitaker opened his desk drawer. He removed a fountain pen, a sheet of paper, a candle, and a box of matches. After he lit the candle, Whitaker tipped it so hot wax dripped onto the corner of the desk. When he was satisfied that there was a sufficient amount of wax on the desk, he upended the candle and placed it in the wax, anchoring it in place. From another desk drawer he took out a shallow bowl, no larger than a tea cup, along with a paring knife. From a third drawer Whitaker produced two lemons. He sliced one of the lemons in half and squeezed the juice out into the bowl.

"Let's try some Shelley, perhaps," said Whitaker, dipping his fountain pen into the juice and drawing a decent amount into the pen.

Robert watched as the little man scribbled a few lines on the paper. When Whitaker handed him the sheet, he instructed the boy to wave it about so that the 'ink' would dry. The young clerk studied the piece of paper, touching the surface upon which Whitaker had scribbled. The paper felt dry. Robert wondered what sort of madness the little man had succumbed to, what delusion he suffered to think that he had written anything at all.

"Now what?" Robert asked.

"Hold the paper over the flame," said Whitaker. "But not too close. Let the paper feel the heat, but not the flame."

The young clerk did as he was told. Slowly, the words on the page revealed themselves. Robert immediately recognized the immortal verse from Percy Bysshe Shelley's *Ode to a Skylark*. It was one of his mother's favorite poems.

We look before and after,

The first line showed. He kept the page poised several inches over the candle's flame.

And pine for what is not;
With sincerest laughter,
Our pain is fraught.

173

"The juice turns brown when exposed to the heat," Whitaker explained. "A trick my father taught me in the old country."

"That sure is something," said Robert, and blew out the flame. "But how does it help Megan and me?"

Whitaker licked his thumb and forefinger and squeezed the smoldering wick.

"Must I spell out everything for you?" he asked. "Young lady Sullivan's parents will be on the lookout for any more forbidden correspondence, of course. I have given you a gift."

"I should write to Megan with invisible ink?" Robert asked. "But then what? My words of love will be exposed by the flame. Surely, her mother may discover—"

"There is, alas, only one other remedy."

"A suicide pact," Robert said as he collapsed into the chair he had previously occupied. "Why do all the great loves come to that?"

"You need not go to such lengths, Montague," Whitaker told him. "Just tell your love that after she's read your letters she must destroy them."

"Tear them up? Set fire to them?"

"Fire would take care of it," he said, "but it can be hazardous. And a cunning mother would painstakingly piece back together evidence she finds in the garbage."

"What then?"

"There are papers that dissolve in water," said Whitaker. "I shall order a ream."

"You would do that for me?"

"Of course not," he said. "The paper I speak of is quite expensive. I will give you so many sheets at a time and I will deduct the cost from your pay. Unless you would rather risk discovery?"

"I've no fountain pen," Robert confessed.

Whitaker stood up. He surveyed the shelves where he kept on-hand an array of overstock items. He chose a fat fountain pen with an onyx and ivory body, inlaid with two bands of gold, and presented the pen to Robert.

"I cannot afford this," Robert told him.

"There is enough madness in the world already," said Whitaker. "Take the pen. Consider it a gift. Besides, no young man should be deprived of his first love because of an obstacle as odious as money."

"Mr. Whitaker—"

"Go on," he said, "take it."

Robert took hold of the pen. Whitaker held onto the other end.

"There is something you will do in return for me," the store owner announced.

"What is it? Tell me."

"Never let this pen out of your sight," Whitaker let go of the pen now, "and promise to write with it. Not just letters to your first love, but poems, stories, essays, and novels."

"But I am sixteen years old," Robert reminded him. "What would I have to say?"

"Everything in its time, young man," he said. "Now, swear an oath to me."

"I swear never to let this pen out of my sight," he said, solemnly, "and to do my best to create something with it."

"Well done," Whitaker replied. "Now, do you know how to use this thing?"

"We use fountain pens in my composition class," Robert said. "Mrs. Graves said it teaches us not to make mistakes."

Whitaker groaned, as if he had been transported back to his youth. He sat down at the desk.

"Time for you to go, Robert," he said.

The young clerk gathered his schoolbooks and headed for the back door. He paused, feeling the weight of the pen in his left hand.

"When the time comes," said Robert, "what shall I write?"

"Write what your heart says is true," Whitaker said. "You might start with a poem. Women love poems written about them."

"That won't seem..."

"Fickle?"

"Well..."

"All the great poets had several lovers, Robert," he said. "Now, go home and compose your own verse for Lady Sullivan."

Robert opened the back door.

"Good night," he said.

"Wait," Whitaker called to him. He picked up the second lemon and tossed it to Robert. "Don't forget your ink."

For the first time in several weeks, as he made his way home that night, Robert experienced a new sense of hope. At home, after dinner ended, he went to his room to complete his homework assignments. Afterward, he prepared his fountain pen and his lemon ink, and took out a sheet of plain white paper. Robert wrote a few nonsensical lines at his desk. Next, he held up the paper to the light bulb that burned in the wall sconce over his bed. The words he wrote—*never a bluebird, always a picket fence*—revealed themselves in a light brown color.

He took out a second sheet of paper. With his fountain pen poised over the page, he closed his eyes and conjured Megan Sullivan—her fair skin, her auburn hair in the late afternoon summer light at the powder mill picnic. Lost in the spell cast by such thoughts, he never heard his mother open his bedroom door.

"What are you doing?" Helena demanded.

Robert put his pen and his lemon ink into the desk drawer. He picked up a pencil, pretending to write on the paper Whitaker had given him.

"I'm writing," he told her.

"School Work?" his mother asked.

"No," he answered. "A letter."

Helena stared at him. "It better not be for that Irish tart from the mill," she warned.

"Abigail Sweeney?" Robert blushed, remembering her naked form in the moonlight before her cronies jumped him. "Mother, Abigail ran away."

"Not far, I am sure," said Helena. "The nearest bordello is my guess."

"Mother, why do you hate the Irish so much?"

"They are a degenerate race, Robert," she told him. "Prone to thievery, drunkenness, and murder."

"And you have studied the whole of the Irish race to—?"

"Do not sass me," she said. "I know what I know, and that should be enough."

"What if I want to marry an Irish girl one day?"

Helena crossed the room in two steps. She slapped her son hard in the face.

"Never speak of such things to me," Helena's voice rose into a snarl. "Not in this house. Not ever. Do you understand me?"

"Yes, mother," her son replied.

His cheek stung. It was not the first time his mother had struck him, but that night it would turn out to be the last.

"Now wash up for bed," Helena instructed him.

"Ten more minutes, please."

"You have five," his mother said, and exited the room.

Robert took out his fountain pen. He thought about Megan Sullivan some more, about how his heart ached whenever she was within proximity to him; but, try as he might, he could not think of the right words to say.

Part of the problem, as the months pressed on, was that the balance of love's power in the world shifted. A current flowed that turned everything toward the chaotic. The war in Europe pressed on, and Robert, despite his best efforts, could not get Megan to accept any of the secret letters and poems he wrote. The school year drew closer to summer. Then the world tilted full-on toward further madness when The Lusitania was torpedoed by the German navy. Once the story hit the newspapers stateside, most of the boys Robert knew at school were talking about jumping a train and heading to Canada where young men were joining up with British forces, concerned, as were many, that Woodrow Wilson would drag his feet long enough to stall committing any U.S. forces. It was nearly a year later, and nothing was being done about it.

Every week it seemed that more and more American boys, frustrated by America's slow progress, were going this route. From Canada they were shipped overseas to fight alongside their French and British brothers-in-arms.

"It's our duty," Sean O'Malley had said. "My father won't like my fighting on the same side as the Brits, but it beats the Germans bringing the fight to our shores one day."

A man in love may have reconsidered; a man who had fallen victim to unrequited love was a different animal. A few weeks later, when he learned that Sean O'Malley, the son of Seamus the pub owner, lazy-eyed Sean himself, was planning to join a group of boys who would drop out of school, head north to Canada, lie about his age, and become a soldier, Robert suddenly felt as if he too, like O'Malley and the other boys, had outgrown Delaware County and that beyond the ocean his true destiny awaited.

Still, aside from the heartache of Megan, Robert had his future to think about. His third year of high school was drawing to a close. At his mother's insistence, he had applied to several colleges in the Philadelphia area. Only one college, Haverford, was interested, but there was no money to be had. Robert submitted his application anyway and took the entrance exam. The administrators at Haverford College discussed several endowment programs with him and his parents. One of them, a slender man with bifocals and a permanent tubercular cough, paid a visit to the Hyatt residence. He came that day with an official letter of acceptance and an offer.

"If you were to become an educator like your mother," the man said, "There would be a small grant and a stipend."

His name was Braxton. Matilda sat with her family at the dining room table that night. She regarded the Haverford College representative as if he were royalty. Braxton appeared nervous whenever Robert's sister posed a question.

"What about girls?" Matilda asked. "Are they getting the same offer?"

"Some," Braxton replied. "We work closely with Bryn Mawr College. Young women are being assigned to various schools throughout the American South—"

"The South?" Theodore snapped out of a daze at that moment. "Do you mean to say that my boy would move away after he completes his studies?"

"Why, yes," he replied. "Master Hyatt would be obligated to serve four years at a school the program assigns him to, and after that time—"

"Why the South? Why can't he teach here?"

"The federal government mandates that educators serving in the program go where the greatest need exists," said Braxton. "And right now, young, energetic educators are needed in the South."

"Of course," Theodore said. "And then what? After the government is through with him? There's a war going on, and I do not see how—"

"What if I want to go?" Robert asked. "It should be my decision."

"What about the war?" his father asked. "By this time next year plenty of young boys will be joining the army to go fight the Germans."

"Mr. Hyatt," Braxton said. "I fail to see the correlation—"

"Some boys from school are leaving this summer," Robert announced.

"To go where?" Helena asked.

She had remained silent throughout the meeting. Her intention was to hear her son make up his own mind.

"Canada," Robert said. "They said boys will be allowed to sign up with British Canadian forces."

"But they are too young, Robert," his mother said. "Besides, you do not want to go to war. It takes a certain mettle to kill another human being."

"The authority has spoken," Theodore threw up his arms in a supplicating pose. "Please accept my apologies, Mr. Braxton. My wife is prone to hysteria."

"Mother doesn't look like she's in hysterics," Matilda noted.

"Matilda," her brother said, "don't be disrespectful."

"I don't know about you, Mr. Braxton," said Theodore, "but I could use a drink. How about you?"

"Me? Oh no," Braxton said. "No, thank you."

It was eight o'clock. Braxton removed a thickly stuffed envelope from a pocket inside his jacket.

"I will leave you with the acceptance letter and some information about the new education protocols," he said. "The Secretary of the Department of Education extends his deepest gratitude. Separation from family is always hard, but often we make sacrifices for the greater good. I hope, Robert, that you will consider making such a sacrifice yourself."

For weeks afterward, the envelope sat atop his mother's desk in the living room. Helena had read the material six times over by the time her son had gotten around to reading the envelope's contents. Theodore, as ever, remained aloof though he questioned Braxton's reference to 'the greater good,' accusing the young administrator, and the whole of Haverford College, of communistic leanings. Matilda, meanwhile, took on a melancholy demeanor, crippled by the fear that her brother might run off instead to fight in the war.

As the school year ended, Robert became less interested in Haverford College, the New Teachers Program, and his parents' constant bickering about their son's future. What filled his mind were thoughts of war in Europe.

"Robert," Matilda's voice came as barely a whisper as she entered his bedroom one night. "Are you awake?"

"I am now," he told her.

"I do not wish for you to go away," his sister said. "Besides, who will marry Megan Sullivan if you do?"

The name made his heart feel heavy. He felt a sudden sadness and was thankful and relieved that his sister could not see his face in the dark.

"I'm not sure that Megan and I are meant to be," he told Matilda.

"Promise you won't go," she said.

"I cannot do that, Matilda," he replied. "There are people less fortunate in the world, people who need help. It's only a matter of time before the United States joins the war."

Matilda sat on the edge of his bed. A blue moon's light graced her round face. She looked much older for a brief instant, and then, a cloud obscured the moonlight, and Matilda looked like herself again.

"What if you get killed?" she asked. "What then? Am I supposed to remain here? *Alone? With them?*"

"I will stay alive just for you," said Robert. "And when I come home I will write about the war. I will write about you, too. And I will need a good secretary, someone with a keen eye."

"Me?"

"Yes, you. You're my best pal."

"Robert?"

"Yes?"

"When will you go?"

"I don't know," he answered. "Soon, I suppose. Now, go back to bed."

Matilda stood up. She jumped onto the bed and hugged her brother, kissing him on the cheek as she did. No more words were exchanged. As quickly as she had leapt into her brother's bed, Robert's sister slipped out of bed and exited the room.

Later, he lay awake thinking about the day that had passed. Robert and his family had attended another powder mill picnic. He had felt uneasy about Abigail's absence;

something akin to guilt caused him to suspect that someone, perhaps even one of the children, may kick a dead branch on the ground and reveal the bones of the missing Irish siren. Or worse, Megan Sullivan herself may have gone to dip her feet into the creek and stepped upon Abigail's skull. The feeling, though intense, was fleeting. For no sooner had Robert thought about Megan than she appeared near a stream that fed into Cobbs Creek. Seated upon a short rock, Megan dipped her bare feet in the water. Robert started toward her. In his left pocket, he had an invisible letter for her.

"Where do you think you are going?" Helena asked.

Robert ignored her.

When Megan saw him approach, she withdrew her feet from the water. Her smart hat matched the pale blue, gingham dress she wore. A few younger girls stood nearby; among them was Matilda who, upon seeing her brother approach, ushered the other girls further down the stream.

"Hello, Megan," said Robert.

"Is that your mother over there staring at us?" she asked.

"Why would anything change?"

Megan laughed. "Sit with me," she slid to the edge of the rock.

Robert sat down next to her, his back to his mother whose stare he could feel cutting into him.

"My father said that Michael Harter left last night," said Megan, "on a train out of Philadelphia bound for Buffalo."

Robert knew little about Michael, only that he was another boy attempting to win Megan's favor. There were many boys lately who wanted nothing more than to call Megan their own.

"What's in Buffalo?" he asked.

"Michael's gone to join up with Canadian forces," she told him. "My father says they probably will send him home."

"Why?"

"You don't know?"

"Should I?"

"He can't see colors properly," she told him. "I should think that's important in war."

"Do you?"

"You mock me," said Megan. "But it's true."

"I don't mean to offend," Robert said. "Do you consider what Michael's doing to be a brave thing?"

"I think war is senseless," she said. "If women ruled the world, our planet would be decidedly different."

"You are a suffragist."

"Women in Norway can now vote," Megan informed him. "And soon women in Denmark as well. We won't live to see it. But one day a woman will be president of the United States."

Robert removed the letter from his pocket. He slipped it to Megan, clinging to her warm hand when he did.

"Another secret letter?" she asked.

"I love you, Megan Sullivan," he told her. "After college, we could marry."

"I am sure your mother would not approve."

"My mother has nothing to do with it," said Robert. "I will receive my degree and travel south to teach. Would you like to live in Georgia with me? What about New Orleans?"

"What about the war?"

"You think I should fight?"

"No," Megan said. "No American should. It's not our problem. But men always think that war is necessary."

That day Robert did not spend much time with Megan. The letter he had written to her detailed not the love he felt for her, though that love coursed through him as sure as the blood in his veins, but his plan to leave Ardmore and travel north by train.

It turned out that Robert was not alone. The overall mood at the picnic was a somber one. Men spoke in hushed tones about the fate of Europe. Women clung to their teenage sons, spurred by news of yet another boy running off into the night to hop a train in Philadelphia that would carry him toward

Canada and from there into war. Even Robert's father appeared morose. Theodore barely drank that afternoon.

After the picnic, once they were home again, Helena gave Robert an earful about Megan Sullivan. Matilda retreated to her room when her mother began shouting. Theodore took down a bottle of bourbon from a kitchen cupboard, a stash he kept for just such occasions, and commenced drinking in the kitchen alone. He poured over the Sunday Bulletin and The Inquirer, pretending not to hear Helena as she kept after their son. Only after he was certain that his wife had sufficiently run out of steam did Theodore leave the confines of the kitchen. He found Robert sitting on the stairs with his head against the wall. Helena had retreated to the bedroom.

"Pay no mind to your mother," Theodore told his son. "She can't let go of you. That is the root of all this."

"What does she hate the Irish so much, father?"

"Robert," he said, "it doesn't matter that Megan Sullivan is Irish. She could be Siamese, a Negro girl, anyone. Your mother would still feel the same. If one day you marry, it means that one day she has gotten older. And that's something she cannot face."

"How do you do it?"

"That's why God invented whiskey, son."

Robert stared at his father.

"I'm joking," Theodore said. "Now, listen carefully to me. I am only going to tell you this once. Do what you must."

Before Robert could reply, his father stepped past him on the stairs. Theodore rustled his son's hair, something he had not done since Robert was a little boy and went off to bed.

The events of that day ran over and over again in his head. When Robert climbed out of bed, the hour was late. He dressed, turned on the light over his desk, and sat down to write three letters. The first letter he wrote was to Mr. Whitaker, begging his forgiveness for such a resignation. The second one was addressed to Megan. He did not use his secret lemon juice ink; instead, he rendered the words in stark black against the white page. The last letter he wrote was for his family.

> *Dear Mother, Father, and Matilda:*
>
> *It is with some trepidation that I write you these words tonight. I have thought long and hard about my decision. In time, you will understand the choice I have made.*
>
> *Tonight, I am leaving to go north. In a few days' time I hope to cross the border into Canada by rail and sign up with the British Expeditionary Forces. I will cable you when I arrive. The war goes on as you know, and it is not right for American boys to sit back while other countries match their might against German hostilities.*
>
> *Within a few years, the war will end. If I am able, I will return home sooner, but do not count on it. I suppose in many respects I am just like Uncle Myles, born with a traveler's soul.*
>
> *Please do not think of this as a final goodbye. I do not plan to die in some foreign land for the sake of something so vague a notion as liberty. What I must do runs deeper than that. I do not expect you to understand it, but maybe one day you will.*
>
> *Love,*
> *Robert*

When he finished the last letter, Robert placed it into an envelope, sealed it, and left it on his pillow. The remaining letters he deposited in envelopes as well, writing Mr.

Whitaker's name on one and Megan's on the other, and placed the letters into his pocket.

Next, Robert removed a small suitcase he kept beneath his bed. The suitcase had once belonged to a set owned by a family in Bryn Mawr that Theodore had purchased at an estate sale. Robert's father had good intentions that day, upon viewing the listing in the Philadelphia Inquirer, even if his decision was fueled less by some altruistic sense of taking his family somewhere on vacation and more by a particular brand of Irish whiskey that Theodore had developed a taste for behind Helena's back. Theodore was still drunk when he had returned home lugging the set from the trolley stop at Ardmore Junction. It was a crisp February afternoon in 1910. Theodore's intention was to take Helena and the children by rail to Florida where the sun always shined, and summer never went out of season, but the vacation never came to pass. A week after the estate sale Theodore had lost his job with Philadelphia Rapid Transit Company. Angered by replacement workers brought in from New York City, he had taken part in the general strike. The vacation he had dreamed about never came to pass. Shortly after the strike began he picked up a shift at Addison's Powder Mill. Later, he would be hired as a trolley operator for the Red Arrow Lines. The suitcases remained empty, each one stored beneath one of their beds. Five years had passed since Robert's father came home hauling a steamer trunk with four empty suitcases stowed inside it. The trunk remained in the attic.

Robert opened the suitcase lid and paused. He leaned in close, sniffing the odors of another life that had once been lived out of the luggage piece. He found a pale blue ribbon inside a pouch sewn into the underside of the suitcase lid. When he pressed the ribbon to his nostrils, he smelled the slightest hint of perfume. Imagining that the ribbon belonged to Megan Sullivan, and not to a rich Main Line woman he did not know, he stuffed the fabric strip back into the liner pocket. Then he took a change of clothes from a drawer in his dresser, a sheaf of the paper and the fountain pen Mr. Whitaker had given to him, the two lemons he kept stashed behind his desk, and placed them, along with his pair of favorite walking shoes, into the suitcase. He closed the lid, and quietly set the latches.

In the top drawer of his dresser, Robert kept an envelope hidden beneath a drawer liner. He took the envelope from its hiding place, opened it, and counted the money he had saved while working for Mr. Whitaker. The total amount he had managed to squirrel away was thirteen dollars. He was not sure if it was enough to get him all the way to Buffalo. If it wasn't, Robert would travel as far as his money would take him. Some boys at school talked about a number of towns in upstate New York where there were cheap boarding houses. And if it meant finding work to pay the rest of his way into Canada then that was what he would have to do.

The first step toward reaching Canada and joining the British Expeditionary Forces began with his bedroom window. For weeks, Robert had lubricated the tracks inside the window frame with petroleum jelly. Every third night he tested the window, ensuring that it opened with hardly a sound. At school, there were a growing number of boys who had been in Ardmore one day and gone the next. Now, Robert's turn had come. He opened his window. For several seconds, he remained fixed with his hands on the frame, eyeing his suitcase that sat on his bed. He listened to the house settle. The light from the hallway that showed beneath his bedroom door shifted, or perhaps it was his eyes playing tricks on him in that hour, but in that moment he thought he heard his mother weeping in the hallway. He took up his suitcase now and placed it on the porch roof just beneath his open window. He waited for his mother to come through his bedroom door, but she never did. Suddenly, as he looked back over his shoulder, the bedroom looked foreign to him. He imagined Matilda fast asleep in her bed, how she would wake up the next morning and find that he was gone. He could, if he wanted to, go to her room and sit on the edge of her bed. His sister would wake up to find him there, and he would explain to her the steps he had to take, that for once in his life he saw a greater good in the world to which he had to contribute, a good that would ensure a more stable future not just for Europeans but Americans as well, but even as he climbed through the window onto the porch roof, Robert knew that if he had visited his sister one last time Matilda would cling to him and refuse to let him go. The row that would ensue afterward, once his parents had heard Matilda carrying on, meant that his plan would be thwarted, and the war might end before he ever had the chance again. So, with his feet firmly planted on the porch roof, he lowered the window to its original position.

All around him, the night muted the usual sounds of Ardmore. He picked up his suitcase and heaved it at a hedgerow that stood between his backyard and the Graysons' door, and then he lowered himself onto the porch roof. He waited and, when it seemed that no one had heard his movements, shimmied down the wrought iron lattice work on the side of the porch. Halfway down the latticework, he made a short leap to the ground. His suitcase lay wedged inside the hedges. Robert retrieved it, took a deep breath, exhaled, and made his way out of the yard as he considered the war going on somewhere across the Atlantic Ocean: daylight crept over a bombed-out field, gracing the war-weary faces of soldiers who readied for yet another battle, while in the middle of the night in Ardmore, the teen looked up at the stars, wondering if they looked the same on the other side of the world. He felt something else besides the war tugging at his soul that night. He could not name it, not that night, but it was there, pulling him toward whatever future awaited him.

Chapter Twenty-Four: The Land Of Dust And Honey—The Stray Wolf In The Hen House

Most nights Tilly didn't need a fire, nor did she desire food. There was something in the water—an invisible ingredient that sustained her. After she had first arrived, drinking from the lake every day, she gave little thought to food. When she arrived she was starving, dehydrated, half-dead. That was the first day. She was like any other hungry child, longing for food the way flowers longed for the sun, the way wolves in their fashion waited all day for evening to arrive just so they could serenade the moon.

A long time ago, there were wolves around her family farm. She remembered the wolves, how they sometimes got into the hen house or the barn, how her father would take his rifle down from the wall rack he had built in the mudroom behind the kitchen, how her mother would ready a lantern, but her father always turned it down; better to see the night in the dark as the wolves did, her father always said, then to cage yourself in light. On those nights when her father left the house, padding silently over the ground, Tilly would listen to the racket of hens being sized up by a stray wolf. She would wait by a window listening, waiting for the single shot from her father's rifle that would end the noise, but some nights Tilly's father's aim was not true. Then the darkness would carry the whimpering from a dying wolf, the most solitary, mournful call she had ever heard, a predator reverting back to its pup mind, wondering what thing had brought such pain, wondering why the darkness absorbed *all the shapes and edges around her, no longer that great killer that once roamed the hills that bordered the farm. There would be a second shot before some sense of calm returned and on these nights her father remained out there in the dark, reluctant to return to the house, and the light that waited for him.*

Tilly, long separated from her family and living in a hut by the lake whose waters sustained her, preferred the dark just like her father did. She saw little use for fire, even when the night air became crisp, which wasn't often, for she knew that even the smallest fire might make her drowsy before it was time to sleep. Until that hour she needed to be awake in case her brother approached.

When he came, she heard him long before there was a knock at the cottage door. The footfall was too heavy, belonging to a man and not her brother Cecil. There was no way to keep time by the lake. In the beginning Tilly had tried. She drew marks in the sand, but each morning the marks were wiped clean. When she carved wedges into a tree the bark grew back over the wound by daybreak. Her last effort consisted of breaking twigs into small pieces and placing a twig piece beneath her bunk before lying down to sleep, but when morning came she would discover that someone or something had come in the middle of the night and stolen the twig pieces. After that, since every day and night appeared to be the same, the same clouds, the same bronze moon always full and always looming low over the woods across the lake, Tilly abandoned time and, in return, time gave up on her. When the knock came she was already on her feet. She went to the door and opened it.

A man stood there dirty, haggard, dressed in a uniform that clung to his thin, frail body like a funeral shroud. Behind the man, dusk settled over the land. The sky turned a darker blue, and the woods beyond the lake stood like shadow sentries waiting for their post orders from the stars. Tilly leaned against the door, a pang of remorse rattling her. This man was not the one she had hoped for, but even so she knew that he needed care.

"Are your folks here?" the man asked.

"No," Tilly said. "I am alone. I am waiting for my brother. Would you like to come in?"

"You're American?"

"Yes," she replied.

"How did you get here?"

"Please," said Tilly. *"Come inside."*

Barth entered the hut. He saw a wood pail in one corner with a ladle sticking out of it. When he drank the water, it was cold. Once he had taken his share, he collapsed on a low bunk.

"I have no food," Tilly announced. *"Are you a soldier?"*

"My regiment," he began. *"We took a pounding. I think I am the only one left."*

"You're in a safe place," she told him. *"The war can't get you here."*

"How did a young American girl come to live in a hut by a lake in France?" Barth rubbed his eyes with one hand. *"Or is this Belgium?"*

"Neither," Tilly said.

"Excuse me?"

"I don't think this is Europe."

"Where do you think we are?" he stared at her as he lay on his back.

Tilly drew a small stool from a corner and placed it beside the bunk.

"My name is Tilly," she said as she sat down. *"What's yours?"*

"Barth," he replied. *"Have you seen any German patrols in this area?"*

"Germans? No," she answered. *"I was lost. That's how I ended up here."*

"Lost?"

"My family's from Acton," Tilly said. *"Acton, Maine. You know it?"*

Barth shook his head.

Tilly went on to tell him about her brother, about how the storm came when they were playing in the woods near the caves.

"A light?" Barth sat up when she reached that part of her story. *"And you followed it?"*

191

"Yes," she took his hand in hers. "And you must have done the same thing?"

"Are there others here?"

"I have seen no one but you," Tilly admitted. "Though I am waiting."

"You live here alone?"

"My brother Cecil," she went on. "He was lost with me, near the caves—"

"Your brother is here?"

"No," she said. "In the woods near our farm there are caves. I used to tell Cecil that the caves were inhabited by trolls so he wouldn't wander out there alone. We were playing in the woods when a storm came. After that we became separated.

"I followed the light," Tilly went on, "as I already explained. And there was music, chiming bells. I don't know how much time I spent in the cave. I kept following the music until I came to the forest. It was night. I remember that. I kept calling out Cecil's name. Then the dreams came after I couldn't search anymore—"

"Dreams?" Barth asked. "Did you have them too? I mean, in the forest near here?"

"I only learned later how those dreams came to be," she said.

Tilly turned her attention to the only window in the cabin. Beyond the uneven glass the sky was dark. Stars appeared over the forest opposite the lake.

"It's the Madri," Tilly said. "That's where those strange dreams originate. The Madri is the queen of the lake. Her attendants are water nymphs, just like in old fairy tales. The water nymphs rise after dark to sing. Their songs form a mist that travels into the forest. That much they told me. I don't know how the mist gets inside our heads, but if you experienced them too then they must somehow seep into our dreams and change them. Of course, I don't know what the woodland animals dream of at all. But I do know that I will never sleep in the forest again."

"How did you find this place?" Barth asked.

192

"I am not sure," the young girl said. "I came out of the forest one day when I saw the lake. The cabin was here. The Madri and her nymphs allow me to stay here."

Barth stood up.

"Are they out there now?" he asked.

"No," Tilly leapt from her stool. With both hands she took hold of Barth's right arm. "You mustn't."

"Why not?" he asked. "I want to see if what you say is true."

"The Madri forbids it," Tilly led the soldier back to her little bed. "Lie down now. It will be okay. I promise."

"I don't think I want to sleep."

"You must, Mr. Barth," she pleaded. "Now, take off your boots and sleep."

Tilly busied herself now lighting a fire in the fireplace. Once the fire was good and warm she removed her dress and put on a nightgown. She waited for Barth to make room for her on the bed and climbed in beside him.

The soldier and the little girl lay with their backs to one another. Tilly turned on her side, throwing her left arm over Barth's chest, and rested her chin on his shoulder.

"The wind blows westward through the forest," she whispered. "The song mist cannot seep into your head here."

"How can you be so sure?" Barth said as he yawned.

"What year is it?"

"1917."

"That cannot be."

"I would not make up something like that, little one."

"That means it's been what? Seventy years I've been here waiting for Cecil?"

The wood hissed and crackled in the fireplace. Barth could feel the girl's breath quicken.

"Maybe time is different here," he offered. "You're still a young girl."

"When I think of time I picture Cecil," said Tilly. "And my heart aches."

"You shouldn't think of such things, Tilly," he told her. "What happens if the wind shifts?"

"I beg your pardon?"

"The wind," said Barth. "It might shift. What if the nymph's song seeps into the cabin while we sleep?"

Tilly propped her head up on her right hand and stroked Barth's grizzled face with her left.

"The songs won't get you here, I promise," she told him. "You have to trust me."

"I want to, but I can't take any more of the dreams I had in the forest," he said. "How can you be so sure?"

"Because," said Tilly, "I stopped dreaming long ago."

Part Four:
Stones of Old Earth

Chapter Twenty-Five: The Woman In The Dark Coat—Haverford Township PA, 2012

May Weldon woke up from a sound sleep at twilight, hours after Miller had left. Floorboards creaked overhead.

Since taking ill, May had retreated to the confines of her bedroom to sleep. For years she had slept on the ground floor, less out of fear, more out of allowing those powers ever-present in her house to occupy the second floor as they saw fit, as well as Hyatt's third-floor apartment. Then the day came when she woke up on her sofa and opened her eyes to find one of the curious creatures that had frequented her home standing before her. To read about the fantastical in novels and stories was one thing, but to witness it first hand was quite another. The human psyche had long ago lost its ability to interpret such things—a hidden knowledge now reduced to the echoes of mythology and folklore. No words were exchanged, but it was understood that she might be more comfortable, in her final days, resting in her bedroom instead of sleeping on the couch. Over time, she became accustomed to the strange goings-on in her house. It was all part of the preparation. Within a week or two, she felt less like an alien in her home and more like its rightful owner again. Every day from then on, she withdrew to her bedroom on the second floor an hour or so before dusk fell, giving ground to those who were there to make her transition an easy one.

A few weeks beforehand, May's nurse Beverly had stayed until nearly dark. Beverly had remarked, May recalled, that the house had given her the chills. The nurse was convinced that the old place was haunted. Her constant questions and impromptu explorations of the home had upset the order of things. May kept a strict regimen every day as the sun set, no matter the season. As dusk approached, she retreated to her bedroom, leaving the house to fend for itself; susceptible as May's house was to fluctuations in temperature, the way many old houses were, and to the procession of invisible visitors that populated her home from sundown to sunrise every day without fail. Two months before all the activity began in earnest (for there had always been, over the span of the decades that had passed since Hyatt left the world, peculiar sounds in the house, such as shadows that moved swiftly in the corner of her eye), May had first experienced the pain. After her diagnosis, the treatment followed. There was not much time left for her and a change was due—one world for the next. Then came the day Beverly had nearly ruined everything. Fortunately, for May, there were greater powers at play, but there was a downside. She had to feign exhaustion, retiring to her room long before the appointed hour arrived.

Beverly's meddling aside, what mattered most until May's final day was the water. Every morning, just after the sun rose, May would open her bedroom door and find a pewter pitcher filled with water and a drinking glass. The rule was simple: three glasses of water a day before noon. That had been the agreement. At first, May remained unaware of any changes. She continued her latest round of chemotherapy. Earlier that day, the dose that Beverly had administered had been her last. The following week she was due to visit her oncologist. In some part of her, in the place where the soul dwells beneath the roof of the heart, May already knew what her diagnosis would be. The water had been a gift that would make the original Magi jealous with envy, though it was slow to work in the beginning, but in the weeks that followed she experienced profound changes. Her hair had grown back considerably, but she kept it shorn and hidden beneath her kerchief so as not to arouse suspicion. Make-up went a long way to give her the washed-out look Beverly and her neighbors had come to expect from a woman losing her battle with cancer. And that morning, before Miller showed up at her front door, she had begun menstruating again. In the beginning, there was some concern that the transference between places would render the water useless. It may not have worked as strongly or as fast, considering how far it was from the source, but it worked all the same. May did not concern herself any longer with keeping up her charade. In a few days, it would all be over.

In the decades that had passed since Hyatt himself had gone over to the other side, there were several considerations to be made. After considering all possible options, when she consulted with lawyers May decided that the money from Hyatt's literary estate would be put into an endowment at Haverford College where Hyatt's papers were kept. As for the house, May would take care of that.

Presently, May entered the walk-in closet to her left. It had been another bedroom, her original from when she was a young girl. On her fiftieth birthday, the old bedroom had been converted. A double-door was added in the master bedroom and the original doorway in the hall closed off. In the walk-in closet she went to seek a bundle of letters she kept secured in a small, fireproof safe. The envelope to one of the letters still bore a thumbprint, Hyatt's thumbprint, a dark smudge that had been created, she imagined, by an oily residue left on his hands after cleaning his rifle, before hastily stuffing the letter into the envelope and passing it on to the company executive officer to be sent back to the States. May had periodically gone into the safe to read the contents of that letter, written long before she had been born, and struggled then, as she did now, with a perverse desire to keep it hidden from the public, as well as the yearning to share its contents with the world. In the end, as she did now, May removed the letter that was several pages thick, penned in Hyatt's careful, deliberate hand, from the bound stack and put it back in the safe before taking the other letters into her bedroom to read them once more.

Her original intention was to outline a draft of the essay she had promised Howard Miller she would write. She would base it on the letters she had chosen to keep for herself: some addressed to her and others to Hyatt's family while he served with the 4th Canadian Division in France during The Great War. There was also her diary from when she was a young girl. May opened it and the pages were brittle, yellowed with age, but the ink, she was pleased to discover as she thumbed through the delicate pages, was still legible.

January 25, 1939

His name is R.J. Hyatt, and he plans to rent the apartment above our home. Mother told me that he is a novelist and a poet. She talked about him like he was one of the great poets of our age. I don't know much about poetry except to say that it bores the hell out of me. If my mother knew this it would break her heart. Mr. Hyatt barely said two words to me...well, maybe three. No, four. I can recall them now: 'Hello. How are you?' Never in my short life so far have I heard a voice like his. Mr. Hyatt is at least twenty years older than me

Two days before Mr. Hyatt showed up at our house, my mother rode the trolley to Philadelphia. She returned late in the afternoon. I was already finished with school for the day. So, I sat on the porch and waited...and waited...and waited. Mother was all agog when she walked up just before 4:00 p.m. She showed me a book of poems by Mr. Hyatt. Later, when my father came home from work, my mother showed it to him. Then she spent the early evening reading the poems aloud. This man Hyatt is supposed to be a genius. My father said Mr. Hyatt fought in the Great War. He also told me that Mr. Hyatt published a novel some years ago. It was very popular, my father said. And because of that Mr. Hyatt made a lot of money.

April 15, 1939

    Mr. Hyatt has vanished.

    I wish I could write more in my diary but between schoolwork and my chores I never have time. So much has happened. I heard Mr. Hyatt tell my father that his novel was going to be reprinted. I suppose that means Mr. Hyatt will have more money. He is an odd bird. A few days a week he goes to the market for my mother, buying fresh fruit, vegetables, and chicken (Mr. Hyatt's favorite).

    One day I tried to visit Mr. Hyatt in his room. I knocked on the door in our second-floor hallway that led up to the third floor. When he opened the door, he scolded me. Mr. Hyatt said that it isn't proper for a young woman to visit a man in his flat without a chaperone. He has changed since the first time I met him. I don't remember what he said after he had scolded me. I was too saddened that he had turned me away.

    At night, when Mr. Hyatt sits with us at dinner, I don't like looking into his blue eyes for too long. There is so much pain in them.

It's been two weeks since we have seen Mr. Hyatt. My father said our tenant left a note saying he had to tend to business out of town. I am scared that Mr. Hyatt won't be back. I guess I miss him, even if most days he acts like I'm not there.

I just wish Mr. Hyatt would come back.

May 10, 1939

My mother and I went to the library on Darby Road today. I had all but given up on Mr. Hyatt. During our walk, I asked my mother if she had heard from our tenant. She told me no, and she added that I needn't worry.

When we arrived at the library my mother went off to find something to read. Her flavor in books was much different than mine, always reading romances from Victorian times.

I sat at a table and started my homework assignments. A few minutes later I looked up and saw a familiar face. I must have let out a gasp because the librarian gave me a stern look. There was Mr. Hyatt, standing at my table. He held a volume of Virgil in one hand and an ancient, leather-bound book in his other. I couldn't see the title of the second one. Mr. Hyatt placed the leather-bound book down on the table and slid it toward me. The other book was Ovid's Metamorphoses. Start with this, he told me.

I didn't want to read. I didn't want to complete my assignments. I was bursting with questions. My mother appeared at my table, and my inquiry was cut short. She showed Mr. Hyatt the book she intended to check out. It was an old copy of The Land of Dust and Honey. Mr. Hyatt's novel. I wanted to crawl beneath the table and die.

My mother said Mr. Hyatt has sad eyes. She doesn't know anything about him.

One day, he told my mother, I'll give you a signed copy. My mother went all weak in the knees. It was embarrassing.

And to me Mr. Hyatt said, Read your Ovid. Then we'll move on to Virgil.

The three of us walked home to Chelten Road. On the porch Mr. Hyatt ruffled my hair.

It's good to be home, he said.

In that instant I knew one thing: I loved him. And I never wanted him to leave again.

May placed her old diary back into the box. She decided to pass it on to Miller, along with all but one of the remaining letters, so that he could use the diary and the letters in his biography, as long as he agreed to give them over to Haverford College Library Special Collections Department when he was finished with them. The letters in her possession, along with her girlhood diary, had remained a secret to Miller the first time he came calling all those years ago. Now, as she sat on her bed, opening one letter after another and spreading them out before her, she was not so sure that she wanted him to have them at all.

Among the letters were those that Hyatt had written to his mother during the war. Other letters belonged to May. They had been placed inside unmarked envelopes and slipped beneath her bedroom door when she was a teen. Some of the letters Hyatt had written to her later, during May's time at Bryn Mawr College, caused her to blush. These letters, like the previous ones slipped beneath her bedroom door, were also placed in their plain white envelopes. Later she would find them in her dormitory room at Bryn Mawr beneath her pillow. May had never figured out how Hyatt had walked into a women's dormitory, climbed the stairs to the third floor where her room was located, gained access to her room behind a locked door, and placed such missives beneath her pillow without having ever been seen, much less accosted by old Miss Worthy, the matron charged with keeping the dormitory free of the brutish sex that sought to spoil the virtues of young, intelligent women. And Hyatt, no matter how much May pressed him in those days for an answer, would never give her any indication of how he had detected the gap in Miss Worthy's intricate web of defenses that enabled him to come and go as he pleased.

"Tell me," May had pleaded with him one winter night.

It happened on her Christmas break during her second year at Bryn Mawr. She stood as she always did, at the entrance to Hyatt's rooms on the third floor of her parents' home, while the writer occupied his desk, staring at a blank page in the thick ledger that lay open before him.

"Some magic," said Hyatt, "should remain a secret."

His hair had grown long, nearly reaching his shoulders. And there were more wisps of gray than May had remembered. After high school until that day, there were moments when she thought she loved him, though his letters and notes made no claim that he felt the same way—never once a broad declaration of love, nor for that matter, the slightest hint of love; instead, only his own musings coupled with questions about her studies at Bryn Mawr, and recommendations concerning what writers she should be reading, as opposed to those assigned to her by her professors.

"What are you working on?" she asked.

"A new novel," he told her.

His words struck her hard, as if he had revealed a secret; the weight of this new knowledge left her breathless.

"Is it almost finished?" she asked.

"No," he turned to look over his work. "I am still waiting to see how it all will end."

"But it's your work," May said. "How can you not know how you want your story to end?"

"There are variables," he said, "that will need to work themselves out."

There were days, and long nights, when young May suspected that the writer had not been telling her the truth, that every time she visited him in his rooms the scene had always been the same: poised over his desk, often unaware of her presence (a fact that May found disturbing), and an old ledger opened before him. Hyatt, at times, appeared as if in a trance, his fountain pen poised an inch or two over a blank page. More peculiar than Hyatt's blank pages were those rare times when May ascended slowly to his rooms, pausing on the stairs long enough to hear the distinct sound of his pen scratch against the page, at times slowly, at times in a furious pace. The times she cherished the most were those when she heard him recite lines he wrote, or, given the lack of evidence where written words on the page were concerned, lines he intended to put down on paper, his voice melodic and baritone, Hyatt weaved intricate and complex sentences aloud that carried a music all their own. Those rare moments, however, never lasted long.

As she grew into her late teens, May found it increasingly more difficult to remain apart from Hyatt. Whenever she padded up the stairs, in warmer weather choosing to go barefoot (a practice her mother admonished her for, warning her daughter that the sight of a woman's naked foot led some men to consider lascivious thoughts), she listened for the sounds that became familiar as the years passed. The shy tenant had become as permanent a fixture in her life; as fixed as her parents and the first-floor furniture that her mother was forever rearranging; Alice was convinced that unseen forces had populated their home and nudged chairs and tables ever so slightly out of place.

Toward the end of eighth grade and throughout her high school years, May discovered that Hyatt did not live in a vacuum, as much as she wanted to believe it so. Some days she returned from school to find that Hyatt had visitors—young men and women who traveled far to meet the author. Some wanted nothing more than an autograph inside whatever copy of *The Land of Dust and Honey* they toted to her house; others interviewed him for various magazines and journals, and they were always dismayed when Hyatt refused to have his photograph taken. Her mother always made these visitors feel welcome, going out of her way to prepare tea and to feed them, and she insisted that Hyatt hold court in her living room. Once a man and a woman from Scandinavia showed up at the front door with recording equipment, intent on interviewing Hyatt for a radio show back home. The woman, like so many others who had come to Haverford Township to meet the author, was pretty. May was convinced that Hyatt might run off with her and live out his days with the Scandinavian woman whose name was Greta, or Helga, or some other name that made May's blood run cold. The writer stayed, and May prayed that no more beautiful women would call on him in the future. If God was listening, it was only half-so.

One wintry night, another woman called upon Hyatt. The hour was late, beyond any other that May could remember his so-called 'followers' had come to visit. Her stark expression had remained with May always, though she never learned the stranger's name. The woman was at least twenty years older than Hyatt. Alice had invited the woman into the living room. Then she sent her daughter to the third floor to retrieve Hyatt.

"There's a woman downstairs to see you," said May.

"Who is she?" Hyatt asked.

"She won't say," she replied. "Mother has given her tea. Bad night to come out for an autograph, don't you think?"

"Stay here," he told her.

May waited until Hyatt had descended the stairs before she kicked off her shoes and padded after him. When she reached the landing between the first and second floors, she paused. Her mother passed from the living room into the dining room. May held her breath, as if the act would render her invisible.

Moments later, she slowly made her way down the remaining steps. She could hear her mother toiling in the kitchen. Her father glimpsed his daughter as he sat at the dining room table reading the newspaper. He nodded at the stairwell behind her, indicating that she should go back upstairs. May ignored him. She learned forward, close to the living room doorway, and listened to the strange woman and Hyatt converse.

"It's closed," Hyatt was saying. "Lost for good."

"There is no other way?" the woman asked.

Hyatt said something, but he spoke in a whisper and May could not hear him.

Suddenly, she felt a presence behind her.

"Upstairs," her mother hissed in May's ear.

May jumped. Her mother grabbed her by the arm and ushered her daughter up the stairs to the second floor.

"Honestly, May," was all her mother said.

When they reached the second-floor hallway Alice led May into her bedroom, sat her down on the bed, and closed the door when she exited the room.

Minutes later, May watched from her bedroom window after she heard the front door shut. The hooded woman walked to a waiting car idling at the curb, climbed into the back seat, and vanished into the snowy night.

Following the incident, it was no secret that in Hyatt's presence May felt renewed; in his absence, her heart hardened. For there remained long stretches of time—days, weeks, sometimes two or three months—when Hyatt would be gone. And in the spring immediately following the strange woman's visit, May worried that Hyatt might succumb to her charms. May never asked Hyatt about the woman. And he never mentioned her. So much the better, May thought as the years passed. The woman in the dark coat never returned. For this, May felt grateful.

That spring there were trips to New York—Manhattan where Hyatt's publisher was located—and once Hyatt had invited May to accompany him for the day, taking the train from 30th Street Station in Philadelphia to Pennsylvania Station, but May's mother refused.

"It's not you, Mr. Hyatt," Alice had told him. "You are a good man, a gifted man. It's just that I do not wish for my daughter to be anywhere near 42nd Street."

The matter was settled. It was one of the longest days a then sixteen-year-old May spent, counting the hours until Hyatt returned.

The announced trips May learned to tolerate. But those days when Hyatt slipped out of the house unnoticed infuriated her. When pressed, her parents offered no help.

Her father remained indifferent. "A bachelor," he said one night at dinner, "is permitted to come and go as he pleases."

Her mother was more optimistic. "Writers are eccentric," she told May. "One never knows why they do what they do. He's probably researching his next book."

This would become the position her mother maintained as the years passed and Hyatt continued to vanish and reappear on a whim. Her father, on the other hand, seldom spoke of their tenant's comings and goings, as if he understood too well the needs a man faced living the way Hyatt did.

When May turned eighteen two things happened that nearly ruined her friendship with Hyatt. The first happened during one of Hyatt's vanishing acts. May had come home from Bryn Mawr for the weekend in late October. She found out from her mother that Hyatt had gone off again without so much as a word. The only reason Alice knew this for certain was because she had entered his rooms on the third floor, as was her custom every Thursday to dust and straighten his furniture, and she discovered that his backpack was not in its usual place hung from one of his bedposts. Respectful of the writer and his tools, Alice made sure that she never touched any of Hyatt's belongings on his desk. Enraptured by some private memory as she espoused the virtues of good housekeeping to her daughter, Alice could not, or perhaps refuse to detect how quickly May's mood turned from one of elation to one of bitterness upon hearing the news.

Soured by the prospect of spending a weekend at home without Hyatt, May sulked and stomped around the house for the remainder of the afternoon. In the kitchen she opened cupboard doors and closed them, searching for nothing, until her mother shooed her off. In the living room, May thumbed through some new books her mother had purchased, among them were *The Member of the Wedding*, *All the King's Men*, and *Titus Groan*; but found that the books did not hold her interest.

"I thought you might like the Peake novel," said Alice as she stood in the living room doorway now, drying a plate with a dish towel.

"Honestly, mother," May replied. "Another British tale of an heir and the poor servant bent on doing him in?"

"Peake is getting a fair amount of attention in Europe," her mother told her. "That's what Mr. Hyatt says."

"Then I shall hate it," her daughter declared.

Alice sighed. "I don't know what's gotten into you," she said. "Are all the girls at Bryn Mawr as morose as you?"

"Some are worse," May informed her.

"What's the point of sending you to college," said Alice, "if all you learn how to do is show contempt toward everything?"

"Maybe utter scorn suits me."

"I have to go to the market," her mother announced. "I think you should come along."

"Do I have a choice?"

"You can stay here and wallow in your misery, or you can get some fresh air."

May chose the former and, after her mother left the house, went upstairs. The door at the end of the hall leading up to Hyatt's apartment was ajar. In that instant, her disposition transformed, and hope filled her as she raced up the stairs to Hyatt's flat.

Chapter Twenty-Six: Love's Passing—

France, 1917

When he arrived in England, fresh from a tumultuous trip across the North Atlantic aboard a troop ship, Hyatt learned that other Americans were easily recognized because they appeared larger than life compared to the Tommies who served in British outfits that had recently returned from the front. He was assigned to the newly formed 4th Canadian Division that was composed of existing units already standing by in England and the one he traveled with from Canada, the 78th Battalion of the Winnipeg Grenadiers. The soldier's life was one that suited young Hyatt well. No aspect of his time had been left to his own devices; at least, not thus far, and, for a seventeen-year-old, it was better for him that way. He made friends among members of his unit, though the dozen young men he called friends would not live to see the war's end. His closest mate was Walter Jenkins, a rich farm boy from Montana whose family owned thousands of acres where they raised horses and cattle and invested in the steel industry 'back east.'

"Why would you leave all that behind?" Hyatt had asked Jenkins one night.

The Montanan was a full head and shoulders taller than Hyatt, broad-shouldered where the seventeen-year-old was narrow, and his square jaw and big white teeth drew stares from women everywhere he went.

Hyatt had posed the question one night as he and Jenkins stood on the deck of their troop ship, a converted ocean liner named the RMS Northridge, as the vessel plowed the harsh dark waves.

"I want my own fortune," said Jenkins. "When the war is over I have plans."

"What do you plan to do before the war ends?"

"Not get killed."

Their conversation, no more than a distant echo, surfaced now and again, especially as the 78th Battalion began training in the English countryside where mock trenches had been excavated. During training, Jenkins and Hyatt, who served in the same platoon, were inseparable. Other members of their unit wondered if the two soldiers had been brothers separated at birth. A developing pastime for Jenkins was taunting one of the training sergeants, a Brit from Devon named Barrett.

"Sergeant Barrett," Jenkins said one day at the rifle range.

"What is it now, soldier?" Barrett screamed.

Barrett liked to scream. He screamed morning, noon, and night. At chow, on the rifle range, during early morning marches, and especially when it came time for inspection, the training sergeant kept at it. Hyatt had never heard Barrett use a normal tone of voice, and he avoided speaking directly to him because the sergeant was hard on the few Americans who served under Canadian command.

"I have to go to the loo," said Jenkins.

Barrett spread his arms out wide. "Do you see any goddamned loos?" he screamed. "No, I suspect you do not. And do you know why?"

"No, sergeant. Why?"

"Because, you big ox, we have no loos in the field. That's why."

"Latrine?"

"Get a load of Napoleon Bonaparte," said Barrett.

He launched into a curse-laden tirade concerning the degenerative nature of the French, their filthy habits, their ridiculous superstitions, their seemingly ineffectual attitude toward war, and a host of other shortcomings. The more Barrett worked himself into such a state, the harder it was, given his strong Devonshire accent, for anyone to understand him.

"I really have to go, Sergeant Barrett," Jenkins told him.

"Piss off, ape!" Barrett screamed.

"You mean," the Montanan said, "right here?"

Hyatt pretended that his rifle was jammed so he wasn't looking when Jenkins proceeded to relieve himself on the spot.

Barrett leapt toward Jenkins, stomping one booted foot down and then another, unaware that Jenkins had taken the opportunity to piss on the sergeant's boots.

"I would beat your monkey brains in with this tin hat," the sergeant removed his Brodie helmet, "if it wasn't a waste of his majesty's military supplies."

Hyatt finished shooting, stood by waiting for his rifle to be inspected, and bit the inside of his cheek as Barrett made Jenkins run back and forth behind the firing line with his rifle held high.

"What do you see in that gorilla, private?" Barrett asked as he snatched the Lee-Enfield rifle from Hyatt's grip.

"He's a good man, sergeant," he replied.

"Another Yank?" the sergeant screamed. "What is it with you fucking cowboys anyway?"

"I am not a cowboy," Hyatt told him. "I am from Philadelphia, sergeant."

"Oh, cradle of liberty and all that," he replied. A smile cracked beneath his moustache. "You mean Philadelphia where those criminals plotted against the Crown?"

"We have a different version," he said. "They say the victors always write history to suit their needs."

"Get out of my face, mongrel!"

211

Hyatt, Jenkins, and the rest of the unit suffered Sergeant Barrett's wrath for several more weeks. In all of the madness, there was supposed to have been some message about survival. When training ended, Hyatt felt a sense of relief. Little did he know that neither Barrett nor all that training in the English countryside could prepare him for what was ahead.

Soon after he had arrived in France, Hyatt learned that Sergeant Barrett had been killed at the grenade range by one of his own trainees—an Italian-Canadian from Toronto, or so the story went, who lacked the threshold to endure Barrett's constant barrage of ethnic slurs.

Unfortunately, Barrett's passing was not the only bad news that awaited Hyatt upon landing in France.

The 78th Battalion had been granted R&R when they arrived in Paris.

The news that Hyatt would learn struck him hard. He had not heard from his family in some time. Letters from home were far and few between during his time in Canada and then England.

In early February of 1917 the executive officer from Hyatt's company handed him a bundle of mail. There were several from his family. He had not heard from his father since running off to Canada to join the army there. In the latest batch of letters none of the envelopes bore his father's handwriting.

The first letter Hyatt opened was from Matilda.

December 4, 1917

Dearest Robert:

Under The Bronze Moon

I hope that this letter finds you well. For many weeks, anger quelled my sensible faculties and I hated you for lighting out like a thief in the night and abandoning me. Father says that men often do things that have no rhyme or reason. Mother says that father is an expert in that field. Right now, she's hovering near the kitchen table where I write these words. She says I should practice proper grammar and structure when I write my letters to you. Mother says that letter writing will one day go the way of the Dodo bird; that no one will take the time to properly correspond with each other. Father just joked that in the future we will send messages all around the world in pneumatic tubes that will dangle in the sky like so many hanging vines. Can you imagine such a thing? Now, Mother just picked up a rolling pin. I am going up to my room to finish this letter...

Anyway, back to mother. She says, where grammar and structure are concerned, that I should know the rules before I break them. She is so tiresome at times with her constant preaching. I want you to know that I am so sorry for not writing before now. I truly was angry, but I don't want you to hate me for it. Honestly, I knew that Ardmore was too small for you. One day, when I am older, I would like to travel. Perhaps when this war ends you can take me to Paris so I can go to Notre Dame and pray for stupid men and their brash decisions. I mentioned earlier that I was angry after you left. Mother said I let the lesser angels get the best of me. She worried that my anger might manifest itself in some other way. Lately, she's been reading books on psychoanalysis and driving father crazy. Honestly, Robert, you could not have picked a worse time to go off to war. So, I mentioned my anger. And as much as I hate to admit it, mother was right. There's a girl at my school—Ula Veryshkov. She's new. Father said that Ula's father tried to

213

get a job at the powder mill, but Mr. Addison let it be known that he had no room for 'Bolshevik' agitators. Ula was in the schoolyard one morning—she's very pretty, shapely already with big hips and breasts to match (mother says that Ula comes from 'good stock' whatever that means) while the rest of us wait around for the gods to grace us— and she, that is to say, Ula, started talking about how Germany had been in the right to sink the Lusitania and that everyone who volunteered to fight in any war must be a fool. Well, we had words after that. Our conversation turned heated and the next thing I knew Ula was pulling my hair and slapping my face. I kicked her in the shins and stomped on her foot. She let go long enough for me to rip her dress and knock her to the ground. It was dreadful. My principal wanted to kick me out of school. Father raged about reformatories and God knows what all, but it was mother who straightened everything out. Ula and I are now friends. Sometimes we talk about boys, but we agreed not to talk about the war. Find me a postcard to send back to the States so that I know you are doing well. Our house feels empty without you here. Every night I pray for your safety, and I hope your officers are treating you with dignity. We had snow recently, and now it's just beginning to melt. Father and the men at the mill are worried that the dam behind the mill may not hold another spring. He says that Mr. Addison and the mayor's office argue over who's responsible for the dam's upkeep and meanwhile the dam weakens. Mother chastises father more now than ever before. I think she's angry too that you left, but she will never admit it. I don't know if you have received Mother's most recent letter, but Uncle Myles visited a few months back. When he learned that you had run off to fight in the war he became furious. He argued with father for an hour and afterward he left. Mother was in hysterics; as if, and I know this seems strange, she favors Uncle Myles more than our father. I think perhaps that mother has always been in love with Uncle Myles. I know what you are thinking. I am just a silly girl. Forget I said that. This war is stupid. Come home, Robert. The very thought of you sticking your neck out for another country does not sit well with me. Oh, did I mention we have a new parish priest? His name is Father Malachi. The girls at my school call him Father Handsome. I started going to mass. Father Malachi came to Ardmore by way of Londonderry. That's in Ireland. They say British soldiers killed some peaceful protestors there last year. Oh Robert, help me understand the world. It confuses and saddens me. Anyway, Father Malachi says killing another human being is a grave sin, a mortal sin, even in war. How much better would the world be if men learned to plant flowers and stop shooting bullets at one another? I did my best to get Mother to go to mass with me, but you know how she feels about the Irish. Well, I am sure you have chores or drills or whatever to do so I shall not keep you any longer. Be safe. And don't be a hero. Heroes get monuments erected in their honor, but I cannot hug a statue and tell it 'I love you.' Send me a postcard from one of those cute little shops in Paris so I can show it to Ula. I will write again soon.

Love always,
Matilda.

The next letter Hyatt opened was from his mother; her handwriting, as always, composed in a meticulous style. After he had received his mail he had gone out to a café to read. It was a small establishment tucked between two empty buildings on a side street near Le Café de Flore. Hyatt happened upon the place by accident; none of his fellow brothers-in-arms went in for places near Boulevard Saint-Germain so there were plenty of girls about. At Poirot Café, where he sat presently, he ordered a glass of pinot from the owner's daughter. Her name was Marie Jeanette Poirot. Belgian by birth, she had moved to Paris with her parents when she was a toddler. Marie had a round face that was pale like the moon on a clear night, and rich, dark brown, sorrowful eyes that made Hyatt blush whenever she stared at him for too long.

"*Courier?*" Marie nodded at the small bundle on the table where Hyatt sat.

"From home," he told her.

"Where is home?"

"Ardmore."

"*Amour?*" Marie arched her left eyebrow.

"No," he replied, embarrassed.

"Oh," she looked disappointed. "From your *Petite amie?*"

"My what?"

"Girlfriend."

"I don't have a girl," Hyatt told her.

"*Quel dommage!*"

Hyatt's French was questionable at best; what he did not understand he could see in Marie's expression. The look on her face was one of mock pity. She leaned forward, bending at the waist, and held his face as she kissed him on each cheek. As she did so, he peeked down her blouse and saw her left breast, a hint of areola. In an instant, Marie was gone, tending to another patron—an old man who sat at a table in the corner reading a newspaper. Marie and the old man exchanged words in their native tongue. Something the man said caused Marie to laugh before she turned to peer over her shoulder at Hyatt.

His face flushed as he turned his attention to the letters. He opened the one his mother had sent.

December 31, 1916

Robert,

I trust this letter finds you in good health. It is with a heavy heart that I must impart terrible news to you. I pray that you will be able to cope with what I am about to write since you are so far away from home.

Shortly after you left, your friend Megan Sullivan took ill. She developed a fever, a very high fever that left her lingering between here and the hereafter. Neighbors who lived nearby said that Megan had suffered blindness during her illness. A doctor named Gorman had surmised that Megan had contracted an infection that had caused her brain to swell.

On Christmas Day, your father received word from Mr. Sullivan that Megan had passed away. It is such a sad thing when the young pass away. No parent should bury their child. When I heard the news it made me think of you, of course, and how much you will miss Megan. I know I have been harsh in the past about the Irish. I have my reasons, reasons which, now that you are a soldier and a man fighting Germans over God knows what, I will share with you when you have put the war behind you.

Megan was buried at St. Denis Cemetery. When the war is over, or you come home safely, whichever the case may be, I will take you to visit the spot the Sullivans have picked for their daughter. It is a pretty place where a brook runs toward the rear of the cemetery beneath an old hawthorn tree whose exposed roots appear ancient and otherworldly in the late afternoon light.

Your father sends his love. Despite my best efforts to persuade him to write you a letter, he refuses to do so. Production at the powder mill has increased since it will be only a matter of time before President Wilson declares war on Germany. Mr. Addison has hired some new men and he has placed your father in charge of training them.

This will be no small feat since most of the men came from Salerno and not a one speaks English. As you might imagine, your father is quite frustrated.

I will continue to write to you as often as I am able. Until then, may God bless you.

With love,
Mother

The light outside the café shifted. Hyatt stowed his letters away in a map case he kept with him. The case contained no maps, only a few letters he had received so far, and other curios that included a photograph of a nude Chinese woman said to have been taken at a famous Parisian brothel called La Colombe Bleue. Hyatt and a few of his platoon members had gone to the brothel with the hope of spending some time with the Far East beauty whose name was Shie Wu. The other men settled for heavy-breasted French whores, each one more rotund than the next, when they learned that Shie Wu's husband had discovered where she worked at night and, in a jealous rage, stabbed her to death and dumped her body into the Seine. Hyatt sought no company that evening, but he kept the photograph of Shie Wu; this simple act was less a reminder of a missed opportunity, and more a remembrance of all that had gone wrong in Europe. That murder occurred in the streets of Paris while a war was being fought and astounded Hyatt. His reasoning had less to do with youthful naiveté and more to do with what he felt was a strong undercurrent of distrust among the French. The people of France needed allies to ensure their liberties. There was no denying that fact. Still, foreigners who came to France of their own free will, especially the Chinese and the Arabs whom Hyatt saw with more frequency as the days progressed, or those refugees seeking asylum from the might of Germany, were treated as less than livestock.

"It will be dark soon," Marie said. "My shift is over. Walk me home?"

"At your service," Hyatt said as he leapt to his feet.

"Papa?"

"*Oui?*" Marie's father Jean-Claude stepped out from behind the bar.

"I am going home now," she said.

"*Avec soldat l'américain?*"

"Yes, papa."

"*Eh bien...si vous devez.*"

"Papa!" Marie exclaimed. She turned to Hyatt. "He likes you," she lied.

"How can you tell?" he asked.

"Papa can be mean to boys I know," she told him. "He thinks I should become a nun."

"What about you?"

"Me? I want to make love when I please," Marie told him. "Shall we go?"

Hyatt followed her out of the I. Long shadows stretched toward the east; a premature night released by the buildings that lined the narrow street. Marie laced her right arm through Hyatt's left.

In different doorways that faced the street stood men whose faces were masked in shadow. Some were in the company of young women Marie's age and others with older women. After another block Hyatt espied a couple between two houses—the woman squatted before a young man who was not much older than Hyatt, working the young man's cock in her mouth.

"*Touriste!*" Marie whispered in Hyatt's ear. "Don't stare. It's so rude."

"Sorry," he hurried along, dragging her further up the street.

"My flat is just around the corner," she said, indicating another narrow street. "I can give you refreshment before you head back. Maybe we can dance if you like."

219

Marie touched his face. She leaned in close and kissed him.

Hyatt was about to say something before she did. Instead, he rubbed his hardness against Marie's pelvis as they kissed.

"*Ce que l'enfer? Pervert!*" a woman's voice cried out down the street.

"I sure am sorry, XXXaddie-mozelle," the unmistakable voice of Walter Jenkins responded. "I thought your beau was someone else."

"Jenkins?" Hyatt shouted.

"Hyatt, for shit's sake," he said as he approached. "I've been looking for you all afternoon. We're shipping out."

"When?"

"Right now."

"Who is this?" Marie asked.

Hyatt made the introductions. After he explained to Marie what was happening, she kissed him again. Then she kissed Jenkins on each cheek.

"*Que Dieu vous bénisse!*" she said.

"Come on," Jenkins said. "We've no time to lose."

"How did you find me?" Hyatt asked.

"How many American boys do you see in this neighborhood?" he inquired.

"Not many, I suppose."

"Well, that's all about to change," Jenkins said. "American Gis are on their way to Paris!"

"Wilson declared war on Germany?"

"Well, no," he replied. "But it's inevitable. Say," he nodded at Marie, "I didn't mean to..."

"*Au revoir, Robert,*" she said and turned on her heels.

Hyatt and Jenkins watched her walk away.

"Pretty close, huh?" Jenkins asked.

"More than you know," Hyatt told him.

"Come on," he said, taking him by the arm. "We don't want to get shot for desertion."

"Wait," he watched as Marie entered a doorway half-way up the street.

"Don't worry, buddy," said Jenkins. "I won't let the Germans kill you. Not while you're still a virgin."

"I've made love to girls."

"No, you have not."

They double-timed it back down the street. A taxi waited for them, blocking the intersection.

"Is it obvious?" Hyatt asked.

"Yes," Jenkins told him. "Anyway, when we get to the front I'll find you a nice farm girl. I know all about farm girls."

"But you don't speak French."

"The language of the land is the same everywhere, buddy," he said. "Now, let's go to war."

Chapter Twenty-Seven: Bearded Men And Boars—Haverford Township PA, 1946

The main room was empty. A door leading to Hyatt's bedroom was open. Inside the bedroom, the covers on the bed were twisted. May smelled the single pillow, stroked the sheets with her hands. She thought she would make Hyatt's bed for him but chose to leave it the way she had found it. Her mother changed bed linens throughout the house every Friday, including Hyatt's. There was no sense in stirring suspicion. That afternoon she would remain a wraith, coming and going unnoticed. Behind the bedroom, at the back of the house, there was a small bathroom. May opened the medicine cabinet, took out a bottle of aftershave, unscrewed the cap, put the lip of the bottle to her nose and breathed in slowly, deeply, and closing her eyes now, she imagined a decidedly different world—one in which she lived in her house alone with Hyatt, a world where she and the author sat on the back porch, watching the sun set through the tall cedar trees that lined the property's edge; one that meant going to bed with Hyatt every night not long after the sun went down. Afterward, May replaced the cap, put the aftershave back into the medicine cabinet, and made sure she did not leave anything out of place.

On the way to the stairs, some minutes later, May passed Hyatt's desk. A stack of ledgers, four in all, lay atop the desk to the left. Another ledger lay on the desk's center with a bookmark sticking out. May opened it. The ledger was blank. She was careful to make sure that the bookmark, a flimsy pale blue ribbon frayed at either end, remained in place. As she placed the book back on the desk a hair stuck to her hand. Startled, May shook her hand thinking it was a spider, at first; in warmer months, the upper floors of her home seemed to be infested with Opiliones—*daddy longlegs* that her father referred to as *harvestmen*. Most insects she tolerated, but ever since she was a little girl the *daddy longlegs* were the pests she feared; the way they brushed over her skin ever so lightly made her blood run cold. From the corner of her eye she saw that it was not a spider at all, but a single strand of hair that fell to the floor and vanished between two floorboards. Relieved, she made her way back downstairs.

A few days later, the memory of her visit to Hyatt's rooms faded. May returned to her dormitory at Bryn Mawr on Monday. The next day, Tuesday, she returned to her dormitory room after classes to find an envelope beneath her pillow. Inside the envelope was a letter from Hyatt.

Dearest May,

I returned this morning after your father had gone off to work. Your mother was on her way to the market, and then to the library before lunch. She was kind enough to prepare a wholesome breakfast for me before she left. I was of a mind to write, and you know better than most, better than anyone, that I do my best work on a full stomach.

After breakfast, I went up to my room and discovered that someone had been toying with the items on my desk. I prefer not to get your parents involved, and I implore you to let me know if you were at my desk while I was away. I know this because of the measures I take, primitive and ritualistic as they may be, to ensure that

223

nothing is disturbed; as such, I am able to tell if someone has gone through my things.

Please know that I am not angry. You are of an age now when others expect you to play an adult role and along with the responsibilities of adulthood comes the tenacity to own up to wrongdoings.

When you come home this weekend I will be here. Let us find some time to talk about my things, and how one must be honest and respectful of property that does not belong to you.

I look forward to seeing you soon.

Always,
Robert

May granted Hyatt his wish the following weekend. She was relieved to discover that he was indeed not angered by the intrusion. The conversation that took place in Hyatt's rooms, however, had brought her to tears; overcome by guilt, she stood there sobbing until Hyatt took her in his arms.

"Dearest May," he said. "Don't cry. We understand each other now. That's all that matters."

May looked up at Hyatt; their faces only inches from one another. She boosted herself up on her toes and closed her eyes, her lips parted ever so slightly, anticipating his. Hyatt kissed her gently before he let go. He took hold of her hands. His eyes, two dark stars that obscured everything else around her, stared deep into hers.

"Now, if you will excuse me," Hyatt said, abruptly, "I have work to do."

"It's Halloween," May exclaimed.

"So it is," he retreated to his desk.

"I was going to go out after dinner," she went on. "I thought it would be fun to watch children trick-or-treat."

Hyatt remained silent. May took a step closer, and then another.

"Robert," it was the first time she had ever addressed him by his first name, "I..."

When she placed her slender hand on the back of his neck he looked at her.

"I know," he told her.

"You don't know what I was going to say."

"You're sorry. I understand."

"That's not it at all," said May. "I love you. I have always loved you."

Hyatt stood up. At first, May thought he might storm out of the room. Instead, he held her face in his hands.

"Dearest May," he said, and kissed her a second time. "I love you, too."

Tears filled her eyes for the second time that afternoon. She looked at her feet as she rubbed the tears away.

"What do we do now?" she asked.

"We wait," he said, and let her go.

"What about tonight?"

"Excuse me?"

"Halloween?"

"Oh that," said Hyatt. "What is this renewed interest in such a pagan ritual? Aren't you getting too old for that?"

"You can be my escort."

"We can never marry."

"I liked it better when you were kissing me," May told him. "Less of a chance to say something we might both regret."

"I am serious, May," he said. "There are some things in my life I have to work out."

"Another girl?"

"No, dearest one," said Hyatt. "Nothing like that."

May put her arms around his neck, tilted her head, and waited for another kiss. If Hyatt had thrown her in his bed in that instant, she would not have protested. Hyatt kissed her gently again. In turn, she pressed her face into his, pressing her lips hard against his as she slipped her tongue into his mouth. When he groaned she thought she might wither in his arms.

His hardness pressed against her lower abdomen, as her left hand reached for him, struggling with the trouser fly fasteners.

"May!" Alice shouted from the foot of the stairs. "Are you bothering Mr. Hyatt again?"

"No," she broke free from his grip. "We're just talking."

Whatever implied guilt came with her statement; her mother chose to ignore it.

"Leave Mr. Hyatt alone, May," her mother called from the second floor. "Come down to the kitchen. I need your help."

Hyatt kissed May once more.

"She's probably coming up," she whispered. "I can't stand this."

"May! Now!" her mother shouted.

"Coming, mother!" May replied as she headed for the stairs.

The second thing that almost ruined their relationship occurred several months later. It happened in the spring, after exams were over. When May arrived home, her father informed her that he and her mother had invited some friends and family over for a barbeque. On the menu were steaks, hamburgers, chicken, and a pig on a roast—in short, all the foods that May despised. The 'family' that her father had invited was relations from his side; like May, her mother had been an only child, while her father's kin was an ill-mannered, brutish lot whose origins began in the tenements of Hells' Kitchen (her father's grandfather) and Fabric Row along 4th Street near Bainbridge in Philadelphia; and before that, from Ireland and the Ukraine respectively. Dark, dreary places, May imagined, that brought out the worst in people. There was certain pressure on May; no one could deny that. She loathed the idea of being paraded around her yard, like some prize cow, as the first in the family to complete an entire year of college. May's cousin Colette had gone to City College of New York, exactly one year after that school finally admitted women to their student ranks, the year May began high school; but, according to Alice, Colette was stricken with what the family genuinely regarded as a 'weak will.' Ultimately, Colette ended up leaving City College and went to live with distant cousins in upstate New York where she gave birth to a baby boy named Elijah who was as vicious and feral as a child could be. Some family members speculated that it was a curse put upon Colette for having a child out of wedlock; other relations, echoing back to the ancestry who came from County Clare, Ireland, maintained that Elijah might be a changeling—a Fae creature switched with Colette's real baby shortly after birth—and one whose purpose was merely to disrupt the lives of mortals who encountered him. The father of the boy, the story goes, was an Italian student from City College named Amerigo Vicci who, once evidence of Colette's pregnancy became known to all, had disappeared. Fellow students believed Amerigo had been called back to Sicily on urgent family business; New York City's finest kept the file open, but made no real efforts to locate a 'guinea' who, like so many others before him, had probably ended up at the bottom of the East River. In all of this there was, May supposed, some lesson in the woeful tale of Cousin Colette, something to do with virtuous women, the suave seduction skills of Sicilian men, and the trappings of co-ed higher education. At the time the story was told, May was only fourteen years old. Sex was something on the periphery of her life like the muffled cries of her mother late at night and squeak of bedsprings. Above all else, intercourse was something to be avoided before marriage, and then only as necessary if she became a wife. For these reasons and more, May took great offense at being lumped into the same category as Cousin Colette, scoffing at the notion her mother suggested when she went on to pontificate that the wanton blood that ran through Colette's veins was in fact the same that coursed through hers. And now, having completed her first year at Bryn Mawr, with her own hymen still intact, at least for the time being, May was forced to endure the whole clan that included Colette and her bastard Elijah.

"But you have to go!" she pleaded with Hyatt.

He had told her that he would not be attending the party, stating strangers made him nervous. But May, distraught over spending even less time with him, would not hear it.

"I have work to do," he said.

His rooms were hot. May felt perspiration coat every inch of her body, but the feeling was nothing new. It happened no matter the season whenever she remained in Hyatt's presence for too long.

"You cannot expect me to go alone," said May.

"If I wasn't a tenant—"

"But you're not just a tenant, Robert," she countered.

"I meant to say if I wasn't here, then—"

"My whole life would be different," she cut him off. "And you know that."

Hyatt took her in his arms. He kissed her forehead.

"What would you do?" he asked. "Introduce me as your lover?"

"Robert," May blushed as she pushed free from his grip. "Don't say such things."

"I am sorry."

"It's because I will not, right?"

"No," said Hyatt. "It's because I have work to do."

"Do you go with other women, Robert?" May asked. "When you are away? Are they whores who take money?"

"Where is this coming from?"

"I want to know."

"Are you asking me if I will save myself for you?"

"Don't be like that," she snapped. "I am not stupid."

"Listen, May," he said. "I love you. You know that. Do I pressure you? Do I force you? Take you against your will?"

"I want to," she told him. "It's just..."

"What?"

May stood before him, her head lowered. "I want to know if...if I am doing it right," she whispered. "That's all."

Their conversation lapsed into hurried kisses and caresses after that, the way it increasingly did when they were alone together. They collapsed on the small sofa beside the desk. May slipped the shoulder straps down from her dress, freeing her breasts. With one hand behind Hyatt's neck she drew his face into her bosom, while she fumbled with the zipper on his trousers. Hyatt slipped free, stood up, and unfastened his belt. He slid his pants down around his knees, his erection only inches from May's face. She took his cock in her hands, and kissed it once, twice, three times before taking the tip into her mouth. When Hyatt grabbed her head she moaned but did not resist. His ejaculate tasted bitter when he came in her mouth. Afterward, she lay back on the sofa, lifted her skirt up around her waist, and pulled off her panties. She took hold of him, guiding his again-erect penis toward her wet vaginal lips. Hyatt lifted her buttocks with one hand and slipped a small blanket beneath her. When her hymen broke the pain was sharp, but brief. Minutes later, Hyatt pulled out and ejaculated on her thighs.

After May cleaned up in Hyatt's bathroom, she returned to where he sat at his desk. The bloodied blanket was gone. Her breasts were still exposed, not for any seductive reason, but because of the heat in the room. A small fan blew on an end table beside the sofa, stirring hot air around the room. May leaned in close, allowing the artificial breeze to play over her skin.

"I will come back tonight," she said. "When my parents are asleep."

"Too dangerous," he said.

The hour eventually arrived when May found herself in the backyard, surrounded by family she hardly knew, as they congratulated her, told her crazy tales of New York and Philadelphia in the old days, and all the while the only thought that ran through May's mind was how good it felt for Hyatt to fuck her; true, she was sore, but she wanted more. And she wanted it soon.

At some point in the late afternoon she stood facing the back porch. May spotted Hyatt, through a window, as he passed through the kitchen. She left her cousin Colette standing there with five-year-old Elijah who gnashed his stunted, crooked teeth.

Inside the house, May found the door leading from the kitchen down into the basement had been left open. Her first thought was Elijah. Her cousin's bastard had a knack for getting into trouble. What if he had gone into the house alone and fallen down the stairs? She smiled, picturing the accident as divine providence, but her musings didn't last long. A scraping sound came from the basement. May darted down the stairs.

The air downstairs was cool, sweet-scented. Hyatt, May soon realized, was not there. Had he gone into the basement at all? At the far end of the basement, there was the old-fashioned arched door that marked the entrance to the root cellar that Hyatt and her father had constructed when she was a little girl. The late afternoon sunlight shined through the basement windows to her left, casting long luminous shafts across the stone arch that outlined the door. The dark and polished keystone rippled with shades of green, blue, and purple. Minute carvings in the rest of the stones were visible now. Until that day May had never noticed them. Her parents had forbidden her to enter the basement alone. On those rare occasions when she went against her parents' wishes the basement was never lit by the late day sun the way it was now. Her father had placed several steamer trunks and other boxes forward of the root cellar door. May moved closer, winding her way around the trunks to get a better look. Each stone in the arch offered simple bas reliefs of designs that appeared Celtic in origin— spirals and intricate knots, bearded men and boars, horses and snakes, and Fae-like creatures that defied any association with mythologies May knew. Her fingertips rubbed each stone slowly, savoring the feel of each carving. Pressing her nose close to one stone in the arch, she smelled old earth, antiquity, a portion of feral history before the Cross came to tame the pagan countryside. Her eyes followed the wild ripple of the door's wood grain as she felt the room slip away; casting her gaze further to the right she saw that the latch was undone. The black iron padlock that had always kept the door secured dangled uselessly from the latch's end.

"Robert?" May called out once she had opened the root cellar door.

Beyond the threshold, there was no light. A pitch that mirrored those places in the heavens, the darkest dark, stretched wide and deep between the stars; a darkness that smelled of damp earth and woodland decay. A void, May saw now, shifted in waveform, blackness stirring against blackness that was, when she cautiously reached out with one hand, cold against her fingertips like a wrought-iron gate in winter. She took a step forward. Behind her, whatever light that had come in through the basement windows, the light she hoped would illuminate the immediate vicinity just inside the root cellar, stopped at the threshold, as if acknowledging the strength of that darkness that was older than the sun itself. If May closed the door behind her she feared she might not only become trapped in the frigid dark, but become part of it, that the absence of everything which dwelled there might consume her and doing so reduce her to base elements that would be dissolved into this strange local void. And then, rendered immovable by whatever had gripped her in that place, there came through that utter darkness a shimmering that took on the shape of the man she loved, as if he had walked a great distance along an empty noonday desert road, fading in and out of view against the rising heat. Seconds later, though to May it felt as if hours had passed, he joined her where she stood.

"May," Hyatt said, matter-of-factly. "You should not be here, dearest one."

He carried an ochre-colored ceramic jug plugged with a cork and sealed with wax. The moment he set the vessel down May fell into his arms, shaking as she sobbed; unable, as she was, to process what she had just witnessed.

"I was looking for you," she confessed.

"You mustn't come after me here," he told her. "Never. Do you understand?"

"What...what is out there?" she nodded past his shoulder.

"Later."

"I want to know."

"Soon."

"No," said May. "Now. Do my parents know what's out there?"

Hyatt kissed her forehead. "Even if they did, they would not understand," he said.

"Why won't you show me?" asked May.

"I was your age when I saw it the first time," he told her. "Younger, actually."

"What is it?"

"Stay here," he instructed her.

The scant light pooling at the threshold vanished once Hyatt closed the root cellar door and locked it from the inside.

May jumped when Hyatt took her by the waist, holding her tightly against his side as they walked further into the dark. She had no idea of how far they had traveled. It felt to her as if they had covered a great distance. She felt nauseous, but it soon passed as she kept her body pressed against his.

Then it happened. The first star she saw called to mind the one that guided the three wise men toward the manger of the baby Jesus. Growing up, it had been her favorite story at Christmas. Soon, there were other stars to the left and the right. A great void blocked out stars that should have been directly in front of them. Bright and strange constellations drew her attention away from the void. Beneath her feet, plush wild grass brushed against her ankles. Hyatt led her further until they reached the bottom of a low hill. What looked like rows of natural rock turned out to be exposed tree roots, some of them thicker than the trolley cars along Darby Road. May did not speak until Hyatt led her back to the root cellar where he unlocked the door, and they returned to the basement.

"It's better in the daylight," he told her. "Or when the moon is—"

May kissed him. "Promise me we will go back?" she asked.

"We will," he assured her. "Soon. But if you tell anyone of this—"

"Never," she said, and kissed him again.

Footsteps sounded overhead. The basement door opened at the stop of the stairs.

"May?" her mother called out. "Are you down there?"

"Just me, Mrs. Weldon," said Hyatt. "I am on my way up now."

He secured the padlock on the door latch and pocketed the skeletal key.

The basement door closed.

"Now what?" May asked.

"I go upstairs," he told her. "Then I will distract your parents while you slip past them and pretend you are out for a walk."

"Or?"

Hyatt lay her down on top of one of the old steamer trunks. The second time he made love to her hurt more than the first. When they finished, Hyatt left her alone and went up to the kitchen. May stood there, listening and waiting until she knew it was safe to return to the party. By the time she left the basement, twilight had fallen over the neighborhood.

Chapter Twenty-Eight: Keeper Of The Eastern Door—Vimy Ridge, 1917

One night, a low fog covered the pasture where the dead were laid out according to rank. Somewhere in the dark, a few soldiers vomited. A lone tenor sang an old Irish ballad. When Jenkins put his hand on his friend's shoulder, Hyatt jumped.

"Jesus," he said. "You scared me."

"Look," Jenkins pointed at the sky.

A single flare ignited and drifted downward. Sporadic machine gun fire sounded some distance away. When the flare went out, the shooting ceased.

"We're close," Hyatt said.

"What the hell is wrong with you, Hyatt?" a voice called out of the dark. It was Sergeant Lattimer, the platoon sergeant. "You're going to give away our position."

"Sergeant, you don't think the Germans can hear O'Malley singing?"

"Just keep your voice down."

"Sergeant Lattimer," Jenkins said. "Does anyone know where the reserve trench is?"

"I should have known," the platoon sergeant said. "Punch and Judy. Will the two of you shut the fuck up?"

"Eventually?" Jenkins asked.

"Or right now?" Hyatt added.

"I could have you both court-martialed," Lattimer stepped out from behind a tree. "No noise, remember?"

"I love this part," Jenkins cupped his ear to get a listen at the end of the ballad O'Malley sang.

"I am serious."

Jenkins loosed a loud fart. "A peace offering for our Kraut friends," he said and winked at Sergeant Lattimer.

"Have you no manners?" Lattimer asked.

"Sorry," he said. "I wouldn't want to face the firing squad over something as—"

"Will you shut the fuck up?" Lattimer hissed. "You're going to get us killed!"

"But we're behind friendly lines," said Jenkins.

"Right," Hyatt said. "Who would kill us here?"

"Well, not you and me," he said before he slowly turned his gaze upon the platoon sergeant.

"Shut your face!" Lattimer finally shouted. "That's an order!"

Somewhere near midnight, Hyatt's unit arrived at the reserve trenches. The 78th had been picked to relieve their British counterparts from the IV Corps. Upon arrival at the reserve trenches, the 78th's orders were changed. With an assault on Vimy Ridge imminent and more British artillery guns being put into place, Hyatt's company was attached to another battalion from the 4th Division already in place at the support trenches forward of the reserve trenches.

Since January, officers from Canadian and British forces had met with French officers who had been present at the Battle of Verdun to learn what they could about German defenses and attack strategies. On the faces of those Canadian soldiers already manning the support trenches was a look of dread and fatigue, the knowledge of a pending large-scale assault, and the bombardments from the German long-range guns—aimed at British artillery units toward the rear of the front—that shook the earth. The concussive poundings desecrated shallow graves nearby, dislodging corpses of the fallen who, exposed to the winter air, froze in contorted positions, making them appear as if the artillery bombardment had awakened them from death. The deteriorating conditions of the trenches themselves—blasted to hell and manned, for the most part, by gaunt young men—did not give the new men much hope. The faces of those veterans already in the trenches appeared sallow from stress and malnutrition. The wonder with which sad and disbelieving eyes stared at Hyatt, Jenkins, and the other new reinforcements who were freshly fed, healthy, and devoid, for the time being, of fear, convinced, perhaps, that the new men were not real at all, but part of some greater war-induced hallucination. All of this, coupled with the constant work on the 'subways' forward of the front line and the ever-present threat of disease that lurked everywhere despite the frigid winter temperatures, pointed toward some great and calamitous conflagration whose light and torrential energy threatened to make the myth of the Angel of Mons a child's fairy tale, a pending event of obliteration from which there would be no escape.

"At chow earlier I heard some Brits talking about a trench raid that was executed the other day," Jenkins said. "Nearly seven hundred Canadian soldiers were killed. You believe that?"

Hyatt had stowed his gear beneath the firebay where he and Jenkins had been posted. He stood on the fire step, peering out into the darkness over the front-line trenches and into the barbed-wired No Man's Land that lay between them and German trenches. A high-pitched whistle sounded somewhere overhead followed by the concussive faraway boom of a long-range German gun. Hyatt thought it odd, in that brief instant, that he could hear the shell coming in before the sound of the cannon's fire, but any further musings were interrupted by an explosion far to the left, beyond the edge of the forward support trench. The ensuing wave of dirt and debris knocked Hyatt off the fire step. He expected soldiers to be running helter-skelter as men screamed out in pain. But no one moved. The British artillery battery at the rear fired a volley of shells, five in all, that lit the distant ridge for an instant until darkness reigned once more.

"Jenkins," Hyatt said as he climbed onto the fire step. "Are you all right?"

The other American did not move. Jenkins's hands gripped a sandbag in front of him. His rifle lay in the dirt just outside the trench.

Hyatt patted him on the shoulder. Jenkins slumped forward, and his knees buckled. Hyatt pulled him backward to get a better look. Where Jenkins's face should have been was a large steaming chunk of shrapnel. Hyatt screamed, letting Jenkins go in the process, and vomited.

"Hyatt!" Lattimer shouted. "Is that you?"

"It's Jenkins, Sergeant," he said. He was unable to look away from his friend's ruined face as Jenkins lay upon the fire step. "He's dead."

"It's war, Hyatt," his platoon sergeant said. "It happens."

"What do we do now?"

"Now? Now we cart his carcass to the rear," said Lattimer. "So he doesn't stink up the place come morning."

The distant thunder of German guns sounded once more. Hyatt counted six volleys and countless whistles. As he crouched down, holding his helmet tightly against his head, he counted the seconds until the first round hit somewhere toward the rear. The next three shells landed one after another, their explosions going off in the woods that separated the trenches from some ancient farmland. Several more artillery rounds exploded in rapid succession—two near the support trenches and four along the front line. Men cried out in the dark. Something sailed through the air, arms flailing, and landed atop the dugout behind him.

"Shit," Lattimer said, and spat.

He wiped blood from his face.

"Are you injured?" Hyatt asked.

"No, it's from this guy," Lattimer pulled down the lifeless torso of a dead soldier. "What's left of him, anyway."

Somewhere someone blew a whistle as the British guns fired back at the ridge.

"In the dugout," Lattimer tossed the soldier's torso aside. "Now!"

The last volley of artillery rounds from the German side was short but precise. Dirt rained down on Hyatt and Lattimer as they lay in the deep dugout along with other members of their squad. Within minutes, it was over.

"I'll be right back," said Lattimer. "Stay put."

Hyatt kept his rifle at the ready, pointed toward the fire bay he had just abandoned. One by one, the other squad members followed suit.

Lattimer returned to the dugout with two medics and a litter in tow.

"Ready?" he asked.

"What?" Hyatt replied. "Now?"

He followed Lattimer and the medics out of the dugout.

Faceless Jenkins lay on the fire step. The legless torso of the other soldier was on the duckboard where Lattimer had deposited him.

"Are you injured?" one of the medics asked. He looked odd in the trench. A short, thin Sikh with thick-lens eyeglasses that were dirty and scratched. "Are you bleeding?"

"No, I—" Hyatt started to say.

"He's not injured," the Sikh said to the second medic.

"Make sure, Hajj," said the second one. "He may be in shock. Or he may be faking it. You know how these Americans are."

"Toomey," said the Sikh. "My name is Dhuda."

"Right, Dudley—"

"Dhuda."

"I am not hurt," said Hyatt. "It's Jenkins."

He nodded at his friend who lay against the trench wall, one leg dangled from the fire step.

Toomey stepped forward to get a closer look. Then he took a step back.

"This man's face is missing," he said.

Dhuda crouched next to Jenkins to examine him. He held a dry cell flashlight and shined the light into Jenkins's ruined face.

"This man is dead," said Dhuda. "I am only a medic, not a magic man."

"You can use the litter, sergeant," said Toomey. "Now, if you will excuse me and Duckworth here. We have—"

"Dhuda."

"—actual injured men to attend to."

"Wait," Lattimer said. "You mean we have to haul him out ourselves?"

"I won't tell you how to run your squad, sergeant," Dhuda said, "but perhaps your man here and another private can carry the corpses out."

He nodded at the legless corpse that lay on the duckboard near the body of Jenkins.

"Corpse and a half, really," Toomey said.

"I see what you did there," said Dhuda, toeing the legless corpse on the duckboard. "Very clever, indeed."

"How kind of you to notice," the other medic replied.

Dhuda turned off his light. He and Toomey ducked into a connecting trench and vanished into the dark.

Hyatt and Lattimer struggled with Jenkins's body as they placed him on the litter. This was no small feat for them, owing to the litter being no more than two poles with a blanket affixed to it and the dead soldier's size; a giant in life, Jenkins weighed more as a dead man.

Lattimer took hold of the legless corpse next. He laid the dead man down atop Jenkins's legs, careful not to allow any more of the dead man's innards to fall out.

"That wasn't so bad," he remarked afterward as he washed his hands with water from Jenkins's canteen before he tossed it aside.

They moved through the connecting trench. Soldiers sat in the dark on fire steps. Some whispered to one another. Others sat alone smoking cigarettes. All of them averted their gaze as the two men hauled Jenkins past.

"Set him down," Lattimer said. "You! What's your name, soldier?"

"Bennington," the soldier answered.

"Who's your squad leader?"

"Sergeant Raven."

"Sergeant Raven?"

"I am here," a voice called out of the dark.

"Need to borrow Bennington, here," Lattimer said. "Bringing out a dead man."

"Who is it?"

"Jenkins."

"I will help too," Raven said. "Come on, Bennington."

The four men each took hold of the makeshift stretcher and hauled the corpses through the support trench. Behind them, over No Man's Land, forward of the front line, a flare went off overhead. German machine gun fire erupted followed by the machine guns on the Canadian side. They kept moving. By the light from the flare drifting over the support trench, Hyatt saw Sergeant Raven's face. Before shipping out to England he had heard rumors that the Canadian army had allowed Native Canadians to volunteer to fight. Until that night, Hyatt had never seen any North American natives, Canadian or otherwise.

"Where are you from, Sergeant Raven?" Hyatt asked.

"Canada," Raven answered. "Like you."

"I am from outside Philadelphia," he told him. "That's in—"

"I know where Pennsylvania is, private," he cut him off.

"Easy, Hyatt," said Lattimer. "You don't want to make Chief Stompin' Mad angry."

"Fuck you, Lattimer," said Raven. "I am Tom Raven of the Ka Nee-en Ka people, a member of the Iroquois Confederacy, Keepers of the Eastern Door. And what are you, son of a white whore?"

Lattimer grinned. "See, Hyatt," he said. "Sergeant Raven's people here are the very ones James Fennimore Cooper wrote about."

"Mohican?" Hyatt asked.

"I say," Bennington chimed in, "these corpses are quite heavy. What say we take a break?"

The flare faded out. The machine gun fire stopped. And despite Bennington's wish, the four men kept moving.

Soon, they ascended from the support trench and walked across the pockmarked earth past the British artillery battery and their cold steel cannons that stood silent in the dark. Beyond the artillery guns they came upon small groups of British soldiers—each one beyond the reach of Saint George, far from the Crown, battered and shell-shocked—who stood about, hollow-eyed and haggard, fresh from several months on the front line, silent as they dreamed of remote Albion where loved ones waited for their triumphant return. In the dark they appeared like wraiths behind a thin veil, lost and scared. At last Hyatt and the others reached a hedgerow that marked the boundary between the war-torn land of the living and the realm of the dead.

"Not much dignity in this," said Lattimer when they set down the litter.

They stood now at the edge of a mass grave. Hyatt glimpsed Jenkins's ruined face as it faced the stars, a gross cavity of splintered bone and nearly frozen blood that had already blackened. He looked away. Raven chanted a song, yet none but the Native Canadian understood the words, but for Hyatt and the others, a lament was a lament in any language.

The air was crisp, cold, and carried a faint hint of the dead mixed with chloride of lime and lye. On the far side of the mass grave waited tall mounds of frozen earth that would be pushed back over the fallen when there was no more room.

"Does anyone know if Jenkins was a Christian?" Lattimer asked when Raven's song had ended. "I feel like maybe the chaplain should be here."

241

"He is here," Raven nodded at the mass grave. "Killed three days before we arrived in this place. I see his spirit atop the mound over yonder."

"Are you serious?" Bennington asked.

"No," his squad leader answered. "Only a madman would profess to see ghosts in this place. No spirits linger here."

"You want to say something, Hyatt?" Lattimer asked.

"I am not particularly religious," Hyatt answered.

"You were chums, right?"

"Sure."

"Say something," he said. "Anything. Don't let the last thing Jenkins hears be the pagan song of this savage."

"Keep it up, Lattimer," said Raven. "I will gut you where you stand."

"Jenkins was the first friend I made after I joined up with the Canadian forces," said Hyatt. "May the angels never let him look back on this place."

"Touching," Lattimer said. He gripped the litter handles at Jenkins's feet. "Now, let's get this done. I am cold, I am tired, and I am hungry."

"Back to normal," said Bennington.

"Stow it, private."

Raven and Bennington took hold of the litter handles where Jenkins's ruined head lay. Hyatt joined Lattimer at the dead man's feet.

"On three," said Raven, and counted off.

When they tilted the litter toward the grave, the big man's body and the remains of the other soldier slipped off. Jenkins tumbled against the frozen slope. The legless torso slid to a halt half-way down. Jenkins's body rolled over a few times. His arms pin-wheeled against the hard earth. The sound reminded Hyatt of potatoes getting dumped from a sack onto a picnic table. At last the dead man's body came to rest beside the others that lay there, his ruined face no longer visible.

Chapter Twenty-Nine: Cold Comfort—Pittsfield MA, 2012

Elinor unlocked the door to her father's house. The moment she stepped over the threshold she was reminded not of her childhood, but of her own mortality, for the prevalent odor that struck her was one she associated with the elderly— the aroma of decay and death in small doses. Beneath the smell of her father's advancing years, an odor that wafted from the coats he kept on a rack in the foyer, a scent that had slowly permeated everything he wore, there was another aroma. She detected the advance of mold that lay hidden beneath floorboards, behind the walls, and in other invisible places. As she held her breath, Elinor picked up several letters from the foyer floor. Each envelope addressed to her father came from some organization or another related to academia seeking donations. As she made a fan of the letters, and waved them beneath her nose, she wondered if her father had ever sent money to them, or if he followed her practice and simply deposited them into the trash without opening them.

As she moved deeper into the house, Elinor was struck by the bookshelves that lined every wall. In the living room were the original shelves she had known as a child. Now, though she could not recall a time when her father had informed her that new ones had been installed, additional bookshelves lined the walls from floor to ceiling in the dining room as well. Perusing various titles, she realized that her father no longer kept his books in any order. This was an anathema to her, as unlike her father, Elinor sought order among her books—both at home and in her office on campus. Moreover, the bookshelves, new and old, reminded her that she had been the only girl in grade school whose family did not own a television. Instead, her childhood had been spent immersed in the poetry of Cummings, Pound, Moore, Stevens, and Crane. Later on, adrift in the throes of adolescence, her tastes would lean toward her mother's books—Plath, Olson, Creeley, and Bly, as well as novelists that both of her parents admired like LeGuin and Camus, Forrester and Dinesen, Dreiser and Faulkner, Porter and Wolfe, Stegner and Styron. But sincere satisfaction had not come to her until she pulled down a copy of *The Savage Mind* by Claude Levi-Strauss, a book that neither her mother nor her father remembered purchasing.

After reading Levi-Strauss's book, Elinor had written a series of short stories, seven in all (modeled after Dinesen's *Gothic Tales*), about a faraway planet whose history had been altered by a manned spaceship and the meddlesome humans who crash-landed there. She mailed the first two stories to Asimov's Science Fiction and Weird Tales respectively, and when the rejection letters came back she took the letters and stories into the backyard and burned them on the grill. Her focus afterward was no longer a life in imaginative fiction, but in the life of the primitive mind.

Over time, Elinor's fascination with the past translated to a PhD in archaeology. What little free time she had in graduate school was spent reconciling her adolescence with a therapist. Several months into her sessions Elinor disclosed that the only reason she had written those ridiculous stories, as she often referred to them in the years that followed her brief attempt at the literary life, was to somehow win her father's favor since she was convinced that he had kept none of the mementos she made while growing up that included grade school drawings and poems, hand-made birthday cards, and notes composed in her penmanship; not even a photograph of Elinor and her father together existed from the time she had first come into the world.

Presently, as she deposited her father's mail on the kitchen table, Elinor dismissed, at least for the moment, any thoughts of her past. She dialed her father's cell phone number from the old phone on the kitchen wall.

"Elinor?" Miller said when he answered.

"Where are you?" Elinor asked. "Are you all right?"

"I am at the hotel."

"In Philadelphia?"

"Where else?"

"It's just that I haven't heard from you."

"I feel good," he said. "What are you doing at the house?"

The way her father referred to the place where she had grown up as 'the house' was unsettling, as if neither he nor anyone else ever put personal stock into it. In truth, the house in Pittsfield had never been *home*. Growing up there, Elinor was strictly limited to so many rooms—her own bedroom of course; a small room off the kitchen that served as a family room, offering a loveseat, an armchair, a coffee table, and an old television that did not work; and the kitchen itself where her family took their meals (the dining room was used only when her parents entertained other adults). The living room in the front of the house was a veritable museum that no one ever visited. The room from which she was absolutely forbidden was her father's study.

"I wasn't sure when you were coming home," his daughter said. "I thought I might surprise you."

"That's not like you," Miller said.

"Maybe I am turning into a sap in my old age."

"Elinor, that doesn't suit you at all."

"I am up for sabbatical, soon," she said. "I thought—"

"What?" her father snapped. "You thought you could escort me to various doctors to find out if I am losing my memory."

Elinor drew a deep breath, held it for a second or two, and exhaled.

"No," her voice wavered when she spoke. "I thought you may want help updating the Hyatt biography."

"Elinor, I am quite capable of handling this work myself," said Miller. "Besides, Heddings came by to visit me just now—"

"At the hotel?" she asked, choosing to ignore the fact that her father may have imagined the whole thing.

"Yes," he replied. "It appears the updated biography may not be a done deal. I mean on Heddings's end."

"I never liked him."

"No one likes Schuyler Heddings, my dear," her father informed her. "Anyway, May Weldon has given me some letters from her private collection along with an introduction she wrote for the biography."

"That's great news."

"Yes, she asked me to call on her tomorrow," he went on. "A few days ago, she looked as if she would die any day—"

"Dad, don't say such things."

Miller laughed, and said, "You sound just like your mother."

"I am sorry."

"Don't be," he replied. "So, it was all very mysterious."

"What was?"

"Ms. Weldon," he said. "It appears she's one of those rare creatures that has overcome her life-threatening cancer. It's uncanny, really."

"Remission?"

"I'm not sure, Ellie. Perhaps something altogether different."

"You said you are going to see her once more?"

"Oh yes," her father said. "Tomorrow. Then I plan to catch an early afternoon train back north. I may not make it home until after nine in the evening."

"Dad?"

"Yes?"

"Do you want me to meet you at Penn Station?"

"Don't be ridiculous. How does one get lost on a train?"

"I was thinking about the city at large."

"You are just like your mother, Ellie," said Miller. "You worry too much. My car is at the station in Springfield. I will be fine."

"Dad?"

"Yes?"

"Will you make an appointment to see Dr. Moran?"

There was a long pause. When her father did speak again there was no fight left in his voice.

"I have been writing notes to myself as of late, Ellie," he said.

"Oh, Dad," Elinor said. She bit her lower lip a moment. "For how long?"

"With any frequency? The last month or so," her father replied.

Now it was Elinor's turn to pause. If she pushed, she worried she might lose him for good.

"Dad, this will not get better on its own," she said. "You have to see a doctor."

"Do you know what scares me most?" Miller asked.

"I cannot imagine."

"Being put out to pasture, Ellie," he announced. "Reaching a place in my life where I no longer recognize you, where I no longer remember the work I have done over the past four decades."

"You will still have me," his daughter said. "If it comes to that, I can remind you."

"A cold comfort, but good to know," he told her. "Say, aren't you teaching this week?"

"I can cancel my class tomorrow," she said. "I will be here when you get home."

"There's no reason to burden yourself," her father said. "Right now, I am—"

"But I want to."

"Very well."

"Dad?"

"Yes?"

"I love you."

"I love you, too," Miller said. "You were always my pride and joy. I know I never showed it much. But you are. Good night, Ellie."

After the call ended, Elinor wandered through the house. Her father's words followed her like some relentless ghost, a specter of the life that could have been. Sentiment was one thing. Truth was something entirely different. On the second floor she found the door to her father's study ajar, the room dark.

Chapter Thirty: Thunderheads And Dark Spaces—Vimy Ridge, 1917

Two weeks later, the cold spell broke. In the French countryside, that meant rain. The coming of spring also meant the rising stench of stagnant water that remained in the trenches despite the troops employing water pumps several times a day to keep the trenches from flooding. A few hundred yards from the support trenches, the mass grave remained open; the bodies in it gave off a rank odor.

There were other changes that came with the warmer temperatures. The Winnipeg Grenadiers were ordered to relieve, at last, their British brothers-in-arms on the front line and for the 78th Battalion, the process took an additional week. Hyatt's company, however, was the first to move and they completed their transition in a single rain-sodden night.

After disposing of Jenkins's corpse, Hyatt had learned that his company commander had been killed on the same night. His new company commander was a short, thin, uptight barrister back in the real world named Cruddup. Captain Cruddup was accompanied by his Quartermaster Sergeant: a hulking, mean-spirited, square-jawed Irishman by the name of McCool. On the first morning of being positioned on the front line, Hyatt was awoken by Captain Cruddup and Sergeant McCool before dawn.

"Stand up, soldier," said McCool.

Hyatt had been dreaming at that moment when Sergeant McCool shook him from his sleep. In the hours before stand-to, he dreamed not of dead men but his sister Matilda who was grown now, out walking in a field at twilight, the first stars showing in the sky, darker shades of green in the woodland that bordered the pasture, the air around Matilda festooned with fireflies, blinking miniature stars that mimicked the unseen constellations waiting patiently for the sun to acquiesce, to give over its reign on that side of the world. Cicada songs were adrift in the near night and his sister was humming to the music. As he followed her, Matilda was unaware of his presence. Thunderheads laced with lightning colored purple and white, flashes revealed hues of pale green and blue in the dark cloud columns, drifted in from the west. Before the storm arrived, there was the pregnant fragrance of the coming rain. Drafts of cooler air cut through the humidity, causing Matilda to rub her arms as she walked across the field dotted with dandelions. When the rains fell in voluptuous drops, Hyatt's sister walked on, heading for the shadows between the trees at the field's edge. In those dark spaces lurked something that compelled Matilda onward through the lightning and the pouring rain. Whatever called her toward the wood, Hyatt did not know, for it was a thing both timeless and feral, something as ominous as it was eternal. Gone now were the fireflies, silent the cicada song; foreboding the thunder that crashed and cracked overhead. His sister stepped over the threshold where opposing branches from two Hawthorn trees formed an arch, and, having done so without looking back, she vanished. Hyatt called out her name, but each time his voice was drowned out by thunder, each time he shouted louder and louder until his voice became the thunder itself that rattled the Hawthorn trees.

"All right, laddie," said McCool, "Quit your hollering before you wake up the Krauts."

Hyatt lay on duckboard beneath the fire step. He slid backward until his back pressed against the trench wall, the dream a dull ache in his heart now. McCool kicked him in the leg.

"Up, Yank," he said. "One day when this war is over you can tell me all about this Matilda who makes you shout in your sleep. She must be something."

"Matilda's my sister," Hyatt said.

"Whatever you say," the Quartermaster sergeant replied. "Now if you don't mind, Prince Charming. It's time for stand-to."

As if on cue, sporadic machine gun fire sounded from the German side.

"Dirty Hun sons of bitches!" McCool cried.

He climbed onto the fire step, unslung his Lee-Enfield, and returned fire as others began shooting along the fire step.

Hyatt climbed to his feet, using his rifle to brace himself. Just as he stepped up onto the fire step and was about to peer over the top of the trench, cold dirt, kicked up by German machine gun fire, temporarily blinded him. Someone gripped his collar as mortar rounds exploded nearby and pulled him down onto the duckboard.

"Kraut bastards got up on the wrong side today," McCool said.

A gurgling, choking sound caught the sergeant's attention. Hyatt peered past McCool and saw Captain Cruddup holding his neck as blood spurted out from between his fingers.

"Captain," Hyatt started toward him.

McCool pushed him back. "You just stay low," he said.

Cruddup's eyes went wide as he stared over the two men at the sandbags that lined the top of the trench. He spat blood and slumped to his left.

"Is he dead?" Hyatt asked.

"He's with the devil now, boy-o," McCool said, and spat. "Fucking officers are bullet magnets, nothing more."

Somewhere a whistle blew. Hyatt followed McCool's lead and donned his gas mask. McCool fastened his helmet over the mask. Hyatt followed suit.

Further down the line, yellow smoke wafted past two soldiers manning their fire step. Only one of the soldiers put his gas mask on in time, while the other, experiencing the burning in his lungs as the gas cloud lingered about him, scrambled up and out of the trench. Hyatt watched as the soldier ran blindly into No Man's Land and became ensnared in barbed wire. Several mortar rounds rained down behind Hyatt. Just as he was about to duck into the dugout behind the fire step, he witnessed the soldier tear himself free from the barbed wire and fall face-first into the mud where he triggered a landmine. A parabola of body parts and blood arched upward. Then the dead man's remains rained down into the soft wet mud.

The mortar barrage ceased. Less than a minute later, the German machine gun fire stopped.

"You see one of the Kaiser's cocksuckers," McCool shouted at Hyatt, "you shoot. Otherwise, save your ammunition."

A single shot from the German side knocked the Irishman sideways. McCool landed flat on his back against the duckboard.

"Sergeant?" Hyatt was down at his side now.

A fresh volley of gunfire erupted, Canadians and Germans shooting at one another across the wide No Man's Land that separated the two lines.

Another whistle blew. To Hyatt's right, further down the line, someone gave the all-clear. Hyatt kept his gasmask on.

"Don't fetch the chappy yet, private," said McCool, removing his helmet and then his gas mask. "I am still alive."

"The chaplain's dead," Hyatt told him.

"Figures," he said. McCool examined his helmet. "I'll be damned."

"Are you ok?"

"I haven't gone west yet. Look at that. A Kraut round stuck in the steel. Feel that!"

He offered Hyatt his helmet. Hyatt took it and rubbed his hand over the surface, feeling the round that had pierced halfway through McCool's helmet. He took off his own helmet after that and removed his gasmask to get a better look.

"You want to stay down here and chew the rag?" McCool asked. "Or you want to join the fight?"

Hyatt and the sergeant climbed onto the fire step once more and joined the others who continued shooting at the Germans. The night sky turned a dark shade of blue during the thirty-minute exchange. Just before it ended, Hyatt spotted a silhouette in the forward-most enemy line. He aimed at his target and fired. The silhouette dropped out of sight. When soldiers on either side of No Man's Land became weary of shooting, they began lobbing hand grenades. The battle lasted until daybreak. Whistle blasts, in three quick successions, signaled the end of the firefight.

"Hyatt," sergeant Lattimer appeared next to him now. "Some fight, huh?"

"Private Hyatt?" McCool said, and laughed. "No offense, boy-o, but—"

A single shot from a distance ended the conversation. The bullet caught McCool beneath the left eye, blowing out the back of his head. He fell backward and lay on the duckboard below with his legs splayed.

Lattimer grabbed Hyatt by the arm and pulled him down off the fire step.

"Just stay down," the sergeant told him. Small arms fire continued unabated. "Jesus Christ, Hyatt," said Lattimer, nodding at McCool whose lifeless eyes stared back at them. "No offense, but you are bad luck."

The following week, the front-line trenches were invaded by frogs. For three days, the frogs were Hyatt's only company. Other members of his unit refused to man the fire step near him, fearing that by some unexplained and paranormal phenomenon their fate would turn out just the same as Jenkins, Captain Cruddup, and Sergeant McCool. Intermittent freezing rain fell. Hyatt worked alongside others in his unit, lifting sections of the duckboard and clearing out excess water via pumps and helmets along with the frogs that seemed to multiply by the hour. The work was done as needed, always between morning and evening hate. Hyatt was grateful for the camaraderie. When the troops weren't busy ridding the trenches of rainwater, there were other chores that were performed. Sandbags were filled and used to reinforce the trenches, rifles and other weapons were cleaned, and reams of barbed wire were moved to the forward-most trench to be used under cover of darkness to reinforce the barrier constructed ahead of the front line. This last chore, stringing fresh barbed wire between poles, was one Hyatt had never executed. The task was reserved for soldiers who had proved their mettle in No Man's Land at night when they established listening posts, crawling one hundred yards or more through the mud on their bellies for the chance to eavesdrop on German activity. When morning or evening hate came around, and gunfire erupted between opposing forces, Hyatt was once more left alone to man his fire step.

That other members of his platoon shunned him in the days after they lost Jenkins and McCool was no surprise—for none of the enlisted men thought much of Captain Cruddup, or any of the other officers, and they did not count the captain's loss as one close to their hearts. Enlisted men and non-commissioned officers, however, were another matter. Such isolation weighed heavily on Hyatt; but, unlike other members of the platoon, Hyatt worried that he might be called upon to take part in some fool's errand of a mission from which he might not return. Just north of the trench his unit occupied, a portion of the tunnel that had been excavated by German forces collapsed during the heavy rains. A squad was called upon to investigate one dark, rainy afternoon. Their orders were to capture any survivors who may have found a way out.

"Hyatt," sergeant Lattimer said as the squad prepared to leave the trench. "I want you to go there with them."

"Sergeant?"

"It's that or latrine duty," he said. "Besides, there are only five guys in the squad including Corporal Chumly."

"So, I make six."

"Yes, a nice even number," said Lattimer. "Take your rifle and some ammunition. Leave the rest of your gear."

Hyatt removed the pack around his waist that contained his gas mask and tossed it aside.

"Jesus Christ, Hyatt!" the sergeant exclaimed. "I think you might need that."

Minutes later, with his gas mask pack secured, Hyatt caught up with Chumly and the others. They were congregating at the ladder at the north end of the trench. Chumly and another soldier were discussing in detail which one of them should go up the ladder first. Hyatt interjected to let Chumly know that sergeant Lattimer had assigned him to the patrol.

"Great," said Chumly. "It's the accursed kid. Now it's a suicide mission, boys."

No one laughed.

"I'll go up the ladder first," Hyatt said.

"Wait," the corporal told him.

In order to keep the enemy occupied, a mortar barrage commenced. The explosions were inconsequential compared to the heavy British guns, but long-range artillery, as Chumly explained, was out of the question for their venture.

"Can't spare the shells for a corporal and a few privates," said Chumly. "That's the truth of the matter."

The attack on forward German positions on the other side of No Man's Land proved no more of a nuisance for the 16th Bavarian Infantry Division positioned near Souchez, owing to how well-fortified their trenches were. All of this would change in the coming weeks, but that day the mortar barrage sounded weak compared to the usual artillery bombardments conducted by the Canadian Corps and their British complement.

Chumly signaled to Hyatt. He and the others followed him over the top. Once they exited the trench, they double-timed it to a stretch of woodland a few hundred yards to the north.

No one but Chumly spoke to Hyatt. He was a short, chubby redhead with pale blue eyes and a pencil mustache he had fashioned after the style of British officers.

"I sure hope you learned something from your boy getting killed," said Chumly.

"My boy?"

"Jenkins," he answered. "I saw the way he took you under his wings. That was a right, proper thing to do."

"Thanks, I guess."

"But his sin was arrogance," Chumly went on. "If he hadn't been so full of pride, he might still be alive."

"With all due respect—"

"Save it," the corporal told him. They stood at the edge of a small grove now. "You're an American. Why don't you tell me why your country is dragging her heels? Is your president a coward? Or aren't American soldiers up for the challenge?"

"I don't know President Wilson, personally," Hyatt told him. "So I couldn't say."

"We'll continue this conversation later," he said. "Everyone spread out!"

The grove separated the pasture where they stood and the next one. A Grenadier scout had spotted the place where the tunnel had partially collapsed. He had informed the battalion commander that morning that he had spotted four German soldiers who had attempted to dig their way out. In the process, the soldiers further weakened the walls of the tunnel. The heavy rains did the rest, causing their escape tunnel to collapse and effectively trap them in chest-deep mud.

"Hyatt," Chumly waved his hand, indicating that he should get down on the ground.

For several minutes, the squad lay in wet grass, just a stone's throw from the grove's center. The other squad members looked pensive and averted their eyes from Hyatt's gaze.

"I need a volunteer," Chumly said. "Hyatt, why don't you go in there and see what's what?"

Hyatt slowly stood up. "I am not sure you understand the definition of volunteerism," he said.

"We can discuss that later," the corporal said. "Stay low and stick to the trees."

The grove was dark, wet. Hyatt made no sound as he moved slowly from tree to tree. When he reached the place where the German soldiers remained trapped, he saw that they appeared unarmed. Behind him, Chumly and the others approached. Hyatt watched as the corporal kicked one of the Germans in the face.

"That's for Sergeant McCool, Hans," he said.

The Germans were in a depression between three trees. One of them had managed to clear away enough mud so that only his legs and waist were still trapped underground. The others were wedged chest-deep in the muck—one of them bleeding profusely now from his nose as a result of Chumly's kick.

"Steinhart," the corporal spoke up. "Ask these krauts how far they've tunneled."

Private Steinhart was thin and nervous-looking in the same way the Tommies had been when the Canadians had relieved the British. He conversed with the German soldiers a moment while Chumly huddled close to the other squad members. Hyatt stood alone.

"So," Chumly said. "What's the story?"

"Corporal," Steinhart spoke up, "I thought our orders were to free them and take them prisoner?"

"The tunnels?"

"Just this one," he said. "He said it ends here."

"That's bullshit," Chumly argued.

The remaining squad members stepped close to one German whose arms were free. They unfastened their pants and proceeded to urinate on the man.

"Corporal," one of the squad members said. "The kraut covered his face with his hands."

"Withers," said Chumly. "You and Dearborn hold his arms. Powell?"

"Corporal?"

"Hold that kraut's head back and keep his mouth open," he said, and smiled at Hyatt. "I have to shit."

"Corporal Chumly," Steinhart said. "Don't."

"Whose side are you on, Steinhart?"

"I am Canadian."

"Why don't you keep Hyatt company over there," the corporal said.

Steinhart sidled over to where Hyatt stood. They kept their backs turned away from the scene.

"I'm going back," Steinhart whispered. "This is insane."

"He'll probably shoot you," replied Hyatt.

"Now, Powell," Chumly said. "Make sure he chews that up real good."

Hyatt turned and saw Chumly fastening his pants. The other Germans started cursing.

"Shut them up!" the corporal cried.

Withers took aim with his rifle and shot two of the Germans dead. A third one prayed. The fourth one, the one Chumly and the others had assaulted, continued to vomit through his nose as Powell kept his hands clamped over the man's mouth.

"This is madness," Steinhart told Hyatt.

"Withers," Chumly shouted. "I didn't say shoot them. Hyatt, Steinhart. You two dig that last man out. We'll bring him back for interrogation."

"Hey, corporal," said Powell, nodding at the German who wiped his mouth clean once his hands were free. "What about shit-breath here?"

The German spat and cursed in his native tongue.

"Steinhart," said Chumly, "what did shit-breath say?"

He quit digging for a moment. "I don't know, corporal," he answered. "It's a dialect I do not understand."

"Kraut is kraut, Steinhart," he told him. "Now, tell me what he said."

Hyatt had managed to free the third German's left arm. He shot Steinhart a look, ever so slightly shaking his head.

Corporal Chumly leveled his rifle at Steinhart.

"Well?" he asked.

"He said your mother sucks leprous cocks," Steinhart told Chumly.

"Leopard dicks?" the corporal asked, shouldering his rifle now. "That doesn't make any sense. Steinhart, your German sucks."

"Leprous," said Powell. "You know? Like leprosy?"

Chumly grinned. He tossed his rifle to Powell. Then he pulled his bayonet from his boot scabbard and charged the foul-mouthed German who struggled briefly before Chumly pinned his arms. The corporal waved his bayonet just inches from the man's face now. Then he proceeded to stab the German in the neck, the eyes, and the sides of the man's face until all that was left was a battered, misshapen, bloodied unrecognizable mess.

"Shit," Chumly exclaimed. "You hear that? I think this prick is still alive."

"Corporal—" Withers began.

It was too late. Chumly went back to work on the man with the bayonet. He didn't stop until the man quit breathing and died.

Hyatt saw that the prospective prisoner's right arm was almost free. He turned his attention deeper into the grove for a moment, unable to look upon the man that Chumly had killed. The prisoner suddenly freed his right hand from the mud, pulling a Luger pistol out and firing it at Chumly, Powell, Withers, and Dearborn.

The first round struck Chumly in the neck and blew out the base of his skull. The corporal collapsed in a lump where he stood. Powell was struck in the chest. The third and fourth

259

rounds caught Withers in the abdomen. Dearborn caught the last round in his face.

Steinhart raised his rifle to shoot the remaining German, but his weapon jammed. A sixth shot from the German's pistol went wide, peeling through bark on a tree close to where Steinhart stood.

Hyatt leveled his rifle and fired, shooting the German in the face. A spray of blood, bone, and brain matter splashed against the mud behind him. The Luger in the German's hand fired a seventh shot, in response to the man's death throes; the bullet grazed Steinhart's helmet.

"You killed him," Steinhart said.

Withers had collapsed on the cold, wet ground, curled up in a fetal position and barely breathing.

Hyatt moved into action. Withers slapped his hands away each time he attempted to check the soldier's wound.

"Go find a medic," Hyatt told Steinhart. "Now!"

Withers gripped Hyatt's hand. His eyes went wide as he gasped for breath.

Steinhart ran full-tilt through the grove, heading back the way they had first traveled.

"Stay with me, Withers," Hyatt said. "The medic will be here soon. Right now, I need to apply pressure to that wound."

"They're waiting," Withers gasped.

"No," he told him, "it's going to be alright."

Withers sucked in a breath and coughed up blood. "I can see them," he grunted.

"Withers, there's no one here but me," Hyatt assured him. "Just listen to my voice. And you have to let me put pressure on that wound."

"Don't let them get me," he said. His breathing became shallow now. "The one with no...eyes..."

Withers loosened his grip on Hyatt's hands. His eyes clouded. His mouth stretched open as he attempted to draw a breath. Then he died.

Hyatt remained among the dead as he waited for Steinhart to return. The rain changed over to sleet and snow as thirty minutes passed. Still, there was no sign of Steinhart. Hyatt scanned the trees around him, careful to not let his gaze linger too long on the man Chumly had cut to ribbons, and he saw that there were no ghosts in the grove.

After the grove incident, sleep came in fits and starts. When Hyatt did manage to slip into unconsciousness he dreamed of Withers who wandered lost in a primeval forest permanently lit in a deep blue light, a place where mist shielded ghosts from the weary eye. In one dream, Hyatt glimpsed Withers as he made his way through the eventide forest chased by the dead German soldiers. Hyatt followed. A tall fir blocked his view as he heard Withers scream. When he stepped around the tree, Hyatt came face to face with the fourth German, the one Chumly had killed with his bayonet. The German's eyes were missing and in their place two dark sockets ringed with dried blood; dual hollows that stared back at Hyatt. When the German opened his mouth his breath reeked of fetid excrement. Hyatt awoke in a fevered panic. It was still daylight. He had fallen asleep composing a letter to send back home. The memory of the grove stayed with him, including how he found his way back to the trench on his own to find Steinhart a hysterical mess surrounded by Lattimer and a few of the officers. In those first hours after he had returned to the trench there was speculation and fear concerning the events that had unfolded within the grove. Sergeant Lattimer was the one who took on the voice of reason, insisting that a team of NCOs go out and investigate. He took Sergeant Raven with him and another sergeant. When they returned, Hyatt and Steinhart were cleared of any wrongdoing. That was days ago. Awake now, the dream image slowly faded of the eyeless German, the other three who had brought down Withers the way lions did their prey, and how the hollow-eyed German hissed his wretched breath at Hyatt before turning and running toward the kill where they tore strips of flesh from Withers' body. How Withers screamed and pleaded with his God to take him from the one place in all the world where he was doomed to remain forever.

Part Five:
The Rule in No Man's Land

Chapter Thirty-One: Swedish Fish And Tilapia—Haverford Township PA, 2012

When Miller awoke he knew by the light coming through the hotel window that it was late morning. He could not remember if he was supposed to call May, or if she had told him that she would contact him. As he climbed out of bed, he thought of his daughter. Elinor worried too much. He had a good mind to call her just to say he had not forgotten where he was, that he was not lost, that everything was normal. Just then the room phone rang beside his bed. Chastising Elinor would have to wait.

"Hello?"

"Dr. Miller?" a man asked.

"Yes."

"It's Victor Cardin," he said. "The photographer. I am down in the lobby."

"Yes, of course," said Miller.

"We are due at Ms. Weldon's house for a shoot today," he said.

"See you in fifteen minutes," he replied.

"Dr. Miller?"

"Yes?"

"It's after eleven," Cardin told him. "I'd like to get some of the noon-time light for the exterior shots."

"I am on my way," Miller said, and hung up.

Next, he dialed May's house. There was no answer. Shit, he thought, and tried the number again.

"Hello?" May answered.

"Good morning—"

"It's after eleven in the morning, Dr. Miller," she cut him off. "I was beginning to think you stood me up."

"I'll be there shortly," Miller told her.

"We're having tilapia for lunch," said May. "I hope you like fish. It's very good for you."

"I will be bringing a photographer," he informed her.

Miller winced at the ensuing silence. He was certain that she would protest.

"For what?" she finally asked.

"Some exterior shots, mostly," he told her, "with your permission, of course. I am sure there's some paperwork involved." May said nothing. Then, he added, "I thought I might implore you to allow a few photographs of the third-floor rooms."

"Dr. Miller," May said, "I haven't been up there in a couple of years, now. There's hardly—"

"No matter," he said. "I am sure we can use the old ones from the first print run."

"Oh, I don't see why not," she told him. "If it means that much."

"Thank you."

"But the photographer must leave when he's finished."

"I understand—"

"No, Dr. Miller," she said, "you do not. I wanted to wait to tell you, but here it is. I have completed the introduction that you and that editor of yours wanted me to write. I hope you don't mind, but it's almost thirty pages long."

"Splendid," he said. In one night, he thought. His next words he chose carefully. "I am sure it is perfect."

"Do you patronize your students in the same fashion?" May asked. "You can change it as you see fit. I will see you within the hour."

Twenty minutes later, freshly showered and dressed; Miller rode the elevator down to the lobby. Near the main entrance a heavyset man sat sleeping in an armchair. A camera strap around the man's neck was festooned with dollar store pins, atop his protruding stomach, a Hasselblad camera. At the big man's feet, a tripod and camera bag lay on the floor.

"Mr. Cardin?"

The big man stirred, opened his eyes, and looked Miller up and down.

"Miller?" said Cardin. He yawned like a sated lion after the kill. "I dozed off."

"I am sorry to keep you waiting."

"I just got here," he confessed. "Traffic down from the city was a bitch. I hate New York."

"Well," Miller replied. "You're here now. That's what matters most."

"So, this writer," he said, slowly getting to his feet. Cardin exhibited such difficulty in doing so that Miller almost extended a hand to help. "He's not camera shy, is he?"

"I wouldn't know," Miller replied. "R.J. Hyatt's dead."

"The widow?"

Miller pursed his lips. "What exactly did Schuyler tell you?"

Cardin fished a mangled Snickers bar from his back pocket. He peeled the wrapper like a banana skin, and bit the Snickers bar in two, consuming the top half.

"Who the fuck's Schuyler?" he said, chewing the candy bar as he breathed through his nose.

Traffic along City Avenue crawled past road crews working on either side of the street as Miller's rental car approached Saint Joseph's University.

"Hey, I appreciate you driving," said Cardin. "Truth is I should be sitting in the back seat. I get car sick if I am not driving."

"Where are you from?" Miller asked, attempting to change the subject.

"The thing about car sickness," the photographer went on, "the thing that most people don't know, is that it has to do with depth perception."

"Is that so?"

"You like Swedish fish?" Cardin pulled an oil-stained brown paper bag from his camera bag.

"No, thank you," he replied. "Ms. Weldon is making tilapia for lunch."

"I hate fish."

"But you are...oh, I see."

Miller's stomach churned as he watched Cardin upend the paper bag and wolf down candy fish; a few of the Swedish fish missed the photographer's mouth and fell to the floor. Undeterred, Cardin bent over, picked up the candy fish, popped them into his mouth, and kept on chewing. The exertion from contorting his body into the position, the simple act of leaning forward, caused his face to turn the same shade as the candy he consumed.

"Are you all right?" Miller asked.

"Diabetes," Cardin informed him. "Or so my Hindu doctor tells me. Chopra, her name is. She looks like she's twelve years old. Big tits, though. I could do worse."

They drove in silence for the remainder of the ride.

Miller saw May standing on the porch when he pulled to a stop.

Cardin balled up his oil-stained brown paper bag, looking left and right as he did, and rolled down the passenger window. He tossed the bag. It landed on the curb.

"Shit," Cardin said.

"I wouldn't have done that," Miller warned him.

May descended the porch steps and marched through her sunlit yard.

"Excuse me," she said to Cardin as she approached the car, "I don't know where you are from, but I'd appreciate it if you refrained from throwing your garbage into the street."

Miller sighed. "I told you."

Cardin closed the window.

"I thought you said this broad's dying from cancer?" he asked.

"She is," said Miller.

"Chemo?"

"Yes."

"I'll be damned."

Miller climbed out of the car. May was no longer wearing a bandanna. Her hair, still white gray, appeared full though short and even the color of her face stunned him. Gone was the pallor he had witnessed the previous day, calling to mind for him the May he had known years ago.

"Hello, May," he said. "You look well."

"It's a good day," she told him. Then, pointing at Cardin, she asked, "Who's this?"

"Victor Cardin," the photographer popped out of the passenger seat. He shot out his meaty right paw. "Pleased to meet you."

May kept her hands at her side.

"Likewise," she said. "You should know, Mr. Cardin, that it is not proper to offer your hand to a lady unless she offers you hers first."

"I admit," said Cardin as he rubbed his nostrils with his right hand now, "I am a little short on manners. I came from a broken home."

"Your parents separated when you were young?"

"No, ma'am," he answered. "My wife left me for a woman. Doesn't that beat all?"

"So, you're the photographer Dr. Miller told me about?"

"That's me," he said. "Nice house. You live here alone?"

"Get your things," May said as she did an about-face. "And don't forget your litter on the curb."

Inside the house, a few minutes later, May showed Cardin the garbage pail in the kitchen. Miller marveled at how she treated the big man like a child. What perplexed him even more was the fire that had returned to May's eyes. Her complexion was healthy, too, and her arms appeared more toned than he remembered, but it was her eyes that belied her condition.

"I suppose," May opened the door that led to the basement, "we should start downstairs. Mr. Cardin?"

"Yes?"

"Did Dr. Miller tell you about the root cellar?"

"No, I don't think—"

"Never mind," she nodded at the basement stairs. "Down you go."

Chapter Thirty-Two: The Daunting Moon—Vimy Ridge—April 7, 1917

"Hyatt!" Lattimer shouted. "Are you feeling alright, private?"

It was near dusk, two weeks after the grove incident. Hyatt was preparing for evening stand-to when the sergeant approached.

"I'm fine, sergeant," replied Hyatt.

"Good," he said. "I want you to go out into No Man's Land tonight."

...and bring back Withers...

"Sergeant?"

"You won't be alone," Lattimer assured him. "Breckenridge and Murphy will be with you."

"But I've never been on patrol."

"You worried about that curse?"

Hyatt remained silent.

"Well, don't," Lattimer went on. "What happened out there in the grove was hard. You did what was right. Shit, even Steinhart's been singing your praises. And he's a fairy."

"Sergeant Lattimer."

"Fine," he said. "I shouldn't talk about your friend like that. Allow me to rephrase it. Steinhart is a fickle boy. He's afraid of his own shadow, beyond shell-shocked if you ask me. But we need every swinging dick in the field. And you, you're a kraut killer. The curse has been lifted. You've been baptized, born anew."

"I don't feel different," said Hyatt.

"Of course not," he said. "That killer instinct lies dormant in you now. Don't believe me? Ask that injun Raven. He'll tell you the same thing. Now, get some shut-eye after stand-to. Sleep in the dug-out if you have to. If we're overrun by krauts, I'll come get you beforehand."

"I haven't been sleeping lately."

"Don't slip off your trolley now, Hyatt," Lattimer told him. "I can't have you cracking up on me. We're all in this shit together. Remember that. Besides, you'll get enough sleep when you get to rest camp. I know I will."

"I don't plan on dying here, sergeant."

"Isn't that rich? You been over the rest camp lately? More and more bodies every day. Good men. I am sure they thought the same way you did until Death tapped them and told them otherwise," he said. "I will send Steinhart up here to man the fire-step with you."

Not long after dark, the small arms fire began. The absence of the static report of machine guns on either side was disconcerting to Hyatt. He noted the look on Steinhart's face who kept his head below the parapet, refusing to fire his rifle. Somewhere on the other side of No Man's Land a whistle blew, a German's whistle. The gunfire stopped. From a distance, Hyatt heard Lattimer calling out for a ceasefire. The night grew still. The silence agitated Hyatt.

"Maybe things are changing," said Steinhart.

He had not bothered to take part in the evening hate, not that he would have been much good. Ever since the grove incident Steinhart had developed a nervous tick; his hands trembled all the time, even when he slept which was seldom. The artillery thunder, the white-hot lightning of explosions, the whizzing bullets like so many mosquitoes, the brutality of Chumly before the German sent him to rest camp for good, all of these things pushed him over the edge. In the midst of it,

Steinhart had experienced a revelation, a moment of clarity, a vision of sanity within this present insanity-reality.

"Maybe God is finally listening," he told Hyatt. "Not that God from our churches, not the Jew's God, not the Mohammedan's Allah, none of these. I am talking about the real one, the God of all things. He who cast the original darkness, the one who retreated before the imposter God came along and breathed over the still waters and created the worlds. There was a dream I had recently. In it, I saw the far reaches of—"

"Steinhart," said Hyatt. "Get a hold of yourself, man. There's no God to it. At least, none so far as I can see."

"You are an atheist?" he asked. He cast his rifle aside and spread his arms out wide. "Amidst all of this?"

As Steinhart posed the question, Hyatt remembered Matilda's letter and how she had wanted him to take her to Notre Dame when the war was over. He never gave divinity much thought back in Ardmore, especially not the God said to inhabit the churches and the synagogues there. For Hyatt, the Creator may have existed in places like that, back home where petty crimes and the occasional murder wasn't enough to keep Him away; but here, in Europe, amidst the wholesale slaughter, amidst the very undoing of sanity itself, God had removed Himself from the hearts and minds of Europe's people. What frightened Hyatt more than the prospect of God abandoning the war-weary was that the Devil himself had vacated the premises, unable to comprehend how such evil between men could overshadow the cold dark of Lucifer's heart.

"I am not sure what I believe anymore," said Hyatt. In the trench, the last thing he wanted was a fellow soldier who had slipped off his trolley. "Why don't you tell me about home instead?"

Steinhart's voice was high-pitched and hoarse, a cold, rusted chain creaking in the wind. The more Steinhart spoke, the further Hyatt became lost in his own thoughts. Home was always at the forefront of his mind, though it was so far away.

271

Richard J. O'Brien

Some nights Hyatt wondered if Ardmore had been a place he had known only from dreams, some vague variant of the world he knew now—a world fractured by war, a world given over to the sweet taste of deception and madness rather than the saltlick pillars of truth and peace. For daylight hours, cold and gray in that pasture, rendered something different than the dark. In bleak daylight there were reminders—simple shapes and forms of a tree root here, a distant bird with wings outstretched there, that reminded him of home, a place barely more concrete than the phantasm he conjured each night. In darkness, all things appeared fleeting—life, love, everything the mind knew to be true; in the dark, one could imagine the stars were angels in full retreat, an abandonment of the divine on a cosmic scale—devoid of free will, those heavenly warriors followed their Creator into the furthest recesses, into a place that no human could ever hope to reach through prayer and devotion. In the dark, a man questioned his faith. Doubt reinforced the fears he carried as well as those fears and superstitions handed down to him by ancestors that all the reason and all the logic in the world could not hope to conquer. For more than daylight, the night stripped bare the fragile sense of self, and coupled with war, such darkness diminished a man's veneer. It wore away the exterior of existence until it reached the coveted prize—the vulnerable soul that longed for God in any of His guises, the bastard of the Creator's light left to fend for itself. For what was man in the dark but an animal? What worked at Hyatt's soul was something more sinister than the devil himself, something born beyond God's domain, something made manifest in the cold dark amidst the smell of cordite, the rounds that ricocheted off heavy metal artillery guns and plotted courses to finish death's work; the very thing at work in the world that propagated war was also, or so Hyatt surmised as the days and nights in the trench bled into a pool of quiet despair, the thing that sought to erase from every soldier—Canadian, French, or German—the remembrance of home.

Under The Bronze Moon

Some time later, as thin clouds gave way to an abundance of stars, each man in the trench put away thoughts of home. The watch order was established. Sappers and those soldiers destined for patrol ordinarily took first watch so that they could catch up on sleep, however fleeting such a thing may have been, before crawling across the borderland of the living and the dead. But that night, as the hour grew late, a new energy surged through the trenches. Steinhart's rich tapestry of unrequited love (for he had spent nearly an hour delivering a soliloquy concerning Mirabel Rosencrantz, the Jewish siren who called young Steinhart toward ruin not with song but with flaxen hair, full hips, heavy breasts capped with chocolate brown nipples, and a penchant for sexual deviance that would have made Lot's wife blush), a woeful tale of rejection indeed, was interrupted now by the appearance of Sergeant Lattimer.

"Sorry, boys," he said. "I hate to break up the pow-wow, but we're moving."

"Where?" Steinhart asked.

"Patrol," said Lattimer.

"I dreamed I would be killed on patrol," he told him.

"Don't worry," he replied. "I will personally see to it that you live long enough to see your girlfriend Mirabel. She sounds like a keeper."

"Mirabel wasn't my girlfriend, sergeant."

"I'll say," he replied. "I've been listening to you drone on about this whore all night—"

"Mirabel's no whore—"

"Listen, Steinhart," Lattimer said. "Any girl willing to wet a fellah's wick for a nickel is a whore in my book."

"What about you, Hyatt?" Steinhart asked. "You have a girl at home?"

"There was one girl," Hyatt began.

"Swell," said Lattimer. "You two grab your gear and let's go."

"Where?" Steinhart asked.

"You shell-shocked?"

273

"I don't think so," he replied. "Well, maybe. How would I know—"

"For Christ's sake, Steinhart," the sergeant said, "Give it a rest. We're venturing into No Man's Land. Now, get a move on. The squad leaves in an hour."

"But we—"

"Haven't been trained?"

"Well, yes."

"It's simple," Lattimer said. "Stay low and move slow."

"In the mud with the bugs," Hyatt replied.

"Exactly," he said. "I might add that you pray you don't get shot to shit or crawl across a kraut landmine."

"It's an exercise in futility," Steinhart said. "That's what it is."

"If it wasn't war, Steinhart, they'd call it something else," said the sergeant. Then, he asked, "You speak German, right?"

"I do."

"Perfect," said Lattimer. "Steinhart, I want you on forward listening post. I want you close enough to hear those kraut bastards fart."

"Any more good news?"

"Now, listen," he said, ignoring Steinhart's remark. "Just so you two don't think I am sending you on some kind of suicide mission, you will be out there with Sergeant Raven. Is he a crazed Injun? Sure, but he can kill quietly and effectively. Something you both will learn if you live long enough. Understood?"

"Just the three of us?" Hyatt asked.

"More than three there's too much noise," the sergeant informed him. "Stow your gear in the dugout and get some sleep if you can. I'll man your fire step. Sergeant Raven will come around for you when he's ready to move out."

Hyatt did not sleep. He sat in the dugout listening to Steinhart talk about the inefficiencies of the Lee-Enfield rifle. Before long, Sergeant Raven appeared in the dugout. Hyatt wasn't sure if the Mohican had slipped in unnoticed, or if Raven had been concealed in the shadows the whole time.

"Time to go," said Raven.

Steinhart slung his rifle over his shoulder. He started for the entrance, but the sergeant stopped him.

"Leave your rifle," Raven told him. "That goes for both of you."

"Are you nuts?" Steinhart asked. He kept the rifle slung to his shoulder. "I am not going anywhere without it."

Steinhart headed for the entrance. In one fluid motion, Raven withdrew his Bowie knife from his boot and pressed the blade against the soldier's neck.

"Too much noise," he said. "Take only your bayonet."

Once they left the trench, it took Hyatt nearly an hour to crawl into No Man's Land at Sergeant Raven's side. Steinhart had gone on ahead of them, moving ever so slowly toward the ruts in the ground that served as listening posts positioned dangerously close to enemy trenches. Out there in No Man's Land, Hyatt thought about death with every inch he moved. He worried that Steinhart was not up to the challenge, that a Bavarian sapper would snuff the life out of him. Within that hour Hyatt had twice crawled over the rotting corpses of two different British sappers with their bodies in a terrible state of decay. The rule in No Man's Land was that if you came upon the enemy, you did not shoot for fear of drawing down fire from either side. Instead, a soldier was expected to dispatch his combatant by means of hand-to-hand combat. Killing another man with your bare hands was hard work. Sergeant Raven preferred to use his knife. Before they had left the trench the sergeant explained that some soldiers liked to choke a Kraut to death; but this, he pointed out, was folly, for many soldiers new to combat did not know how to conserve their strength. Raven argued that at times it took powerful might to overcome the enemy face to face with bare hands. The knife, he reasoned, did the work for you; in the dark, the knife was an infantryman's best friend. The blade was the covenant between the enemy's blood and the earth.

"Well, here's to a quiet night," Hyatt whispered to the sergeant.

"Don't bother stabbing him repeatedly in the chest," Raven explained. "It's better to drive your blade through the eye, or into the throat and tear the flesh away."

"You killed many men out here like that?"

"These Krauts are not men," he answered. "They are demons."

Hyatt was about to say something in reply, but Raven held a muddied finger to his lips.

Before long, Hyatt and the sergeant crawled away from one another, separating themselves by ten yards or more. A low fog entered the barren zone from the west as Hyatt lay there. From his position, he could no longer see Steinhart; for the first time since he had arrived in France, Hyatt wondered if he might die alone. He remembered the first corpse he had crawled over early on that night, how Sergeant Raven had told him that Sturmtruppen sappers had stolen the uniforms of the dead, how the Krauts did so for the sole purpose of posing as corpses in No Man's Land.

"When in doubt, use your knife," said Raven. "Turn the living German demon into the corpse he pretends to be."

Exhaustion forced Hyatt to question whether he had the strength to knife someone to death, much less know the difference between the real dead and the murderous intent of an enemy soldier. As the night pressed on, and the fog thickened, he was sure that before his time in No Man's Land had ended he would meet Death face to face. Lying there in the cold mud, his eighteenth birthday gone by without so much as a nod from anyone he knew in the trenches, this notion of the end plagued him. He suspected that it would start with severe yet abrupt pain before he experienced firsthand the domain of the hereafter; his end brought about not by either the morbid stealth of the Sturmtruppen nor the errant shrapnel of enemy mortar fire, but something else. That night, Hyatt did indeed glimpse the hereafter, the next world beyond the veil; only, it did not occur the way he had envisioned it.

He had lost track of time, or perhaps the truth of it was that time had instead lost track of him. As the fog thickened, he could no longer see Sergeant Raven or Steinhart, their supine forms were lost in the foggy dark. Nor could he call out to them, for this was another rule, his survival depended on it, and soon Hyatt resolved himself to the fact that he was alone. Before long, however, he discovered that from far across the North Atlantic, all the while invisible until that night, a ghost had followed him. In the dense fog that enveloped No Man's Land, she was there, dressed in a sheer gray smock, her pale, heavy breasts visible through the mist-sodden and threadbare fabric. Her bare feet were caked with mud and in the dark her red hair looked black, but he knew her by the way her hair fell forward, covering the right side of her face as she trained her left eye on him—a hollow socket filled with dark storm clouds. Overhead, a flare ignited, fired by Bavarian troops. As the light lingered over No Man's Land, and Abigail Sweeney remained where she stood, her fingers encrusted with mud like her feet as she pulled one strap down on her smock and then the other, baring her gypsum breasts with taut pink nipples. Her arms undulated as she beckoned him to join her, to leave No Man's Land, to put the war behind him once and for all. The enchanting smile that in life had lured him toward ruin was her only feature that remained the same, her hollow-eyed face a pallid satellite, feral and daunting like the moon. How easy it would have been to appease her, to please himself in her cold unloving arms, but then, as the flare's light flickered and faded and No Man's Land gradually darkened once more, Abigail's form dissipated like smoke carried away in the shifting fog.

Moments later, another form came walking through the fog. Hyatt reached for his bayonet.

"Hyatt," the shadow hissed.

"Steinhart?" he whispered back.

"Where's Sergeant Raven?"

"Here," Raven said, appearing out of the fog as he crept low toward the two young men. "Steinhart, get down."

Steinhart did as he was told. Just as he did, another flare fired from the enemy side. Its pale white light formed a dome over them.

Raven signaled the soldiers to remain still. Before long, the flare drifted past and went out.

"Let's move," said Raven.

The long crawl back to the trench took nearly another hour. Along the way, they met up with two British sappers who had also been in No Man's Land, listening from points further north. A sentry in a forward position outside the trench challenged them with a password.

Once they were back in the trench, Raven instructed Hyatt and Steinhart to get some sleep. At the dugout, Lattimer intercepted Steinhart and took him to the company CP to find out what he had heard from the Germans. Alone once more, Hyatt collapsed in the dugout. He slept a dreamless sleep all the way through morning hate.

Chapter Thirty-Three: The Wild Country Is Real—Pittsfield MA, 2012

The Land of Dust and Honey, locked inside a barrister bookcase behind her father's old mahogany desk, lay as far out of touch as her father had been throughout the years of her life, flanked by two garish stone gargoyles (a gift, those gargoyles were, from one of her father's graduate students given to him several years ago). The first edition remained there as it had throughout Elinor's life. For decades, the novel stood locked away, untouched; a mystery to Elinor much like the fascination her father harbored toward the book, setting its importance higher than anything else in his life. She peered through the glass now, studying the novel's cover—a woodcut print of a multi-branched tree colored black against the pale tan cover. She recalled how the book held no interest for her, no interest, that is, until the summer after she completed her first year of graduate school. In June of that year, Elinor slogged her way through Europe, staying at various hostels, including a firetrap in Amsterdam where, as if some divine providence had been at play, she discovered that the room's previous occupant had left behind a battered paperback copy of Hyatt's novel. Elinor read the first one hundred pages, but she never finished it, nor did she take the paperback with her, choosing, instead, to leave it behind so as not to upset whatever order was left in the universe. She smiled, thinking about the hostel in Amsterdam, about how superstitious she had been over the whole affair, and stared at the hardbound book behind glass. *The Land of Dust and Honey* was a holy relic in her atheistic eyes, a thing whose sanctity existed beyond her comprehension, and the book, like its author, remained an enigma to her father, no matter how much research he performed, a veritable riddle he had wasted his life trying to figure out.

From the beginning, there had always been the word or, in her father's case, a book. For the uninitiated, *The Land of Dust and Honey* by R.J. Hyatt was a thick seven-hundred-page tome replete with Old World pagan references that depicted a place far and away from the reality the main character had known. Elinor recalled now how the prose had a hypnotic effect on her, how the stream of consciousness narrative (at least in the beginning chapters that she had read) had disturbed her thoughts for days on end, long after she put Holland behind her and moved on to Denmark, and how her father had exalted this one work above all others. Her father had devoted his life to teaching and writing about the novel, to deciphering nearly indecipherable arcane knowledge that, by all accounts, a novelist as young as Hyatt had been when he wrote the book, could not have learned or even researched in the time between The Great War's end and his return from Europe some years later with the completed handwritten manuscript. This much she knew from what her father had told her, though in her adult life Elinor had tried desperately over the years to forget. Most adults looked back on their childhood with good and bad memories, at times experiencing an imbalance in recollection, but all Elinor could recall of her father was how he spent his life annotating Hyatt's famous novel, exploring with an obsessive-compulsive candor obscure references within the text, cataloguing anthropological, mythological, and scientific references (these last were speculative in Hyatt's time, but came to be understood as scientific facts later on), and, on her eleventh birthday, celebrating the publication of his book-length companion guide to the reclusive writer's dense work.

Since that day Elinor had come to realize that her life was one that existed in the shadow of R.J. Hyatt's great work. Her childhood consisted of quiet time that she divided between her studies, the numerous books that filled those rooms to which she was allowed access, and creating homemade cards out of construction paper that she slipped beneath the door to her father's study while he worked. In all those years, from the time she learned how to spell at age four until shortly after her ninth birthday, a pivotal moment in which she gave up her clandestine campaign at communicating with her father via those homemade cards and random notes, Elinor could not recall a time when her father had ever acknowledged her gestures. At an early age she had learned her place in her father's world. And by the time she reached adolescence, she became as much a mystery to him as the novel to which he had devoted his life. When Elinor began her undergraduate studies, she realized the impact her father's work had on the academic world; though, try as she did, she remained incapable of reconciling her personal life with her father's professional persona. As people put two and two together, realizing that she was the daughter of *that* Harold Miller, Elinor became something of a Sybil, a prophetess whose sole purpose was to share her father's knowledge. In graduate school, English professors cornered her in the library and stopped her on campus seeking to know more, extending informal invitations for her father to come and visit the university as a guest speaker, as if her father's work had somehow turned him into the closest link to, if not a forgery of, R.J. Hyatt himself. No matter how she struggled she could never outrun the long shadow of her father's reputation and that goddamned novel.

In the end Elinor forged her own life as best that she could. When she read any fiction at all she limited her tastes to the realists of every epoch. In her life, there was no room for fantastical tales of mythic, timeless realms. She discovered that the great R.J. Hyatt was one among many writers whose works garnered legions of devotees. Her chosen field of expertise—archaeology with a special concentration on the Bronze Age, gave her a luxury, a panoramic view of ancient people and their ways of life that helped shape the human mind and influenced storytellers around the world. Her father's view was much more concise; life, indeed all of history, hadn't begun until, as a teen, he stumbled upon *The Land of Dust and Honey.*

"And you maintain this position?" Elinor's therapist had asked her earlier that year.

Her therapist's name was Kala Banerjee. She was a lithe, dark-skinned woman of pedigree with a Jungian background.

"I do," said Elinor. "It's as if my father is happier in the world Hyatt created."

"But it is a story," Dr. Banerjee said. "It is not real in the sense that the wild country does not truly exist."

Elinor stared at her therapist. "You know this book?" she asked.

"Of course," she beamed. "My brother wrote his doctoral thesis on it when he was at Yale."

"Oh Christ," her patient muttered. Then, she asked, "How old is your brother?"

"Karthik is sixty years old. It was a long time ago," Dr. Banerjee responded. "But this isn't really about a physical book or the world it contains."

"Then what are we talking about?"

"Borders," she replied, "and boundaries."

Elinor considered this for a moment. "I always thought that my father wished the story was true."

"And if it was?"

"Dr. Banerjee, please."

"No," she countered. "Please, indulge me. Let's say for argument's sake that this novel your father devoted his life to turned out to be a true testament. Pretend for a moment that this other world R.J. Hyatt wrote about was a physical place in space and time. Would that have made a difference in your life?"

"But it is not," said Elinor.

"For the moment, pretend it is," Dr. Banerjee said. "Would it have made a difference in your life?"

"No," she replied.

"And what about your work?"

"What about it?"

"From this chair," the therapist told her, "it could be argued that your field of study is just one big 'I told you so' to your father."

"You think I have *daddy issues*, is that it?"

"All that digging into the earth," she went on. "Archaeology. Bronze Age, right?"

"Yes, but—"

"In my professional opinion," said Dr. Banerjee, "it would appear that you have spent your adult life digging not for relics from a lost age, but proof that this is the only world. You could have chosen any field of study. You are intelligent. And yet, here you are."

"So, I do have daddy issues?"

Dr. Banerjee laughed. "Oh, Elinor," she said. "All women have daddy issues. And men, well..."

The women shared a good laugh. In truth, Elinor felt uncomfortable talking about her profession. There was a time when she did go on digs, but in recent years she devoted her time to teaching undergraduates. She was even now further removed from her chosen field of archaeology than she cared to admit.

"One last question because our time is almost up," the therapist said. "Let's go back to that perfect world for a moment. Let's just say that if your father could bring you to that place R.J. Hyatt wrote about in his novel. Never mind whether you think it's a work of fiction. The rules of this world are as follows: the wild country is real. Your father found a way there. Would you go if he asked to?"

"Dr. Banerjee—"

"Yes or no, please."

"No, I would not," Elinor said.

"Why?"

"Because it doesn't interest me."

"Do none of your father's passions interest you?"

"That's the thing," she told her. "He kept my mother and me shut out—"

"Elinor, never mind your mother," Dr. Banerjee cut her off. "She was an adult who chose to marry your father. That is very different from being a child dependent on the love and attention of her parents."

"No, it never interested me."

"The book? Or your father's association with it?"

What Elinor had always wanted was the same as any girl: a close relationship with her father. She would have abandoned him by the time she was sixteen years old, had it not been for her mother's insistence that she do otherwise as if her mother harbored some premonition of her own death and was desperate to keep intact what remained of their family after she was gone. Her mother's greatest fear had always been that her father would be utterly alone in the house that never quite became a home.

Downstairs in the kitchen, after a long search on the second floor for the key that would unlock the barrister bookcase, Elinor spotted a note tacked to a bulletin board on the wall. *Second drawer*, the note read, *in Ellie's old desk.*

In the basement, she discovered less clutter than she had anticipated. Elinor's old desk stood near a wall to the left of the furnace. The second drawer was empty, though she detected the slightest hint of those old aromas that she remembered from high school, erasers and pencils, when the desk was in her bedroom. Elinor snapped, yanking the drawer out of its slot. She was about to hurl the drawer across the basement when she glimpsed a small Ziploc bag taped to the underside of the drawer. In the bag was a small skeletal key along with another note scrawled on one of her father's UMass business cards. *Bookcase in study*, the note read.

The impulse overwhelmed her. Some hidden part of Elinor understood that what was about to happen was more than simply reading the book she had shunned her entire life. It needed to be a ritual, a cleansing of the decades of bad blood between her and her father, but she needed not any old paperback copy of Hyatt's book. She needed to open the tabernacle in which the original source sat for all those years.

In all the years that her father had kept his prized possession locked away in the barrister bookcase behind his desk, though the book's presence caused both temptation and trepidation, Elinor had never considered removing the novel without her father's permission. Picking the lock or breaking the glass were out of the question, not for fear of punishment from her father—her mother had always been in charge of disciplinary action—but retribution from a higher plane, as if damaging the sacred space in her father's study might unleash some malevolent force that would haunt her forever.

Chapter Thirty-Four: Put Down Your Glass—Vimy Ridge, April 8, 1917

A joint artillery operation began when British and Canadian batteries bombarded Bavarian and German forces dug in at Vimy Ridge. The shelling lasted throughout the day, every day for a week. In that time Canadian infantry forces readied themselves for the pending offensive. As soldiers of the 78th Battalion attached to the 4th Division prepared for the final push against the enemy stronghold, they endured retaliatory bombardments from German forces.

Four days into the artillery exchange, a new company executive officer made his rounds through the trenches after evening hate. Two privates accompanied the XO, carrying mail that had been delivered from the rear. The new officer's name was Guillaume, a thin, dark-skinned man whose family, Hyatt had learned, emigrated from Bombay to Montreal.

"Hyatt," Guillaume called out.

In a previous conversation, Hyatt had discovered that the XO had been a Frenchman. So, he practiced his French, as did many of the other men in the company, whenever Guillaume made his rounds.

"Bonsoir, *monsieur*," said Hyatt as he waved to the XO. "*Belle nuit, non?*"

"*C'est des conneries,*" Guillaume replied. A German shell exploded in the middle of No Man's Land, sending dirt and debris flying in all directions. "*Quan cette foile fin?*" Then, he held out an envelope. "Sorry, private. There's only this one. I hope it is a good one."

Hyatt grabbed the letter. The return address was from his home in Ardmore. He scurried into the dugout and used a flashlight to read his mother's letter.

February 2, 1917

Dearest Robert,

It seems every time I sit down to write to you I assume the role of the bearer of bad news. I would have sent a cable, but from what I have read lately it was doubtful that a telegram would reach you. The international mail system offers little more insurance in that respect, so I hope this reaches your hands.

Today, I write for two reasons: the news I share is not meant to be read in a printed cable. It is my hope that your mother's penmanship, such as it is, will ease the burden of what I am to tell you, just as the very act of writing serves for me as a form of catharsis.

My dear son, I am alone now. One week after I sent my last letter your sister fell ill with a fever. Did Matilda mention in her last letter that she was sick? Poor girl. Her resolve knew no bounds, but in the end the Good Lord took her away. Matilda lingered for nearly two weeks before her fever bore her from this world. I would have transported your sister to the hospital, but Dr. Gorman, the very same who had treated Megan Sullivan, had informed me that Matilda was too fragile for such a move. Your sister passed away shortly before eleven in the evening.

And where, you may ask, was your father in all this? Once Matilda had taken ill, your father sequestered himself to the confines of O'Malley's Pub. Every night for those two gruesome weeks your father drank himself into oblivion, returning home when he saw fit.

On the night your sister died, I had to leave Matilda's corpse in her bed and go retrieve your father. I went straight through the front door of that wretched saloon. The room was crowded with many of the ruddy-faced denizens of O'Malley's no-good race. And there, amidst the Fenians and the rest of the drunkards, your father sat at the bar. He was quite tight that night. I am sure through the smoke and noise of that room he didn't recognize me at first; imagine his own wife appearing like a stranger in his sodden eyes. 'Put down your glass, Ted,' I told him. 'Your daughter has died.' As you may imagine, your father was utterly destroyed by the news. I had to employ Mickey McMaster's assistance to help get Ted home. Honestly, I had prepared myself for a showdown at O'Malley's Pub that night, but it never came to pass. Once I made the news known, your father left the bar stool, staggered toward me, remaining as stoic as his drunken state could allow, and put his arm around me. It was only after we made it out of that saloon when things got worse. Fortunately, Mickey McMaster was outside micturating into the gutter.

Matilda was buried at St. Denis Cemetery not far from where Megan Sullivan lay at rest. I would have preferred that your sister had been buried in a Methodist cemetery, but Matilda insisted, while she maintained her faculties before the fever damaged her brain beyond repair, that she be buried there in accordance with her growing fascination with the Catholic faith. And so, with Matilda's dying wish and a sizable donation to the church, your sister's wish was granted.

Robert, I wish you well. You are my remaining child. Be safe, my one and only. I pray the war ends soon.

All of my love,

Mother

For Hyatt, there was no time to grieve. He stowed his mother's letter in the map case where he kept his other letters stored. Nearby, several enemy artillery rounds exploded. The earth shook, dislodging chunks of dirt from the dugout ceiling. Further down the line, as Hyatt exited the dugout, a whistle blew.

"Gas!" a cry went out.

Three more artillery shells exploded to his left. Hyatt donned his gas mask. He climbed onto the fire step, his rifle at the ready.

"Fix bayonets!" Lattimer shouted.

Through the fog of chloride gas, they approached; a small cadre of German Sturmtruppen who ran through No Man's Land headed for the front-line trench. Hyatt watched as one after another triggered land mines. Enemy bodies were torn to pieces and catapulted high into the air. The remaining Sturmtruppen continued their advance, running full-tilt toward Hyatt's trench. There were perhaps one hundred in all, each one's face hidden behind a gas mask.

Machine gun fire cut down the closest wave of the Kaiser's army before Hyatt could expend a single round. By the time he emptied his cartridge the first of the Sturmtruppen were at the sandbag wall. For a moment, Hyatt saw the silhouette of one German soldier armed with a flamethrower. Orange, white light ignited in the dark, the fire doused a dozen Canadian soldiers, including Sergeant Lattimer. When the remaining Sturmtruppen charged the sandbag wall Hyatt thrust his rifle forward, catching one of the Germans in the gut with his bayonet. After the German soldier fell, Hyatt snatched the dead man's rifle, aimed it at the flamethrower operator, and fired. The Sturmtruppen lost his grip on the gun as he fell backward. There was a brief flash beneath him before the Sturmtruppen flamer was consumed by fire as fuel sprayed all over him. Another German soldier breached the sandbag wall.

Hyatt shot him point blank in the face. He fired another round after that, hitting a third enemy soldier in the chest. After that Hyatt dropped the German weapon and retrieved his own rifle. Along the duckboard to his left, six enemy soldiers advanced on him. Hyatt had no time to reload. As he prepared to meet his end, those men fell one by one until the last one halted within arm's reach of Hyatt and fell to his knees. Behind the kneeling German, Sergeant Raven ripped off the soldier's gas mask as he continued to stab him in the back with his Bowie knife. Within minutes, the assault was over. Hyatt manned the fire step once more. He reloaded his weapon and looked out into No Man's Land.

With Lattimer dead, and two platoons decimated, Sergeant Raven became Hyatt's platoon sergeant. He informed Hyatt that the German Sturmtruppen continued to seek a point of weakness in the line. Before dawn, the Sturmtruppen pulled back across No Man's Land. The front line on the Canadian side remained intact. It was Sunday morning, Easter. In less than twenty-four hours, the Battle of Vimy Ridge would commence.

Chapter Thirty-Five: Life After Fire—Haverford Township PA, 2012

After Cardin finished photographing the root cellar door and the stone arch her father and Hyatt had built, including the obsidian keystone at the arch's pinnacle, May escorted the two men to the third floor apartment. Cardin was permitted to take several photographs of Hyatt's old living space. While the photographer worked, Miller tried to remember if all the personal effects he saw now had been in place when he had first visited her before writing his book. What troubled him were not the original desk and other pieces of furniture; no, what confused him was that the quarters looked as if they had been recently used.

"I seem to remember—" Miller began.

"Some of the things were in storage," said May. "It felt empty up here."

"You haven't been up here in a year?"

"Almost."

"There's barely any dust."

May pretended to examine her fingernails. "I have help, Dr. Miller," she said.

"Do you mind if I check out the desk more closely?"

"Let Mr. Cardin work," she said.

May and Miller sat on the narrow stairwell between Hyatt's old rooms and the second floor.

"Do you know," May announced, "that I used to hide on these stairs when I was young? I loved listening to the pen scratch the paper as Robert worked. Of course, back then he was still Mr. Hyatt to me. You see, Robert always wrote in longhand. I suppose if he meant to publish another novel he would have hired a typist. He told me once that he hated the sound of a typewriter. It reminded him of machine gun fire. Don't you think that's odd?"

"Do you think he would have used a computer?" Miller asked.

"You know his work," she replied. "Robert was very much interested in hidden worlds...well, at least one that we know of."

"I beg your pardon?"

May eyed Miller with a sideways glance, smiling.

"From his book, of course," she said. "So, yes, I would say he would have enjoyed the reality of cyberspace; though, I suspect, that he'd still write longhand even if he were writing today."

"It's sad when talented people die before their time," Miller said. "And I mean no offense with what I am about to say, but such tragic circumstances surrounded his funeral."

"Funeral? Oh, yes," May said, and laughed. "I think it's fitting it turned out the way it did."

"It spawned a whole cottage industry," he added.

"If by cottage industry you mean conspiracy nutcases," she countered, "then yes, I suppose it did."

The tragic circumstances surrounding Hyatt's funeral were well-known. Miller had written about it extensively in his biography. Hyatt's cause of death in 1966 was listed as a massive heart attack that occurred when the writer was sixty-five years old. Miller was able to locate an old Photostat of the original death certificate. At the time when he first interviewed her, May was not forthcoming about the details of the writer's death. And Miller did not press the issue. Between newspaper archives and other documents, he was able to piece together what had happened. It was one of his investigative undertakings he was quite proud of, tracking down the doctor who had signed Hyatt's death certificate. His name was Joseph Sadowsky. Miller did not do it alone; however, he had hired a private detective agency in Philadelphia to aid him with some of the research.

That research led Miller to Boca Raton, Florida in 1995 where Dr. Sadowsky, now a widower, was living out his days in a modest bungalow.

"Hyatt?" Sadowsky had asked when Miller showed him a copy of the death certificate. "Of course, I remember him. I called his time of death at his place in Ardmore—"

"Haverford Township," said Miller. "At the Weldon residence, if I am not mistaken."

"Right," he said. "Havertown. His landlord insisted that his body not be moved. Pretty woman, as I recall, striking in a way."

"Ms. Weldon."

"I guess," said Dr. Sadowsky. "Anyway, she insisted on a funeral in her living room. That was against the law. So I put her in touch with a gentleman I grew up with. Michael Graves, a mortician who owned a funeral home."

"Did anything seem odd?"

"That was a long time ago, Mr. Miller," he said. "But there was one thing."

"And what was that?"

"She seemed very impatient," he said. Sadowsky had a faraway look in his eye, as if his next words had to be chosen carefully. "It was as if she had somewhere to go. I knew the neighborhood, knew about Hyatt being a writer and all. He never really got his due. And everyone said he was a loner. I guess it comes with the territory. That's why I chose medicine. Being a doctor meant you always got to see someone."

"Was Hyatt a patient of yours?" Miller inquired.

"Oh no," he said. "Neither was Ms..."

"Weldon," he reminded him.

"I've called the time of death for many people in my lifetime, Mr. Miller," said Dr. Sadowsky. "Friends and family

293

are always nervous in the presence of death. Ms. Weldon seemed bothered by the whole thing, but not in a grieving way. It was more like she was waiting for me to clear out. Things like that you don't soon forget."

"Did you get the sense that Ms. Weldon and Hyatt were intimately involved?"

"No," he cut me off. "Nothing of the sort."

"Why do you think she was in a rush?"

"Mr. Miller," he said, "that was thirty-odd years ago. You may want to follow up with Michael Graves back in Haverford Township. He owns Graves Funeral Home. Tell him Joe sent you."

Dr. Sadowsky's shoddy memory had somehow forgotten that Michael Graves was dead. This much Miller discovered several weeks after he interviewed the medical examiner. The Graves Funeral home in Havertown had burned to the ground in 1966. Michael Graves and his family lived on the second and third floors of the building. An ensuing investigation ruled out foul play. The fire had occurred the day after R.J. Hyatt passed away. There were two bodies in the basement of the funeral home at the time of the blaze; one of them, a male, was believed to have been Hyatt's.

After the blaze, both bodies were transported to the Delaware County Medical Examiner's Office, and, according to a report filed that year, were both interred in the Philadelphia Potter's Field just south of the International Airport.

May never wavered in her belief that Hyatt had always wanted to be cremated.

"In a way," she had said in her initial interview, "he received his wish."

"Did R.J. Hyatt believe in life after death?" Miller asked.

"We never talked about it," came her curt reply.

Given the writer's life of seclusion in his final years, it came as no surprise to Miller that so much mystery and tragedy tainted the writer. R.J. Hyatt remained as elusive in death as he had in life.

A chill ran through Miller as he sat on the stairs with May. He had never been a particularly religious man, but the thought of someone's dead body being caught in a funeral home fire, burned beyond recognition, didn't sit well with him. He pictured the writer's restless spirit moving through May's house, as well as the neighborhood at large, caught between worlds and invisible to everyone.

He knew too well the theories, baseless as they were, that had sprung to life after Hyatt's death. Many fans of his novel believed that his body was not the one in the Graves Funeral Home fire. And a certain contingent of devoted Hyatt admirers, emotionally unstable as many of them may have been, believed wholeheartedly that Hyatt lived on in anonymity until he was nearly ninety years old. The most hardcore base among this fringe lot maintained that Hyatt had somehow discovered a way to live forever, that his novel was nothing more than a roadmap to a world next door. Such notions, for Miller, were preposterous. And it depressed him to no end to think that some people took such ludicrous notions as the truth.

"Sad," May was saying now, "how fragile the human mind can be."

Miller rubbed his face with both hands, looked at his watch, and craned his neck to listen to Cardin's camera at work.

"How is Theresa?" Miller asked.

"Who? Oh, you mean my nurse," said May. "She's fine, I guess."

"Has she been by to see you today?"

"No, Dr. Miller," she replied. "Her services are no longer needed."

"You look remarkably well," he said.

May patted him on the knee. "Are you hungry?" she asked. "I could start lunch soon."

"We could go out," said Miller. "My treat, of course."

Richard J. O'Brien

"That's very kind of you, but no," May said as she stood up. "Come downstairs when the oaf is through. We have some things to discuss."

After she was gone, Miller went back upstairs to the apartment. He found Cardin packing his camera equipment.

"Hard to believe it," said Cardin.

"How's that?" Miller asked.

"This writer," he replied. "That he lived here, wrote here." Cardin nodded toward the small bedroom. "Maybe even got busy with the widow—"

"Hyatt and Ms. Weldon were never married."

"I am being offensive again," Cardin patted his pockets, searching for candy and found none.

"Forget it," said Miller. "It's nothing."

"You know, years ago, after college," the photographer said, "I went out to visit the home of Ansel Adams in Carmel, California. When I was young, studying art and photography, I was fascinated by Adams's work. My classmates thought more about the new photographers like Avedon and others. But Adams, now, he had the mystic's eye.

"Anyway, there I was, twenty-six years old, and I nearly had a nervous breakdown standing in the same home that Adams had lived in, had developed many of his most famous prints. Where he slept and dreamed.

"I should have waited," Cardin went on. "Looking back, I don't think I appreciated the magnitude of it all. You know? Sure, I was moved. And I suppose I experienced something profound, but by the time I left I was a wreck. So much so that I almost chucked the cheap cameras I had bought used in Paterson before heading out west. Can you believe that? I carted my stuff all the way out to California with the hope of taking some beautiful pictures along the coast. Then, wham! One visit to the Adams place and I was ready to throw in the towel.

"Somewhere on Route 66," he concluded, "driving back east, I was ready to quit."

296

"Why?" Miller asked. "I would think such a pilgrimage would be inspiring."

"More like terrifying," he said. "After seeing Ansel Adams's home, the reproduction prints and the dark room where he had worked, I realized that after all that schooling I didn't know shit about photography. And my professors who taught art and photography didn't know a fucking thing either. No offense, of course."

"None taken."

"That's the thing about art," said Cardin. "You can't learn it in a classroom. You have to get out there and do it. Make mistakes. Get cut up, bleed a little. That's how it's done."

"We should head downstairs," Miller said.

He stepped aside and allowed the big man to traverse the narrow stairwell to the second floor. Miller knew men like Cardin, misfits who lacked common graces, hewn from coarse stock with nothing to show for it but rough edges, but the photographer had a point. A place like Hyatt's apartment should be open to the public. The original desk was still there, along with some furniture the writer had used. What would it take, he wondered, to convince May to set up some sort of writer's retreat in her home? Retirement was fast approaching, and Miller could, with May's blessing, help administer such a thing.

Downstairs, Miller found Cardin in the foyer where the photographer stood transfixed before the photograph of May captured in a fit of laughter as she stood in front of a knotted mess of gargantuan roots, thick as telephone poles, which protruded from a ravine. It was a photograph Miller had never seen. May's hair was close-cropped, as it was now.

"Remarkable," was all Cardin could say. "It looks like Autochrome."

"You say that like it's strange," Miller told him.

"Not at all," he replied, his voice no more than a whisper. He continued to stare at the print. "So what if no one's used it since the 1950s. And this looks new."

"I am not sure—"

"That's freshly printed," he told Miller. "I thought you said this broad's dying from cancer?"

"I may be old, Mr. Cardin," May stood in the dining room entrance now, "but I am not deaf."

"No offense, Ms. Weldon," he told her, "but you look good to me." To Miller, he said, "I'd bang her."

Miller stood speechless.

"Ogre," said May. "I'd wear your fat ass out in no time flat."

"How old is that photo?" Cardin jerked his thumb at the photograph on the wall. "A week? Maybe less?"

"Dr. Miller," she said, "I don't think I like your colleague's tone."

Cardin pursed his lips, hoisted the strap on his camera bag higher onto his shoulder, and looked away as his face turned red.

"May—" Miller began.

"Get out of my house," she told Cardin. "Just go. Now!"

Miller followed Cardin to the front door, but the photographer waved a dismissive hand. "It's me she means," he said. "I am used to it." He let himself out, careful not to slam the door.

"Did Schuyler Heddings hire that ape to work with you?" May asked.

"He did," Miller answered. "Or perhaps someone else from the publisher."

She took him by the arm and led him into the kitchen.

"Sit," she said. "I'll have lunch ready soon."

"I feel I must apologize," he said. "If I had any idea—"

"Never mind that, Dr. Miller," May said. "Oh, and I have your essay ready. Do not let me forget to give it to you."

He watched May work as she poured olive oil into a pan atop the range, turning on the burner as she did so, before she cleaned the fish at the sink.

"It feels so final," said Miller.

"What does?"

"After today I will not see you again. Am I wrong?"

May finished cleaning the fish and dropped them into the pan. Afterward, she washed her hands and dried them; all the while staring intently at Miller.

"Are you hungry?"

"No," he told her.

"You know it's been years since I looked at the biography you wrote," said May. "I cannot remember. Did I tell you about Robert's father? When Robert was overseas? During the war?"

"Theodore? Of course."

May sat down at the table.

"You better get out your recorder, Dr. Miller," she said. "I'll have to keep an eye on the fish, of course. But I should tell you about the war. The real story. The one that Robert told me."

Chapter Thirty-Six—The Cresting Moon—Vimy Ridge, April 9, 1917

The tactic over ground was a simple one: Canadian and British forces would advance by leapfrogging over one another. One squad would advance while the other remained in reserve, offering cover fire. Whole divisions broken into smaller units would advance on German positions in unison, until the objective was obtained.

Hyatt's platoon was given a different set of orders. Their objective was difficult as it was clandestine. In the months leading up to the offensive, British engineers, and eventually their Canadian counterparts, excavated tunnels beneath No Man's Land, a vast underground town—the 'subways' that would provide troops to move undetected and bolster the advance on Vimy Ridge. The hard chalk underground made for stability, but the digging had been slow-going, miners managed to move twenty feet a day. When Hyatt learned that his squad would help set large underground mines beneath German positions—the goal was to detonate the mines and allow the earth to do the rest, swallowing German and Bavarian trenches en masse—he expected narrow, dimly lit passageways in which there was barely enough air to breathe in such a tight space. Instead, what Hyatt found underground was a complex maze complete with rooms that included beds and field kitchens. Moving through the 'subway,' there were intermittent rumblings caused by the artillery bombardments above ground that went on unabated, explosions that dislodged chalk dust from the subway ceilings and walls. As he followed the GI in front of him, he remembered something his new squad leader Sergeant Tully had told him before their unit descended beneath No Man's Land.

"These tunnels serve more than one purpose," Tully said. "If the krauts compromise the subway, then they can set off gas canisters. If that happens, the subway becomes our grave."

For everyone at Vimy Ridge, there was risk. Each man destined for the subway carried charges that would be applied to the walls of those vast tunnels. The plan: bring down the tunnels upon exiting and join the battle on the ground.

Hyatt's platoon wasn't underground for fifteen minutes when things went wrong. They had traveled through the maze nearly four hundred yards when an explosion immersed the soldiers in utter darkness. Then, one by one, squad leaders lit up their flashlights. The air was heavy with chalk dust and the smell of cordite as some attempted to press forward, while others wanted nothing less than to retreat all the way to the coast—if only those in favor of retreat could find their way out of the darkened tunnels. The confusion worsened when additional explosions, large and small, filled the tunnel with more chalk dust and rubble.

The tunnel where Hyatt stood had been breached by Sturmtruppen. Now, instead of fire from flamethrowers, the Germans unleashed canisters of mustard gas. Soldiers fought each other to escape the poisonous vapors, their efforts hindered by the thick dust that blinded them and clogged gas masks.

Choking, Hyatt stumbled backward as platoon members pushed back in their attempt to escape the gas. He lost his helmet, tripped, and fell, striking his head hard against the tunnel wall. Hands clawed at him; bodies piled up over him. Before long, he lost consciousness.

Later, Hyatt pushed free from the fallen. He crawled in the direction where his head lay, knowing that had been the way he and the others had first traveled into the subway. Down

301

there in the dark, all was silent. The dense, chalky air smelled of cordite, vomit, shit, and iron. Somewhere he had lost his gas mask. Several times he held his hands in front of his face; unsure, he was, whether he could see his hands or whether his mind had tricked his blind eyes into conjuring the memory of his hands. After he crawled another twenty yards, he reached another wall. There were more bodies piled up there. For a moment, Hyatt resigned himself to the fact that he would die there, then a light shined through the darkness, and illuminated, to his horror, the contorted faces of dead soldiers. He crawled slowly over the pile of bodies that separated him from the light source. Soon he discovered that the light had come from Sergeant Tully's flashlight. Hyatt saw Tully's blood-encrusted mouth move but he could not hear him, as the sergeant's legs were smashed and ruined beneath rubble. He watched the sergeant train the light on his own thigh and cut into it with his bayonet, attempting to amputate his own leg. When Tully sliced through the femoral artery, blood streamed high in an arc and splattered against the wall to Hyatt's left. Whatever life had been left in Tully faded from his face—an expression of surprise at first, then confusion preceded a look of utter despair that became permanently fixed. Hyatt took the flashlight from the dead man's hand and kept moving. After what seemed several hours he spotted daylight—a pale gray shaft of suffused light speckled with chalk dust.

When at last he emerged from underground, Hyatt discovered that the battle had ended. The dead lay everywhere. He stepped carefully among them. Amid the ruined bodies, he found a canteen. Unscrewing the canteen cap, he took a deep breath, coughed up dust, and spat. Hyatt drank, savoring the water, before he lifted the canteen and rinsed his eyes clean. No sound reached him, but movement to his right caught his attention. A band of Austrian soldiers stood in No Man's Land less than thirty yards away. There were seven of them in all. They raised their rifles and fired. One bullet tore through Hyatt's sleeve, grazing his left forearm. He dropped the canteen and ran for the tree line only a few yards away as the Austrian soldiers continued to shoot at him.

The small grove led to denser woodland that gave way to a primeval forest. The late afternoon daylight barely penetrated the expanse of ancient trees there. From where he stood now, Hyatt could see the Austrians that had followed him. He ran south along a ravine where tree roots as thick as his waist protruded and sunk into the ground beneath a shallow stream. The ravine banked to the right and stopped; the stream's source cascaded over a cave entrance there.

Hyatt entered the cave, fearing not the darkness but the enemy soldiers who would surely follow. The cave was damp and cold. The floor sloped toward a cathedral of bright blue stalactite; beyond the vast chamber, past the slick hard stone floor colored dark blue, were three dark openings in the cave wall. The one on the left was no larger than a manhole cover and the one on the right only slightly larger. The aperture in the middle offered an egg-shaped opening, six feet high, lined with pale gray stones that formed an arch. At the arch's pinnacle, was a dark blue keystone.

Once he passed over the threshold of that odd arch, Hyatt discovered darkness deeper than he had ever known. He kept his flashlight trained on the cave ceiling. Prehistoric etchings there depicted hunters and their prey, winged sky gods and assorted mysterious creatures. Further along, the cave ceiling gave way to queer constellations. Wild grass shifted against his shins as the light from his flashlight faded and went out. Hyatt continued forward, heading toward an enormous bronze-colored moon that crested the horizon.

Part Six:

A Labyrinth of Strange Constellations

Chapter Thirty-Seven: Small World— Philadelphia PA, 2012

Driving back to the Hilton Hotel, Miller considered once more the tale of war that May Weldon had told him. There were any number of reasons for the vision Hyatt had experienced at Vimy Ridge, battle fatigue, shellshock, malnutrition, to name a few. Yet, the parallels between the writer's experience at war and those depicted in his novel were too familiar. After years of textual analysis and biographical investigation only one question remained: was it true? Or was May having one last laugh at his expense? The former he had no way of knowing, even if his gut told him that something extraordinary had happened to Hyatt; the latter he dismissed, at least temporarily, until he could visit May one last time. He had recorded the interview he conducted earlier that afternoon. The description May had given him about the Paleolithic paintings inside the cave intrigued him. He needed to find out if those cave paintings had been catalogued by archaeologists sometime after the First World War ended. Whatever the case, whether the tale was true or not, the information he had received opened several opportunities for the biography's revision; moreover, hallucination or not, Miller started to understand more about the genesis of *The Land of Dust and Honey*.

As he entered the hotel lobby, he stopped. There was a brief moment in which he had forgotten his room number. Miller attributed this memory lapse to anxiety, but the truth was that no matter how hard he tried he drew a blank. To compound matters, his mind raced as he considered Hyatt's time in France.

Miller approached the front desk where a clerk wore a name tag that read: Chet. He was embarrassed to admit that he had forgotten his room number.

"How may I help you, Dr. Miller?" Chet asked.

"I left here this morning with Mr. Cardin," said Miller. "Do you know if he's checked out?"

Chet checked the computer behind the front desk. He typed with one hand while he tapped a Bic pen against his big teeth with the other.

"It looks as if Mr. Cardin checked out late today," the clerk told him.

"Thank you," Miller said. "You know what? I seem to have misplaced my room key. May I have another?"

"Wait here, please."

Miller picked up his briefcase that he had set down on the floor. In it were the letters May had given him along with the introduction she had written. He was anxious to get to his room.

Seconds later, a man in a sharp gray suit emerged from a door marked 'Hotel Manager.' He was short, nearly dwarfish, and lean in build with close-cropped gray hair.

"Dr. Miller?" the little man asked.

"Yes?"

"My name is Abel Whitaker," he extended his small right hand. "I am the hotel manager."

"Nice to make your acquaintance," Miller said, shaking Whitaker's hand.

"I am terribly sorry," the hotel manager said. "I am afraid we've had to move you to another room."

"Anything wrong?"

"Not at all," he said.

"What room will be mine?"

Whitaker handed him a new key card tucked into a sleeve bearing the Hilton logo.

"It's a suite, Dr. Miller," he said. "Mr. Heddings paid for it. He will be here later this evening if he has not arrived already. Would you like me to check?"

"Heddings is coming here?"

"He insisted that Wagner-Krauss pick up the tab," Whitaker informed him, "for the remainder of your stay here."

Miller walked toward the elevators. Whitaker trailed him.

"And my luggage and things?" asked Miller.

"Everything is squared away, sir," the hotel manager said.

"Are you from the area, Mr. Whitaker?"

"I am. Why do you ask?"

"What about your great-grandfather?"

"Ardmore," said Whitaker. "It's not far from here."

"Small world," Miller said.

An elevator arrived on the ground floor. The doors opened. Miller stepped inside.

"Will you be dining in the restaurant, Dr. Miller?" Whitaker asked.

"Yes," he said as the doors closed.

As he rode the elevator to his floor, Miller remembered the first day he had met Schuyler Heddings. It started with a phone call. His editor, Muriel Pfeiffer, had telephoned him at his office at UMass. It was a rare occasion, for Muriel was an old-fashioned editor who always used her administrative assistant to field calls and, more often than not, also tasked her with communicating edits to authors. But that afternoon it was Muriel herself on the line.

"Oh, Harold," said Muriel, her voice as raspy as ever thanks to a four-decade steady diet of Pall Malls and single malt scotch. "I am so pleased to find you at work. I tried you at home, but there was no answer."

"I'm working, Muriel," he told her. "What's on your mind?"

"Rhineholt Publishers, as you know, has been going through some changes," she said. "I wanted to call you and inform you personally that several departments are being restructured as a result of the merger with Wagner-Krauss from Europe."

The much-publicized merger he knew about through two sources, the business section of the New York Times and Muriel's administrative assistant Hilda Beauchamp who had telephoned him nearly a year beforehand to inform him of the pending merger between the two publishing houses. Official word came several weeks afterward. Publishing, Miller knew, was a business like any other. Mergers happened now and again. There was always a chance that new authors might have their contracts cancelled; but, given that the Hyatt biography had already seen three printings, Miller was not worried. He was grateful that his life's work had been accepted and published by Rhineholt, as well as the half-dozen 'lost works' of other writers that he had unearthed, and that with a nod from each writer's respective estates, he had been able to share those works with the world.

"You are moving to Europe?" Miller asked.

"No," Muriel replied. "But after careful consideration I have decided to leave. After thirty-five years with Rhineholt, it's time for a change."

"Well, I do appreciate you calling to tell me personally, Muriel," he said. "What will you do? Another publishing house?"

"Oh no, not me," she said. "I am going to retire and move to South America."

"That's wonderful."

"I have a house in Brazil. It's a lovely little cottage. I know it sounds like a cliché, but I intend to write a novel."

Two weeks later, Miller boarded a train headed for Penn Station. He had been summoned by his new editor for a face-to-face conference.

"I want to meet all of my writers," Schuyler Heddings told Miller over lunch. "You live so close to the city I figured this would be a good opportunity."

"I live in the Berkshires," Miller reminded him.

"Right," he said. "Anyway, it's important to know your clients, to understand their needs, and to find out what sort of future we have in store together."

The meeting turned out to be nothing of the sort. Instead, Miller endured a power lunch in a midtown eatery where Heddings divided his time between picking his teeth and praising the Vanderbilt greats like Robert Penn Warren, Allen Tate, and John Crowe Ransom.

"Me?" Heddings asked. "I always wanted to be a poet, but I lack the sensitivity for such high-minded endeavors."

"It's a calling," Miller looked at his watch.

"Right, anyway after Vanderbilt I knocked around Europe one summer," he went on. "Then my daddy called me home and read me the riot act about finding work. I began as a proofreader at a now-defunct small press in Manhattan. After that it was back to Europe. Only this time instead of banging German girls I went to work for Wagner-Krauss in their Paris offices. Fast forward a decade or two and here I am. Your humble editor who is about to savor all that New York has to offer."

Presently, Miller arrived at his suite and found the door ajar. Though the room was his, according to Whitaker the hotel manager, he knocked anyway before he entered. The bathroom door was shut. The toilet flushed. Miller stood in the small living room area.

When Schuyler Heddings emerged from the bathroom he was still singing a song Miller did not recognize. The editor showed no sign of surprise and continued singing until he finished the verse.

"Harold," he said. "I am terribly sorry for barging in like this."

"No trouble," Miller replied. "What's that song?"

"An old R.E.M. song," he told him. "One that brings back fond memories of my days at Vanderbilt."

"What brings you to Philadelphia?"

"I am going to meet with a chef who's written a book and his agent," Heddings said. "The book's a memoir."

"That's not like you to travel, Schuyler," he replied.

Heddings shrugged his narrow shoulders. He moved to the sofa and sat down, crossing his right leg over his left. His bright purple, silk socks matched his cravat.

"The truth is I hate Philadelphia," he confessed. "It lacks the character of New York. And the carnality of Paris afterhours is completely absent here."

"Who is the chef?"

"Some brute who thinks he has an interesting story to tell," said Heddings, examining his manicure. "It's the usual fair. Sexual abuse at the hands of his stepfather, and the inevitable drug and alcohol addiction that follows such a thing. Then he went on to Europe to train under some culinary savant in Provence. Afterward, he found God. Personally, I'd cut that part of the book; but redemption sells. Right?"

"Who does he know?"

"Smart man," he said. "His culinary instructor is the cousin of a big mahoff with Wagner-Krauss in Paris. I know the guy. The whole thing has become political."

"So you are pressed into this?" Miller asked.

Heddings waved a dismissive hand. "It's no bother," he said. "I'll do my part. It's what I am paid to do."

"Is the book any good?"

"The book is remarkable, actually, though I suspect that it will be my luck to sign this guy and then find out that it was all bullshit. There is, however, one curious aspect of this memoir."

"And what would that be?"

"The chef who wrote the memoir is a distant relative of Ryman Kessler."

"*The* Ryman Kessler?" Miller snapped to attention now.

"That's right, Harry," Heddings said. "The author of *Gas Lamp Genie*? Have you ever read it?"

"I've taught it in my early American literature class," he answered. "It's remarkable how—"

"Rumor has it that somewhere in Philly is Kessler's other novel," the editor said. "Imagine scoring two lost manuscripts? This is right up your alley, Harry. Once you cinch the Hyatt manuscript you should get to work on Koestler's trail."

"Kessler and his alleged manuscript went up in smoke at the Liberty Hotel when it caught fire in 1933," said Miller. "That road is a dead end."

"Speaking of lost manuscripts," Heddings switched gears now. "How goes it with Dame Weldon? Has she coughed up anything yet? I mean the piece she was going to write?"

Miller placed his attaché case on the coffee table. He removed the folder that contained the introduction May had written for him. Heddings took the sheaf of papers from him. He shuffled through the pages, making odd noises with his throat, before handing the pages back to Miller.

"That's it?" Heddings asked.

"It's sound," Miller announced. "It's what you wanted. And I have—"

"The other manuscript?"

"I was going to say some new letters."

"But no manuscript?"

"No."

"I want the second book, Harry."

"And what if it doesn't exist? What then?"

"I will tell you what then," Heddings told him. "Without Hyatt's long-rumored second novel, your biography will most likely be dead in the water. Sure some hardcore fans will purchase your book. You may even garner a few decent reviews in college literary journals. But that's hardly worth the time and

310

money. Even if you do see some sales of the updated biography, it will never be enough to cover the advance."

"I thought we had a deal."

"A deal? No," he said. "Harold, we had a conversation. The publishing industry is evolving. People no longer want to read about squeaky clean dead writers. People want to be intrigued by sex and money."

Heddings stood up. He did not offer his hand for Miller to shake.

"Is that the direction Rhineholt-Wagner-Krauss is going?" the professor asked. "Tell-alls about celebrities and redemption tales by line cooks?"

"Chefs."

"Whatever," Miller snapped. "The point is—"

"Christ, Harry," Heddings said as he walked toward the door. "No one reads anymore, at least, not the way they used to. Forty or fifty years ago you could go into the country, meet some kid who dropped out of grade school, and there was a good chance he might wile away his lazy evenings reading Faulkner or Harper Lee or even the Bible, for fuck's sake. Now? Now, we have illiterate little bastards who would rather play video games or watch porn on the internet while they struggle through college because mommy and daddy say that's where they belong.

"And if they haven't gone to college," he went on, "a good number of them sit at home living on welfare while watching Jerry Springer and Maury Povich. Reality television junkies, the lot of them! But business is business, Harry, and I am in the publishing business. That means we have to print what sells, no matter how reprehensible those books may seem according to your academically tainted, ivory tower standards."

"We're talking about two different things here, Schuyler," countered Miller. "And you know that."

"Are we?" Heddings opened the door. He turned to face Miller as he stood in the doorway. "Once upon a time you were good, Harry. But you've lost the fire. Hell, just last week there was a graduate student in the city who unearthed a manuscript by a Harlem Renaissance writer. And that was almost by accident."

"Did you offer him a contract too?"

"Harry, there are a lot of hungry sharks out there," the editor told him. "They are willing to bring this venture into the twenty-first century. Some young academicians like—"

"I used to be?" Miller asked.

Heddings shook his head. "Never mind," he said. "We'll send you word on a deadline. If you make it, we'll consider the updated biography. That's the best I can do."

Miller nodded and shut the door.

Chapter Thirty-Eight: An Emancipation—Pittsfield Ma, 2012

The old fear was gone now. Elinor saw her reflection in the bookcase glass. When she was a little girl she often snuck into her father's study, hiding beneath the desk, sometimes for an hour or more, watching her reflection in the glass, convinced, in her child mind, that her father's barrister bookcase with so many early works of fantastical literature, among them Hyatt's novel, was itself a threshold between the mundane and the magical, an inaccessible egress beyond which her life-long rival yet lived. Day after day, before her father returned home from campus, young Elinor sat beneath the desk waiting for something extraordinary to happen. Later, the adolescent Elinor suspected that the book had inexplicably fed off her; a slow drain that empowered the novel through a science which she could not understand. The magic had always been there, only for Elinor, not in the way she believed. As she continued to stare at her faint reflection in the glass, Elinor listened to the emptiness of the house as she remembered a conversation she had had with her mother when she was eight years old.

A girl at school had made fun of Elinor's name, telling her that it was '*an old lady's name*,' a name for a spinster, and the first name of that woman in The Beatles song who kept her face in a jar by the door. Elinor confronted her mother after school that day, demanding to know the reason for the name her parents had chosen for her.

Ann Miller, always a study in poise and grace, patted the sofa cushion next to her. Elinor sat down. Her teary eyes revealed the hurt of her classmate's cruel words. Even now, she could still remember hearing the grandfather clock's tick that kept time with her mother's voice.

"Your name is an old family name," Ann had told her. "The name Elinor was my great-grandmother's on my mother's side."

"So it *is* an old lady's name," Elinor cried.

Ann laughed as she smoothed her skirt. When next she spoke, she did not smile.

"Your father wanted to name you after a character in his favorite novel," she told her daughter. "Her name was Matilda. Tilly was her nickname. But I didn't like it. So, I told your father that I could not bear to hear someone call you 'Tilly.' It sounds like broken glass being rubbed with tin foil."

Elinor suppressed a laugh of her own. She wanted to be angry; she wanted to be unforgiving.

"But why this name?" she asked.

"All names have power, my love," her mother said. "A person's name often carries the power of those who came before her. That power is strength, a strength you inherit. And your great-great-grandmother was as strong as they came."

At eight years old, young Elinor did not possess the means by which to comprehend what her mother had said that day. As time went on, however, she understood that at least for one moment, though she had yet to be born, she shined brighter than her father's favorite book.

Alone in the study now, bookcase key in hand, Elinor heard the tick of the clock on the wall. For reasons never fully explained to her, her father had never grasped the concept of a digital clock, or at least one that made no noise. She tapped the skeletal key against the palm of her hand, contemplating her next move. All that separated Elinor from her rival was a thin pane of glass. She inserted the key and unlocked the bookcase. She lifted the door up and slid it back into the case, revealing the prized first edition of *The Land of Dust and Honey*. Taking the book in both hands, she considered the weight of the novel, the two-tone dust jacket, and the deckle-edged pages.

Next, Elinor placed the book on her father's desk, turned on the lamp, and sat down in the plush leather chair. Opening the front cover, she found an old Chromatic photograph of her and her father. In the picture she stood on a beach, her father on his haunches behind her; on the reverse side of the photograph, her mother's careful penmanship: Ellie and Harry, Mystic CT, 1969. With each turn of a page, Elinor discovered more mementos from her past. Here, placed between the title page and the next, another photograph of a four-year-old Elinor at Mystic Beach; a red pail embedded in the soft, wet sand as she sat with her legs splayed, a yellow plastic spade in her right hand as she shielded her eyes from the sun with her left; standing at her side, her mother in a one-piece turquoise bathing suit as she peered at the ocean. There, in the middle of Chapter One, a small handmade card of pink construction paper with purple crayon block letters that read: HAPPY BIRTHDAY DADDY. LOVE ELLIE. She spent several minutes looking at each piece of the past her father had hidden away inside Hyatt's novel. In all, she counted seventy-seven photographs, cards, notes, and drawings she had made for her father. Elinor was careful to keep the mementos between the pages where she had found them. She recalled now that her therapist Dr. Banerjee had spoken about a particular part of *The Land of Dust and* Honey entitled 'The Wild Country.' The chapter was located more than half-way into the book. The old clock on the wall to her left continued its tenuous tick-tock. She opened the book, pressing her thumbs against the page edges so her father's keepsakes would not fall out, sat back in the chair, and began to read.

The Wild Country

The long night of aberrant dreams ended the moment Tilly and Barth left the ancient forest behind them; no longer was the former soldier plagued by ruined faces of the dead; nor did he have to sleep at a distance from the young girl for fear of mistaking her for a German sapper, and slitting her throat—an ordeal that nearly came to fruition, the night after they left the cottage, had it not been for Tilly's screams that brought Barth out of his blood rage as he pressed his boot knife against her thin neck. For Tilly, leaving the forest meant an emancipation from the endless subterranean caverns she traversed in the dreamtime; a labyrinth of granite, shale, and limestone that echoed with her lost brother's voice; unable to find her brother in the dark, she woke up shrieking under the stars.

Chapter Thirty-Nine: Other Doorways—Haverford Township PA, 2012

...coming over the low hills, past the scrub brush and rocky outcrops, a plateau offered a wide vista in those pre-dawn hours. The strange constellations became distorted; as if long sections of starry light had been ripped away, leaving fathomlessly dark rents in the otherwise pristine night sky.

Three days into the overland journey it had been Tilly who insisted that they continue to travel after dark; drawn, she was, by some inexplicable desire to head west. Barth had been skeptical, at first; then, on the seventh day, as night gave over to day, he saw it. The first rays of dawn crested over the eastern edge of the plateau, though the sky to the west ahead of them remained a darkish violet; and Barth understood what compelled Tilly to press on each evening after walking all day long...

Miller replaced his bookmark and set aside his battered trade paperback copy of Hyatt's novel. He sat in May Weldon's living room. The chair was a high-back armchair upholstered in forest green leather. Somewhere overhead, pipes groaned as May turned off the shower. When he had arrived that morning,

Miller was surprised to see that she was not ready for his arrival. May showed him into the living room, apologizing for meeting him at the door dressed in her pajamas and bathrobe.

"Long night," she told him.

The twinkle in her eye did not go unnoticed.

"How are you feeling?" Miller asked.

"I'm fine," said May. "I was up late packing. And then I had company."

The expression she wore reminded Miller of how she had looked that one night several years ago when they had slept together. That morning there was defiance in her voice as if the mere mention of 'company' was meant to elicit some crass response on his part. But Miller did not challenge her. Instead, he quickly forced the memory of that night aside, embarrassed that he still lusted for this woman after all this time.

"I am afraid I don't have much to drink," May told him, "except for tea or water."

"Tea will be fine," said Miller.

"There's spring water in the refrigerator," she replied, "if you change your mind. Otherwise, help yourself to some tea."

Presently, floorboards creaked overhead. Moments later, May descended the stairs. Miller tucked his book back into his satchel.

"Did you get your tea?" May stood in the living room doorway now.

She wore khaki pants, a pale blue button shirt, and hiking shoes. Her face appeared fuller than the day before, youthful in a way that defied explanation.

"No, I'm okay," Miller said. He averted his eyes, pretending to be interested in some books on a shelf when he stood up. "I should probably run over to the library and make photocopies of the letters—"

"Keep them," she said, "until it's time to turn them over to Special Collections at Haverford College."

"Are you sure? You made it sound as if you wanted them back right away."

"A girl can change her mind."

"Well, I have to go home today."

"No time for lunch?"

"I suppose I do."

"Good," May said. "We have business first. Did I not tell you?"

"Tell me what?"

"Come with me," she said.

A set of french doors off the dining room opened onto a sun porch that had been converted into an office. It was a space Miller had not seen until that day. Bookshelves lined each wall in uninterrupted rows, obstructing most of the windows. On one set of bookshelves near the french doors were several dozen critical works on Ovid; among those books, the volume of *Metamorphoses* that Miller had given to May. Aside from the numerous bookshelves, furniture was sparse. An old desk stained dark brown was situated beneath the only visible windows, three of them, that offered a scant glance of the backyard. Behind the desk was a brown leather high-back chair and a wood dining room chair had been placed in front of the desk. In front of one of the bookcases to the right was a small loveseat, its cushions piled high with various magazines and journals. What caught Miller's eyes, however, was a first edition hardbound copy of R.J. Hyatt's *The Land of Dust and Honey* atop the desk. The book, upon closer examination, appeared to be in pristine condition.

"I believe you have one of those already," said May.

Miller turned to face her. The late morning light coming through the tops of the windows added to May's radiance. Her face exhibited the healthy color of a woman much younger than her years. Her hair looked longer than the previous day; it was still white gray, for the most part, but now several short strands of dark hair were visible as well. These anomalies in May's appearance troubled Miller, given that in the span of a few days his host had gone from a gaunt, cancer-stricken wraith to a visage of the formerly vibrant and, dare he notice, voluptuous woman he had known in previous years.

"What?" he asked.

"Harold," she said, "are you not well?"

Miller's mind had become a clean slate. He was unable to recall what she had said a moment ago.

"I'm sorry," he told her. "I thought you were saying something to me."

From somewhere in the house came a dull thud. The room shook. May arched her left eyebrow.

"Never a dull moment," she said.

"What was that?" he asked.

"My mover is here," she informed him. Then, she called out, "Arawn! I am in the den, dear!"

Heavy footsteps plodded their way through the house. Miller was not ready for the young man who appeared in the den doorway. He expected some slovenly and perhaps bearish man in coveralls. Instead, the man who stood before him was tall, broad-shouldered, and narrow in the waist. He wore a pale green T-shirt that stretched tightly across his chest, and strained over the circumference of his muscular arms. Miller guessed the man's age to be in his thirties, but it was hard to tell for sure. The young man's hair was dark, laced with strands of gray, and long. A veritable mess of braids and dreadlocks.

"Dr. Miller," said May, "I would like to introduce you to Arawn Yates."

"Aaron?" Miller extended his right hand.

"Close enough," the big man's hand caused Miller's to vanish for a moment as he shook it. "It's Arawn. A Welsh name."

"Y-Yates did you say?"

"That's right."

"There was a man who lived decades ago over in Ardmore—"

"May," said Yates, "I'm nearly finished, save for the business in the basement."

"Thank you, dear," she told him. "We will be on our way after lunch."

Yates nodded and left the room.

"There were stories prior to the First World War," said Miller. "He lived in the woods near the powder mill—"

"Harold," May said, "I told you that story. Remember?"

"Of course, of course," he said. "It's just that..."

"What?"

"Never mind," he told her. "You will think me crazy."

"Good," she said. Then, pointing to the wood chair in front of the desk, "Please, sit."

May went behind the desk. She knelt and rolled back a small area rug. Beneath the rug, was an in-floor safe. After she opened the safe, she removed an old manuscript box bound with leather straps.

"Take this," she handed the box to Miller.

He took the manuscript box from her and placed it on the desk. May removed three more identical boxes and placed them on the desk beside the first one. Miller sat back down on the wood chair, eyeing the boxes. Sweat coated his brow.

"Is this—" he started to say.

"You were always an eager one," said May. She produced a sheaf of documents from the safe and placed it atop the manuscript boxes on the desk. "One thing at a time."

She closed the safe, rolled the area rug back over it, and sat down behind the desk.

"These," May tapped the sheaf of documents, "were drawn up by the firm that represents Robert's literary estate."

"And the boxes?"

"Harold, please," she said. "I am trying to paint a big picture here. So, bear with me."

"I'm sorry."

"There is a contract here as well as some paperwork about my home—"

"May, I don't—"

"Harry, please," she held up a cautionary hand. "There is an agreement within these pages stipulating that neither Schuyler Heddings nor the publishing company that employs him will have anything to do with the content of these boxes. This point I cannot stress enough. The inheritance you are about to receive—"

"Inheritance?"

"I am leaving you my house, Harry," May told him. "I have no one else in this world. It's yours if you want it. There is one condition within the agreement. You must never open this house to the public. Is that understood?"

"Yes, I understand," Miller said. "But I don't see—"

"The agreement also details how, upon your own death, your daughter Elinor will become the owner of this house," she continued. "Your daughter, like you, will not be permitted to open this house to the public for any reason. Lastly, if Elinor bears no descendents to continue ownership of this house—"

"May, wait," he said. "There's something you should know."

"You have already sold your soul to Schuyler Heddings?"

"No, of course not."

"Then what is it?"

"It's my daughter, Elinor."

"Is she ill?"

"No, not at all," Miller replied. After a brief pause, he added, "Elinor fears that I am developing dementia."

"Don't we all? At this age?"

"Said the woman who looks remarkably fit for someone who's recently undergone chemotherapy."

"If it's a matter of reviewing these documents," said May, "then I can give you the name of a lawyer who—"

"Elinor thinks it may be Alzheimer's."

"Is she a doctor?"

"No, but I am having trouble."

May made a steeple of her hands as she rested her elbows on the desk.

"You're forgetting things?" she asked.

Miller wanted to tell her everything, but he held back. It was enough to admit to another human being that his mind wasn't what it used to be. He saw no sense in burdening May with the knowledge of the time he had gotten lost driving back from the UMass campus. For him, it felt like a story that someone had told him; even now he had problems recalling all the details of that night, the night that Elinor had diagnosed him.

"It's worse than that," he said, quietly. "When it happens, I mean."

"Listen, Harry," she said, "why don't we do this? Let's take a walk. There are a few new eateries over on Brookline Avenue. Overpriced and the service is mediocre, but at least it will afford us the opportunity to get out of this house."

"I saw a Japanese place driving into town," said Miller. "I can't remember the last time I had Japanese food."

"Then Japanese it is," May said. "Do you like sushi?"

"Not especially."

May grunted. "New Englanders. You're all the same."

"I am from Chicago."

"A landlocked wasteland of concrete and steel," she joked.

Miller did not laugh.

"I have to write things down these days," he told her. "Otherwise, I forget. It used to be that I could look at a syllabus and remember the classroom number. Now? Now, I have to write down the hall and the classroom number. You should see my office."

"I am sure you have guessed already," May said, placing her hands atop the manuscript boxes. "This is Robert's *other* book. The manuscript comes with the house. That's the deal. And no Schuyler Heddings or that deplorable conglomerate he calls a publishing house. In a nutshell, that's it. You can think about it over lunch."

"If I decide, for health reasons, that I may not be the best person to entrust all of this with," Miller said, "then what?"

"The manuscript vanishes," she replied. "As for the house? It goes up for auction."

Miller shifted in his seat. He nodded at the sheaf of documents.

"May I?" he asked.

Three hours later, Miller stood looking down at a headstone in St. Denis Cemetery. In a tree some ten yards away, a lone Eastern Bluebird emitted its melodious warble.

The headstone read: Matilda Anne Hyatt, born May 19, 1903, died Jan 17, 1917.

At the top of the headstone, a carving that depicted a tree resembling the woodcut used in the cover illustration of *The Land of Dust and Honey*. Miller stooped low beside the headstone to get a better look.

His thoughts now were not of the past, but of the future. Once he had finished reviewing the legal documents over lunch at Sampan Inn, he signed them. May and he drank a small cup of sake each to celebrate. Afterward, they walked back to May's house. It felt strange for Miller to be the legal custodian of the home of the world's only living link to Robert Jonas Hyatt. Now that May was gone, sadness filled him. It happened shortly after they had left the restaurant and returned to the house.

They were in the kitchen when Arawn Yates ascended from the basement. His massive frame filled the doorway.

"Ready?" he asked.

May slid a set of keys across the kitchen table. "You will need them, I suspect," she said to Miller.

Miller took the keys and placed them in his jacket pocket.

"Is there a car coming to fetch you?" he asked.

May and Yates laughed.

"Sorry, Harry," she said. "I am afraid I will be walking."

"I will see you downstairs," said Yates before he turned and descended the stairs.

324

May stood up, gathered the tea cups from which they drank Earl Grey, and placed them into the kitchen sink. She took a deep breath as she kept her back turned to Miller.

"May?" he went to her and put his hand on her shoulder.

"I am fine," she said. "Come downstairs with me before you go."

In the basement Yates waited by the arched door that led into the root cellar. At the apex of the arch, a faint light glowed within the carved onyx keystone. There were several steamer trunks lined against the wall on either side of the door. One of the trunks was open. As he drew near, Miller saw its contents: old bricks from the wall Hyatt and May's father had removed while constructing the root cellar. In front of the brick-filled steamer trunk, three bags of mortar waited on the floor.

Yates opened the arched door. Cool air wafted into the basement.

May laced her right arm through Miller's left.

"Shall we?" she asked.

"What's in there?" he countered.

"Don't be such a fuss-bucket," she had told him as she led him through the doorway.

Miller shivered, remembering, as he looked around the cemetery. He was alone, and the afternoon was pressing forward. Near the base of the tree where the bluebird sang, he retrieved a small stone, placed it atop the headstone, and offered a prayer for Hyatt's sister. After that he headed back to his rental car in which his overnight bag was stuffed with Hyatt's manuscript.

Sunlight dappled through the trees that flanked the cemetery gates. It was a warm afternoon, devoid of humidity, and yet Miller felt another chill. The sensation had started, in earnest, back at May's house (he would not come to terms with ownership for several more months) the moment he entered the root cellar.

May had clung fast to her guest as she guided him through the darkness. She stopped after they had traversed a few yards into the void that connected the familiar world Miller knew and the one waiting beyond that threshold. Miller felt nauseous, dizzy, and anxious. He reached out with his free hand to brace himself but felt only emptiness.

"Don't worry, it passes," May assured him.

They continued forward. Miller was barely aware of the dirt floor beneath his shoes. It wasn't long before the darkness gave over to light. It was faint, at first, but soon there was enough illumination to reveal the walls of a cave where Paleolithic paintings rendered in ochre, umber, black, and red depicted strange animals beneath queer constellations. One section of the long mural caught Miller's attention. A flat part of the cave wall had been reserved for a large rendition in red of what appeared to be a spoked wheel; its center looked like a globe with a tree colored dark brown growing out of its northernmost point. The wheel itself was wide, and where the spokes met the wheel the artist or artists had painted arches in black.

"Harry," May tugged at his arm.

When they emerged from the cave they descended a narrow pass onto a field of thigh-high, wild, green grass. The sky directly overhead was dark cobalt; at the furthest reaches of the horizon, the cobalt sky turned indigo. More than the oddly colored sky, what stopped Miller in his tracks was an immense tree of mountainous proportions. Broad as several city blocks at the base of its trunk, the tree twisted skyward with magnificent limbs that spread out in all directions, as if the tree supported the sky itself and the uppermost reaches of the branches vanished into the haze of high altitudes. By Miller's guess, the tree was at least a mile away. From where he stood, he saw a countless number of exposed roots thick as subway tunnels and as elaborate as the branches overhead.

May let go of Miller's arm and pointed to the wide, green plain ahead of them. A lone figure, barely distinguishable from the great tree in the background, made his way forward. May waved her arm high. The man waved back. More than two hundred yards separated them. As the man closed the gap, moving gradually, his hands stuffed into his pockets, May and Miller pressed toward him. There was less than fifty yards of high grass that separated them now. The man stopped. He was tall, lanky, and his shoulders slouched as he shoved his hands deeper into his pockets. The man did not look at May, choosing instead to be interested in something hidden in the tall grass.

"Is that—" Miller began.

"Indeed," said May. "That's Robert."

Miller drew several deep breaths now. He leaned forward at the waist, thinking he might throw up or pass out, or perhaps both as each second passed. A half-minute later, as May patted his back, Miller recovered.

"I must be—"

"Dreaming?" May asked.

"I was going to say having another episode," replied Miller. He patted his pockets. "I should write this down. Then I will know it's real."

"No need, Harry," she said. "This is all very real. You are standing in *The Land of Dust and Honey.*"

"Do you think I could meet him?"

"Oh, I am afraid Robert's rather quite shy that way," May told him. "It's nothing personal."

She steadied Miller once more as he faltered. Then, satisfied that he would not collapse, she leaned in close and kissed him on the cheek.

"Not a chance in hell?" Miller asked.

"I am afraid not, Harry," she patted him on the shoulders.

Miller waved to Hyatt. The writer kept his eyes trained on the high grass.

"How can he still be alive?" he asked.

"That's a long story," May said. "I think the manuscript will make it clear."

"So, this is it?"

"Arawn will show you the way through," she told him.

327

Unaware that they had been followed, Miller glanced over his shoulder. Yates waited in the grass twenty yards behind him.

When Miller turned to say something to May he discovered that she was already moving through the grass, drawing her knees up high as Hyatt approached her. When they embraced, Miller felt guilty for watching them. As he turned to go, he saw Hyatt look at him over May's shoulder. That's when Hyatt smiled and nodded.

May!" Miller called out.

The couple stood shoulder to shoulder facing him now.

"Harry?"

"What's to stop me from coming back here?" he asked.

May stretched her arms out wide as Hyatt held her by the waist. "Arawn Yates!" she cried.

Outside the cemetery, as he climbed into his rental car, Miller recalled something Yates had told him. The two men were standing in the basement of May's house. Miller could not remember the walk back through the cave into the root cellar. He had succumbed to a depressive stupor almost immediately as May and Hyatt waded through the high grass toward the enormous tree; unable, no matter how hard he tried, to come to terms with failing to speak to the writer he admired most.

"What happens now?" Miller asked.

Yates stood in the arched doorway between the root cellar and the basement. His left hand rested on a latch affixed to the inside of the heavy door.

"May's given you everything you need," said Yates.

"I meant this," he gestured to the doorway, and the carved onyx keystone at the arched frame's apex.

"You leave," the large man said. "I lock this door from the inside. Later, I come back and fill the root cellar with fresh earth. Then I seal the portal for good."

Yates pointed at the bricks inside the steamer truck to his right.

"How will you get back?" Miller asked.

The big man grinned. "There are other doorways," he said. "You just have to know where to look."

When the arched door slammed shut Miller knew he had to do something to ground him once more to the world he knew. He thought of calling his daughter, but she would never believe him, not without proof. So, he went to the cemetery to pay his respects to Matilda Hyatt.

Now, as he sat in his rental car, the air conditioning on full blast, he thought of two things: the long trip by train back to Pittsfield and Yates's final words. *There are other doorways. You just have to know where to look.*

Miller fished his cell phone out of his jacket pocket. He called his home number. Elinor answered.

"I'm leaving now," he told her.

"Why don't I meet you half-way," she offered. "Keep the rental and I will share the cost—"

"No need," her father told her. "Do you know anything about Paleolithic cave paintings?"

"That's random. Are you okay?"

Miller laughed. It wasn't going to get any better. And by the time it was really bad, he wouldn't be aware of it. That much he knew.

"I'll see you when I get home, Ellie."

Chapter Forty: A Daughter's Help—
Pittsfield MA, 2012

Elinor lit two candles in their crystal candleholders on the dining room table. The dinner she had prepared for her father, a simple roasted chicken with potatoes, carrots, and string beans, lay warm in the oven. It was after nine o'clock. Before she began cooking, she cleaned the dining room. There were papers and old mail strewn across the table. These she removed and stacked on a chair in the corner of the room.

At nine-thirty, Elinor heard her father unlock the front door. She wanted to rush him at the door, but she hung back, making noise in the kitchen as she removed the dinner from the oven. Admittedly, Elinor was not the culinary savant her mother had been, but she had picked up a few tricks along the way. She hoped that the meal would suffice, wondering if her father had remembered to eat at all while he was away.

"Dad, are you hungry?"

"Not now, Ellie," he said as he appeared in the kitchen doorway.

"But I made—"

"I said not now," Miller left the kitchen and went into the dining room. "Candles? Excellent."

Elinor followed her father into the dining room. She watched him push aside the serving plates and silverware.

"What are you doing?"

Miller took one manuscript box after another out of his overnight bag and placed each one on the table. As he removed the leather straps on each box, his daughter moved around the table to get a better look.

"Dad, are you feeling okay?"

"Do you know what I have here?"

"Not a clue."

"Take a guess."

"I don't like this game," Elinor told him. "Why don't we eat first."

"Oh, damn," he snapped his fingers. "Before I forget, we have another house now."

"What? Are you moving?"

"No," he said. "It's May Weldon's old place."

"Dad, why would you buy—"

"I didn't buy the house," Miller said. "May left it to me."

"Dad, slow down."

"But this," he gestured to the manuscript boxes, "this is what's most important."

"Let's have some dinner," Elinor pressed him now. Her father's manic behavior was unsettling. If anything, some food might slow him down. "We'll eat. Then you can rest. You must be tired."

"I am not tired," her father said. "And we'll need a safe deposit box for these. Are you staying the night? You can drive me to the bank tomorrow."

"Stop!" she shouted. "Just stop it!"

Miller stared at his daughter. He could not recall a time when she had ever raised her voice to him.

"What are you so upset about?"

"You're going a mile a minute over some old papers," Elinor said and picked up a small stack of foolscap from an open manuscript box.

"Be careful."

"Dad, they're blank."

Miller extended his hand. Elinor gave the papers back to him.

"You're looking at R.J. Hyatt's second novel," her father said. "You know he wrote his first novel in invisible ink as well. If you had read the biography I wrote you would know this by now."

"I am sorry," said Elinor. "But I thought Hyatt wrote only one book?"

Miller picked up the first sheet out of the box closest to him. The fabric on the box lid was torn, but he paid it no mind. After he set the lid aside, Miller held the page over one of the lit candles, careful not to let the foolscap touch the flame.

"Here," he handed the sheet to his daughter once the words started to show. "See for yourself."

Elinor took the sheet. The handwriting she recognized from other samples her father had kept copies of in his files.

Under the Bronze Moon:
A Novel of the Land of Dust and Honey
by
R.J. Hyatt

She handed the page back to her father.

"Is this for real?" Elinor asked. "Wait. Never mind that. Dad, did you steal this?"

Miller sat his daughter down at the table. He pulled a chair close to hers, took her hands in his, and told her of how May Weldon wanted to hand over her house to someone she knew, someone she could trust. He told her of how she needed someone to aid in her next phase of life.

"Did you kill her?" she asked.

"Ellie," his expression soured as he spoke. "Be reasonable."

"All right," she said. "So, May Weldon bequeathed you this manuscript, after swearing up and down for decades that there was no second book. Why?"

"Have you been listening to what I am telling you?"

"It doesn't matter," said Elinor. "In less than a day I bet Schuyler Heddings will get his shitty hands on it."

"Not likely," her father told her.

He went on to explain how Heddings was out of the picture, how May had worded the legal agreement so that neither the boorish editor nor his publishing company would ever get near the new novel.

"New?" she withdrew her hands from his and sat back.

"As in as yet undiscovered," Miller back-pedaled now. He knew that if he had told his daughter the whole story that night she would have him checked into a mental institution by daybreak. And he didn't blame her. Who would believe such a thing? "Anyway, I am not solo on this thing. The law firm that manages R.J. Hyatt's literary estate—"

"So you just march into a publishing house in New York," she said, "and wave those boxes around until someone throws money at you?"

"Ellie, that's not how it works," he said.

"I know that. I just want to hear what the plan is."

She's testing me, he thought. Let her have her fun.

"Typically, something like this will go to auction," her father said. "We'll work with the law firm representing Hyatt's legal estate."

"We?"

"I think you want in on this, Ellie."

"What makes you so sure, dad?"

"Because once this is over," he said. "I am out."

"You're going to retire? I don't believe it."

"Let's eat," said Miller. "I am famished."

They ate at the kitchen table. When they finished, they left their plates and went back into the dining room.

Together, father and daughter worked through the night. Foolscap with the freshly revealed lemon juice ink was spread out in the living room and the den, and up the stairs to the second floor. As they worked they discovered that Hyatt had numbered his pages. Miller insisted that he and Elinor start with the last page of the book, working their way forward, so that neither of them would be tempted to read the book from the beginning as they progressed. When the candles on the dining room table ran low, they moved the operation into the kitchen. There they used the gas range to heat the pages. They took turns, first Elinor and then Miller in front of a lone burner, until Hyatt's invisible ink was invisible no more.

Chapter Forty-One: The Land Of Dust And Honey—Fallen Man

It was early the next morning when Barth woke up from a dream about home. The small cabin interior filled his vision as the sun rose. In the dawn's light the room looked much smaller than he remembered it from the previous evening. He lay perfectly still as he listened to Tilly's soft snore beside him, thinking about the dream that was still fresh in his mind.

Everyone Barth knew in Ardmore was walking through town in a solemn procession. His mother, his father and even his younger sister who had died before the war began were all on their way to the powder mill. Carrie, Barth's sister, was only eleven years old when she contracted tuberculosis and never recovered. When he dreamed of her Carrie never shared any great insight into her older brother's life; if she spoke at all it was about daily chores and school, as if life after death was a carbon copy of the one his sister knew before she died. For Barth, it was a comfort knowing that Carrie was able to live on in his dreams like a normal girl without being burdened with relaying information from the ether, without serving as the conduit between the world of the living and the realm of the dead. In this particular dream, however, Carrie and his parents did not acknowledge Barth. He fell in step with the procession of townspeople and followed them to Cobb's Creek; at the powder mill people waded into the shallow water, moving further out until they went under. No one emerged from the creek on the other side.

"Who's Carrie?" he heard Tilly ask.

"My sister," he answered.

Richard J. O'Brien

Tilly had the cabin door open now. Barth didn't remember her getting out of bed. A gentle, lilac-scented breeze blew into the room. The young girl swept the floor with an old broom fashioned from a tree branch, cord, and twigs that served as bristles.

"She's dead?" Tilly asked, keeping her back to the soldier as she worked.

"A long time ago," he answered. "I want to see this lake of yours."

Tilly put away her broom.

She and Barth left the cabin. High grass gave way to a narrow stretch of sandy beach that bordered the lake on three sides. The water appeared clear to a certain depth, but a few feet below the surface lay dark water.

Barth squatted down at the lake's edge. He used two hands, cupping them, and drank the water. After a few seconds passed, he repeated the action.

"I don't feel anything," he said.

Tilly did not hear him. She sat on a squat rock that served as a bench. Her eyes were closed as the sun shined down.

"I like it here in the morning," she called out. "Did you drink?"

"Yes," said Barth. "Should I feel different?"

"I don't know," Tilly answered.

"How much did you drink?"

"The nymphs say a ladle a day will keep death away," she told him. "But sometimes I get thirsty. I drink more than I should."

Barth was about to ask her about the Madri, the queen of the lake, and whether she ever appeared during the day, for the soldier was very much interested in speaking with the Madri, in finding out more about the magic and the circumstances that had brought him to this strange land, but his inquiry was cut short by the sight unfolding before him.

A man, slight of frame and hunched at the back, emerged from the forest on the lake's far side. He stumbled and fell, sprawling face-first into the sand. The man lay motionless after that, a few feet from the water.

"Tilly?"

336

"Yes?"

"There's a man over there," Barth informed her.

Tilly joined him where he remained on his haunches. They watched the man climb unsteadily to his feet. Tilly gasped when the man staggered to the right, pitching his body at an obscene angle, and fell down a second time. Barth rose to his feet. The man didn't move. Tilly took hold of the soldier's hand. They ran around the lake's edge, as fast as the sand would allow them, until they reached the fallen man.

Motionless, the man remained face-down in the sand. When Tilly and Barth reached him, they turned him over. The man was eighty or ninety years old, by Barth's guess, and from the looks of him severely malnutritioned. Tilly brushed wet sand from the man's face; unsatisfied with her work, she darted for the water, scooped up a handful and attempted to wash away the sand. Barth removed his canteen from his web belt.

"Fill it," he said. "But don't let him drink all of it at once."

Tilly did as she was told. She used more than half the canteen's water to wash the man's face clean. As Tilly poured water over the man's face he opened his mouth, attempting to drink. He managed to swallow a mouthful before spitting out the rest as he was overcome by a coughing fit. Tilly held the old man's face in her hands, soothing him until he was still. She turned then to go refill the canteen. The old man took hold of her arm.

"No," his voice barely a whisper as he spoke.

"The water will help you live," Tilly told him. "It's magic."

"No," he said. "No more magic." He pointed a crooked, bony finger at Barth. "You, help me to the shade."

Barth lifted the man in his arms, cradling him as if he were a child. The man weighed almost nothing, his bones hard against his sallow skin.

Ample shade was provided by a row of trees not far from where they found the newcomer. When Barth propped him against a tree he felt a chill. He wondered if the remnants of the night mist the water nymphs had created with their song the previous evening somehow lingered within the shadows. There were some places, Barth

337

reasoned, better left alone by man. He stepped into sunlight and watched Tilly approach with a canteen full of lake water.

"Drink," she told the old man as she knelt beside him once more.

The elderly stranger batted the canteen away from his lips and turned his head away.

"So persistent," he said. "Father was right. You never listened."

The old man pulled a locket from his coat pocket. He handed it to Tilly.

"Mother used to wear this," he said. "Do you remember?"

Tilly opened the locket. Inside, an old limning, rendered with meticulous skill, of her and her little brother. Tilly was only four years old and her brother not quite two years old.

"Cecil?" Tilly cried.

"In the flesh," he gasped. "Or what's left of it."

"But you are old!"

"And you haven't aged," said Cecil. "How can this be?"

"The lake," Tilly told him. "The water has magical powers, like in my story books when I—"

"No!" he snapped.

A coughing fit seized Cecil. Barth squatted down next to the old man and gently rubbed his back. He offered Cecil a scrap of cloth from his pocket. When Cecil spat dark blood into the cloth Barth was careful not to let Tilly see it.

"I have searched," Cecil said at last. "When I was old enough I went back into the caves."

"Cecil, please," his sister said. "You don't need to say anymore. Save your strength. Take this water. It will save you. I promise. It will."

Her brother laughed. A gurgling sound followed. Cecil leaned to his side. When he spat dark blood out of his mouth a second time, there was no hiding it from Tilly. Beside him, the blood clotted on the cool sand. Blood and phlegm dripped from his chin.

"Tilly," he whispered. "I searched for decades. Once inside the caves I became lost. In my travels I found strange lands, many of them far worse than this place. Did you hear the music? The sweet music? It led me to you."

"Save your strength, Cecil," Barth told him. "And listen to your sister. Take the water."

"May I speak to you privately?" Tilly tugged at Barth's hand now.

They moved a few feet away from Cecil. Barth kept his eyes trained on the old man.

"He's—" Barth started to say.

"Listen," said Tilly, "I was thinking. Why don't the three of us stay here? Just for a short time. Cecil can drink the water and be well. I will stop drinking the water. He could grow young. And I could get older. We could meet—"

"Tilly," he said, "your brother is very ill. There's no guarantee it will work."

Barth saw Cecil lift his bony hand, beckoning them.

Tilly went to her brother. She knelt beside him and held him close. The stench of slow death permeated his ratty clothes.

"Tilly," Cecil whispered.

"Shush," she told him.

"I see the storm," he declared.

"No, Cecil," she told him. "It's going to be all right. The sun is shining. Be still."

"Tilly?"

"Yes?"

"I'm scared."

There were no more words left to exchange. Cecil drew a deep breath. His exhalation was long, slow, and deliberate, as if his body was ready to give up the ghost. A gauzy sheen clouded Cecil's eyes. He died in his sister's arms.

Barth stood a short distance from sister and brother. His heart felt heavy. For a man to witness death, for a woman to bear witness too, was one thing, but for children it was another matter. When Tilly began rocking back and forth, clutching her dead brother in her arms as she sang an old lullaby, Barth had to turn away. He walked to the lake's edge. His distorted likeness in the water stared back at him; below his image, lithe, pale forms swam past and vanished in *the sparkling reflection of sunlight. He didn't know how many minutes had passed when he felt Tilly's hand take his.*

"I will want to give him a proper burial," the young girl whispered. "Will you help me?"

"Here?" Barth asked.

"I can't take Cecil home," she said. "I don't know the way."

"Sure, I'll help you."

"I want him laid to rest in sight of the cabin," she rubbed her eyes with the back of her free hand. "I don't want him in the forest."

Barth let go of Tilly's hand. He went back to the shade of the trees. Cecil felt as light as he did when Barth first picked him up.

Tilly walked a few paces behind the soldier as he carried her brother around the lake. She studied the limning in the locket, closed it, and opened it again. Her younger brother had been older than her parents when she had disappeared. A new sadness filled her now. There was no hope of ever going home.

It took Barth a few hours to dig a proper grave. Tilly helped him wrap Cecil in a blanket and lower him into the ground. Before Barth set about filling the grave back in Tilly offered a prayer to the God she knew before she had come to this strange land. And she invoked the Madris to look after her brother's remains.

At nightfall Tilly and Barth left the cabin. They headed east across an open valley. Storm clouds blotted out the stars in their odd constellations. It wasn't long before they lost sight of the lake for good.

Back at the lake the water nymphs sang a lament for Cecil's passing, a song that rose from the lake's surface like a thick, dark mist. The lament-laden mist blew westward into the forest, and it bestowed on every last living thing there a storm of nightmares.

Chapter Forty-Two: An Unexpected Visitor—Boston MA, 2014

Two years after her father had returned home with the hand-written manuscript, Elinor's life changed forever. Hyatt's second novel was published by a major publishing house in New York, much to the chagrin of Schuyler Heddings and Wagner-Krauss. Elinor assisted her father over several months prior to letting anyone at all know that the novel existed. She transcribed the first half of the colossal book from Hyatt's hand-writing into a legible, properly formatted manuscript. Her father completed the second half.

On that first night when Miller had returned to Pittsfield with the manuscript it was Elinor who ended up heating the first page of chapter one in Hyatt's hidden novel. She read the opening sentence a dozen times then she sat down at the dining room table. She remembered now how weak her legs felt, how upset her stomach felt. That night she did something she rarely did. She went to the cabinet where her father kept his single malt scotch, poured a tumbler, downed it, and poured another.

"Dad," she handed him the final sheet of foolscap, "you need to read this."

Miller took the sheet and sat down next to her at the dining table. The brown ink was faint, but legible.

"Why don't you pour your father a glass?" he asked his daughter.

Elinor obliged him. Miller polished off the double his daughter had poured him and set the glass aside. Then he read the sheet once more.

Chapter One:
Stigmaur: The Tree Palace

A long time ago, a man waited for a woman to grow old like him so that one day, with help from the miller and his daughter, they could grow young again and love each other forever...

The book itself, under the watchful eye of the law firm representing Hyatt's literary estate, went up for auction. The bidding was fierce, including one from Wagner-Krauss that nearly screwed up the whole affair. In the end, Henry Holt Publishers had placed the winning bid. When the book was published, Elinor and her father received credit as co-editors. R.J. Hyatt's second novel included an introduction by Miller himself. Foreign language rights were sold in over thirty countries. The novel itself caused a stir that resulted in astronomical sales. Devotees of Hyatt bought copies, as did new readers, curiosity seekers who, prompted by the press, sought out both *Under the Bronze Moon* and *The Land of Dust and Honey.* There were countless interviews during the weeks of hype following the book's release. Elinor left this task to her father, the resident expert on Hyatt.

One year after *Under the Bronze Moon* was released, Miller suffered a major stroke. He died at home, and was buried at Hillside Cemetery in North Adams, MA next to his wife Ann.

It was a private affair. Elinor and only a handful of the faculty that knew Miller at UMass-Amherst were in attendance.

Miller left behind for his daughter a modest sum of money, including royalties from his role as co-editor of the new Hyatt novel. And the house in Haverford Township, PA that May Weldon had given to Miller now had a new owner.

Elinor had never visited the house prior to her father's death. She had every intention to accompany her father back to Pennsylvania, but the publication of Hyatt's posthumous novel, and the media circus that followed, never allowed her time. In the days following her father's death, Elinor had no desire to do anything at all, least of all travel to the small Pennsylvania town to see the house she had never wanted in the first place. After her father's burial, Elinor returned to Boston to teach. She traveled back to Pittsfield on weekends to pack her father's things and prepare his house for sale.

It was during one of those weekends that Elinor made a discovery. As she packed up various papers in her father's study she saw the old manuscript boxes that had once contained Hyatt's second book. The original hand-written manuscript had been shipped to the Special Collections Department at Haverford College to be housed with Hyatt's other papers there. Elinor picked up the manuscript boxes, contemplating whether to throw them into the garbage, when she saw that the exterior fabric on one of the boxes was torn. A closer inspection revealed that something had been tucked underneath the fabric. Carefully, Elinor cut away a small piece of cloth to reveal a piece of onion skin folded in threes. After she unfolded it on her father's desk, Elinor saw that it had been the top half of a ship's passenger manifest from 1936. Folded inside the manifest page was an old photo of R.J. Hyatt standing next to a young dark-haired girl wearing an egg-shaped locket. The photograph appeared to have been taken on the deck of a ship.

Since her return to Boston, Elinor had resumed her sessions with her therapist Dr. Banerjee. It helped to talk to someone about being left alone in the world, someone who was objective and far-removed from her life. During an appointment shortly after discovering the passenger manifest and the photograph, Elinor sought Dr. Bannerjee's advice.

"It doesn't make any sense," said Elinor.

"But you are intrigued," Dr. Banerjee replied.

"No," she said. "I mean, yes. Of course I am."

"What feelings did this piece of paper elicit when you first discovered it?"

"I was confused," she admitted. "But then the whole thing made sense to me."

"How so?"

Elinor did not mention the photograph. She handed the old scrap of paper to her therapist.

"Here," she said. "See for yourself."

HMS Vertumnus
List of Passengers bound for New York and Boston
From: Belfast and Liverpool
May 1, 1936

Name *Final Destination*	*Point Of* *Origin*
Abramson, Gustav (age 46) *New York*	*Belfast*
Abramson, Johan (son, age 20) *New York*	*Belfast*

Carlysle, Samuel (age 22)	*London New York*
Hyatt, Robert Jonas (age 36) *New York*	*Unknown*
Hyatt, Tessie (daughter, age 9) *New York*	*Unknown*
Jones, Ronald (age 42) *Boston*	*Limerick*
Kirkland, Joseph (age 20)	

"Someone tore this in a hurry," Dr. Banerjee said.

"I know," her patient said. "It's like someone deliberately stole it."

"Hyatt had a daughter?"

"No, he did not," said Elinor.

"A war child, perhaps?"

"If he did, my father would have known about it," she said. "Besides, the girl listed on the manifest is only nine years old."

"Maybe your father didn't know everything about R.J. Hyatt," said Dr. Banerjee. "How does that make you feel?"

"I never said he did," Elinor told her.

She spent the remainder of that appointment in silence. Before she left Dr. Bannerjee's office, she took back the scrap of the HMS Vertumnus passenger manifest.

Several weeks later, the mystery deepened further one day while Elinor was in her campus office on a cold Wednesday afternoon. The door was closed as was her custom lately to ward off unwanted visitors like Reginald Davies. During Elinor's time of mourning Davies had ramped up his campaign to seduce her, attempting to exploit her loss for his gain. And while Elinor had crushed every attempt he made to get close to her, the astrophysicist proved unrelenting. It took him nearly a year before he got the message. During that time, she began closing and locking her office door. In recent weeks, however, with no sign of Reginald Davies, Elinor eased up and left the door unlocked. Had she known that a simple barrier made of wood was enough to ward off the astrophysicist's frequent visits Elinor would have employed the measure sooner than she did.

That afternoon Elinor was preparing a final exam to administer to her undergraduate classes when a knock sounded at the door.

"It's open," she called out.

The door opened slowly. Elinor kept her eyes trained on the paperwork in front of her, hoping that the visitor was anyone but Reginald Davies. When she looked up she saw an elderly woman, slight of frame beneath her dark dress and black hooded coat, with jet black hair and eyes that looked oddly familiar to Elinor.

"Dr. Miller?" the old woman asked.

Elinor stared at the egg-shaped locket the woman wore.

"Please, call me Ellie," she said as she gestured to a chair beside her desk. "Have a seat."

"Thank you, Ellie," the old woman said. She sat down and placed her black purse in her lap, crossing one ankle in front of the other without lifting her feet from the floor. "My name is Tessie Smith. You probably know me by my other name, Tilly."

"Right," said Elinor. "Who put you up to this? Was it Schuyler Heddings?"

"I am afraid I don't know anyone by that name," Tessie said.

"Is there something I can do for you?" she asked. Then added, "Before I call campus police?"

"Water."

"There's a fountain in the hallway."

"No," said Tessie. "The water that springs from beneath Stigmaur."

"The tree palace in R.J. Hyatt's novel? Look, Tessie, or whatever your name is," Elinor said. "I am sure you think you've had fun at my expense, but—"

"So you know it?"

"The tree palace?"

"Yes."

"It's a story," Elinor told her. "Nothing more."

How do writers live with these kinds of fans? Elinor wondered.

"I know," Tessie said. "It's my story. Robert changed my name. I am the one who got lost in the cave."

"Impossible," she countered, developing serious doubts about her own sanity now. *Am I really entertaining this?* She thought.

A hint of a smile flashed on Tessie's face. "I am afraid it's all very true, dear," she said. "The water of Stigmaur kept me young, for a time."

Tessie opened her egg-shaped locket and leaned toward Elinor.

On the inside left was a copy of the photograph Elinor had found along with the portion of the ship's passenger manifest. On the right, a limning of a dark-haired girl and a baby boy.

"I'm sure you know the gentleman with me on the left," said Tessie. "And that's my brother Cecil on the right."

Elinor sat back in her chair. Suddenly, her office, usually cold on winter days like this one, felt uncomfortably warm.

"You said something about water?" she asked.

"I know you have inherited a house," said Tessie. "I was there once for a brief time. And then I returned as an adult. It was many years ago. May Weldon would have been a teenager, I think. I am not after money, if that's what you think."

"May Weldon's house," Elinor said. "What about it?"

"I have reason to believe that somewhere on that property," she said, "is a doorway to the other side."

Elinor reached for the phone on her desk. "You can leave now," she said, "or you can wait for campus police to show you out."

The old woman stood up. She reached into her purse, pulled out a piece of scrap paper, and placed it on the corner of Elinor's desk.

"My number here in Boston," said Tessie. "In case you change your mind."

"What makes you think I will?" Elinor asked.

"You are an archaeologist," she replied. "All of this," Tessie gestured to the walls of the office, "is an artificial construct. You search for the truth. You have already explored worlds long gone hoping to discover new facts. And now you may have inherited a doorway to a world different from ours. Wouldn't you want to know the truth about such a place?"

Tessie exited the office. As she stood in the hallway, she turned to face Elinor once more.

"Anything else?" Elinor lifted the phone from its cradle now.

"Her Majesty's Ship The Vertumnus," said Tessie. "It sailed out of Liverpool on May 1, 1936. Call me later."

Before Elinor could respond the old woman walked away. She set the phone down in its cradle and went to her door. The hallway was empty.

Back at her desk, Elinor picked up the scrap paper with Tessie's telephone number written on it and placed it in her pocket. She sat back in her chair. Countless questions arose in her mind, and she chewed over them to no avail. On her desk, to the right of the telephone, she kept a photograph of her father and herself on the beach at Mystic, Connecticut when she was a little girl. Elinor had treated herself to a silver Tiffany & Co. picture frame when she decided to display the photograph in her office.

"Could it hurt to poke around?" she asked the photograph, already knowing the answer.

The educated, rational adult side of Elinor wished, even now, that she had never become involved in the Hyatt novel business, but there was the little girl who once sat under her father's desk, entranced by the fantastical books inside his barrister bookcase; back then, she had been convinced that the bookcase served as a doorway between worlds. It was this little girl inside her, the one with her father in the photograph on her desk, that had agreed to help him prepare Hyatt's *Under the Bronze Moon* for publication and the little girl who once knew, beyond any doubt, just like her father did, that magic and mystery still thrived in the world. The little girl in Elinor knew something else to also be true. Tomorrow, she would pick up the phone and call Tessie Smith.

The End

About The Author

Richard J. O'Brien lives in New Jersey. Once upon a time, before the Berlin Wall came down, Richard served in the US Army. He attended Rutgers University, and he holds an MFA in Creative Writing from Fairleigh Dickinson University.

Richard's books include *The People's Republic of New Arkaim, Rejoice for the Dead, Aleph Café: Stories, The Accidental Hero of the City of Brotherly Love, To Dream the Blackbane, Under the Bronze Moon,* and *The Garden of Fragile Things*.

Readers can find Richard on Twitter @obrienwriter and online at https://obrienwriter.com/.

You can also follow his author page on Facebook at https://www.facebook.com/obrienwriter/.